W9-AFU-675

"Anya Bast is a professional at writing stories that keep the reader in a . . . state of suspense. Her reputation is well deserved."
—*Romance Junkies*

"The atmosphere that Anya Bast portrays is intricate, dark, and highly erotic."
—*Just Erotic Romance Reviews*

PRAISE FOR

DARK ENCHANTMENT

"When I was first introduced to Anya Bast a couple of years ago, I quickly became enchanted with her work. It seems that I cannot read her work fast enough to satisfy the need. *Dark Enchantment* . . . holds the reader spellbound while in its pages . . . Like all her books, *Dark Enchantment* is well put together and a pleasure to read. I hope you take the time to get lost in a 'Dark Enchantment' yourself—you will not be disappointed."
—*Night Owl Reviews*

"Readers will recognize many characters. Bast has created a charmed world of faeries, brownies, witches, goblins, and more. You won't want to leave this beautiful world . . . Seriously sexy."
—*RT Book Reviews*

"This is the third installment in the Dark Magick series and it does not let you down . . . Charlotte is surprisingly sassy [and] Kieran is droolworthy! . . . As with Bast's previous novels, there is plenty of action in this novel as well . . . You will not be disappointed or bored!"
—*ParaNormal Romance*

continued . . .

WITCH FURY

"Full of action, excitement, and sexy fun . . . Another delectable tale that will keep your eyes glued to every word."

—*Bitten by Books*

"Hot romance, interesting characters, intriguing demons, and powerful emotions. I didn't want to put it down, and now that I've finished this book, I'm ready for the next!"

—*Night Owl Reviews*

WITCH HEART

"[A] fabulous tale . . . The story line is fast paced from the onset . . . Fans will enjoy the third bewitching blast."

—*Genre Go Round Reviews*

"Smart, dangerous and sexy as hell, the witches are more than a match for the warlocks and demons who'd like nothing more than to bring hell to earth and enslave mankind. Always an exhilarating read."

—*Fresh Fiction*

"A story that will captivate its readers. It will hook you from the first few pages and then take you on a wild ride. It is a fast-paced story but it is also a story that will make you feel emotion. Anya Bast uses words like Monet used paint. It's vibrant. It's alive. Readers will be able to see the story come to life as it just leaps out of the pages."

—*Bitten by Books*

WITCH BLOOD

"Any paranormal fan will be guaranteed a Top Pick read. Anya has provided it all in this hot new paranormal series. You get great suspense, vivid characters, and a world that just pops off the pages . . . Not to be missed."
　　　　　　　　　　　　　　　　　　　　　　—*Night Owl Reviews*

"Gritty danger and red-hot sensuality make this book and series smoking!"
　　　　　　　　　　　　　　　　　　　　　　—*RT Book Reviews*

WITCH FIRE

"Deliciously sexy and intriguingly original."
　　　　　　　　　—Angela Knight, *New York Times* bestselling author

"Sizzling suspense and sexy magic are sure to propel this hot new series onto the charts. Bast is a talent to watch, and her magical world is one to revisit."　　　　　　　—*RT Book Reviews*

"A sensual feast sure to sate even the most finicky of palates. Richly drawn, dynamic characters dictate the direction of this fascinating story. You can't miss with Anya."
　　　　　　　　　　　　　　　　　　　　　　—*A Romance Review*

"Fast-paced, edgy suspense . . . The paranormal elements are fresh and original. This reader was immediately drawn into the story from the opening abduction, and obsessively read straight through to the dramatic final altercation. Bravo, Ms. Bast; *Witch Fire* is sure to be a fan favorite."
　　　　　　　　　　　　　　　　　　　　　　—*ParaNormal Romance*

continued . . .

Titles by Anya Bast

WITCH FIRE
WITCH BLOOD
WITCH HEART
WITCH FURY
WICKED ENCHANTMENT
CRUEL ENCHANTMENT
DARK ENCHANTMENT
MIDNIGHT ENCHANTMENT
EMBRACE OF THE DAMNED

THE CHOSEN SIN
JEWELED
JADED

RAVEN'S QUEST

EMBRACE
OF THE DAMNED

ANYA BAST

BERKLEY SENSATION, NEW YORK

THE BERKLEY PUBLISHING GROUP
Published by the Penguin Group
Penguin Group (USA) Inc.
375 Hudson Street, New York, New York 10014, USA

Penguin Group (Canada), 90 Eglinton Avenue East, Suite 700, Toronto, Ontario M4P 2Y3, Canada
(a division of Pearson Penguin Canada Inc.) • Penguin Books Ltd., 80 Strand, London WC2R 0RL,
England • Penguin Group Ireland, 25 St. Stephen's Green, Dublin 2, Ireland (a division of Penguin
Books Ltd.) • Penguin Group (Australia), 250 Camberwell Road, Camberwell, Victoria 3124, Australia
(a division of Pearson Australia Group Pty. Ltd.) • Penguin Books India Pvt. Ltd., 11 Community
Centre, Panchsheel Park, New Delhi—110 017, India • Penguin Group (NZ), 67 Apollo Drive,
Rosedale, Auckland 0632, New Zealand (a division of Pearson New Zealand Ltd.) • Penguin Books
(South Africa) (Pty.) Ltd., 24 Sturdee Avenue, Rosebank, Johannesburg 2196, South Africa

Penguin Books Ltd., Registered Offices: 80 Strand, London WC2R 0RL, England

EMBRACE OF THE DAMNED

A Berkley Sensation Book / published by arrangement with the author

PUBLISHING HISTORY
Berkley Sensation mass-market edition / May 2012

Copyright © 2012 by Joanna Mackens.
Cover art by Tony Mauro.
Cover design by Rita Frangie.
Interior text design by Tiffany Estreicher.

ISBN: 978-0-425-24796-9

BERKLEY SENSATION®
Berkley Sensation Books are published by The Berkley Publishing Group,
a division of Penguin Group (USA) Inc.,
375 Hudson Street, New York, New York 10014.
BERKLEY SENSATION® is a registered trademark of Penguin Group (USA) Inc.
The "B" design is a trademark of Penguin Group (USA) Inc.

PRINTED IN THE UNITED STATES OF AMERICA

10 9 8 7 6 5 4 3 2 1

ALWAYS LEARNING　　　　　　　　　　　　　　　**PEARSON**

For James

PROLOGUE

A.D. 1012, NORWAY

Other people's blood seeped into Broder's wounds, making every slash and scratch on his body burn.

He was alive. He'd survived.

His muscles were weak from disuse, but the drive to live—the drive for revenge—had made him deadly for the time he'd needed to wreak this carnage. Now that it was over, the will to kill leaked slowly from him, not unlike the last decade of his life.

It didn't matter. Nothing mattered anymore. The moment he'd set foot in this enclave his life had been worth nothing. Before then, even. . . .

Ignoring the fiery pain of his injuries, his chest heaving and his eyes wild, Broder turned in a circle, a sharp sword clenched in one sticky hand, an ax in the other, and surveyed the bodies around him. The sight gave him no pleasure, no peace, but he didn't regret any of it. He'd do it again if given the chance, even though the act itself was more blur than memory.

He'd delivered retribution.

He barely remembered it. He'd heard tales of men caught up in battle carnage, wild with bloodlust, unknowing of the deeds they committed. Man, woman, child, it mattered not to them; all fell beneath the crazed warrior's blade. That was how he'd spent the last five minutes . . . had it been ten? Or had it been an hour? He wasn't sure. Images flashed through his head—blood, bone, flesh—the sharp, silver edge of his blade rendering it all into so much meat.

Movement caught his eye. He turned, ready to launch into another attack, and caught sight of a decapitated body sliding slowly from an ornate gold and green chair to the floor, making a lifeless heap. He relaxed.

It was over. Soon, he, too, would be over.

Blinking barely focused eyes, he lowered his sword and lifted his head, stretching muscles of his body that had long gone unused. He limped to a nearby chair and sat. He needed to leave this place because he didn't want to die here and he didn't have much time, but now that the insane rage that had animated his half-dead body had ebbed, he could barely move. His nose twitched, stinging from the stench of unwashed bodies and death.

Slumping against a heap of silken pillows, his blood staining them dark brown, he closed his eyes. Just for a moment. His hands still gripped his weapons, as though secured there for eternity. One wound burned brighter and hotter than the rest. He looked down at his side and examined the crescent-shaped slash.

He wouldn't survive it.

Every movement made the congealing blood covering him—his own and other men's—crack like dried mud. The images of what he'd done crowded his mind, made him sick, but he didn't want to take it back. He looked around, his lip curling with hatred. If anything, he wanted more.

"Broder Calderson!" His name echoed through the quiet chamber.

In spite of his wounds, Broder leapt to his feet, turned toward the voice, and reflexively threw the ax in his right hand. The man who stood at the entrance of the chamber didn't move, didn't even blink, as the weapon circled through the air, swooping end over end lazily, as if time had slowed it, the blade headed straight for his forehead.

The ax passed through the man as though he were made of mist.

The man—tall, slender, with black hair slicked back from his angular, handsome face—smiled. He swished his forefinger back and forth, grinning. "No, no, Broder. Bad boy."

Broder frowned at the strange language and accent and backed up, the sword dropping from his hand and clattering to the marble floor. The man wore outlandish clothing.

He looked him up and down. He wore no tunic and his trousers were more than passing strange. There was an odd, sharp cut to his garments and his shoes were too shiny. Some sort of extra-long bit of material that served no purpose hung from his neck. He'd never seen the like of such attire—or fabric—in all his life. A black swath of some hard material Broder couldn't identify balanced on the man's nose and wrapped around the upper part of his face, concealing his eyes.

"What are you?" Broder asked in a voice that hadn't been used in a very long time. It came out broken and rough.

"Not what, *who*. You don't recognize me? I am Loki." The man walked toward him, strange footwear crunching broken pottery, treading through pools of blood. His strange, shiny shoes never seemed to be affected. His voice held a strong note of derision. "Surely you must know who I am. I am known for the tricks that I play, and I have played many of them." His voice went serious. "But I am not playing now."

Of course he knew Loki. Broder felt the blood drain from his face. He'd just tried to kill a god. "Am I dead, then?"

Loki laughed. "Not hardly. Not yet, anyway." He removed the odd black thing covering the upper part of his face and his cold blue eyes skirted Broder's body, taking in the parts of him covered with Broder's own blood. "You won't be dead for a very, very long time. If ever."

Broder struggled to make sense out of those words. It was clear to Loki and to himself that he'd be dead in a few hours. It had only been a need for revenge that had kept his body full of life up until now. He'd had his revenge; now it was time to join his loved ones. He welcomed it.

Loki took a step forward, his polished shoe crunching on the remains of an invaluable piece of pottery. "You've had more than a little fun here, I think. You must be thirsty." He gestured to a half-broken pitcher on a nearby table, sitting in a pool of the blood he'd shed. "Need libation, perhaps?"

"It wasn't . . . fun." Broder frowned, trying to translate the odd manner of his speech. "I had reason for this violence."

"You offend the gods, you ungrateful barbarian!" Loki's voice boomed from him, echoed into the reaches of Broder's head, made the blood leak from his ears. Broder swiped at it and stared at the coating on his fingers. *"You'll not avoid reprimand!"*

Broder staggered backward, his head and side pounding out an intense rhythm of pain.

"You must be punished for this. You know that, don't you, Broder?"

Punished? He'd just spent the last ten years of his life in torment. And before that . . . hadn't he had enough torment?

"Wah, wah, wah," Loki sneered. "Don't think I can't read your thoughts. If you offend the gods, you suffer for it." He pointed at Broder. "And you, sir, have offended most heartily."

Broder winced, pain flaring through the wound in his side. He just wanted to die. He wanted to collapse to the floor, close his eyes, and never wake up. However, he had a very bad suspicion his wish would not be granted. There were punishments worse than death. Anyone who believed in the gods knew that much, and this was Loki, the most deceitful of all the gods.

Loki held up a hand. In his palm a small blue light sputtered to life and formed the shape of a sword, then narrowed to a sharp, pointed sliver that looked like a narrow spear.

Broder tensed. Surely that supernatural weapon was meant for him.

"I'm impressed you don't run," said Loki. "Most of them do."

He threw the blue sliver at Broder. Even though he moved to avoid it, the sliver found his chest, burying deep like the thinnest dagger made of pure ice. It pierced his heart, spreading agony to every part of him. Freezing and burning in equal turns, it dropped Broder to his knees, snapping his head back, arching his spine. A bellow of torment ripped from his throat.

The sliver formed a cold hollow of nothing in the center of his chest, shearing away all the flickers of humanity he'd managed to hold on to during the last decade. Soon nothing remained.

Nothing. And nothing truly meant *nothing*—no warmth, no love . . . but no fear or anger, either. It was . . . peaceful. He breathed into it, relaxing completely for the first time in years. Yet at nearly the same moment the pain ebbed, something else rushed in to fill up the serene emptiness. Something foreign. Something that didn't belong there.

Something from Loki.

In the center of his soul a mark of despair burned. He knew without being told that he was Loki's—his possession—and that could not be a good thing. He'd traded one Hel for another.

Broder pried his gummy, blood-crusted eyes open and saw that he'd fallen on his hands and knees to the floor, shards of pottery cutting into his shins and palms. Grunting with effort, holding one arm to his chest as though he could compel the icy sliver and Loki's mark out of him, he forced himself to look up into the grinning, gloating face of the god.

"You are hereby punished for your crimes, Broder Calderson. Eternally."

Broder had no doubt of this, but he could barely rouse himself to care.

"Don't be disheartened," Loki continued. "I am not an evil god with no sense of the human heart. Exactly one thousand years from now, if you have been a worthy warrior you will have a woman. Not just any woman—the woman of your every desire."

And then Broder truly knew he was damned.

ONE

ONE THOUSAND YEARS LATER . . . TO THE DAY

Jessamine's boots clicked on the pavement of the parking ramp, echoing through the empty structure. It was late and she was alone. If she'd had any other choice, she would have been home and in bed right now with a good book, rather than walking through this creepy parking garage with every bad movie cliché about such places riffing through her already freaked-out mind.

Her tote bag, stuffed with all her paperwork, rested over one shoulder. Her hand was secured in her pocket, pepper spray unlocked and at the ready. She didn't take any chances. Not these days. Life had suddenly grown too unpredictable for that.

Her hands still trembled from what she'd just done. She wasn't certain she could ever do it again. How she'd managed to do it at all still eluded her. She hadn't received any concrete answers from the risk she'd taken tonight, but sometimes lack of information was meaningful, too.

And, wow, she'd taken a huge risk.

Now all she wanted was to get home, sort through the confusing results of the evening, and figure out what to do next.

As she rounded one of the thick concrete walls, a man stepped out from near the elevators. Jessa hesitated, watching him carefully, her hand ready on the pepper spray. He was a good-looking guy dressed in a black linen shirt, a pair of jeans, and black boots. His face had a *GQ*-handsome quality to it, light blue eyes and well-trimmed facial hair around his sensual mouth. His hair, black and slick, was styled to perfection. Her best friend, Lillie, would have swallowed her tongue. Just her type.

Normally she'd think *yum*. Tonight he set off every warning in her body. He was the type of polished man that usually put a woman at ease, but her mind never strayed from *Ted Bundy*. He'd been a handsome, polished guy, too.

He watched her with attention beyond that of some guy waiting for an elevator. His fascination with her every move did little to flatter her. She walked past him, doing her best to hide her impulse to break into a run.

"Be careful tonight," said the man in a rich voice that reminded her of warm chocolate.

She missed a step, tried to smile but was too on edge. "Excuse me?"

"They know what you are." He paused. "They've been watching you."

What I am? She pulled up short, stunned by his words. The comment sent a shiver through her, a jolt of fear followed by a sharp jab of anger. "Are you trying to scare me or are you just crazy?"

The edges of the man's mouth quirked up and he slid his hands into his pockets. "My name is Dmitri. I'm a friend."

"A friend, sure. The kind of friend who wants to rape and murder me, maybe." Her hand clenched hard on the pepper spray. If he took one step in her direction, he'd get it full in the face.

For a moment it appeared as though his eyes went completely black. It rocked her back a step. *Impossible*. "I'm not the one who means you harm. I'm just trying to warn you, Jessa."

Now she was really scared. How the hell did he know her name?

Jessa bolted, breaking into a run, checking over her shoulder constantly to make sure he wasn't following her.

What that man had said made a kind of sense she didn't want to examine. She had no idea who Dmitri was, but it was possible he was telling the truth. Maybe they *were* watching her. Maybe they did know what she was. Maybe they did mean her harm. It wasn't paranoia if they were really after you, right? She just wished she knew who *they* were.

How much strangeness could a woman handle before she went insane? She was afraid she might be about to discover the answer.

When she determined Dmitri wasn't following, she slowed her pace, rounding the corner that brought her to the lot where she'd parked her car. Her heart pounded fast enough to make her eardrums thrum and her hands were shaking. She needed to get home, to the safety of her well-locked apartment. She needed time to breathe, collect her thoughts.

Jessa approached her black sedan with a sigh of relief. No echo of a man's measured footsteps had resounded behind her; no gloved hand had covered her mouth and drawn her into the shadows. There was her car; she was safe. Yay. She tried to muster some enthusiasm for that happy news and failed. She was exhausted and frightened.

Pulling her keys from her other pocket, she unlocked her doors remotely. Just as she touched the door handle, someone cursed loudly. Her head whipped up and she spotted a man with medium brown hair holding a briefcase on the opposite side of the row of parked cars. He looked harmless, like some accountant or businessman who'd been working late.

In one hand he held a briefcase and he was using the other hand to shade his eyes as he peered into the driver's-side window. He swore again, his voice sounding squeaky and distressed.

She almost ignored the worried man, got into her car,

and drove away, but she hadn't been raised that way. "Are you all right, sir?" she called loudly from her safe place beside her car's driver's-side door. Her voice held a nervous, distracted tremor. She didn't want to deal with this right now.

The man glanced at her, seeming surprised to find her there. He adjusted his glasses on the bridge of his nose. "I locked my keys and my cell phone in the car. Stupid," he muttered. He turned back to the automobile, staring into the window as though he could reach through the glass and grab his stuff. "It's late, the building is closed, and—"

"No problem," Jessa called to him. "I've locked my keys in my car before, too. I'll call a locksmith for you. I'll tell them it's a green Impala on level three of the Handburg parking garage. They should be here soon, okay?"

She opened her car door, intending to sit down and fish out her phone to make the call, but the man walked over to her instead.

No. He didn't walk, he ran . . . or something. Damn, the guy could move *fast*. One minute he was way over there, now he was right beside her.

She backed away from him, alarmed. Had she imagined that?

"Wait. That will be expensive. Do you mind if I just call my wife? She's got an extra key."

He flashed a bland smile at her, a bland smile on a bland face. She looked down and saw the gold wedding band on his left hand wink in the dim light.

She must have imagined it. "Sure." She dug into her bag and pulled her cell phone out. "Here you—" The cell phone clattered to the cement as bland suddenly turned brutal. The veneer of nice, harmless man peeled away like an aging patina.

Oh, no.

Jessa stepped backward as the man's thin lips peeled into a gruesome smile, revealing sharp white teeth and . . . were those . . . *fangs*? How could that be?

"Jessamine Amber Hamilton?" Even the man's voice had

changed. He ripped off the glasses and threw them to the pavement.

She shook her head, unwilling to answer, and took another step back. Her fingers closed around her pepper spray. He was between her and her car. That needed to change. Getting to her car meant she could make it out of here alive.

Rage blossomed inside her. *She just wanted to go home!* Jessa stopped retreating. "Get the hell away from me right now." Her voice came out a whole lot stronger and more assertive than she felt, but she needed to treat this man like the dog he was—and show him who was alpha. If she didn't act afraid, maybe he'd back off.

The man tipped his head to the side, looking oddly alien. Then he smiled a waaaay creepy smile and said, "No."

"Fine. You asked for it, asshole." She pulled the pepper spray from her pocket, aimed it at the man's face, and pulled the trigger. The pepper spray hit him straight in the eyes, but he didn't flinch. All he did was swipe a hand across his face and leer at her. It was as if she'd shot him with a water pistol. Then, if the fangs weren't weird enough, his eyes bled black . . . *completely black*. Hell-spawn obsidian *black*.

Okay, that was not normal.

The smell of the pepper spray stung her nose, made her eyes water. It was potent. Any normal human would be writhing in agony on the floor of the parking garage by now. Why wasn't he?

The man narrowed his creepy black eyes and smiled, revealing—unmistakably this time—two shiny sharp fangs.

It appeared she had her answer; this thing wasn't human.

A growl issued from the back of his throat that raised the hair along her nape. She dropped her bag, turned, and ran. He tackled her immediately, rolling her over and looming above her. She fought him—punching, biting, scratching—but his strength was as unnatural as his teeth. And his grip was cold, *freezing*. Where his skin touched her, she went numb.

His mouth, with those shiny fangs, descended toward her face, ice-cold saliva dripping from their knifelike points.

She screamed.

He could feel her.

Her presence burned through every fiber of his body, screaming at him to find her. It had rushed through him the moment Loki had untwisted the cosmic laws that bound him—unlocked Broder's ability to be with a woman. His chastity belt. That's what the Brotherhood of the Damned called it, a darkly comedic term for the magick that kept them from intimate contact with any other person.

You could call Loki many things, but not a liar. At least not this time. It was exactly a thousand years since the day Broder had been taken for the Brotherhood. Just as Loki had promised, he was free—at least for a time—to taste the fruits he'd been forbidden.

He could feel her.

From the moment he'd been freed, she'd pulled him toward her. This was the one woman allowed him in all the world and nothing was going to keep him from her.

He raced his cycle down the rain-slicked streets of Washington, D.C., the reflection of the lights from the intersections he rode through gleaming on the wet pavement and the ends of his long, rune-laced leather coat flapping behind him.

His blood sang hot with the supernatural scent of her. She wasn't far, just a few blocks away. His body tightened with need, his heart rushing with adrenaline triggered by her nearness. She would be human, that was always how Loki did it. Not Valkyrie, not witch. *Human.* It complicated things for the Brotherhood and amused Loki, the bastard. He never made things easy.

One thousand years he'd been in the Brotherhood of the Damned. One thousand years of offing Blight, one by one, hoping to find that single agent from whom the sliver had been taken that pierced his soul. If he could find that one agent of the Blight, he would be free to die.

Most humans dreamed about immortality, but most in the Brotherhood dreamed of death—of peace, of rest, of change of any kind. Love was just a dream . . . death, something to strive for.

Immortality for the Brotherhood was hell.

Kill the agent of the Blight from whom Loki had extracted the sliver lodged in Broder's soul and the sliver would die, too. The countdown clock of his physical life would resume.

But this. This was a new goal. This was different from the last thousand years of his life. This woman promised warmth, companionship . . . pleasure. A respite from the endless cycle of killing and death.

He was close now. He gunned the engine of his cycle, ran a red light. The city was empty, winding down into night. To his left was a parking garage. In it was his woman.

Broder gunned the motorcycle inside, his blood a torpedo headed straight for her.

TWO

Fangs scraped Jessa's throat and the man's huge body—he'd seemed so harmless a few seconds ago!—anchored her to the parking garage floor. No amount of screaming seemed to help and the only thing going through her head right now was *oh, shit* on repeat.

She'd always wondered what her last thought would be.

Suddenly the man was gone. No, wait, not gone—*launched*.

One moment another drop of freezing-cold saliva dangling on his fang had been about to drip onto her cheek; the next moment . . . nothing.

Pushing up on her elbows, she watched as the man careened through the air like a wadded-up piece of paper to land near a big black motorcycle, apparently her savior's mode of transport. A huge guy with dark hair and dressed from head to toe in a long, ancient-looking leather duster strode after the man . . . thing . . . whatever it was. And he looked *pissed*.

Biker Guy grabbed Fanged Thing by the front of his shirt and hefted him. They struggled and she wasn't sure who was going to win. Fanged Thing was stronger than he seemed. Alarmed, she crab-walked backward until she hit the tire of a nearby car. Fanged Thing growled and snapped at Biker Guy, but he wasn't taking any guff. Then Fanged Thing punched Biker Guy in the side and wiggled out of his grasp.

Okay. Time to go. Wrong guy winning.

Her breathing came out harsh, panicked. After taking a moment to collect her thoughts, she scrambled up, going for her tote bag, her fingers scrabbling on the filthy pavement to collect her car keys.

Good etiquette might dictate that she remain and thank her liberator, but she'd had a good look at Biker Guy and, frankly, even if he were victorious in this battle, the cure looked just as threatening as the illness.

Hands shaking, she scooped her cell phone up and opened her car door. Portions of her arms and shoulders burned with cold. Where Fanged Thing had touched her or dropped saliva, her skin had turned a light gray. *Whatever.* She'd deal with it later. Right now, she had to get out of there.

A distance away, she saw that Biker Guy had cornered Fanged Thing. Fanged Thing cowered in Biker Guy's presence, raising his hands to shield his face and yelling, *"No, no!"*

Biker Guy pulled a huge gleaming silver dagger from somewhere on his person; it had been hidden by his long coat. The blade flashed in the light, swooped . . . and was knocked away as Fanged Thing completed a tricky move by sweeping Biker Guy's legs out from under him. Biker Guy went down hard and Fanged Thing was on him, inhuman growls issuing from his throat and dangerous jaw snapping.

It didn't look good for her leather-clad savior.

Okay, *really* time to go.

Jessamine sank into the driver's seat and started her car engine with shaking hands. The sound made Fanged Thing's head snap up. In that same moment, the silver dagger flashed upward and sank into Fanged Thing's chest. Fanged Thing exploded into . . . glass? Or was that ice? Were those *ice* pellets? Could it really be . . . she squinted, watching the ice, or whatever it was, settle onto the biker dude and the floor around him in glimmering shards and tiny chunks.

Biker Guy looked up at her, the blade he'd used to explode Fanged Thing dripping with water . . . or melted ice.

Eyes wide, hands shaking, mind blown, Jessa gunned the engine of her car. Tires squealing, she was out of there.

She raced around the levels of the parking garage, hands white on the steering wheel, going as fast as she could without careening into parked vehicles. The sound of her tires squealing on the pavement echoed throughout the parking structure. Just as she'd nearly reached the exit ramp, the rough sound of an engine reached her ears and a black motorcycle appeared in front of her car . . . and stopped, blocking her path.

Jessa slammed on the brakes, sliding on the pavement, hot rubber scenting the air, and stopped the car a breath's space from Biker Guy's leg—he looked completely unworried.

Her breath shuddered out of her. She gripped the steering wheel and stared through the windshield at the man, taking stock. A chunk of her long hair had come free from her ponytail and lay over her face. It rose and fell with her panicked breaths.

Her savior was good-looking. Intimidating, for sure. Dangerous seeming, no doubt. Not *GQ* handsome like Dmitri. This guy looked like he'd just been sprung from prison with that heated scowl on his face.

He was tall and he was ripped. The roll of his muscles could be seen easily underneath his clothes. What was worse, *and completely inappropriate*, was how he made her respond—like a woman to a man. It was instant, primal, and wholly unwelcome. This man made her whole body sit up and take notice.

Even so, he was definitely not someone she'd want to encounter in an empty parking garage late at night.

Yet, she'd thought Fanged Thing had looked completely harmless before he'd vamped out on her, and this man had probably saved her life. She thought about that Dmitri guy and his creepy warning—which had turned out to be true. Could it be that this was Opposite Night, when all the decent-looking men were dangerous and all dangerous-looking men were decent?

Biker Guy swung off the cycle, leaving the admittedly beautiful thing blocking her way, and stalked toward her, long worn leather coat trailing behind him like the wings of a fallen angel. He walked with anger set into his shoulders and a hint of menace and easy arrogance in his swagger. That anger made his body seem like it would be hot to the touch, as if he identified so strongly with rage that it affected him physically.

She hoped his eyes didn't bleed black. She'd have a heart attack and save everyone the trouble of having to kill her.

"You!" he bellowed through the window. She jumped at the commanding sound of his voice.

"I don't know you," she said in a shaky voice, glancing at him, then moving her gaze to fix on the cycle blocking her path. "Move your bike. I gotta go."

"No." He paused. "Roll down the window." Absently, she noticed he spoke with an odd accent she couldn't place.

Jessa took a deep breath and tried her mojo—funneling all of it she possibly could at the man. She didn't know exactly how it worked, why she could do it, or really *how* she was even able to do it, but if she concentrated hard enough, she could make people bend to her will. Sort of like a Jedi mind trick—*This is not the woman you're interested in. Move away from the vehicle.*

The man lifted his brows. "Roll down the window," he repeated, slower this time, as if she were an idiot.

Damn it! Why wasn't it working?

When she remained still and unresponsive, completely freaked out and unmoving, he tapped the glass. With effort, she peeled her fingers off the steering wheel and rolled down her window a crack. She glanced up at him. God, he was stunning. Sculpted, strong jaw; full lips that compelled a girl to want to suck on them; deep, oddly expressive brown eyes.

"Uh, thanks . . . for your help. I appreciate it." She looked at his motorcycle. "Really. I have to go now. Can you move that, please?"

"Why was he targeting you?" The man's voice was deep

and rough, like he didn't use it very much—like honey and gravel.

"Who? That guy back there? Listen, I'm still processing all that, okay? I have no idea who or *what* he was, let alone what he wanted to do with me." She set her jaw. Savior or not, gorgeous or not, this man was starting to piss her off. "Look, buddy, I'm all out of pepper spray, but I'm sitting in a car and I'm not afraid to use it." She looked meaningfully at the shiny, expensive Harley blocking her path.

His gaze traveled over her, catching on the painful, damaged sections of her skin. "You need healing."

"Yeah. I'll go to the hos—"

He reached out and pulled her car door off the hinges, then threw it aside as if it weighed nothing.

"No. *Just no.*" Jessa shook her head and scrambled into the passenger side. "No, okay? *No.*" She opened the passenger-side door and prepared to run.

But he was there, blocking her path. "You don't understand. Where there is one of those things, there are more. You are in danger."

The man radiated a palpable aura of menace as he loomed over her. She gave him an up and down sweep of her gaze. He still had ice in his hair. "Clearly."

"You're not in danger from me."

"And my father was the Easter Bunny."

He grabbed her wrist, right below one of the light gray expanses of skin; the area had the imprint of Fanged Thing's fingers on it, as though she'd been marked with frostbite by his skin touching hers. She yelped.

The man laid his hand over the injury and it warmed immediately. When he lifted his fingers, her skin was back to its regular peachy tan color.

Jessa took a step back, her eyes wide. "I didn't just see that. I didn't—"

He grabbed her other arm.

"Stop doing that!" By the time she'd uttered the sentence, her other arm was healed. Then he pressed his fingers onto the few places where Fanged Thing's saliva had dripped on her.

"Anywhere else?" he growled at her.

She shook her head, blinking rapidly with nervousness.

"You're healed."

"Thank you." She tried to step away, but he held her fast. "Uh, you can let me go now."

He stared at her as though he hadn't heard a word she'd said. Tipping his head to the side, he examined her with thorough interest. A strange, intense light had entered his eyes and she took a step backward.

There was something about this man that told her to back off—apart from the outward signs, the cycle, the leather, the scowl. There was something inside him that screamed *danger, cross to the other side of the street.*

She had the urge to rip her arm away from him, but she stood her ground. He was so close to her that his breath stirred the fine hairs around her face. Heat rolled off him and she absorbed it into her own skin. Despite the threat he emanated, her body started a slow, sexual burn. She tried to ignore it, push it away. Now was not the time and this was definitely *not* the man.

And man, *oh, man.* He was every inch a man.

The lines of his face were hard and cold, set in an almost cruel expression. This was a man who was both brutal and beautiful. But even though his expression was harsh, his brown eyes were filled with heat and emotion. It softened him.

As he stood staring at her, his eyes clouded, becoming distant, and a muscle worked in his jaw. As though he might be warring with himself over something. She'd never known brown eyes could look that hot. It made her whole body tighten with sexual awareness. Worse, his gaze probably mirrored her own.

Well, hell.

Then the man reached out, snagged her sweater with one big hand, and pulled her flush up against his chest. His body heat rolled off him and enveloped her, making her heart rate speed up.

A huge, strong hand grasped the nape of her neck, the other hand going to the small of her back. She made a small noise in her throat, but it wasn't of fear—not exactly . . . not totally. She should have been frightened, should have been fighting him, but there something inside her that thrilled at this man's touch. She didn't want to get away, even though that desire made no sense at all. Her libido really did *not* have her permission to misbehave right now, but she couldn't seem to stop it.

Pulling her head to the side, he exposed the column of her neck, then slowly lowered his mouth to it. His tongue flicked out, tasting her skin. Gooseflesh erupted all over her body and a shiver traveled up her spine.

This was wrong. This was so, so very wrong. She knew that, so why was her body reacting this way to him? He was a forbidding stranger and—

He gently bit her throat, almost as if he wanted to mark her, and she moaned, closing her eyes.

She should have been worried that fangs would suddenly erupt in his mouth. She should have been having posttraumatic mental explosions of blood and flesh tearing—of icy, frostbite-giving skin and freezing saliva. Yet all she could think of was bare skin, tangled limbs, a bed. . . .

What kind of magick did this man possess?

Kissing her skin, he murmured words in a foreign language that sounded tender, almost like endearments. His hand traveled up to cup the back of her head, his fingers raking through her long hair. He made a noise in the recesses of his throat, his body tensing, as though holding himself back from tearing her clothes off her.

She wasn't sure she wanted him to resist his impulse.

Maybe it had been so long since she'd had sex, her libido was overriding her good sense. Maybe a one-night stand with some stranger in a dirty parking garage was—

Her mental facilities returned with a roar. Her eyes flew open and she pushed away from him. He released her with a groan that almost sounded anguished, but he let her back away.

She blinked and hugged herself. "What the hell was that?"

The man stood completely—almost eerily—still, eyes closed, fists clenched. "I won't hurt you or do anything you don't want me to do."

"Uh, okay, good to know. I'm leaving now." She dropped her arms to her sides and went for her badly damaged car. "Forget the door. I'll just tell the insurance company . . . hmmm . . . well, just forget it."

He grabbed her by the upper arm as she passed. Making her jump. "We need to talk. Come with me."

She ripped her arm away from his grip. "No. You saved my life, then killed my car. I think that must make us even . . . I guess. And it's true that we just shared . . . a moment, or something, but now I'm out of here."

"Come." He turned and walked toward the cycle. All she did was stare at his back. She could run, but she didn't have any illusions she'd actually get away. He'd just torn the door off her car, after all. He turned toward her expectantly.

Barely able to look at him, she gave her head one little shake. Seriously, this was all a bit too much.

He stopped, looked up at the ceiling as though summoning patience, then walked toward her. "My name is Broder Calderson."

"What kind of name is that?"

"A very old one."

"My name is—never mind. I'm not thinking." She put a hand to her forehead. Clearly she was in shock. She'd almost just told him her name. Of course, maybe that didn't matter. Dmitri of the jet-black eyes had known her name without her revealing it.

"I won't hurt you, but I won't let you leave alone, either. Are we going to do this the hard way or the easy way?"

She narrowed her eyes. "That sounds like a threat."

"I'll do whatever I need to do to keep you safe and right now you are not safe."

She blinked slowly and wavered on her feet. Her whole world had just been tipped on end, all her illusions about reality destroyed by a flash of fang, a poof of ice, and the introduction of Mr. Gorgeous Incredible Hulk.

But, really, her world had begun to tip into strangeness way before tonight, hadn't it? Either she was delusional or the world was not all it appeared to be. And, honestly, she didn't think she was delusional.

She considered him as she mulled her options. She was powerfully curious about Fanged Thing, and this man, Broder, was the only one with the answers. If the only way to get those answers was to have a conversation with him, then that was the risk she had to take.

But before she agreed to go with him, she'd put all the odds in her favor.

Her gaze slipped to his leather duster. "Fine. Give me the big, shiny dagger you're hiding in that archaic piece of clothing and I'll go with you."

His eyebrows rose into his hairline. "Excuse me?"

She spread her arms. "I need some kind of a way to defend myself, don't I?"

He looked at her like she'd spoken Greek.

She sighed. "You're superstrong and you're a stranger, no matter that you saved me from some sharp-toothed monster with frozen slobber issues and an eye disorder. I have no weapon and no assurance you won't hurt me." She looked at him pointedly. "I'm not going anywhere with you until you give me that dagger."

His eyes narrowed. He hesitated, but then reached into his duster and pulled forth the blade in a heavy leather sheath. It appeared to have a special holder secured inside his coat. "I see your point," he answered slowly, handing it over.

The dagger felt heavy in her hand. Enclosed in thick black leather with a *B* and a *D* in script at the base, the sheath itself was lovely, but when she pulled the blade free, she gasped. "Wow." It seemed made of pure light—if light was as sharp as a new sword and could draw blood.

"Be careful with that."

She raised her gaze to his and narrowed her eyes. "Who are you?"

THREE

Broder had thought the last thousand years of his existence had been hell. He'd been wrong. *This* was hell. Having to sit across from this woman, who heated his blood like water on a stove, and not jump on her like an animal in rut—*this* was hell. He drew a breath and concentrated on her face, tried to pay attention to what she was saying.

He'd been without a woman for a thousand years; he'd been forced to learn control and he had a lot of it, but there was something about this particular female that made him crazy. Perhaps it was because she was available to him, but he wasn't convinced it was the only reason. It made sense that Loki had chosen a woman that was beyond average well suited to him.

And, *fuck*, she was beautiful. Long, straight, dark blond hair that framed a heart-shaped face with big brown eyes and full, rosy lips. She was curvier than the current notion of what was beautiful—but perfect for his personal notion. All those curves were in exactly the right places. All of them begged for exploration, by both his hands and his mouth.

If Loki had fashioned this woman for him alone, Broder would not have been surprised. It was hard, very hard, to concentrate on what she was saying as she sat across from him in the booth of the diner.

Even despite the danger she was in.

As soon as he'd arrived at the parking garage, he'd known

something was wrong. When he'd reached her and found that agent attacking her, he'd gone insane. If he'd had all his wits, he would have kept the demon to interrogate, but his blood had rushed through his ears, all rationality had fled, and every part of him had demanded the demon become ice. Now he had no idea why it had been targeting this woman—*his woman.* He already thought of her that way.

". . . and then you pulled my door off the hinges!" She let her arm fall to the top of the table as if in exclamation. She gave him a slow, narrow-eyed blink that screamed irritation. "You ruined my car."

He said nothing in response.

She twisted her full lips and his groin ached. He shifted in his seat to relieve the pressure. This woman was going to be the death of him—and he'd thought he was unkillable.

"You never explained who you are."

"Think of me as a soldier in a war or a policeman."

She raised her brows. "*Think of you as?* What are you really?"

"Unclassifiable."

She studied him for a long moment. "I figured out a while back there are mysteries in this world."

"Mysteries and monsters. There are both. You found that out today."

"I knew it before," she muttered. Lowering her gaze and drawing a finger across the top of the table, she said, "My name is Jessamine, but everyone calls me Jessa."

That was a gorgeous name. It fit her well. "Of course it is."

"What?"

"That name suits you."

"Oh." She scrunched her face up. "You don't talk very much."

He shrugged. He was about to talk a lot—much more than he usually did. "What were you doing in that government building so late at night?"

"Why do you want to know?"

"I'm trying to figure out why you were targeted by that man."

"What was he, anyway?"

"A monster."

She gave him a withering look. "Thanks, figured that out already. More info, please?"

"All in good time. Why were you in the parking garage of a government building after hours?"

She took a sip of her coffee, then stared out the window at the empty city street. "It's personal. I'd rather not discuss it."

"Any detail at all would help me. You don't have to tell me everything."

She took a moment to answer. "I needed to look something up regarding my family."

Broder considered her vague answer. Outwardly he had no idea why an agent of the Blight would go after her. There didn't appear to be an obvious reason. Maybe she'd just been in the wrong place at the wrong time, had run into a hungry agent. Yet the Blight were usually much cleaner in their feeding habits than that. If their prey resisted the way she'd been resisting, they usually let it go. The Blight, like the Brotherhood, had compelling reasons to keep their presence secret from humanity.

"The building was closed for the day, locked. It was well past working hours. There was no one there and you didn't have entry."

"All true." She refused to meet his eyes.

"Do you work there?"

She glanced at him, eyes flashing. "None of your business. You know, I'm not much for interrogations."

Hmmm . . . in his opinion, that meant *no*. Interesting.

She was hiding something, but did it have anything to do with why the Blight had sought her out . . . *if* the Blight had sought her out? She seemed legitimately ignorant of the presence of Blight in the world, even if she was taking the supernatural occurrences back in the parking garage better than most humans would. Maybe she was just a really good actress.

There was no end to the tricks Loki played on the Brotherhood. Clearly there was something special about this woman. He just needed to figure out what it was and hope it didn't bite him in the ass.

He narrowed his eyes at her. Was the woman worth all of this? He could just leave the diner right now, leave the woman to whatever fate would befall her. Reject Loki's "gift." He'd gone this long without sex, what was another thousand years?

His gaze traveled across her creamy skin and over her lush mouth. He imagined those lips touching his, traveling lower. He imagined undressing her, one offending piece of fabric at a time, spreading her lovely thighs and tasting her. He closed his eyes, turning his head away. He clenched his fists as his body tightened.

Yes, she was worth it.

Damn Loki and his games. The petty god had known that this woman was his every dream and he'd never be able to walk away from her.

Jessa sipped her coffee and cocked her head to the side. "Are you all right?"

"Yes," he ground out. He sounded pissed off, but he couldn't help it.

Her eyebrows rose up into her dark blond hairline and she muttered, "Okay, then," under her breath. Opening her purse, she extracted a long box of what looked like candy, opened it, and popped a brightly colored . . . thing into her mouth.

"What are those?"

She flashed the yellow box at him. "Jujyfruits." When he gave her a blank look, she gawped at him. "Jujyfruits? You've never heard of them? Never, I don't know, *gone to a movie in your life*?"

He frowned at her. No, he hadn't.

She sighed as though he was hopeless. "They're candy, usually consumed at cinematic events, a.k.a. *movies*." She stared down at the box. "When I was depressed about something, or feeling anxious, my aunt would take me to the movies and buy me these. I guess they're sort of like a drug for me now. I eat them when I'm really sad or stressed." She snorted. "I've been eating lots of them lately."

For a moment Broder considered what it would be like to have someone take him to the movies, then mentally shook it off. "They look disgusting."

She offered the box to him. "Try one."

He considered the brightly colored candies for a long moment, then chose a red one and popped it into his mouth, chewed, and swallowed. "They taste disgusting, too."

She shrugged and selected another. "More for me. So, what's your favorite candy?"

"I don't eat candy."

"Big surprise," she muttered, then eyed him suspiciously. "You know, you don't strike me as a very well-rounded individual."

He stared stonily at her.

"You seem, I don't know . . . like you're all work and no play. Not that I know what your work is. . . ." She trailed off, eating another Jujyfruit.

"Anyone ever tell you that you talk a lot?"

"Anyone ever tell you that you don't talk enough?" She set the candy box aside and closed her arms over her chest. "Okay, I showed you mine, now show me yours. What was the deal with that fanged thing back in the parking garage?"

"We can't discuss that here."

She snorted and rolled her eyes. "If you think I'm going anywhere with you that's not a very public place, you've got another think coming."

He twisted his lips. He'd always found that turn of phrase to be odd. "If I am meant to protect you, you will go where I say and not complain about it."

Her pale brows rose. "Oh, really, Mr. Caveman? I think not. I can protect myself just fine on my own. I've taken self-defense classes and I carry pepper spray."

Catching her gaze, he held it steadily. "You're kidding,

right?" The woman had no idea what she was dealing with. "Your self-defense classes and your pepper spray mean zilch against demons and you know it."

"Demons?"

"What else would you call a man with fangs who wants to suck all the blood from your body?"

She visibly paled. "Uh, well, normally I'd call him a vampire."

"There's no such thing as vampires."

"No vampires . . . yet demons exist?" She grew a little paler.

"He froze your skin. That's what demons do."

She blinked. "Tell me more."

"Not here."

She nodded, her jaw working in her rage. "Okay, you won't give me any answers? I'm out of here." She dug into her purse and slapped a dollar and a quarter on the table to pay for her coffee. "Thanks for your help in the parking garage. Have a nice life."

Letting his head fall back against the plastic seat behind his head, he grunted. So, she was going to be a pain in the ass. *Great.*

The bell on the door tinkled as she left and through the plate-glass window of the all-night diner he could see her step to the curb outside to hail a cab. It was raining again and it quickly soaked her raincoat and plastered her hair to her head. They'd left her doorless car parked at the garage. It would have been tricky to explain to the security guards at the exit of the ramp.

He tossed a few bills on the table, then, slowly, he rose and followed her.

"You can't go home," he said, yelling over the sound of the pelting rain. "How many fucking times do I need to tell you it's not safe?"

She paused and looked at him, her hand still up in the air to signal the passing cars. "I have no reason to trust what you say."

"Yeah, only the fact that I saved your life."

Lowering her hand, she turned toward him. "Yes, you saved my life and I'm grateful for that, but you aren't being straight with me, either. I need to know what your motives are. Your secrecy is not making me feel secure." She turned back to the street, muttering under her breath, "I'm done with secrets." Then, louder, "Taxi!"

A yellow cab pulled over to the curb and she climbed into the back. Broder climbed in after her. She wasn't going anywhere with his dagger. She'd probably forgotten she had it tucked into her enormous purse.

She turned toward him, a look of pure indignation on her face, tendrils of her wet hair plastered to her pale cheeks. "Get out!"

"No."

"You are *not* going to follow me home. I'll never feel safe in my apartment again."

He bared his teeth at her in frustration. "You have no reason to feel safe now. It's possible you're being stalked by demons."

"And I'm supposed to think being stalked by you is safer?" Making a frustrated sound, she rolled her eyes and leaned forward. "The nearest police station, please." She gave him a smug look, which he ignored.

The cab pulled away from the curb and started down the street.

"What do you intend to tell the police when we arrive?" Broder murmured, gazing out the window at the rain-slicked streets. "That you were attacked in a parking garage by a vampire who tried to suck you dry and were saved by a leather-clad man with superstrength who is trying to follow you home? That should get you pretty far . . . far as the nearest mental hospital, anyway."

"Don't worry about what I'll tell the police. That's my business . . . and your problem. Hey!" She leaned forward, addressing the taxi driver, a tall blond man with an unruly mustache. "You just turned down the wrong street. There's a police station over on Ash."

The taxi driver remained silent and suddenly Broder went

on alert, the runes in his coat giving off a subtle pulse of power. Something was not—

The driver yanked the wheel, pulling the taxi to the side of the street. The doors snicked locked and then the driver lunged into the backseat with the sinuousness of a snake— straight at Broder. The agent's hands closed with incredible strength around his throat. Broder choked, his air leaving him.

Beside him Jessa screamed.

He grabbed the demon under his arms and slammed him up into the ceiling of the car, trying to dislodge his hold. It was unlikely the agent could kill him, but the demon could definitely put Broder out of commission long enough to kill Jessa. There was no room to move in here, no room to *fight* . . . and Jessa still had his dagger.

Jessa was busy screaming and trying to open the door or roll down the window—both of which were child-locked. No escape for her.

He slammed the agent's body into the ceiling of the car again, but the man's grip still didn't budge. The agent's jaw was opening, fangs descending. The demon hissed, freezing spittle spraying Broder's face, his eyes soulless black. Broder cast a desperate, sidelong glance at Jessa. He was going to be incapacitated and she was going to die if she didn't remember she had the dagger. He tried to mouth the words, but no air came out to give them life.

Black spots appeared in his vision. He was going to pass out. He'd return to consciousness with her bloodless body in his lap. The thought made him insane with rage.

Fighting with every ounce of his will the unconsciousness that threatened, he found the agent's eyes and gouged. The thing screamed, fangs flashing, but still didn't let go. It wouldn't, of course. Once an order was given, these mindless, primal, lower-level agents wouldn't stop until they'd achieved their goal or died trying. The thing's grip tightened, even as its blood ran down Broder's hands.

Jessa was screaming her head off and the black spots

were growing bigger, stealing his consciousness. Soon it would all be over.

The agent exploded into ice.

Broder inhaled, gasping for breath and getting nothing but foul demon ice mist, which made him choke. Jessa had dropped the dagger onto the seat of the cab and was busy trying to climb over the seat, still screaming, "You gouged out his eyes! He's all . . . ice! There were more f-fangs!" In between screaming, she seemed to be hyperventilating.

Now she was acting like most humans did when exposed to the Blight and the Brotherhood. Kind of a delayed reaction, but there it was. Oddly, it made him feel better.

She scrambled for the driver's-side door and opened it, falling out into the rain-filled gutter of the street. Crawling on her hands and knees, she made her way to the middle of the sidewalk and sat down, hugging herself, her dark blond hair tangled and covering her face.

Broder broke the lock on the back door easily and opened it, going to her and kneeling at her side. He sighed. "It's a lot to take in."

She laughed. "You love to understate things, don't you? That thing almost killed you."

"No. I was never in danger." He paused a beat. "It almost killed *you*."

"Why do they burst into ice when they die?"

"They were created in Hel."

"Demons from Hell, of course."

"It's not the Christians' Hell; it's a different realm from that. Hel is a very cold place. The Blight were molded from Hel's ice by the goddess who rules there, in order to wage war on Earth. When they're stabbed by one of Loki's blades and die, they return to their original form. Ice."

She stared straight ahead and let out a humorless laugh. "That must make cleanup a snap."

They stayed that way for a long moment, while he let her absorb everything. The Blight were still after her for some reason that he suspected not even she understood. They wouldn't stop until she was dead. That meant . . . "Do you have any kids, Jessa?"

She shook her head.

"Any pets at home?"

"No." She looked up at him suspiciously, his questions reaching through her shock.

"Do you take any special medications you don't have with you?"

Frowning, she shook her head. "No. Why?"

He sighed, touched her forehead, and let her collapse into his arms, unconscious. "That's why," he murmured, scooping her up and laying her in the backseat of the cab, moving his dagger out of the way first. Then he climbed into the front and pulled away from the curb.

She was going to have to stay with him for a while, like it or not.

Jessa woke slowly, as if waking from a deep, delicious sleep that had nourished every part of her body and mind. Stretching, she smiled, recalling the weird dream she'd had. Vampires that poofed into ice when stabbed with a special blade and hunky, mysterious men coming to her rescue. Shaking her head, she opened her eyes . . . and went very still.

She pushed up, seeing she still wore her clothes and she was not, as she'd presumed, in her own bed. The quilt covering her was fluffy and soft, in tones of brown and gold. The bed was an enormous four-poster—king-size. The room was huge, with a massive creek stone fireplace dominating the opposite wall. A comforting fire flickered there.

The place was sparse with furniture, despite its size. A large brown-and-gold-toned area rug covered the polished wood floor. A couch, table, and chair rested to her right, in front of a large bay window. To her left were two darkened doorways—a walk-in closet and a bathroom, she surmised by the look of it. Two chests of drawers stood on either side of the massive bed.

Where the hell was she?

Unfortunately, she suspected the answer once she'd examined her most recent memories. Broder had touched her head and she'd slipped straight into dreamland. Neat trick. The trick of someone not human.

This had to be his house.

Pushing the blankets away, she slipped out of the bed. Her bare feet touched the cold floor and she spotted her socks, shoes, and bag along one wall. Padding across the room in the opposite direction, she pushed aside the drapes and peered out the window at a large, manicured lawn with a heavy treeline shielding the house's view of its neighbors.

She let the drape fall back and immediately crossed the room to the door and found it open. Broder had kidnapped her and brought her here for some reason—she still wasn't sure she bought his "protecting her" shtick. After all, he didn't know her; why would he risk his life for her? One thing was for certain: She needed answers.

He probably wasn't human. She understood that, but she wasn't ready to deal with it yet.

She put on her socks and shoes, grabbed her tote bag, and slipped out into the hallway, her feet meeting a long runner rug of blues and silvers. Whatever Broder was, it appeared he had money. Tasteful artwork decorated the neutrally colored walls and accent tables set with fresh flowers sat periodically down the long corridor that was filled with doors.

Scratch that; maybe he'd brought her to some kind of hospital or halfway house. That would mean that either she—or he—was crazy. At this point she wasn't ruling out any explanations for recent occurrences.

At the end of the corridor, she found a sweeping staircase and followed it down into a huge foyer with marble floors and a set of heavy double doors. From a room on her right, she could hear the sound of murmuring voices, all of them male. She stopped in the middle of the floor, shivering in the cold air of the house, and considered the front doors.

They might be unlocked, just like the door to the bedroom she'd been placed in.

She might be free to leave.

Yet she'd been attacked—twice now—by fanged monsters Broder claimed were demons. Who was to say she wouldn't be attacked again, and without Broder and his magick dagger to fight the things off, what chance would she have?

The primal part of her brain that sought her survival told her that maybe leaving this house wasn't the path to take, even though she felt scared here.

"Hello," said a deep voice from her right.

She tore her gaze away from the doors to meet a pair of startling blue eyes that were attached to one of the most gorgeous men she'd ever seen. If she was hallucinating this, between this man, the mysterious Dmitri, and Broder, her insanity had *good* taste. Maybe she'd stay awhile.

She blinked and the apparition didn't fade. "Uh. Hello."

"You must be Jessamine."

The man possessed the same accent that Broder had— clipped vowels and slightly strange pronunciation of some words. It was the kind of accent that occurred if one spoke another language before learning English, yet spoke English flawlessly. She couldn't place the accent at all, but that was such a mildly odd thing in a sea of bizarre that it barely even registered at this point.

She stared at him, taking in the full impact of the gorgeousness. Thick, tousled tawny hair, piercing blue eyes, tanned skin, chiseled features—and the powerful body of a god. The same body Broder possessed.

This man was light to Broder's dark, though there was something every bit as forbidding about him. Broder and the stranger both had an edge to them, something impossible to define, but that marked them both as dangerous to deal with. Despite this man's attractiveness, she'd normally go out of her way to avoid him.

She shifted on her feet. "Yes. I assume Broder told you my name. Is he here?"

He shook his head. "He had to go out."

"When is he expected back?"

"Soon." The man looked at the front door. "Going somewhere?"

She glanced at the door and shouldered her bag a little more securely. "I don't know. I guess I'm still deciding."

"You can leave if you choose, but that wouldn't be a good move. You're being targeted by forces you can't control."

"Yeah, I kind of figured that out last night."

"My name is Tyr."

She made a face. "Tyr?" Then she realized that had been rude. "I'm sorry. It's just an odd name."

"It's a very old name."

Interesting. That had been almost the same explanation that Broder had given. There was something really peculiar about these men. Of course, it didn't get any more peculiar than supernatural strength, healing through touch, and the ability to put someone to sleep with the brush of a hand.

He motioned to her. "Come with me."

"Why?" she asked, suspicion clear in her voice.

Tyr smiled and spread his hands. "Because I want to keep you from leaving, if I can. It's a dangerous world out there for a woman on the demon hit list."

With that smile, even though it didn't quite reach the man's eyes, he really set himself apart from Broder. She couldn't even imagine a smile on that man's face. His skin would probably break apart if he tried.

He walked into the room from which she'd heard all the male voices, leaving her alone with the front door. Should she take door number one, which may lead to demons, or door number two, which led to . . . well, the verdict was still out.

She hesitated for a moment, then walked over to door number two and peered into the room. Within, ranged on various chairs and couches, was an endless array of men, all of them with their gazes focused on her. They'd gone silent in her presence.

Some of them were pretty, some weren't pretty, but all

of them were compelling. All of them were muscular, either leanly or more of the beefcake variety. It was a festival for the eyes and female senses. All of them seemed intent on her, though it wasn't in a physically appraising or sexual way. Their regard seemed dangerous on some level that spoke to her primal, lizard brain and told her to flee before she was crushed like a bug.

Jessa took a step backward. Door number one was looking better right now. "What is this place and who are all of you?"

Tyr leaned against the wall and slid a hand into his pocket. "Broder hasn't told you?"

"No."

"He will."

She counted to five and did her best to control her temper. "Why don't *you* tell me?"

"Not my place."

"Whatever." She took another step backward. This was just weird. What were all these men doing in this house? She glanced at the door. "I think it's time I took my chances on my own."

"Do that and you'll probably die."

Her lips curled back from her lips as she edged toward the door. "I have more resources than you might think." She did. Strange, new ones that she shouldn't have, yet which were there anyway. All she needed to do was remember to use them when they were called for. "See you around, Tyr."

She opened the heavy front door and found Broder on the other side. He looked unsurprised to find her fleeing.

Glancing at her tote bag, he drawled, "Where do you think you're going?"

FOUR

"I'm leaving. You have a whole house filled with beefcake and no explanation for it."

He narrowed his eyes and tilted his head to the side a little. "So you're fleeing because of beefcake?"

"No. I'm fleeing strange, inexplicable beefcake in a big fancy house because every last one of you gives off a don't-fuck-with-me vibe. So here I am, obeying the vibe. As in, *leaving*. Right now."

"I'm afraid I can't let you do that."

She glanced back into the foyer, where Tyr was still standing, arms crossed over his broad chest and his full lips twisted as though enjoying the show. "He said I could leave whenever I want."

"He's not your protector. I am."

"Protector? What the hell is this, the Middle fucking Ages? What era are you from, anyway?"

Broder didn't answer right away and suddenly she wondered if she'd hit upon something she might not want to know. "We're from the era in which we guarded the lives of women with our own." His lips peeled back to show sharp white teeth. "Was I the only one in the cab last night?"

"I know that I'm in trouble. It's just that I'm not sure I'm in less trouble by staying here."

He stared at her for a long moment, his jaw clenched. She

stared back, her will strong. "Go back inside," he said
finally. "You can get something to eat. I'll introduce you to
the . . . beefcake." He paused. "More importantly, I'll tell
you exactly who is trying to kill you. Useful information, no?"

Her stomach growled at the thought of food, but it was
the offer of knowledge that hooked her. "Fine." She backed
away, into the foyer.

Broder led her back into the room with all the men.

They were still ranged across the room in various dis-
plays of beefy goodness, all still focused on her with eerie
intensity. Jessa folded her arms across her chest and scowled,
determined not to be affected. The testosterone in here was
a little too much to take.

"You've already met Tyr." He motioned to the tawny-
haired man on her right. She nodded at him, shifting uncomfortably on her feet.

Broder motioned toward a dark-haired man slouched in
a chair who sported a vicious-looking scar down one side
of a brutally good-looking face . . . good-looking if it hadn't
been for the glower. "That's Grimm."

She tried a smile. "Of course you are."

"Over there is Stig." Broder pointed at a leanly muscled
man with sandy hair and green eyes who wore a duster a lot
like Broder's. Many of them, she now noticed, wore similar
items of clothing. "And that's Dag, Leif, and Keir."

She glanced at all the men Broder indicated. "May I just
say that you all have very unique names."

"They're Norwegian," said Tyr.

One of the men, Leif, she thought his name was, shifted
on his chair and she caught sight of a sheathed blade.

"Unique way of . . . dressing, too," she added, clearing
her throat. She'd make a bet all these men were armed. She'd
make another bet there was a reason for the propensity
toward longer coats in their fashion decisions.

Broder nodded at a godlike man who seemed to take up
more space in the room than the others even though he really
wasn't any more muscular than the rest. She'd noticed him

before, but had purposefully skated her attention over him. Of all the men in the room, even Broder, this one seemed the most threatening. "And that's Erik, the oldest of us and our leader."

She examined the man in question. He didn't look old at all. In fact, he looked about the same age as Broder. "He looks very young for the way you speak of him."

"He was the first of us. Perhaps that's a better way to put it."

That just confused her more.

Erik stood from where he sat on the edge of a polished desk. He nodded at her. "We're pleased to have you among us," he said in that same odd accent. "You are safe here. Never doubt that."

Oddly enough, when a dangerous-looking muscle-bound man told her she could trust him, it didn't automatically put her at ease.

"Hungry?" asked Broder.

She was too uneasy to be concerned with food, but she nodded anyway. She just wanted to get out of this room and away from all these mysterious men.

Broder led her out of the room, and she cast a final suspicious look over her shoulder, wondering like crazy what the hell was going on in this place. Was it a halfway house for wayward underwear models? Some secret organization of crime-fighting superheroes? Oh, crap, the set of a Norwegian porn movie?

He led her into a huge industrial-style kitchen. She could probably fit her entire bedroom into the enormous stainless-steel refrigerator alone. She guessed she shouldn't be all that surprised. After all, men as built as these guys must need to consume a lot of calories.

Broder set some bread, jam, and butter on the table, then went for silverware and plates.

She eased onto a chair at the center island. "Are you an Olympic sports team of some kind?"

He returned to the island and set a plate in front of her. "Is that what you think? Do you always pair bobsledding with vicious monsters that move like snakes, have irises that turn jet-black, and sprout retractable fangs?"

She gave up her attempt to make rational sense of it all. Swallowing hard, she pushed the plate away, suddenly not very hungry anymore. "So you're saying those things and the men in this house are connected?"

"Blight."

"Excuse me?"

"The fanged monsters, they're called the Blight. Yes, we fight them."

She digested that. "So this is like some kind of superhero club."

He frowned at her. "Super to a human, maybe. Definitely not heroes."

"Blight are demons. Correct?"

He nodded. "Spawned from the depths of icy Hel, which holds the same name of the goddess who keeps that realm. Hel is Loki's daughter and she's imprisoned there. You could say she and Loki have a troubled relationship."

"You mentioned Loki before. I remember him from my mythology class at school. He's a Norwegian god, right? A trickster god. Kind of a prick?"

"You sum him up nicely."

"So the Blight are trying to kill me." She chewed on that for a moment, breathing deep and trying to remain calm. Apparently demons and Norwegian gods were real. Shock was keeping her from running around the room, holding her head in her hands. "So what do they want? Why are they here?"

Broder selected a piece of bread and began to butter it. "The mission of the Blight is to bring about Ragnarök." He glanced up at her. "Sort of like the Christians' version of Armageddon. Ragnarök is an apocalypse for the gods."

"Apocalypse for the gods," she repeated numbly. This just got weirder and weirder.

"Yes."

"Do we care if the gods have an apocalypse?"

Broder shrugged. "I hate all the gods I've ever met, so I

don't care if they live or die. However, their war would be bad for the world. There would be a series of natural disasters that would result in the destruction of the planet. Basically, Hel is trying to kill her father. Humanity is in the way."

A little puff of air escaped Jessa. She gave him a slow blink. "Are you fucking crazy?"

"I wish I was. I also wish I didn't have to tell you this next part, which is likely to blow your little human mind."

"My little hum—wait a minute, you're trying to make me angry, aren't you? Well, forget it. You can't. Tell me the rest of your whacked-out story."

He set the butter aside and moved on to the jam. When he was finished with that, he folded over his piece of bread and calmly dipped it into his glass of milk. "We are the Brotherhood of the Damned, a group of men who committed brutal acts in our days as Vikings and have been punished by the god Loki to an immortal life battling the Blight."

Jessa stared.

Broder took a bite of his bread. "Why aren't you freaking out right now?" he asked around the mouthful.

"I'm freaking out on the inside." At least now she knew why her mojo hadn't worked on him. He wasn't even human . . . if he was telling the truth.

He cocked his head to the side. "You don't look like you believe me."

"You have to admit it's a little hard to swallow."

"So you didn't see the two agents of the Blight last night? You missed the bloodthirsty fangs, the freezing touch, the huge cobra mouth, all that stuff?"

"Yes, but you're telling me that the god Loki is real and that you're over a thousand years old. You're saying that you're some kind of . . . prison inmate for life, but instead of making license plates, you're forced to fight demons. You're also telling me that Loki and his daughter, Hel, are locked in some epic family squabble and the fate of the world hangs in the balance. Gee, what's not to believe? By the way"—she gave him a head-to-toe sweep—"for a thousand, you're looking really good."

He bit into his jam sandwich, unfazed. "Humans," he said after he'd swallowed, "never believe anything outside their tiny, limited sphere of experience."

"You're not human, then? So I was right."

"I was, once. Then Loki stabbed me with a sliver of Blight and I became something else." He paused. "Brotherhood."

"So everyone in this house is suffering from the same mass delusion. Perhaps something happened to each of you in your past, something in which you felt out of control or helpless, so you decided to give yourself *special powers* and *immortality*"—she made air quotes around the words—"so you would never feel out of control or helpless again. I get it." She pushed from her chair. "But I don't want any part of it." She turned and went for the door. Nothing was going to stop her from getting the hell out of here this time.

"I know you don't want to believe this, but walk out that door and you will die, I guarantee it. I don't know why the Blight want you dead, but they do. You don't stand a chance against them."

She halted, clenching her hands at her sides. "Why does everyone presume I'm so helpless?"

"Because you're human."

"That doesn't mean I'm stupid."

"You're not stupid; you're just not prepared. Don't you remember last night? In the cab? All you did was flail and scream."

She whirled. "I killed that thing!"

"*With my dagger*, yes. You don't have my dagger any longer."

That was a good point.

She put a hand on her hip. "Prove to me that you're everything you just said you were. I want honest-to-god, irrefutable evidence that you're not delusional and insane."

"More proof than demons?"

"Okay, maybe I need proof *I'm* not delusional and insane."

He set his bread down and rounded the island to walk

over to her. He stood so close, she could feel the warmth of his body radiating out and enveloping her. He smelled good, like leather and the faintest whisper of cologne. Reaching down, he picked up her hand, his strong, broad fingers closing around it, and pressed it palm-first to his chest.

Her breath caught at the feel of his strong chest under his shirt and the warmth of his skin. He was hard beneath the soft skin, all muscle.

"Close your eyes and reach out with your mind to the center of me," he said.

After shooting him a look that clearly conveyed how futile she thought this exercise, she closed her eyes and sought the "center of him," whatever that meant.

She expected to find nothing, but it hit her almost immediately. In her mind's eye a long sliver of blue pulsed. She knew without a shadow of a doubt that it was lodged in Broder's soul. It gave off a pulse of danger, of darkness, that made her want to back away from him, but she stood her ground.

Suddenly she was whooshed away to some building she didn't recognize. She understood this was happening in her mind, but it seemed completely real. The chill in the room dissolved into her bones; the shift and rustle of material filled her ears.

Gasping, her eyes open, she turned in a circle, taking in the scene. Strong, big men, all in the clothing of Vikings, ranged around her. She recognized a few of them from the room downstairs. All of them were being addressed by a sleek, handsome man dressed in a suit. Loki? She could hear nothing, but she sensed that all the men in the room possessed pulsing slivers of darkness in their souls.

As soon as the vision had engulfed her, it spit her back out. She stumbled backward, disoriented, her hand going to her head. Nausea filled her. "What was that?"

"I shared with you one of my earliest Brotherhood memories. Proof that I am what I say I am."

She took another step back, the world going fuzzy. Her breath came in short, panicky little pants and her chest was tight. She turned in a dizzy circle, eyes wide, wanting this awful feeling to pass.

Her vision went dark and she collapsed.

Broder watched Jessa as she lay on his bed. She looked fucking good there. Too good to be true. She lay on her back, her head lolling to one side, her riot of thick, dark blond hair loose on the pillow. He'd covered her with a blanket and was keeping a close eye on her. When she'd passed out, she'd bumped her head on the floor.

Her body made an intriguing form under the cream-colored blanket he'd tucked in around her. He tried not to concentrate too hard on the pout of her lips or the tiny mole that marked her cheek just beneath her right eye.

All the makeup she'd been wearing was gone now. She hadn't been wearing much of it to begin with. Jessa was one of those women who didn't need it. She was a natural beauty, though not a perfect one. Her nose was a little bigger than what normally might be considered classically attractive, her body a size or two more curvaceous, and her two front teeth had just a slight gap . . . a gap he really wanted to explore with his tongue.

In his opinion, she was gorgeous, just his type, as Loki had known she would be. If, after all these years, it could be said he had a type. He was a little out of practice.

He pressed his hand to her forehead again, frowning. The bare amount of healing ability he possessed told him that she was okay. No concussion, even though she'd given her head a good knock. She should wake up all right. All right at least physically. Mentally and emotionally he wasn't so certain how she'd fare.

Broder hated telling humans the truth—breaking their tenuous illusion of a world that made sense. People wanted things to make sense, went out of their way to create theories and philosophies that explained everything that was scary in life, or things they just didn't understand.

The cold truth was that nothing made sense. Everything

was chaos and they were all just fish swimming around in it—an ocean of chance whose tides swelled at the fickle whim of the gods.

His gaze skated down the length of her for the millionth time. He wanted to lift the blanket and ease his hands beneath her clothes. He wanted to stroke his fingers down her smooth skin, find the places she most loved to have touched, and make her moan. It had been so long since he'd had a woman to touch, to care for, to stroke and to please. The last woman had been his wife.

Broder clenched his hands, holding himself back from jumping on her. Curse whatever situation Jessa was in. If she'd had no target on her back from the Blight, he simply would have seduced her, brought her back here, and fucked her until they both couldn't walk. Now they were in this mess and he'd been forced to shatter her safe little world.

Somewhere, Loki was laughing right now.

Jessa roused, her eyelids fluttering open. Her big brown eyes locked with his. "If you're not crazy, then I must be." Then she winced and touched the back of her head. "Ouch."

He leaned back in his chair and sighed. "It's not you or me who's crazy, it's the world. Just relax. You bumped your head."

She spotted the glass of water on the short dresser at the edge of his bed, pushed up, took it, and sipped. "Okay."

"You're taking this better than most humans do."

She shrugged. "I don't think having a panic attack and passing out qualifies as taking it well."

"That wasn't from shock; it was a reaction to sharing a memory with me."

Setting her glass of water on the table, she cocked her head to the side and studied him. "So all the members of the Brotherhood are being punished for a brutal crime?"

"Yes."

"What did you do to merit a sliver of demon stabbed into your soul?"

Broder turned away from her. *Fingers slick with blood clenching the grip of the sword, ax handle sticky and heavy*

*in his other hand. Turning in a circle, bodies every-
where. . . .* "None of your business, woman." He stood.
"Want an ice pack for your head?"

She stared up at him, eyes glittering with anger. "I think
it's totally my—"

"I'll go get the ice pack." He left the room and went down
to the kitchen. Anything to get away from her questions and
the look in her eyes.

When he returned to the room, she was standing at the
window and looking out over the grounds. He handed the
ice pack to her and she pressed it to the lump at the back of
her head.

She cast him an irritated glance. "Did you just call me
woman a minute ago?"

He rubbed his hand over his mouth. The scent of her was
driving him insane and the warmth radiating from her body
only compounded it. He'd done an excellent job of suppress-
ing his lust over the centuries, but there was something
special about this woman that made it hard to control.

He didn't answer her question. He figured it was rhetori-
cal. Most modern women didn't like being called that, but
he wasn't a modern man. That was clearly evidenced by the
thoughts he was having now, the slip of his gaze over the
swell of her breasts and the flare of her hips.

He wanted her clothes off her. He wanted her beneath
him, his cock inside her. *Right now.*

He closed his eyes, his body going tight. "You should
move away from me."

She turned toward him, closer to him, *fuck it all.* "Why?"

"Can't you just do as you're told?"

She huffed out a breath, dropping the hand with the ice
pack to her side and putting her other hand on her hip. "No,
actually, I'm not really the type to bend to a man's every
command."

He stared at her, the curve of her hip, the press of her
breasts against her sweater. Her brown eyes were flashing
with temper and that only made them more beautiful. He'd
developed superhuman control where women were con-

cerned over the centuries, but Jessa was shredding it like tissue paper in a tornado. She didn't understand the danger, had never met a man like him.

"Back away, Jessa," he growled.

She shifted and leaned in toward him. *"No."*

The slim tether he had on his control snapped. He lunged at her, sweeping her up in his arms. She yelped and dropped the bag of ice, but he barely noticed it.

He wanted her. On the bed. *Naked.* Not in that order.

He pulled at the hem of her shirt. "I warned you to get away from me."

"What are you doing?" There was a note of alarm in her voice, but the note of musk in her scent said she wasn't exactly scared—not totally. That note of musk only made him need her more.

He cupped her face in his hands, forcing himself to stop tearing at her clothes. "It's been a very long time since I was with a woman and *I want you.* You, above all others. If you don't want me touching you, get the fuck out of this room and away from me *right now."*

She went very still, staring up into his face with wide eyes.

"Last chance," he gritted out.

The scent of her was strong now, though he could clearly see the conflict on her face. She wanted him, but knew she shouldn't. If he were a gentleman, he'd back away right now. Except he wasn't a gentleman; he was an immortal Viking who hadn't touched a woman in a thousand years.

"Are you sure?" he managed to force out.

She gave him an almost imperceptible nod.

FIVE

What was she doing? She'd wanted so badly not to give in to him and here she was, giving in to him. Worse, her body was humming with need. There was no way she could say no. Not now. Not with his hands on her and that look in his eyes—like she was every Christmas he'd never had, like he would die if he didn't get to touch her. Her libido had trumped her mind.

All that mattered right now was his hands on her body. Everything else was going to have to wait until later.

With a growl of pure lust, he yanked her around and dragged her to the bed. His fingers worked to free her clothes the moment he tossed her down. "I want you bare," he breathed against her mouth. "I want your skin on mine."

She wanted that, too, wanted more than that. She wanted her hands sliding over the warm, hard muscle of his chest and arms, desired his body flush up against hers, hot and intimate.

Her fingers caught in his shirt, finding the hem and yanking upward, as desperate to find bare flesh as he. Her hands slid over his muscled stomach and he groaned at the touch of her fingers. Her breath caught at the white crisscross of ancient scars, her fingers tracing a couple of them. It made sense he had them, but they were still jarring—so deep, so brutal, such blatant evidence of his violent existence.

"You're making me crazy," he murmured. "I'm trying to hold myself back from you, but you're making it hard. *A taste*. That's what I need. Just a taste."

"You can take more," she breathed against his lips. *Please.*

She pushed her sweater over her head and he tossed it to the floor. Next came her jeans, off and discarded. Now she was clad only in her black bra and underwear. Pausing, he leaned back and seemed to soak in the sight of her, as though memorizing the lines of her body. A moment later and his ferocity returned. He came down over her, forcing her thighs to spread and slipping his hand between them. She let out a shuddering breath of surprise mixed with arousal as his fingers found all the places where she was hot and excited through the thin panel of her underwear.

He stroked his thumb over her clit through the slick fabric, back and forth until she wanted to scream. In no time the little nub became swollen, sensitive, wanting more of his attention. A little whimper escaped her throat as her need built. His touch excited her in ways no other man's ever had. It had to do with his masterfulness, his aggressiveness, or maybe it was simply his sexual appetite—so great and so obvious.

"I remember this," he rasped. "How a woman feels. I want to make you moan with pleasure, Jessa."

She gasped as a powerful wave of sensation radiated through her. "I'm already there."

Broder shuddered against her. "No. I want more from you. *More.*" He lowered his mouth to hers, almost kissing her. "You feel so good, so hot and sweet. I could get drunk on you. Let me make you come."

Jessa shivered as his words rolled over her. "Oh, I don't think you'll have a problem with that, Broder." Her voice came out breathless. He could probably do it in his sleep, or just by looking at her the right way. His hands on her made her feel close to catching fire. Every little movement he made rasped the silky material of her bra across her stiff, sensitive nipples. A slow, sweet ache began between her thighs.

His huge, muscular arms slid around her, his hands easing down her back to cup her buttocks. With a natural inclination she didn't even think about, she wrapped her legs around his waist, pressing herself against the bulge in his jeans.

Broder's head dropped to her collarbone as he groaned. "Jessa, you're killing me." His voice came out a low rasp, tortured sounding. Women must drop at his feet, yet he managed to sound as if she was the only woman in the world worth having.

He lifted his head, caught her gaze with his, and held it. The way he looked at her—with such intense need—made her stomach muscles clench with anticipation.

This was totally wild. Her entire world had exploded with craziness the moment he'd stepped into it. Yet that didn't stop her body from needing and wanting the touch of this man, or the slow slide of her hand up to unhook her bra and fling it across the room.

No going back now.

He groaned in the back of his throat as her breasts fell free. Cupping one in his big hand, he rasped his callused thumb across the nipple, making her gasp with pleasure. She reached out to touch his chest, wanting to feel again the delicious bunch and pulse of the warm muscle under his shirt, but he grabbed her wrists—one, then the other—and pressed them to the mattress above her head. It made her spine bow, her body arching toward him, as if she was offering her breasts to him.

He took the offer, lowering his head to her nipple and sucking it into his mouth. She gasped as his hot tongue curled around it, sliding over every bump and ridge of the aroused peak. Pleasure radiated out from that point and engulfed her, sending her straightforward into a sexual haze that stole her cognitive ability. She felt drugged.

His tongue eased over the opposite nipple after thoroughly laving the first, while his hand slipped down over her stomach and found the soft hem of her underwear, then slid past it, seeking the tenderest part of her. His big hand explored her sensitive places, as though touching a woman for the very first time, with a thoroughness that left her panting. He explored every hill, every aching valley of her with his fingers, as though trying to memorize every inch.

His cock was as hard as steel and pressed into the outside

of her thigh, yet any attempt she made to touch him was denied, frustrating her. He wanted to touch her, *only*, for reasons that baffled and disappointed her.

Then he found her aroused clit and all other concerns disappeared. As he stroked her, his mouth moved from her breast, past her collarbone and chin, to her mouth. His lips hovered over hers.

At the last moment, seeing what he wished of her, she turned her face to the side.

This crazy sexual abandon she'd slipped into was one thing—but a kiss . . . it felt too intimate. A first kiss was a doorway, a promise of hope and, just maybe, of love to come. She knew the sentiment was old-fashioned, but that was how she felt. The rest of this was just hormones flaring. It was base, animalistic. A kiss was . . . emotional.

She wasn't ready to share that much of herself with him.

He made a soft sound of disapproval, but didn't press the issue. Apparently he had other things on his to-do list. Yanking her underwear down and off, his thick fingers slipped deep inside her, first one and then another.

Pleasure blossomed through her, unraveling her ability to think clearly, and she let out a long, slow moan. She would have given him anything in that moment if only he kept touching her that way.

"You are so beautiful," Broder said roughly, staring down at her.

Her body clenched in near orgasm, wound up tight, then slowly untwisted as he thrust his fingers in and out of her. His thumb found her clit and applied just the right amount of friction and pressure. He meant to make her come, and he meant business. It was almost as if he was forcing it out of her.

Pleasure exploded from the center of her sex-starved body and rolled out, making her gasp and then moan. Tears pricked her eyes as her spine arched and ecstasy poured through her. She cried out, closing her eyes and turning her head away from his eyes.

He nestled his nose in the curve of her neck and thrust his fingers in and out of her, drawing it out, wringing as much pleasure from her as he could possibly force from her body. She shuddered with waves of pleasure, the muscles of her sex pulsing and contracting.

When her climax had finally passed, Broder reached down and unbuttoned his jeans, pushing her thighs apart. He meant to take her right here, right now. She barely knew this man. Oh, she wanted him . . . but this was not right. Her desire for him had blinded her in the beginning, but now that the reality was here she knew she couldn't do this.

Panic shot through her. She didn't know this man. They had no condom.

This could not happen.

"You said you wouldn't hurt me," she whispered, now genuinely afraid. "You said you wouldn't do anything I didn't want you to do."

He went still. After a moment he rolled away from her, sitting on the side of the bed with his head cradled in his hands.

She sat up slowly, feeling lethargic, drained from the powerful climax he'd given her.

Now that the heat of the moment had passed, she felt exposed. This wasn't her gig, having intimate relations with men she didn't know. It just wasn't her.

"Look, I'm sorry. Normally I'm not a tease. I didn't mean to be one today. It just happened." She pushed a hand through her hair and pulled the sheet up to cover herself. "You touched me and lust took over. I couldn't say no once you started touching me. I *should've* . . . I just couldn't. Please forgive me."

Catching the edge of the quilt, she rolled herself up into it. Broder didn't move, didn't say a word. After a moment, he simply stood up and left the room.

She stared at the closed door for a long time, trying to gain a handle on the moment. It seemed like she'd been doing that a lot lately.

She'd teased him and she'd teased him *bad*, by the looks of it. She wished she could say it was all his fault and she hadn't had a choice in the matter. Of course that wasn't true. He'd been the one to get aggressive, but she'd given him permission to touch her and had known full well what he'd wanted from her. The lust had been mutual, but she just hadn't been able to consummate it.

Pushing up from the bed and taking the quilt with her, she entered the bathroom. It was a huge room, much bigger than she'd presumed. There was an enormous shower and a huge corner tub, plus a sink with two basins. Plush brown and gold rugs covered the floor and a small dresser with towels graced one corner. She could live in here.

Apparently if one was stabbed in the soul with a demon sliver and damned to live for an eternity, at least one did it in style.

After securely locking the door, she dropped the quilt, and started the shower. She loved the water. It calmed her in the most stressful of circumstances. Today, she took her time, washing as much of the tension down the drain as she could. Broder had made it clear that she shouldn't leave the house, so she guessed she needed to make herself at home.

The shower was divine, a large walk-in affair with multiple spigots. She washed her body thoroughly, then did it a second time. The filth from her encounter with the demon from the parking garage still clung to her. She shook her head under the water, trying to absorb that truth.

She'd been attacked by a demon. Twice.

Skin polished to a soft pink, and feeling refreshed, she toweled off and wrapped herself in the huge bathrobe that hung on the back of the door. Then she exited the bathroom, still drying her hair.

Her clothes were still lying scattered where Broder had thrown them and there was no sign that the man had ever returned. Sighing, she began cleaning up.

Broder's bike shot out of the mouth of the garage and sped down the long driveway leading to the main street. The trees that lined either side of the quarter-mile drive whipped past as he accelerated.

He needed to rid himself of the powerful lust he had for Jessa and this was one of the only ways he knew how to do it—speed. The other way was demon hunting; he might do some of that, too.

He hit the main street and accelerated again, weaving in and out of traffic with practiced ease, headed for Maryland where he could drive unimpeded. Maybe the wind could blow some of this tension from his body.

He wanted her so much he ached. Being denied that way—it had cut through the layers of numbness he'd cultivated—straight to the bone.

There had been a precarious moment when he'd almost pushed her. Not so hard it would have been rape—he would never do that to any woman—but he'd considered seducing her into saying yes. He'd sensed the desire in her, had been able to scent it on her skin. He'd known that if he touched her just a little more—*just the right way*—she would have given in to him easily. She would have melted and let him do anything to her that he wanted—and he *wanted* so much.

The temptation had ridden the edge of his control, but in the end he hadn't been able to do it. When Jessa wanted him to take her, he wanted her to want it with everything she was—and not to regret anything afterward.

It was going to be hard to wait for her to come to him and he couldn't be sure he'd be able to resist her in the future. Her skin was too smooth, her lips too full, and her body too curvaceous and inviting.

Tonight he'd won the battle with himself. Tomorrow all bets were off.

Jessa turned out the light on the bedside table and snuggled under the blanket, closing her eyes. Too nervous to face the other odd men in the house, she'd stayed in Broder's room all day. One of the hunky guys had brought dinner up to her, something her stomach had been incredibly grateful for, but Broder had never returned.

She'd spent the day going through his books instead. She'd found an incredible library of them in a large cabinet in the walk-in closet. Tomes of all kinds, from all across the centuries.

If Jessa hadn't already been convinced that Broder had been telling her the truth about his age, the library would have done it. Either he was very, very old, or he was an incredibly wealthy book collector.

Jessa had a degree in American literature. Even though her aunt had warned her to stay away from such a useless tract of study, she'd pursued the subject anyway because she loved it so much. Before her aunt's death and her subsequent discoveries had sent her into a tailspin, she'd been attending graduate school at night to further her studies. Until recently she'd worked as an accounts receivable clerk for a manufacturing company—hardly exciting—but one day she hoped to teach American literature at a university. She needed her PhD to do that.

She'd spent the entire day propped against the wall in the closet, carefully flipping through the aging pages of the books with a tissue to keep the oil from her fingers away from the precious paper. She was going to have to talk to him about preserving these tomes. Broder had first editions of Emerson and Hawthorne. She'd nearly wet herself when she'd found a copy of William Hill Brown's *The Power of Sympathy*. For the first time since her ordeal had begun, she'd been at peace—totally calm and centered—as she'd immersed herself in *Walden* and *Moby-Dick*.

It was ironic that Broder had given her that gift.

When her aunt had died, the grief had been overwhelming. Then the other things had begun to occur, the strangeness . . . the photos. She'd been forced to put everything on the back burner—work, school, all of it.

Luckily she'd received a handsome life insurance settlement that had allowed her to quit her job for the time being—she'd loathed it with a bone-deep hatred, anyway. Giving up school for a year had been a harder decision to make, but it had been necessary.

The closet contained far more books than clothing, but

she had managed to find a pair of sweatpants and a sweater to wear. Both were incredibly—comically—too big for her, but it was better than lounging around in his bathrobe all day.

Too bad every single article of his clothing smelled like him—leather and the barest whiff of his cologne. It was downright intoxicating. She had to resist the urge to throw all his clothes on the bed and roll around in them like a cat in nip.

Someone had sent up dinner, consisting of a steak, potatoes, and a salad. She'd eaten everything but the steak—she was a vegetarian—then selected a battered first edition Edith Wharton novel and curled up in bed with it. She'd read until she could barely keep her eyes open and then had surrendered to the inevitable; her body needed sleep.

She wondered if someone like Broder needed it.

Rubbing her cheek against the cool pillow, she tried her best to banish him from her thoughts and endeavored to ignore the fact that the pillow also smelled like him. The scent of him relaxed her, made her feel protected, though she tried to deny it.

After her encounter in the parking garage, she felt pretty secure in this house . . . although she wasn't too sure of all those men. She'd locked the door before she'd slipped into bed with the book and lodged a chair under the doorknob just for good measure.

But Broder made her feel safe.

The man was all sorts of contradictions and made her feel all sorts of contradictory things. It was as though her head and her heart had begun warring the moment she'd laid eyes on him.

In fact, she was so distracted dealing with all these new problems that she wasn't thinking very much about her original ones. And she really needed to get back to those.

Her heart squeezed, thinking of her aunt . . . or her non-aunt. Jessa wasn't sure anymore. No matter who Margaret had really been, she'd been the only mother Jessa had ever known. No matter what Jessa found out about her true identity, Margaret had been a good parent . . . and Jessa missed her so much.

Soon she hoped she would discover just who Margaret

Hamilton had been, and that bit of information, in turn, would lead Jessa closer to discovering who *she* truly was.

And why she had these strange abilities.

Broder woke with the warmth of another body at his side. He closed his eyes again, trying to make sense of the odd sensation in his chest. It was warm and full, such a contrast to the cold black hole that usually resided there. He'd slept well.

He couldn't remember the last time he'd slept well.

Pressing a hand to his chest to dispel the warm oddness, he turned over carefully. Jessa probably didn't even know he'd slipped into the bed with her. The night before he hadn't been sure he could do it—sleep in the same bed with her this way. It had been a challenge not to give in to temptation and touch her.

Now she lay on her back, one arm thrown up over her head and her dark lashes shadowing the creamy skin of her cheeks. He knew just how creamy that skin truly was and his fingers itched to stroke it again . . . all the way down her body.

He pulled the quilt down a fraction, then stopped himself.

Clenching his fists, he forced himself to sit up, get away from her. It was hard to be a gentleman when you weren't one in your darkest heart. He was still a Viking warrior, even after a thousand years. He still felt compelled to take what he wanted. To plunder and pillage.

It was hard not to touch her when he knew he could make her moan, make her like it. The memory of the way he'd made her come the day before made him crazy. No amount of fast motorcycle rides could force away his intense desire for her. No amount of demon slaying could wash away his intense need to touch her, hold her, to make her his.

And, fuck, how he wanted her.

He pushed up to his feet and gazed down at her. After a moment he turned away and went into the bathroom, where he showered and changed. She'd taken a shower in here. It was odd to see his things displaced; he'd lived alone for so long.

Emerging a short time later dressed in a pair of jeans and scrubbing a towel through his damp hair, he found Jessa awake and sitting up in the bed, her wary gaze slipping down his bare chest to his feet and back up again. Heat flared in her eyes and his body answered, his cock responding to that naked flash of desire in her eyes.

She jerked her head toward the door, where the remains of the smashed chair lay strewn on the floor. He'd found the chair lodged under the knob when he'd tried to enter the room the night before. "I'm not sure if I should be more concerned that you did that, or that you did that and I never heard it."

Tossing the towel over the back of a nearby, intact, chair, he replied, "You were sleeping like the dead when I came in."

Her gaze landed on a couple of shopping bags on the floor by the fireplace. "What are those?"

"Clothes. Toiletries. Stuff like that. Things I figured you'd need."

She stared at the bags for a long moment. "How did you know my size?"

"I didn't. I guessed." To determine her clothing size, he'd had to recall the shape of her under his hands. It had nearly wrecked him.

Her eyes found his. "Somehow I have trouble seeing you shopping, especially for . . . toiletries."

"I didn't go shopping. Someone else did. A woman I know."

Her eyebrows rose. "Your girlfriend?"

He ground his teeth together. "No." He'd like to tell her who the woman was, but he thought she'd had enough revelations to rock her world for a while. She'd probably find out soon enough, anyway. "Don't worry about it. It's done. Hope your new clothes fit."

And now she could get out of his clothes. They were driving him insane because it mingled their scents—hers with his. He had a nose not unlike a wolf's, thanks to the Blight sliver embedded in his chest. Smelling their mingled scents on the clothes she wore, on the mattress she'd slept on, reminded him of sex.

"Well, thanks for the stuff, but I can't stay here for a long time or anything. I had a life, you know, before the parking garage. I was busy . . . doing something. I need to get back to that."

"Have you not heard a word I've said in the last twelve hours? You won't *have* a life if you leave here, woman."

She glared at him. "I heard you and believed you, even though it all seems impossible. That doesn't change the fact that I was engaged in very important activities before you entered my life, ones I can't abandon, not even if it means I'll be risking my life. I'll be careful. I won't go back home, I'll use cash, I'll arm myself well. I won't be putting myself in danger."

"You're already in danger. We need to figure out why." He clenched his fists and made a low growling noise. He wasn't going to lose her yet.

Never, a deep, dark part of him growled.

She calmed his soul and no one had done that in centuries. One day Loki would make him give her up . . . but not yet. "No. You're not leaving. I won't permit it."

She leapt out of bed. "Listen, Mr. Caveman, do you not know anything about the modern-day woman? Giving us orders only makes us want to kick you in the junk."

He closed his eyes and counted to ten. She reminded him of a Viking woman; they'd never had much trouble going toe-to-toe with a warrior, either.

"Stay for the day at least. We'll go over everything, figure out what's going on with you, what makes you a target. You can tell me what 'activity' it is you're so engaged in that you'll risk your life for it. Maybe we can help. To do that, though, you're going to have to tell me everything. No secrets."

She stood with her hands on her hips and considered him for a long moment. "A day."

"A day."

She shrugged a shoulder. "I guess a day and a little conversation wouldn't hurt." Then she went for the bags and retreated into the bathroom, closing the door firmly behind her.

Great. He had a day to figure out a way to keep her from leaving.

He finished dressing and by the time he was done, she'd emerged wearing a pair of jeans, a black sweater, and a pair of black boots. Her hair fell loose around her shoulders, looking like gold and silver spun out into threads. She even wore a little makeup. The Valkyrie who'd done the shopping had excellent taste.

Broder tried not to swallow his tongue. Instead, he turned toward the door and grunted, "Breakfast," at her.

Jessa couldn't tell from one minute to the next whether Broder liked her, was simply enduring her company, or downright hated her. His face held pretty much three expressions only—brooding, pissed off, or lustful. All and all, she couldn't say she minded the lustful one. She enjoyed that one way more than she should've. In fact, seeing him come out of the bathroom wearing only a pair of jeans had nearly made her brain melt.

She'd never been in the same room with a man like him, all lean muscle and leashed strength. He had cavemanlike ways that she chafed at, yet there was something dark and primal in the center of her that thrilled at it. There was something in her female lizard brain that recognized Broder was good mate material, could protect her against all comers. Danger, beware! Here was a man who could keep her safe, give her strong babies, all that base, animalistic stuff.

The fact that he lured her so powerfully said a lot about the strength of her reasons for wanting to leave him.

They traveled through the empty house in silence, Broder tromping a little in front of her and her trying to match his strides. "Where is everyone?"

"The rest of the house is sleeping. The Blight are nocturnal, so we are, too."

"The Blight." She was still trying to get her head around what they were. Her mind had cordoned off everything she'd learned in the last twenty-four hours and she was dealing with each item one at a time. Apparently that was helping to keep her sane. "How do you hunt and kill them?"

They reached the kitchen and Broder began pulling things from the refrigerator as he'd done the night before. Apparently she was supposed to dig in and make something from the offerings. He didn't seem to be much of a cook, did Broder, despite his many years on planet Earth.

"Remember that dagger you killed the agent with in the cab?"

Stomach growling, she selected some bread, jam, and peanut butter and nodded as she sought a butter knife. "It's forever emblazoned in my mind."

"We each have one of those. They're blessed by Loki to kill the spawn of his daughter, Hel."

"They alone make the demons go poof?"

Broder nodded and leaned back against the sink to watch her make a sandwich. "Pretty much."

"So . . . how do regular Loki-dagger-less folk kill them?"

"They don't. Regular folk just die. Look at the missing persons in your country and you'll discover who the Blight feed on. Mostly they go for the vulnerable, the people who won't fight back. Indigents, children. People they can make disappear easily."

The bite of peanut butter and jelly went dry in her mouth. She swallowed hard and set the sandwich down on her plate. His voice had been so matter-of-fact. "That hardly seems fair."

Broder shrugged one broad shoulder. "If life was fair, I would have been rotting to dust in the ground centuries ago. We're what makes it fair, the Brotherhood. We fight them, kill them, so the Blight don't kill so many of you."

So many of you. Technically Broder was still human, but he didn't count himself that way any longer. It made her sad. "So what do you do if you get caught without your dagger?"

He took a bite of his bread and chewed. After he'd

swallowed, he said, "We try not to let that happen, but if it does, we can decapitate the demon. That will kill it."

"Do the Brothers of the Damned ever die in the line of duty?"

His lips twisted in a cold, hard smile that didn't even begin to reach his eyes. They were haunted and tormented. "If we could die in the line of duty, we would."

She blinked and looked down at the granite countertop. "So immortality isn't all it's cracked up to be, then."

"No." His voice came out cold and hard. There would be emotion there, if she scratched at the surface; she was sure. He moved to pour himself a cup of coffee and offered one to her, which she declined. "Your turn to share now."

"There's not much to tell."

"There is." His voice brooked no disagreement. "Think of it this way: The faster you tell me everything, the faster I can figure out why the Blight want you and the faster you can get out of here."

A spark of rage made her straighten and meet his eyes. "I'll leave when I want, since I'm not a prisoner here."

His lips peeled back in a feral grimace to show his white teeth. The action seemed almost animalistic—territorial. "Don't kid yourself. You'll leave when I deem it safe. Now talk."

She sensed this was the moment to back down. Settling into her chair, she gave in to it. She was going to have to tell this man what she'd never revealed to any other person in her life, not even Lillie. She had to hope she could trust him.

"Okay, fine. Here it goes." She drew a breath and let it out slowly. "My aunt died three months ago. I was devastated. I held her funeral; I grieved; a part of me died inside. She was my last living relative. My parents died in a car accident when I was just a baby, so she'd been a mother to me. Her death hit me harder than I thought it would. I had to take a leave of absence from work and school to deal with it all. I had to manage the sale of her house and decide what to do with all her things. As I was going through the attic, I came across . . ." She stopped.

What she was about to say wasn't as strange as the tale Broder had told her, not really, but it was personal and painful.

"Yes," prompted Broder in his dark, deadpan voice. It only made her not want to tell him even more. She wanted to scream at him to show some of that emotion she knew teemed under the surface. To act human in some way. She knew he had it in him.

She drew a breath and plunged on. "In records stored in the attic, I found a file of documents and pictures that led me to believe my aunt wasn't really biologically related to me, that she'd lied to me my whole life. That would be disturbing enough, but the pictures I found of my mother and father made me wonder . . ." She swallowed hard and gave a laugh. "It's totally impossible. . . ."

"I believe in the impossible."

"Good point." She pressed her lips together and tried again. "I thought maybe the pictures were staged, or they were for a play, or maybe my parents were into historical reenactments, but the photos seemed genuinely old and there were so many of them. So I had them assessed by an expert—two experts, in fact, to get two opinions. Both of them said the pictures were very, *very* old. That means that the people who were supposed to be my birth parents, they lived a long time ago. The pictures showed they should have been my great-grandparents, not my parents."

"How do you know the pictures weren't of some long-lost relatives or even two random people not related to you?"

"Photos of folks who just happen to look *exactly* like my mother and father? No way."

Broder bit into an apple and studied her with his head cocked to the side a little. He looked as if she'd just told him she planned a trip to the library later.

She glared at him, pissed off that he wasn't as mystified as she was. "Sounds crazy, right?"

He raised an eyebrow. "I'm a thousand-year-old Viking who fights demons. Not much sounds crazy to me."

Pressing her lips together, she continued, "There's more.

I've had some odd . . . abilities . . . cropping up lately. They surfaced right after my aunt Margaret died."

He zeroed in on her, hawklike, apple forgotten. "What kind of abilities?"

She swallowed hard and glanced away. Saying this stuff aloud—something she'd never done before—made it all seem completely insane. "Uh, I can make people do what I want them to do. I don't know how I manage it, but all I have to do is will them to perform some task and they will. Everyone but you, anyway."

"That's why you were at the Office of Vital Records so late at night? You were breaking in to do research? Compelling someone to bring you restricted records?"

She nodded, her cheeks growing warm. "His name was Roger. Divorced. He had a six-year-old son. He was really nice. He searched for my parents' records of birth and couldn't find them." She slumped against the counter. "He found my aunt's records, but they didn't tell me much."

He studied her. "Anything else?"

"Yes." She hesitated, and then just plunged right into the heart of it. "It appears I have an affinity with certain types of electronics."

"Excuse me?"

"Apparently I can adjust the electrical flow of things, stuff like toasters, radios, et cetera." She paused. "I, uh, managed to fix my aunt's DVD player with my mind."

Broder stared at her.

She babbled on. "I'm thinking maybe the two things are related, the ability to control and redirect electrical impulses in both humans and inanimate objects. I have no idea what that makes me. A temporary zombifier?"

He kept staring, apple limp in his hand.

Sighing, she rolled her eyes. "A penny for your thoughts," she said with no shortage of sarcasm.

He hesitated a moment, then threw his apple to the counter and moved toward her with purpose. Suddenly alarmed at the raw need in his eyes and on his face, she jolted from the counter and retreated backward as he approached her.

She put the center island between her and him. "What are you doing?" He was way too close.

He caught her up in his arms and whipped her around, pressing her to the counter. His thigh slid between her thighs as one broad hand cupped her nape and forced her to look into his eyes. "Hold still," he murmured.

Her heart thudded in her chest, ready to break through her rib cage. Hold still? Was he kidding? She was scared—and excited—right out of her mind. "I thought I made it clear last night. No k—"

His mouth came down slanted across hers. His lips, warm and searching, tasted her slowly, gliding over her mouth so thoroughly that it made goose bumps rise all over her body. Then he parted her lips and slid his tongue within her mouth to stroke slowly up against her tongue. Broder kissed her the way she imagined he probably made love—deliberately, methodically, over and over his tongue colliding with hers.

He tasted like coffee. Her knees went weak and she gripped the counter behind her to hang on so she wouldn't fall—even though she was certain Broder would catch her. Desire rose up from the center of her like a flower blossoming. Her body ripened for him, became warm and willing.

He kissed her deeply, his hands roving her body in a territorial way. His smooth yet hard body pressed against hers, making her shiver. His hands eased their way over her arms, stomach, and outer thighs, rubbing and massaging, until Jessa felt breathless, until all she could think of was the big bed upstairs and all the ways she wanted him in it.

She twined her arms around his shoulders as he deepened the kiss, greedily slanting his mouth over hers. He brushed his palm over one of her breasts, making her nipple pebble instantly, and she arched into him, a moan caught in her throat.

If he'd forced her jeans off her right now and taken her up against the counter, she wouldn't have raised a syllable in protest. Instead, he released her so fast she nearly collapsed, then turned away.

"Witch," he snarled.

SIX

"Wait. . . . What?" She was still holding on to the counter and feeling sluggish and warm from his kiss. The word barely made it through the drugged haze. "Witch?" The insult registered and she stood up straighter. "Wait a minute! There's no reason to throw insults. None at all! You're the one who's been aggressive, not me."

"No, I don't mean it like that." He pushed a hand through his hair and stalked away from her, as though trying to work out what he was going to say. Stopping a short distance from her, he let his hand drop to his side. "I mean, *you're a witch*. Literally. I can taste it on you."

There were so many things wrong with that statement that she couldn't even form a response. She stood, staring dully at him and resisting the urge to screech *Are you crazy?* at him.

He could see that he'd lost her. "A witch," he replied patiently, "a woman or a man who possesses magick."

"I know what a witch is."

He shook his head. "You're a Nordic witch, not like anything you've seen in popular culture or in myth . . . well, other than Nordic myth, anyway. I don't know what you're doing so far away from your people." He said that last bit under his breath, as though talking to himself. He looked pretty shaken up by this revelation.

She was going to remain calm. Her life had shattered into ten thousand pieces of strange in the last few months, but she was going to hold on to her sanity, goddamn it all to hell . . . or Hel, as the case may be.

Absurdly, she wondered what witches tasted like. Then she knew she wasn't dealing as well as she'd thought and sat down.

"I guess . . . I guess me being a witch could be true. It actually sort of makes sense. It's bizarre, but bizarre is now a staple in my life." She took a moment for the news to sink in, and it was a little as if the universe had somehow aligned. "I've always been out of step with people, my classmates, my friends. I've always felt different but never knew why."

"As a witch raised away from your kindred, I'm not surprised to hear you say that. You would have always sensed there was something a little unusual about yourself."

"You're not kidding." She paused. "You could taste it on me?"

Broder nodded. "As you told me your story about your birth parents, the pictures, the special abilities, I realized you were probably either witch, elf, or Valkyrie. A kiss told me all I needed to know."

"Did you just say *elves*?"

"Yes, they exist, but you're not likely to ever meet one."

"Wait. No, seriously, you just said elves."

Broder looked like he might be counting to ten. "Yes. I did."

"I didn't know elves were a part of Nordic myth, let alone witches," she replied, feeling numb.

"You are seidhr, one of the rare Norse witches and shamans left in the world. The Blight have been systematically wiping them out because the seidhr are a powerful force in preventing Ragnarök. That's why they want to kill you. Somehow you've been hidden to them all these years, but something you've done lately—probably in pursuing this mystery about your birth parents—has revealed you to them. Now they have your scent, so to speak."

"And they've set the Hel hounds on me."

"Low-level demons." Broder nodded. "They won't stop until you're dead."

And the good news just kept on coming.

She blinked. "I can see how this explains my special powers, but how does it explain those pictures I found of my birth parents looking all young and beautiful back in the eighteen hundreds?"

She could still remember kneeling there in the attic, a spread of papers and files all around her . . . her birth certificate listing different names than she'd expected, names she didn't recognize. Then she'd found the photos, all kinds of them, all of one couple . . . all of them with the same names written on the back that had been on her birth certificate, listed as her birth parents.

And the realization that she looked just like them.

Broder was suddenly standing right next to her. She hadn't even noticed he'd moved. He tipped her chin up to force her to look into his eyes. "Why do you think that is?" His voice was gentle, at odds with his demeanor and the ever-dark look in his eyes.

She drew a breath, licked her lips. "Seidhr are immortal, aren't they?"

He nodded. "As good as immortal." Something emotional moved across his face. "My condolences."

"I think I need a drink. Something strong, something that will make me wake up tomorrow morning and realize all this was just a bad dream."

"How old are you? Around twenty-two?"

"Twenty-five."

He nodded. "Your biological clock has already slowed down. That's how it works for the seidhr."

"I'm not sure I want to live forever."

"You won't live forever, just for a very, very long time."

She paused, blinked, did her best to digest his words. Her mind was full of questions she was afraid to ask. "So, elves. Really? Did I hear you right?"

"The seidhr, elves, the gods and goddesses from Nordic myth are not myth." He paused. "Dwarves don't exist, from what we know."

"Oh, good. I'm so relieved."

"I detect a note of sarcasm."

"You detect right, buddy." She rubbed her temple. "So that explains my ability to make people do what I want them to do?"

"Yes."

"And various household electronics?"

He nodded. "All part of the same skill. That must be your inborn talent, since you need no spell. I believe they call it compulsion."

She nodded, tired. This was just too much.

"You know nothing of who you are. For whatever reason, the seidhr lost you or buried you for a reason. If we find your biological parents—"

"They're dead. Died in a car accident when I was an infant. At least, supposedly." She snorted. "Not so immortal after all, I guess."

"The seidhr age very slowly, but they can die from wounds at any time, just like a human."

Grief welled up dark and thick from somewhere deep inside her. She'd never known her parents, but she missed them all the same. Would she ever know why her aunt—if she could call her that—had lied to her all those years? She'd deserved to know the truth.

Her aunt had been good to her, had loved her with all her heart. Jessa had never wanted for anything and they'd been incredibly close, as close as mother and daughter. Her aunt had seemed to cherish her. Perhaps she'd been protecting her from something—maybe from the Blight.

Jessa had to believe that or she would go insane.

Anyway, it was hard to imagine friendly, loving Margaret Hamilton as a kidnapper or as having some dark, nefarious purpose.

But why, oh, why hadn't she told Jessa the truth?

Broder stared at Erik from across the room. Erik had his massive back to him, one hand on the mantel of the enormous creek stone fireplace.

"Seidhr. I haven't seen one in decades," came his low, bass voice.

Broder gritted his teeth. Of all the types of beings Loki could have paired him with, seidhr was the worst. It had been no accident, of course. The moment he'd kissed her he'd known and had squelched the urge to thrust her away from him, even though she'd tasted good—a little like peppermint and roses. Just like a witch . . . just like how Loki had taught the Brotherhood to recognize them. He'd never kissed one before today, of course.

Erik turned. "Loki sent you to this woman? She's to be your reward?"

"Yes, but apparently this is more business than pleasure. She'll need protecting."

Erik nodded. "So nice of Loki to be clear with us."

Broder shrugged. "We're well accustomed to the games he plays."

"And the ways in which he likes to watch us squirm."

"Except the Brotherhood doesn't squirm."

Erik cracked a smile. "Fuck Loki and his games. This is the first time in a thousand years you—"

"Yeah, I don't really want to talk about it."

Erik nodded.

"I'm taking her to Scotland."

"To the seidhr enclave. They won't like that. Remember, we're not allowed on their lands."

Technically the seidhr and the Brotherhood were allies, but that didn't make them friends. There was an icy tension between them and a serious lack of communication. The seidhr were isolated, protective of themselves . . . to a fault.

"I know."

Erik rubbed a hand over his mouth. "But they'll be happy to recover one of their own. They should forgive you if you're forced to enter their territory. You should take her there right away."

Erik didn't know about Broder's history with the seidhr and, if Broder had his way, he never would. Erik had no idea that the seidhr wouldn't appreciate him riding up and dropping off one of their precious wayward witches—even if he could do that.

"No. Not right away. We still don't know anything about her, don't know why she's been hidden the way she has. It's not like the seidhr to do that, not without good reason. I'll take her to my keep. Call a Valkyrie, train her."

Erik regarded him with speculation, his icy blue eyes sparkling. "You want to keep her."

A muscle in his jaw worked. Yes, he wanted to keep her. Forever. That was the problem. Yet the woman was seidhr. Even if Loki hadn't put a time limit on his relationship with her, that alone would be grounds for no touching.

It was going to be hard not to touch her.

"Safe," Broder answered in a clipped tone. "I want to keep her safe."

"Ah." Erik paused. "I have no doubt Loki has selected the right man for the job."

"We're leaving immediately."

"Does the woman know that?"

"Not yet."

"Remember, I met her." Erik smiled. "Good luck with that."

Jessa leaned against a wall and watched Broder get the pat-down from hell at airport security. Before they'd gone through, she'd bet him a drink at one of the bars on the other side of security that he'd be flagged. Of course he had been. No TSA agent in their right mind would let a dangerous-looking guy like him pass without close scrutiny, yet she was beginning to doubt the female agent who'd flagged him had done it for strictly security reasons.

Finally Broder was let through and he joined Jessa on the other side. "Did you get her number?" she asked, falling into step beside him.

"What?" He looked genuinely bewildered.

She rolled her eyes and repositioned her bag on her shoulder. "That agent back there. A bomb wasn't the 'package' she was trying to discover."

Broder gave her a blank look, then checked his boarding ticket for, presumably, their flight number so they could figure out their gate. Gah. He was hopeless.

"So you never notice it when women find you attractive? Do you miss all the female heads that turn when you walk past them? How is it that you've lived so many years on this planet and not realized the effect you have on the opposite sex?"

He shrugged and guided her onto a moving walkway. "I don't pay attention to such things. No reason."

She gave up. He was too busy killing demons, maybe.

She spotted a bathroom and veered toward it once they were off the walkway. "I'll just be a minute." It was a long flight to Glasgow from Dulles Airport. She hated the idea of leaving the country and had made her opinions known, but going meant answering questions.

And she really needed those answers.

So, like it or not, she was getting on that plane.

Broder narrowed his eyes at her, looking from her face to the bathroom. His thoughts were clear.

"I'm pretty sure I'll be all right just five minutes out of your care," she called as she neared it.

"Stay alert."

She nodded. She remembered the incident in the parking garage with perfect clarity. "I will."

After she'd finished and had washed her hands, she took a second to give herself a critical look in the mirror.

So this was what a Nordic witch looked like. She turned her face this way and that, running her fingers over her cheeks. Her face didn't look any different from anyone else's, yet according to Broder she wouldn't have to worry about wrinkles for a very, very long time.

The idea of possessing magick was odd enough, but possessing what amounted to immortality was almost brain numbing. She hadn't thought much about it since she'd been told, mostly because she had no frame of reference in which to judge the news. She couldn't even imagine being so long-lived. Her only measure of immortality was Broder and judging by him, it wasn't going to be all that much fun.

How could Margaret have kept these things secret? It was possible, of course, that Margaret had never known about her background, or even that her parents had been seidhr. That seemed unlikely, though, considering the photos she'd found in her attic. Perhaps she'd been waiting to tell her about her strange genetic makeup.

Margaret's death had been unexpected. She'd died of a heart attack while out jogging. Otherwise, at fifty-three years old, she'd been the picture of good health. That was one reason her death had hit Jessa so hard—the suddenness of it. It had rocked the foundations of her world.

And those foundations had just kept on rocking, but she refused to let the building fall down.

Broder had told her that the reason her magick had begun to show so abruptly was probably because of the depth of her emotional response to Margaret's death. Even without training, he'd told her, a witch's or shaman's abilities could manifest if some dramatic or transformative experience occurred.

She stared into her brown eyes in the mirror's reflection. Ironically, she wished for her aunt's presence in her life right now more than anything. She just wanted to curl up in her arms and sob, tell Margaret all her fears. Margaret would stroke her hair and tell her everything would be all right.

Grief welled up in her and she tamped it down. Overwhelming emotion was one thing she couldn't afford right now. Gritting her teeth against the urge to cry, she lowered her head for a moment. Suddenly she realized the busy bathroom had gone eerily empty.

She raised her head, frowning. That was odd, considering how packed the airport was right now. A toilet flushed behind her and a woman emerged from the stall, trailing a rolling carry-on behind her. She gave Jessa no notice as she washed her hands, gave herself a once-over in the mirror, and then left.

Jessa relaxed. She was being a little too paranoid. She gave her reflection one last glance, making sure no tears could be seen in her eyes, fluffed her hair, and headed for the door.

She'd only gone a couple of steps when a woman burst from one of the bathroom stalls and collided with her. Jessa fell back against the bank of sinks with a surprised yelp.

It was no woman; it was a demon.

She had a millisecond to figure that out before the demon was on her, fangs descended and flashing, eyes bled black. Sharp teeth nipped at her shoulder, catching the fabric of her shirt. Her skin burned from the thing's touch. Jessa pushed back with every drop of strength and panic in her body, managing to rock the demon back on its heels. She lifted her leg and kicked her boot solidly into the demon's chest.

The demon slammed back against one of the stall doors and staggered inside, nearly falling into the toilet. Jessa made a mad dash for it, but the demon, fast as a blink, tackled her from behind. They scuffled on the floor, Jessa punching and kicking, doing everything she could to avoid those wicked, snapping jaws.

She landed a solid punch to the demon's throat. It made a gagging sound and its eyes bulged. She followed it up with a hard shove to the side and she managed to wiggle away from the thing . . . but she was on the wrong side of the room. She scrambled to her feet and watched the demon do the same thing, blocking her path to the exit. Slowly she backed away from it, her mind frantically casting about for ways to defeat this thing.

She had no dagger and neither did Broder. He'd sent his blade by special courier to Scotland, knowing he'd never get it onto the plane in his carry-on and not trusting his suitcase wouldn't get lost. The only way to kill a demon without a special Loki dagger was to decapitate it . . . and the only weapon she had were her bare hands.

Jessa stared in horror at the demon, who was circling her, hissing, and blocking her way out. "Broder!" she screamed. She had no idea if he could hear her.

God, she hoped he heard her!

A bare half second later and Broder was there, swinging the demon around to face him. The thing made an inhuman squeal of terror at the sight of him. Immediately the demon's offensive became defensive. It didn't matter. Broder's huge hands closed around either side of its head and prepared to twist.

Jessa turned her face away. Even though the demon had wanted her dead just moments before, she couldn't bear to watch the brutally cold way Broder dealt with it.

Soon the demon was so much ice sliding across the floor. Jessa stared in horror at a chunk of the demon that had come to a rest at the toe of her boot, then slowly raised her gaze to Broder.

He stood staring at her with fierce protectiveness in his eyes, his chest heaving and his dark eyes shining with rage.

Wide-eyed, she stood shivering. The patches of her flesh where the demon had touched her burned with pain.

Broder closed the space between them and in a few moments every trace of her injuries was gone.

Behind him a middle-aged woman trailing a rolling carry-on entered. She stopped short near the doorway, taking in the odd sight of an unmistakable male in the women's bathroom and the ice on the floor. "Uh, everything okay in here?"

"Everything is just great," Jessa answered a little too brightly. "Dropped my drink. Be careful not to slip."

The woman's gaze slipped to Broder and she raised her eyebrows.

Jessa took him by the arm. "He just got confused and wandered in here. Doesn't speak English." She offered a friendly, probably slightly crazy-looking smile to the gaping woman and led Broder out of the bathroom.

Once out, she grabbed her carry-on—luckily no one had spotted it unattended and tried to blow it up—and they headed to the gate. Every molecule of her body was on high alert now. Every person she passed was a potential demon.

"I thought you said you'd be okay out of my protection for five minutes," Broder growled, falling into step beside her.

"Yeah, apparently I was wrong. No more bathroom breaks for me." She was still shaking.

SEVEN

Jessa shifted in her seat, but she couldn't shake her unease. Funny how being stalked by demons could set a girl on edge. Here she was in first class and headed to Scotland. Too bad she couldn't enjoy it. Too bad this trip wasn't a vacation.

She'd lied about this trip to those close to her. After all, she'd had to explain her absence, right? Her best friend, Lillie, had pressed her for details, wondering about her spur-of-the-moment decision to visit a country she'd never expressed any interest in. She'd had to fib a little and it had hurt her heart, but she needed to protect the people she loved.

Lillie had clearly also been hurt, wondering why Jessa hadn't called earlier and why she wasn't leaning on her more for support. Lillie thought this trip had to do with her aunt dying, that Jessa felt she needed to get away for a while. That was a conclusion Jessa was happy to foster because it was more believable than the truth . . . but she hated that her friend thought she wasn't needed. She needed Lillie more than ever right now and it hurt somewhere deep inside not to be able to pour her heart out to her.

She settled back into the comfy airplane seat; she hadn't known they even existed. At least they were traveling in style. She couldn't complain about that.

Broder had dressed in a low-collared black linen shirt and a pair of tight-fitting jeans that he made look damn good. He'd managed not to get a drop of demon blood on himself in the bathroom. He looked ready for first class, despite the casual dress, although Broder still looked awkward. He was too small for the seat, even though by airplane standards there was a lot of room, and kept shifting uneasily.

Perhaps a man like him, raised in the time he'd been raised in, would never be truly comfortable with air travel. Broder would probably be much more at ease at the helm of a Viking longship. Jessa could totally see him there, too, battling the icy tempest of the northern seas, water glistening on his bare chest, his hair long and trailing—

"What?" he barked at her, clearly on edge and with a glare in his eyes.

Jerking her gaze away, she muttered, "Sorry." Apparently she'd been too busying imagining him half naked on the stern of a longboat, ocean mist caught in his hair, to realize she'd been staring. She shook herself mentally. "Just wondering why you're fidgeting so much."

"I hate planes. It's not natural to be up here in the air like this." He reached across her and slid the blind down to block the view of the clouds below them. "Give me a boat and the ocean any day."

So she'd been right.

"You did really well back there," he grumbled. "In the bathroom. Not many untrained humans or witches could hold off a demon that way."

"It's amazing the skills that come to the fore when you're fighting for your life." She thought about his words, then said, "You said *untrained* human. Does that mean there are humans who know about the Blight? Are there humans who fight them?" The cabin was dark and quiet; everyone was sleeping. They could talk about this now without fear of being overheard.

He nodded. "There are. Not many, but groups of them."

"Where?"

He shrugged. "All over. We'd prefer they didn't mess with the Blight, but can't stop them."

"Interesting."

He shifted in his seat again. "They get killed a lot."

Yes, she could imagine. Snaking a hand out from her travel blanket, she rubbed a gummy eye and glanced at the little progress airplane on the map at the front of the cabin. "We're almost there."

He moved in his seat again, as if trying to stretch his back. She'd been to Europe once with her aunt, so she knew that the flight attendants would begin serving breakfast soon and everyone would start waking up. She hadn't managed one second of sleep during the flight and she knew Broder hadn't, either. They had no idea if any demons had come along for the ride or not; that really didn't bode well for napping.

At least he'd taken off his duster. It wasn't far, though. He'd stuffed it under the seat in front of him. She pointed at it. "What's the story with the ancient coat?"

He hesitated a moment, then pulled it from under the seat and opened it for her to see. It smelled like leather and his cologne. "Look here." He pointed at a few faint markings, swoops and swirls done in a very light black.

She leaned forward to examine them. They gave off a very faint pulse of energy. "What are those?"

"Runes placed by the seidhr. Every brother has some object or piece of clothing imbued with this type of magick."

Something of the seidhr. She reached out and touched the markings. They sent a slight throb of magick up her arm. "What do they do?"

"These runes let me know when there are demons about. They also provide me with a small amount of protection from the coldness of their touch. The coat also allows me a place to hide my dagger."

"That's . . . amazing."

"That's what you are." He held her gaze for a long moment . . . then finally tore his gaze from her and replaced the duster under the seat in front of him and settled back into his chair.

She glanced at him. "What happens when we get there?"

He hadn't exactly been forthcoming with the details, and she'd been too set on getting to Scotland to further discover who she was to worry about it too much. She understood the seidhr enclave was there and she was thrilled by the possibility she might finally get some answers.

He studied her in the dim light. "I'll take you to my keep in the Highlands. It is one of the most protected buildings in the world against the Blight. There you will be well defended and you will learn more of who you are. You will also train. You need to learn how to defend yourself."

"I did pretty well in the bathroom. You even said so."

"Not good enough."

"What the hell is good enough?"

"Good enough is taking a demon's head off on your own."

"I'm sorry I asked."

That light had entered his eyes again, the hungry one. Since discovering she was a witch, he'd been holding himself back from her, it seemed. She wondered about that. She wondered if, perhaps, the seidhr were somehow sacred in this new, strange world, if the Brotherhood were discouraged in some way from touching them.

Jessa wasn't sure if she should be relieved or disappointed at that possibility.

She pressed her lips together and concentrated on information gathering, in order to calm the beat of her heart at the look on his face. She wanted very much not to want him, but that didn't seem to be a realistic desire. "The members of the Brotherhood are Nordic, right? So why would you have property in Scotland and not in Norway?"

"My roots are in Norway. The weight of my past." He paused. "Sometimes roots hold you back, hold you down. Some weights are too heavy to carry."

She considered that. Broder obviously had more than one dark secret and a hell of a tortured past. Of course he didn't want much to do with the country where his bad memories had been made. She should have thought about that before she'd opened her mouth. Just because she was interested in her roots didn't mean everyone else was.

"Of course," she replied softly.

"The Vikings settled in Scotland, as they settled in many places. Your people lived there primarily, even in the old days. That's why their enclave is located there now."

Her people. God, she had *people*. It was a heady thought for someone raised thinking she only had one living relative.

"Aside from all that, it's beautiful there. And remote, which I enjoy. It's not so crazy to think I would keep an abode there, is it?"

An abode? Once in a while Broder said these archaic things. "No, of course not."

"The Brotherhood resided in Scotland before coming to the United States. For centuries we were in the Highlands. Long ago I bought a castle there. It's my primary residence when I'm not in Washington, D.C."

She blinked. "Castle?"

"What did you think a keep was?"

"Not a castle."

"It's more of a fortress, guarded in every manner against the Blight. Most of the property is crumbling and under renovation, but the keep, which is the main tower, is habitable."

She nodded, feeling, once again, a little overwhelmed. "I've never even seen a castle before."

"It's probably not like anything you're imagining."

That was true. When she imagined a castle, she imagined turrets and elegance. Sort of the movie and book rendition of what a castle would be like. In real life she bet it was far less glamorous. With most of the place under renovation, it sounded a little like they'd be camping. As long as it was safe, she didn't mind.

"Why did the Brotherhood decide to set up in the U.S.? Why didn't they just stay in Europe?"

"There is still a force of Brotherhood in Europe, but Loki moved a bunch of us to America in the seventeen hundreds. The Blight were moving in and we came to counter them. If we hadn't, today the Blight would have a huge foothold in the States."

"And you chose Washington, D.C., as your base because it was the center of government?"

He smiled. "Do you want to know how many demons live in Washington?"

"You don't have to tell me. I can imagine."

"The Brotherhood is scattered everywhere, but you saw one of the largest concentrations back at the house. Where the Blight are, so are the Brotherhood."

"That makes sense."

He leaned in close to her and she looked up at him in surprise. His gaze was intense, caught with hers, vaguely threatening. "You tempt me, woman."

Shrinking back in her seat against the subtle threat in his voice, she whispered, "That's a bad thing?"

"Yeah. It is."

"I don't mean to."

"I know, and that makes it all the worse." His gaze dropped to her mouth. He studied it like he was starving and she was a bowl full of cherries.

The look on his face and the intentness in his eyes spoke volumes about all the things he was thinking—all the things he wanted to do to her. It made lust slip over her body, driving her into a lassitude that made her limbs heavy and her sex warm and excited. Her reaction to this man was always swift and immediate. It was as if Broder had some kind of switch implanted in her brain.

"What I said before, about you not doing anything I didn't want you to do . . ." She licked her lips, her gaze focused on his mouth. "There isn't much I don't want you to do right now." It was a bold statement, but a safe one. After all, they were in a public place.

He made a low sound in the back of his throat that sounded like a growl. "Don't give me permission, *skatten min*." After hesitating a moment, he pushed up from his seat, driving a hand through his hair in a gesture of frustration, and headed back toward the lavatories.

She sank down into her seat and let out a careful breath.

Spending so much time alone with this man just might kill her. Wouldn't the Blight be pleased by that?

After a few minutes, Broder returned. She thought he'd be cooled down by now, but apparently his little foray to the bathroom hadn't helped him snuff his desires—for whatever reasons he wanted to snuff them.

"What does *skatten min* mean?" she whispered, taking in the aroused way he stared at her with a little shiver.

"My treasure." He leaned in toward her, snaking a hand under the thin airline blanket covering her and pushing up the armrest that separated them. Her breath caught as he pulled her against him, under him, and his hot mouth came down on hers. His lips slid methodically, slowly, against her mouth, as though savoring the taste of her.

Oh, God, she was going to melt from his heat.

His big hand slipped under the hem of her sweater and ran over her breasts in their satiny bra, making her nipples peak. She shuddered against his mouth, her body tingling.

He nipped at her lower lip and growled, "Spread your thighs for me, *skatten min*."

She did it, her mind caught in a haze of lust. He unbuttoned her jeans and unzipped them, his hand well concealed under the travel blanket. As he ran his fingers along the hem of her underwear, she shivered and kissed him back harder, her body practically turning itself inside out in its desire to be touched by him.

"I want to make you come," he murmured roughly against her lips. "Right here, right now."

She almost swallowed her tongue.

He continued to run his fingers along the hem of her underwear slowly and she cursed her jeans, which were far too tight for him to get his huge hand down. But instead he dropped to the hot place between her thighs and rubbed her swollen clit through the material.

A low moan of absolute pleasure escaped her throat and he slanted his mouth over hers, consuming it. His tongue eased between her lips and skated up against the length of her tongue as his thumb moved back and forth in the same tempo. Back and forth, the pleasure mounted. She struggled to keep quiet, her breath coming in little pants.

"You like that?" he murmured against her mouth. "Do you like it when I touch you, Jessa?"

She nodded shakily.

"Do you know what I'm thinking about right now?" His thumb applied just enough pressure on her clit to make her mouth go dry.

"What are you thinking?" she managed to ask.

"I'm thinking about the last time I touched you. You have the sweetest curved behind I've ever seen. I want to trace your elegant, slender back with my tongue."

Her breath came out in a little agonized pant. "That sounds good," she breathed.

"I want to fuck you, Jessa. I want a night of pure, down and dirty sex with you. I want to make you come over and over." He took a shuddering, shaky breath. "I want to hear you scream my name at the top of your lungs. Now you know what I'm thinking about."

"Yes," she panted, "now I know. Tell me more."

He groaned deep in his throat and sealed his mouth to hers. Back and forth he stroked, until her breath caught in her throat and she shuddered in pleasure. He increased the pressure of his mouth on hers and she felt the rub of his stubble against her skin.

Nipping her lower lip, he demanded that she open to him. Her sex seemed to catch fire when his tongue slid in to leisurely stroke against hers. She felt every caress of it between her thighs.

The kiss was soft, then demanding, then a tease, and then the promise of something more. The man could kiss. His tongue played with hers and then slipped out as he alternated nipping at her lips and then slanting his mouth across hers to penetrate once again. It stole her breath, made her feel dizzy and made her needy as hell.

It made her want *more* with everything she was. A proper bed. His bare skin against hers.

"Come for me, woman," he whispered against her lips,

his thumb pressing a little harder, rotating just a fraction faster.

He was pushing her straight into an orgasm, right there on the airplane, surrounded by sleeping passengers. Everyone would hear her. But there was no way she could hold back.

Pleasure exploded through her and she gasped against his mouth as it washed through her. He kissed her hard, his tongue plunging over and over into her mouth as she fought not to make a sound.

When it was over, he leaned back in his chair and looked satisfied with himself. He pushed a hand through his hair and signaled one of the flight attendants for a drink, cool as anything.

Disheveled, lethargic, and floating on a cloud of postorgasmic bliss, Jessa slumped back against the seat and drew the blanket to her chin. Yes, being alone with this man was definitely going to do her in.

Just as the cabin was waking up and being prepared for breakfast, Jessa dropped into a satisfied sleep.

Broder slammed the door of the rental car shut and watched Jessa make her exhausted way into the restaurant. It was a long drive from Glasgow International Airport to his keep, north of Inverness, and he was starving. He followed behind her, opening the door and leading her to one of the booths in the back, where they'd have privacy. She was tired, but still managed to look alluring in a loose-haired, rumpled kind of way. She looked like he imagined she might after a night in bed.

He so wanted to give her one, a very long one. The encounter on the plane had sated him for a while, but, ultimately, touching her only inflamed his need for more.

As they passed through the place, more than one pair of male eyes turned in her direction, though Jessa remained oblivious to the attention. He gritted his teeth and forced himself not to rip off the faces of the offending men. He couldn't stop this dark claim of *mine* that echoed through him whenever he looked at her—a witch.

If Loki showed his face, he was going to do his level best to tear it off. Wouldn't be the first time he'd tried. Wanting to claim Jessa and resisting the urge was making him crankier than usual.

They reached the booth and slid into it, Jessa letting her head sink into her hands.

"What's wrong with you?" He reached for a menu and opened it.

"Jet lag, I guess." She dropped one hand to the tabletop and stared at him. "But, being Superman and all, you probably don't get that, right?" Something moved in her eyes and he sensed she was keeping something from him.

"What else?"

She went silent.

He snapped the menu closed and leveled his gaze at her from across the table. "Woman, you have to stop keeping secrets. Do you not realize the danger you're in? Tell me what else is going on with you."

She shrugged and leaned back against the seat. "I don't know for sure. Ever since we landed, I've felt strange, that's all. Like a buzzing electrical current is running through my veins."

He grunted in response and wondered if it had something to do with the fact that the seidhr enclave was located in the far northern portion of the county, a fair bit north of Ullapool.

"What's that supposed to mean?" She grabbed a menu and snapped it open. "Words are nice. Use them."

"I'll tell you when I know for sure. Right now, I don't." He paused. "Okay?"

"Whatever," she grouched.

The waitress came over and they placed their orders.

"Tell me about yourself." She leaned back and crossed her arms over her chest. "I mean, I figure you and me are close, right? What with you giving me two orgasms now."

She looked directly into his eyes when she said it and barely even blushed.

She'd blush for certain if she knew how much he'd loved giving her those two climaxes, how hard it had made his cock—how much more he wanted to do to her. The memory of the taste of her as she orgasmed on the plane was still there on his tongue, as was the look on her face as he pulled as much ecstasy out of her as he could.

"Nothing more to say. I battle the Blight. That's what I do, what I am."

"No girlfriend?"

"If I had a girlfriend, do you think I'd be jumping on you the way I have?"

"Sure." She gave a slow blink. "Wouldn't stop most men."

He muttered in Norwegian under his breath. "Then you know the wrong kind of man, *skatten min*."

She studied him without saying a word. "You really do come from another era."

"The truth is I've been unable to be with any women. At all." He growled, "Ever. Loki has denied me."

"What? Are you kidding? For a thousand years?"

"I've grown accustomed to it. My control is incredibly well developed. Although you"—his gaze dropped to her mouth for a lingering moment—"stir me like none ever has."

Now she blushed. "How did Loki do it? Did he deflate everything"—she glanced in the direction of his crotch and blushed even harder—"down there? Or what?"

"Deflate—" *Oh.* He grimaced. "No. He simply puts in place powerful, painful deterrents if we pursue intimacy with a woman. I learned quickly that women were off-limits."

"Were you still able to . . ." She trailed off, lifting her eyebrows suggestively. "You know, for yourself?"

"Yes, but it's a far cry from the touch of a woman. The scent of her skin, the softness of her lips, the sweet give of her—"

She cleared her throat loudly to interrupt him. She was

now a fascinating shade of scarlet red. "It's cruel of Loki to keep you celibate."

"That's Loki, but I can't blame his punishment of me. What I did—" He choked off the last word.

"What did you do?"

"Not a topic open for discussion."

"Oh, my God, did you rape someone?"

"No!" He barked it. "I never did. Not even back then, when such forms of control and domination were common and accepted."

"Rape and pillage. Happens a lot these days, too."

The waitress delivered their drinks and Broder took a long swallow of refreshing beer. Ah, that was better.

"And the rest of the Brotherhood? Are they also denied the pleasures of the flesh?" She sipped her soda.

"Depends on their original offense to the gods. There are varying punishments given. This happened to be mine."

"What do you mean, *happened*? You just used the past tense. Clearly, you can engage in . . . relations now. Are you out on furlough or something like that?"

"Something like that."

He didn't want to tell her that Loki had chosen her to be his reward for a thousand years of service and she hadn't figured it out. Luckily just then their food came and he avoided answering her by digging in. That didn't stop her from staring at him speculatively over her plate as she picked at her food, knowing full well he was withholding.

Damn Loki to the frozen depths of Hel. He could spend eternity there with his daughter who hated him.

EIGHT

Jessa had been awake for nearly twenty-four hours and she had that tired-yet-wide-awake feeling one got when one had been awake for that long. Yet she'd soaked in everything on the ride from Glasgow. The Highlands had always been beautiful in her imagination, but she realized now that she hadn't done the place a bit of justice. It was gorgeous, even on a dreary, rainy day like today—though Broder had informed her that this sort of weather was the norm, not the exception.

It was chilly, but the grass was green and the hills were many and rolling. Every once in a while, she would get a glimpse of a loch through the trees. She needed to get her sightseeing in now, since she had a feeling once they reached Broder's place, she'd be on serious lockdown.

Broder had had both his dagger and a car—one of his cars—waiting for them at the airport. The dagger was now once again secured in his leather duster. The car had left her speechless. It was an American muscle car. According to Broder, it was a '66 Pontiac GTO. Cherry red and in perfect condition, it drew a lot of attention here in Scotland.

As they traveled down a narrow road, Broder's "keep" broke through the gray mist as though misplaced in time. While they approached, she studied the gravelly gray walls, rising all around the structure, its turrets and tower reaching from the center toward the clouds.

To own and maintain a place like this must mean Broder had a fortune vast enough to land him on those lists of wealthy people. Yet she had a suspicion that his name would never appear anywhere publicly. Somehow he was off the world's radar, disconnected from the grid—a lonely ghost.

The car made its way up the serpentine road leading toward the keep on the hill, finally reaching a set of iron gates. Broder stopped at a small electronic box to punch in a security code and Jessa felt the pull of the machine. It called to her, wanting her to tamper with it.

Feeling freakish, she directed her gaze away from the box to watch the heavy gates swing wide and allow the car through. The road curled around in a loop, with a huge nonfunctioning stone fountain in the middle. The statue in the middle was a lion, a fitting animal to represent its owner.

A large, block-shaped building rose directly in front of her. To the left and right were archways with drives leading beneath them to other, separate structures. Scattered about were tools, scaffolding, the detritus of workers who'd clearly been doing construction recently. Broder had been mostly silent for the trip and had returned to his silently pissed-off overall demeanor. She didn't want to ask about it.

He stopped the car in front of the central tower, got out and opened the trunk. This had to be the famous "keep." Jessa got out, too, inhaling the fresh air, and sighing, as the sound of the gates clinking shut met her ears. It was pretty, but it was prison all the same.

Broder took both their suitcases like they weighed nothing—she could barely manage one—and entered the structure.

She followed him in. "You don't keep your door locked?"

He set the suitcases down. "Not normally. The place is locked down with magick. You don't have to fear here."

She barely heard him; she was too busy gawking. "This place is amazing."

The foyer was not big, but it was beautiful. Obviously remodeled, rather than restored, it reminded her more of a mansion than a cold, drafty castle. The walls and ceiling were all made of stone, but the floor was polished wood and covered with rich blue and gold rugs. Matching tapestries covered the walls, and small, polished wood accent tables dotted the circular area. Three archways led to either corridors or other rooms, all of them dark. A large chandelier hung from the center of the ceiling.

This was nothing like how he'd made it sound. The way he'd described this place, she'd expected to be sleeping in a cold, drafty, crumbling ruin. This was a wealthy man's home.

He grunted, picked up the suitcases again, then walked up the stairs. She guessed she was supposed to follow and hurried after him.

One hand on the smooth, carved stone of the railing, she mounted the stairs, her gaze still riveted on the beauty of the place. "Did you decorate this yourself?" She couldn't see him being that kind of man, fussily choosing just the right area rug to accent the polished floors.

"Do you think I did?"

She smiled. "No."

He didn't reply, just continued his relentlessly strong progress up the stairs. At the top was a small hallway, also dark. He flipped on a light with his elbow, revealing a long corridor lined with doors and graced with a long runner rug that matched the one in the foyer. Stomping to the first door on the left, he wrested it open and entered, then dropped her suitcase on the floor.

He turned to find her right behind him. They stood about a breath's space from one another. The heat of his body radiated out and warmed her, the scent of him filling her senses. For a moment she thought he might lean forward and kiss her, but instead he stared hungrily at her—seeming to put everything he'd done to her in the airplane into his eyes, plus some.

Then, without another word, he hefted his suitcase and left the room.

She let out a slow, careful breath. *Well, okay then.*

Turning to the switch by the door, she flipped it on. The light revealed a room not unlike the one at the Brotherhood house except larger and with more furniture. There was a huge fireplace that was probably meant more for heating the room than for ambience, a big four-poster bed draped with heavy dark red velvet curtains on all sides, and an array of couches, chairs, dressers, and tables. There was a window on the far side of the room covered with drapes that matched the bed. A huge wardrobe stood sentinel in one corner of the room. The only door led to a large bathroom with a sunken tub that had an attached showerhead.

Leaving her suitcase where it was, she collapsed on the bed, let out a long breath, and closed her eyes. If she concentrated, she could feel the hum of magick all around her. She wondered who had set the net of protection—for that was what she assumed it was—and how they'd done it.

But even with the magickal safeguards in place, she still felt a draw to mess with the electrical systems. It was frustrating to know she could, that she had the drive and the instinct, but she had no one to tell her how to truly master the skill.

The next morning Jessa ran her fingers over the rough, uneven stone walls of the corridor, heading down the stairs. The place was incredible, such a mixture of the ancient and the modern. Sort of like the castle's owner. Although she was beginning to think that Broder had somehow missed out on a lot of modern things—like fun, for example.

This was a man who was truly in the world and not of it. A part of her ached to show him what life could be like. He never smiled and a laugh coming from him, well, it would be shocking. She couldn't see him enjoying a movie or attending a carnival or a fair.

Even before he'd been punished by Loki for whatever mysterious deed he'd committed, she didn't see him as having a fun and carefree type of existence. She wondered what his life had been filled with for the last thousand years—just hunting? Only death? Only demons?

If so, her heart ached for him.

The low hum of . . . whatever it was had not abated since they'd touched down, nor had it grown more powerful. She was growing accustomed to it, but she had to wonder what it was from. Was it low-level magick coursing through her, unsummoned by her? That was what it felt like. If so, where was it going?

She was sick of mysteries.

Broder said that when it was safe she would be connected with her people. She wanted that. Wanted her questions answered. Wanted to finally know who she was.

Her explorations of the keep soon revealed a sizable living room with a bunch of antique furniture, including a beautiful gilded full-length mirror and lots of bookshelves, a workout room filled with equipment, a library, and a huge kitchen stocked with food. Broder was nowhere to be found, but he'd kindled a fire in every hearth and now the place was cozier. The keep during winter was probably frigid, despite all the massive fireplaces.

She paused for a moment in the lushly decorated living room. It was all modern and comfortable, overstuffed couches, polished wood tables, bookshelves, and chairs. There were more of the first-edition books. A perusal of the collection revealed fewer American authors and more European. She supposed that made sense considering their location.

Again she reminded herself to talk to Broder about proper storage for these treasures. It was as if Broder didn't know what he had, and maybe he didn't. A decade for Broder probably seemed like a month to a human. Perhaps the passage of time didn't register with him the way it would with another person.

She'd never seen Broder reading any of the tomes, not that they'd had a lot of leisure time. She wondered if he was more of a collector than a reader. After all, the man had to have some kind of hobby other than killing demons. He'd existed for a thousand years, after all. He needed some type of enjoyable pastime, especially since he hadn't been allowed any women. She was still trying to get her head around that.

The hair at the nape of her neck rose and she spun from the bookshelves toward the entryway. She hadn't heard anything, but she sensed someone was there—a part of her ever-elusive magickal abilities, she assumed. "Broder?"

Silence.

Frowning, she wandered over to the bookshelves to take a closer look. A presence entered the room behind her. Whoever it was, he or she was completely silent. Jessa didn't trust anyone trying to be sneaky.

"Broder!" she yelled again. No response. Where was the man?

Casting her gaze about for something she could use as a weapon, she spotted a heavy iron candlestick and edged over as nonchalantly as she could to grab it.

In the same moment her hand closed around the candlestick and she turned to confront the interloper, a dark shape shot toward her. Jessa yelped as the figure plowed into her midsection, sending her flying backward. The candlestick dislodged from her fingers and went rolling across the floor.

Jessa tried to scramble away, but the figure pounced on her. She brought her knee up and jabbed an unidentified body part. Her attacker grunted and Jessa was able to push her off from beneath and scuttle away. Pushing to her feet beside the crouching person, she saw it was a woman with long red hair, dressed all in black.

"Who the hell are you?" Jessa asked, but the woman didn't answer.

She backed away from her, putting furniture between them. Her attacker stood, flipping hair out of her eyes. The lady was pretty, but her eyes and smile were cold. There was death in those eyes and she was certain this woman was skilled enough to deliver it. Jessa tried to ask her if she was Blight, but she couldn't seem to form any words at the moment.

Whoever she was, this complete stranger wanted to harm her.

A little puff of air escaped her lips. Finally she found her voice. *"Broder!"*

"Oh, no, missy. You'll not be calling for a man to help you," the woman snarled and then leapt across the couch at her. "It's just you and me. Woman to woman."

Jessa backed up, right into a pedestal with a carved head on it. The pedestal tilted under the impact and the statue crashed to the floor, little bits of sculpture sliding everywhere. "Broder!" she screamed again.

The woman lunged for her. Jessa leapt out of the way and spotted the fallen candlestick on the floor. She dove for it, pretending she'd stumbled. When the woman made a second lunge at her, she rolled to her feet and brought it toward the back of her head as the woman passed by her.

"Stop!" A man's voice boomed out. A huge hand reached out, caught the candlestick, and wrenched it from her grip.

Jessa stilled, watching the other woman carefully. She'd leapt to her feet, her long red hair tangled across her face. She wore a feral expression and her chest heaved with exertion.

Jessa gave Broder an exasperated look. "It's about time. That woman almost killed me." She curled her lip at the redhead. Just let the woman try to hurt her now that Broder was there. The redhead looked at her like she was insane.

Broder rolled his eyes and dropped the candlestick with a clatter to the floor. He turned to the intruder. "Halla, what the hell do you think you're doing?"

Jessa frowned. "Halla?"

The woman gestured at Jessa. "Assessing what my workload is going to be." She gave Jessa an appraising up and down. "Apparently it's going to be heavy, since this woman relies on a *man* for her defense."

Jessa's jaw dropped. "Wait a minute—"

Broder sighed. "Halla, Jessa just found out she's a witch and is being stalked by murderous demons. Perhaps sneaking up on her in an empty house wasn't the brightest move. Technically, she's still a civilian."

Jessa snorted, feeling insulted. "Civilian? Are we fighting a war?"

Now Halla and Broder both looked at her like she was insane. Halla crossed her leanly muscled arms across her chest. "Yes, actually, we are. Happy you finally got the e-mail notification."

Halla had a hell of an accent. Jessa's mouth twitched. "Do you mean *memo*?"

Broder motioned to Halla. "Jessa, meet Halla. She's a Valkyrie and she's come to train you."

"A . . . Valkyrie?"

"They play counterpoint to the Brotherhood," Broder explained. "They're long-lived, like witches, and are blessed by the goddess Freyja."

Halla shifted her weight. "But we don't have that nasty punishment gig because we never committed an original crime."

Jessa took deeper stock of Halla. She looked of an age with her, leanly muscled, obviously in shape. *Obviously*. After all, she was a *Valkyrie*, right? She didn't know why she was so surprised. She'd already accepted that Loki was a real, live being and that she herself was a witch. There shouldn't have been much more Broder could reveal that would shock her.

"So what does a Valkyrie do besides run around scaring years off people's lives? I mean, I'm pretty sure they don't survey battlefields and decide who lives or dies anymore, right?" Jessa asked, channeling everything she knew about the Valkyrie of lore. She paused, fidgeted, and blinked. "Or . . . do they?" She couldn't be sure of anything anymore.

Halla grinned. "Once we did. Now we are just warriors like the Brotherhood. Have to change with the times, right?" Her smile widened and actually became genuine. She stuck her hand out. "I am sorry we got . . . how do you say in English . . . off on the mistaken foot."

Jessa hesitated a moment, then shrugged and shook her hand. "That's okay. And it's *wrong* foot."

Halla withdrew her hand. "You really just found out you're seidhr?"

Jessa nodded. "I'm a brand spanking new witch."

She pressed her lips together as if in thought. "You're young, but not a new witch. I can feel you've been using your power."

"You can?"

She shrugged like it was nothing. "It's a part of being Valkyrie."

"Couldn't you tell I was a newbie when you entered the room?"

"Newbie?"

"Never mind."

"No, she couldn't, Jessa," answered Broder. "She meant to take you by surprise to see what sort of combat skills you have."

That would be none. Halla was right; she did rely on Broder and that needed to change.

"You did come here to train, did you not?" asked Halla.

"I guess so." Then she thought about it for a moment. "Not really."

Halla cocked her head to the side. "Then why are you here?"

Jessa thought about that for a moment before answering. "I came here to find myself."

Roan slid out of his car in front of the huge gray stone mansion that was home to most of the world's witches and shamans. He stood for a moment, gazing at the enormous structure of buildings with that familiar cold weight filling his chest.

The place had begun to bother him so much over the years that he'd moved to a cottage at the back of the property, near the high stone wall that hid the enclave away from human eyes, well away from the bustle and commotion of the Big House, as it was called.

Molly stepped out the front door of the mansion and into the faintly gray, misty morning. She was dressed colorfully, as usual, in a short gray gown that somewhat recalled the Victorian age, a black top hat tilted saucily on her glossy hair, and a pair of very high black platform boots. Her blond hair, dyed black on the underside, lofted free and loose around her pretty face. Her expression lit up when she saw him and she bounced down the steps to his car.

"He's called everyone, you know," she told him, hooking her arm with his. She wore a pair of elbow-length black silk gloves. "They're all in the library."

"Yes." He tried not to answer in such a dead, dry voice, but it was hard.

"He's not in a very good mood."

"Is he ever?"

She shrugged. "Some days he's less rotten than others. Today is not one of those blessed days. Today he almost feels manic. There's something big going on. Something important."

They reached the top of the stone stairs and pushed open the heavy wooden double doors. Through the marble foyer, Roan glimpsed the library, a fire flickering brightly to ward off the chill. A shadow moved in the room and low murmurs filled the air. The heaviness in his chest increased.

He and Molly walked into the room and Thorgest Egilson whirled to face them, his long beard braided into two plaits. His rheumy eyes narrowed and his hollowed cheeks were bright pink with temper or excitement, Roan couldn't be sure which yet. He had no idea why they'd all been called.

He pointed a finger at Roan as Molly skirted off to the side to join the other witches and shamans already convened in the room. "Abigail an' Michael's child is alive. A witch, by the feel of it. She's here in Scotland. Her presence thrums through me blood."

The blood drained from Roan's face and he rocked back a step. The mere mention of Abigail's name nearly sent him over the edge and he didn't like being surprised this way. He shifted on his feet and cleared his throat, trying to gain a handle on the moment. Losing your composure in front of Thorgest was a little like cutting your arm open in front of a hungry lion.

"Abigail's child survived?" It was a slow and stupid reaction. He could see the blood coursing from the wound he'd made right in front of Thorgest.

Thorgest quivered with rage for a moment before exploding, "Yes, ye imbecile! I just told ye. She's here in Scotland somewhere. The magick of her quivers through me veins. *Find her!*" He slammed his fist down on the long conference table that dominated the room and lowered his head. He'd roared the last sentence, making everyone in the room flinch.

"We believe you." Roan shifted on his feet, trying not to let Thorgest's raw emotion affect him; he had plenty of his own.

Empathy was a problem for all trained seidhr shamans and witches, but controlling it had always been a particularly hard struggle for him, especially now. Any hint of the woman he'd once loved more than his own life was enough to undo him completely. He directed his focus past the antique furniture in the fussy room to the large picture window at the end and stared as he gritted his teeth against the flow of Thorgest's rage.

The leader of their enclave swung around and speared him with his light blue eyes. "Ye believe me? Ye know she's here? Then find her. Bring her to me." Roan had never seen him so upset about anything, not in the five hundred years he'd known him. That was saying a lot. He wasn't even making sense right now and that was a rare thing.

"I need more details. You say you know she's here, but we thought she'd perished with her parents. We don't know the name she's using, don't know why she's here. She may not even know she's a witch. Without something of hers, material or immaterial, it's going to be difficult to locate her."

Abigail and Michael had disappeared thirty years ago to escape Thorgest's displeasure over their union. Six years after they'd run away, Thorgest had discovered Abigail was pregnant and had pleaded with his granddaughter to return home to Scotland, but the controlling and manipulative things Thorgest had done had driven a permanent wedge between them. Abigail had remained estranged, putting herself and her infant at great peril from the Blight.

Thorgest's granddaughter had been a powerful witch,

just as Michael had been a strong shaman, yet the very fact of their bloodline had made them a target. It was a testament to the strength of Abigail's feelings about her grandfather that she'd fled the enclave and lost herself in the United States.

More than one year after Thorgest and Abigail's fiery final conversation, one of the witches had sensed the death of Abigail and Michael, but they'd not known the fate of the child. They'd assumed the baby had perished in the car accident along with her parents.

Apparently Thorgest had begun to sense Abigail's daughter through trace magick, leading him to believe she'd arrived in Scotland. It seemed impossible. Roan could not yet rule out the possibility of some kind of trick by the Blight, but he couldn't reveal this suspicion to Thorgest without insulting him. Yet Roan was head of security for the enclave; it was his job to be suspicious. They were constantly on guard against demon attacks and sometimes their enemy could be insidious.

The thought of Abigail's daughter present in Scotland was very interesting. He'd tracked every moment of this story, lived it over and over again in his heart and his mind, since Abigail hadn't broken only Thorgest's heart when she'd left— she'd broken his, too. Roan had been the man meant to marry her, the one Thorgest had groomed for her and had tried to push her toward. Roan had hoped for her, had loved her. Her rejection of him stung to this day.

Thorgest studied him with narrowed eyes and Roan steadied his stance. Thorgest was a strong man and ruled with iron not only in his fist, but in his backbone. When he had that look in his eye, it meant he wasn't happy. However, there was no way Roan was going to quail under his scrutiny.

"Last I checked, we were seidhr," said Thorgest. "That means magick, does it no'? Gather the witches, gather the shamans. Do what ye must." He paused. "Break whatever rules ye must, take whatever risks, but *bring my great-granddaughter home.*"

• • •

Broder knew he should stay away, so why couldn't he?

He moved across Jessa's room in the pitch-black of early morning. She was a witch and he . . . well, he was Broder Calderson. The two should never have met.

And then they had.

He shouldn't want her, shouldn't even be in the room, yet there she was on the bed, covers kicked off, T-shirt tangled around her midriff, and her cotton shorts exposing the long, pale length of her legs. He wanted to kiss and lick every inch of them.

Being around her made him crazy, but not being around her gave him the shakes, like a man in need of a fix. Either way he was damned. It was the story of his life.

He hated Loki for this more than he'd ever hated him and that was saying a lot.

Crossing the room, he stood at the end of the bed. She rolled to the side, throwing her arm across her face, and let out a sigh in her sleep. The sound made every nerve in his body sing for her. Without even knowing he was moving, he crawled onto the bed with her.

Moving her hair away from her face, he jerked in surprise when she sighed and pressed her cheek into his palm with a smile on her face. "Broder," she murmured.

Broder went still, the center of his chest warming where before there had only been cold. He rubbed his thumb over the soft porcelain of her skin.

Mine. The thought came unbidden and it was definitely unwelcome, yet there it was anyway, beating fierce in his heart and in his head. *Mine.*

He wanted her to be his for always, no matter what the gods decreed.

Lowering his head, he softly sampled her lips. "I need to touch you, Jessa," he whispered against her mouth.

She made a purring sound of assent, though she never opened her eyes. "Yes, Broder, please touch me," she answered breathily. *"I want you."*

NINE

His cock was already as hard as steel. If it could have, it would've grown even harder. It was the words he'd heard in all his fantasies since the moment he'd met her. He moved down her body.

She hardly made a sound when he eased her shorts down her legs and spread her thighs. In the moonlit room, her skin looked like milk and he wanted to take a long, deep drink. He parted her thighs and she sighed. He lowered his mouth to her and she made a small sound. She liked it—but no more than he did.

The flavor of her spread over his tongue and he groaned. She tasted so damned good. He found her clit and laved it, hearing her pleased reaction. Under his tongue, the small bud blossomed. He'd only wanted a taste of her, but now that he was here he wanted more. He wanted to make her come. He craved the sound of it, the sweet tension in her body. He fed off of her pleasure, since he couldn't take his own. Not yet.

A new sound made him lift his head. Jessa's eyes were open and staring at him. He smiled at her, then lowered his head again. Unexpectedly, she moved. Her foot struck him square in the chest.

With an *oof*, he fell backward. She'd used every ounce of her strength to kick him and it had taken him by surprise.

She yanked the blankets up over her. "What the hell do you think you're doing?" she screamed at him. "It's the middle of the night. What do you think I am, your personal blow-up doll?"

He stared up at her from where he'd landed on his ass. "What? You told me you wanted it."

She gaped, her jaw dropping. "I was sleeping!"

"Sleeping?" He blinked. She'd been talking in her sleep? "You seemed like you were enjoying it."

She stared at him like he'd gone mad. "*I was unconscious*. I wasn't given a choice."

Broder absorbed that. "Who were you dreaming about?"

After hesitating a moment, she leapt from the bed. She looked good wearing only a T-shirt. "None of your business."

Interesting.

He pushed to his feet. "Let's say, hypothetically, it was me. Wouldn't it be just as if you'd been awake?"

"Get out!" she roared, advancing on him.

He stood his ground for a moment. He loved the flash of anger in her eyes. "Tell me you didn't like it, Jessa. Tell me there isn't a part of you that wanted me to continue."

She stalked up to him and stuck her finger in his chest. "That's not the point. This is the twenty-first century, Broder, and in this century women are in full control of their bodies. You touch me when I say you can. *Now get out!*"

He was in hell.

He was in hell and unable to relieve the ache in his balls from touching her. Over the centuries he'd been able to manage his sexual desires—he'd had to learn how or go insane. But Jessa had unraveled every bit of the control he'd managed to amass.

"How can one tiny little woman have that much power?" he growled as he guided his motorcycle into a narrow space between two hatchbacks on a street in Inverness. He kept a bike here as well as in the States.

He found motorcycles gave him speed and maneuverability and that could be a big advantage when chasing down Blight. Of course, a motorcycle wasn't very practical in a place like the Scottish Highlands, where the weather was unpredictable and it was chilly for so much of the year, but such things bothered the members of the Brotherhood little.

He cut the bike's engine, drawing appreciative looks from passersby, and got off to enter the Quill and Dragon, one of his favorite pubs.

The scents of pipe smoke, alcohol, and polished wood enveloped him as he entered, soothing a little of the tumult in his soul.

How the hell was he supposed to know the woman had been sleep talking? She'd been more than willing back in the States *and* in the airplane. It wasn't such a big leap for him to have assumed she'd been willing again, was it?

Women. Apparently they were just as complex and perplexing in this century as they had been ten centuries ago.

He headed to the bar, letting the soft sounds of the place—casual conversation and laughter—filter through the noise in his head and quiet him. He signaled the bartender. "Johnnie Walker Black." The bartender gave him the glass, which he downed in one gulp. "Leave the bottle."

The bartender slid the bottle over to him and Broder tossed him a few bills and a nice tip. He grabbed the bottle and walked back out of the pub with it in hand, ignoring the call of the man behind the bar. The bartender could try to stop him from leaving with an open bottle, but it wouldn't get him far.

He needed to kill Blight and a lot of them.

On his way out, he pushed past a well-built man with dark hair who gave off a tingle of something supernatural through the runes in his coat. Broder ignored it. There were all kinds of supernatural beings in the world, but the only ones who had his attention tonight were the ones who'd been created in Hel.

Inverness teemed with demons and they were nocturnal. It wouldn't be hard to find low-level Blight prowling the streets, preying on the humans who had gone out to party on Saturday night. It was what the low-level Blight had been expelled from Hel to do—create terror and havoc on a base level. They had free rein—well, almost free rein—to feed from whoever they wished as long as they didn't reveal their presence to the masses. That little revelation was meant for later, when Ragnarök grew nigh.

Taking pulls from his bottle, he walked the streets around the pub, tuned into the area, searching for the sensation of the hair rising on his neck—a sure sign an agent was somewhere close—or the little pulse the runes in his coat gave off.

He found his first one dressed in a pair of jeans and a sweatshirt, its hair cut in a swoopy long emo-boy style that made Broder grit his teeth. The cold scent of ice caught his nose and told him more than the unmistakable sensation in his gut that the guy was a demon. He was busy stalking a drunk woman who was trying to make her way to her car.

Soon Broder was busy stalking him.

Waiting for the moment before the agent leapt from the shadows, Broder smashed the now-empty bottle over the agent's head. The demon turned and hissed at him, fangs bared. Broder wasted no time, yanking his dagger from the base of his spine and slamming the blade to the hilt in the agent's gut. He exploded into a shower of ice pellets.

One down. More to go.

The woman being stalked had run at the sound of the bottle breaking in the shadows behind her and had now sped away from the curb in her car, tires squealing. She probably wasn't fit to drive, but that wasn't his problem.

Several figures rushed him from behind. The demon hadn't been alone.

Broder turned and laughed, a cold sound that made the three hesitate. This was what he needed tonight, a fight to help him deal with Jessa's rejection.

The first agent met him with a snarl and Broder laughed again, a frigid, joyless sound, the ecstasy of the fight rising hot and hard within him.

Bring it on.

• • •

Roan watched from the shadows as Broder Calderson cut an ice-scattered swath through the alleys and streets of Inverness. He fought like a wild thing, almost like a dancer. Broder made killing an art form, in holding with his reputation. No agent of the Blight could stand against this man and survive. That was the impression he gave, anyway. He seemed to revel in the destruction and the chaos that the Blight brought, his laughter making the hair on the back of Roan's neck stand up.

But then, he was Brotherhood. Broder hadn't been made for this—but he'd certainly been molded, just as all the Brotherhood had been. Killing the Blight was their *raison d'être*, unlike the seidhr, who had their magick to develop and pass down through the generations.

The continuation of those generations was why Roan was here.

Magick had drawn him to this location tonight, magick put to the use of finding Abigail's daughter. That was his *raison d'être* right now, tasked to him by Thorgest. So he had created runes using birch bark, his chosen element. The scattering of those runes had pointed him in this direction, told him to come here, come now.

It was a risk to use magick this way. The blatant scattering of runes outside the safety of the compound tended to draw Blight. It may very well have drawn the Blight that Broder Calderson now fought with such joyous abandon. It was ironic that he had such a man to thank for his safety.

Following the trail the runes had marked for him, he'd ended up outside the Quill and Dragon when Broder left. He'd been confused about why the runes had led him there until he'd caught the faint peppermint and rose scent, with a hint of fresh lemon, that lingered in the air as Broder passed. *The scent of a witch.* More specifically, that hint of lemon combined with the rest had been the scent of Abigail; Roan would recognize it anywhere.

So it appeared it may be true. It was possible Abigail's

daughter was alive and the lass was with Broder. That was what the runes seemed to be telling him, anyway. Roan's jaw locked as he watched Broder slide his blade into a hulking black-haired agent that poofed into ice pellets.

Thorgest wasn't going to like that Abigail's daughter was in Broder's care. *He* didn't like it, either.

The Brotherhood and the seidhr were uneasy, chilly allies in this war. The Brotherhood kept vulnerable witches and shamans safe when they needed protection and the seidhr provided them with certain types of protective magick in return. It was good that Thorgest's great-granddaughter was in the Brotherhood's care because she would be a huge target of the Blight. However, *Broder Calderson* was not an acceptable choice to be guarding Thorgest's daughter.

Not an acceptable choice by far.

Roan melted back into the shadows. He had unpleasant news to deliver. Then would come the task of extricating Thorgest's kin from the grips of a monster.

Jessa slammed her fist into a punching bag in the training room and pain exploded through her hand. "Damn it!" She cradled her fist and stepped away from the barely swinging bag with a look of righteous anger on her face.

Okay, she was no hard-ass.

After that disturbing encounter with Broder, she'd thought coming in here to work out might help her get into a better frame of mind. All she'd done back in her room was replay the events over and over and that wasn't helping the delicious tingle in her body that still lingered from his touch.

A very unwelcome tingle from very unwelcome touching. Or so her mind told her. Her body was saying something else entirely. She wanted to tell her body to shut up.

Giving the punching bag one last look of doom—as if she could actually deliver doom with her wimpy punching skills—she headed to the bank of cardio machines. She couldn't handle the punching bag and she definitely couldn't handle Broder, but at least she could handle the StairMaster . . . for a few minutes, anyway.

Why did the man have to be so luscious? And why did she shudder every time she thought about the way he looked at her—like she was something he wanted to eat. Yet there was something else in his eyes, something . . . guilty. Whatever that guilt sprang from, it wasn't stopping him from pursuing her.

But no matter how delectable a man like Broder was, or how starved her libido, she shouldn't indulge. Well . . . she shouldn't indulge any more than she already had, anyway. Why? She would illuminate the reasons.

Number one, she had no firm footing here and her life was in free fall. Right now was not the time for her to engage in an affair, no matter how transitory. Number two, she didn't do affairs. Never had. She might want Broder's body and he might want hers, but she needed more than that. It might be fun for a night or two, but in the end she'd just end up feeling like trash. She'd been down that road before; she knew.

Mostly she'd been a good girl. She'd followed her rule of no meaningless flings even though, as a blonde with curves where men seemed to like them best, she'd had plenty of opportunity. There had been only one time she'd broken her rule—Brandon White. She still remembered that horrible feeling when they'd parted after only a few nights together. He'd tossed her away like a used condom wrapper.

So, no Broder. No matter how gorgeous he was.

She felt bad about it. After all, she was well aware that Broder hadn't had sex in a thousand years. But was that any reason to just jump into bed with the man? Wouldn't that be a little like pity sex? Broder deserved better than that. Perhaps since Loki had suddenly decided to allow him a woman, Broder needed to pick a different one. Not her. Not someone who put such a heavy weight on physical relations.

Maybe Broder needed to go find himself a hooker. Or, hell, almost any woman would do. Most females would fight each other for a chance to spend the night with a man like him.

In that exact moment, Broder burst in. He stood in the doorway of the room, looking as though he wanted to fight someone. His clothes were damp, so she assumed he'd been fighting plenty that night—demons. Blood marked the bare skin of his upper arms, his face, and his neck. Clearly he'd sustained more than a few injuries tonight.

His gaze caught hers and she stilled, letting the machine go silent. "It's four in the morning," he grumbled. "Halla starts your training today. What are you doing in here? You should be resting up."

"I couldn't sleep." Her voice came out way threadier and uncertain than she wanted. She cleared her voice and spoke louder, even put a hint of accusation in her voice. "Where were you?" Her gaze flicked over his shirt. Funny how melted ice looked like blood to her these days.

"I needed some distraction." He stalked into the room, full of testosterone and aggression. Apparently spending the night killing things hadn't improved his mood. Wow. Big surprise there.

She walked toward him. "What did you need distraction from?"

He bared his teeth at her, which made her stop dead in her tracks. "You."

"Oh." Even from a distance—which she was keeping— she could smell the alcohol on him. She wrinkled her brow. "Have you been drinking?"

"Yes," he drawled as though annoyed by having to answer her question.

She raised one eyebrow. "Are you drunk?"

"Woman, a man in the Brotherhood can drink all he wants and never get drunk. Alcohol has no effect on us." He touched his chest. "It's the touch of the demon inside us, you see. That thin icy pick in the center of our hearts. I am a black hole. Pour bottles of alcohol down my gullet and the stream will never hit bottom."

His expression was as cold as his tone, but his eyes held

incredible warmth. The heat was dark in nature and undeniable. All she'd done tonight was whet his appetite. In his gaze she saw that clearly.

He wanted her and he was going to have her. It was only a question of time.

She stared at him for a long moment, perfect understanding without words passing between them. Licking her lips, she tried and failed to quell the electric surge of lust through her veins. Broder's pupils widened and blackened, almost as if he could sense her sudden arousal—like an animal scenting wounded prey.

Broder *did* remind her of an animal. She guessed that his life had made him that way, had taught him to live by his instincts and focus on his survival. It had made him strong—primal. Feral. The man had a lot of control, but it couldn't be endless. She wondered for a moment what an out-of-control Broder would be like. Would that experience be sexy and exhilarating, or would it be frightening?

She responded to that feral component of his personality. Perhaps more dangerous, she responded to the flicker of vulnerability he showed only the barest flashes of occasionally.

Broder had loved once. Perhaps he'd even been loved back. But that had been a thousand years ago.

There was something in Broder that needed love; she could feel it. Something inside him that Loki hadn't managed to kill craved it, wanted it from her. However, she was in no position to give it . . . and, sadly, he couldn't accept it anyway.

He collapsed into a chair with his head tipped back and his eyes closed, letting out a long breath. He was clearly exhausted. She could see now that his wounds were worse than she'd assumed. He pulled his shirt off and inspected them. The blood had clotted around the gashes on his upper chest and arms. He had so many scars. They looked old, from his pre-Brotherhood life, presumably.

Her gaze took in the wounds he'd received, tracing the lines of his body. She looked up from his stomach and into his smoldering eyes. "Do you have a first-aid kit some-where?"

He blinked slowly, calculatingly, then jerked his head to the side. Following his indication, she saw a cabinet on a wall near the sink and small refrigerator that stood in the corner of the room.

After retrieving the kit, she approached him, unsure that getting so close to him was a good idea. Too late now. Using the disinfectant and bandages she found in the kit, she patched up his various cuts and gashes. None of them were deep enough to need stitches—not that an immortal Viking warrior would ever need them. She was certain these wounds would be healed by morning.

Just as she was packing everything up, Broder yanked her down into his lap so she faced him in a straddling position. The kit fell to the floor with a clatter, bandages and bottles rolling everywhere. She'd barely seen him move, let alone had time to react. Her initial reaction was to jab him in the eyes and throat, but he grabbed her wrists. Her fear spiked, but he held her loosely. All she'd have to do was twist her wrists down to be free of his grasp. On the heels of her panic rose a much different reaction to being so close to him.

Leaning toward her, he brushed his lips against hers with a gentleness that seemed jarring when compared with his power and strength. She fought through the fog in her mind, trying to grasp some thread of sanity. His touch always made good sense slip away like the memory of a dream in the morning.

His hands moved to her waist and slipped under the hem of her shirt, his thumbs brushing back and forth against the skin of her waist. It was mesmerizing and she knew she had to break it, or risk giving herself over to him completely.

"Let me go," she said carefully. She took measured breaths in and out, calming herself. "Broder, *please*."

He hesitated a moment, stilling with his mouth on hers. Then he released her.

She shot up as though he were made of fire and backed away from him. He held her gaze and in his eyes she saw agony.

Blinking, she tore her gaze from his and headed for the door. She was not the woman to give him what he craved. Not sex, not love. It was time to get out of here before he touched her again and turned all her resolve to mush.

"I cannot satisfy my desire to become mindless and muddled with alcohol, Jessa, just as I have not been able to satisfy other desires for the last one thousand years." He paused. "Now you are here and *you*, Jessa, are the only one I want."

She hesitated in her rapid pace toward the door, but picked it right back up again without turning or saying a word.

"So what if it's been a thousand years since the guy has been laid?" Jessa muttered, kicking up . . . not as high as Halla. "That's not my problem."

Halla had tagged her for a workout that early afternoon. Jessa was jet-lagged and exhausted, but that hadn't mattered to her new trainer—who *was* a serious hard-ass.

"He has made pass at you?" Halla was standing opposite her and was punching and kicking the air. Jessa was supposed to mimic her movements.

"A pass? I don't think Broder makes passes." She took a moment to pant, then punched down low. "He just goes for the gold."

Halla grinned. "I can show you ways to bring him to his knees. No. Not like that," Halla added, seeing the dismayed expression on Jessa's face. She whipped around, kicking her feet into the air to skewer an imaginary opponent while emitting a sharp battle cry. She grinned. "To his knees *like that*."

Jessa grinned back. Maybe Halla wasn't so bad after all.

They went back to the kicking and punching drills. Jessa tried to hide just how much Halla was making her sweat. "I mean, what does he expect, pity sex? I'm not giving him that."

Halla laughed. "You'd have sex with Broder out of pity? Do you prefer woman?"

"It's *women*, and I know he's gorgeous. Most women would probably trip over themselves to jump into bed with him." She narrowed her eyes at Halla. "Why don't you do it?" Even as the words left her mouth, she didn't like them.

"No." Halla shook her head and executed a perfect roundhouse kick. "The Valkyrie and the Brotherhood are not allowed contact in that way."

Jessa contemplated a roundhouse kick, then collapsed to the floor with a groan. "No more, please. *No. More.*"

Halla shrugged. "We take a break." Then she sank to the floor beside her. "You must train well, Jessa. The Blight will want to kill you at the first opportunity."

"They've already tried several times now. I'd be dead now if it weren't for Broder."

Halla nodded. "But you don't need a man to be your shield. You can learn to fight on your own. Defend yourself."

"I want that."

"Good." Halla leapt to her feet. "Then we train."

Jessa bowed her head in defeat and let out a low, slow breath, then climbed to her feet again. "Where are you from anyway?" she asked right before she did a much poorer version of the roundhouse Halla had just done. She eyed the other woman. "The Amazon?"

Halla missed the reference. "I live in Norway. There is a training and housing facility not far from Oslo. I am a training specialist there. I help the Valkyrie get ready to fight."

"The Blight are everywhere?"

Halla nodded. "Loki's daughter, Hel, creates them easily. All she needs to do is scoop up a handful of the snow and ice that makes up her realm and shape into an agent of the Blight. She sends them out into the world to bring darkness here. If she has her way, she will bring about the end of time, the end of the gods."

"What is she so ticked off about?"

"Loki killed Baldur, the most handsome and beloved of all the gods. Hel loved Baldur and attempted to kill Loki in retaliation. As her punishment, she was set to guard the icy underworld. She doesn't want to be the keeper of that realm, so she's trying to bring down *all* the realms. Both Loki's and Hel's punishments come from the death of one man. You should really read up on your lore."

Jessa executed a rather fine imaginary ear slap, in her opinion, and tried not to preen. "Right, because it's all true."

"Not all of it."

"And where do I read up on the seidhr? It'd be nice to know what I am."

Halla stopped moving. She tilted her head to the side and the smooth skin between her brows furrowed. "But you're in Scotland."

Jessa punched in the air, then hopped foot to foot. She was getting her second wind. "Yes. Is there something significant about that?"

"Your people live here, Jessa. In the north. Broder didn't tell you that?"

"Yes, but I'm on lockdown, remember?" She thought about what Halla had said for a moment. "Do you think their proximity explains why I've felt strange ever since the plane set down?"

"It's possible. It could be some kind of magickal link, most likely to a blood relative, but I don't know much about the seidhr. They are very secretive. I do know that Broder should take you there, or call one of the witches or shamans here to meet with you." Halla paused. "I don't know why he hasn't already. If I were your protector that would have been the first thing I did."

TEN

Jessa slammed open the door to the study and found Broder sitting in a chair, reading a book. She blinked at the surprising sight, but that didn't stop the full frontal assault that followed. "Why haven't you called the seidhr yet? A witch or a shaman should have come out here to meet with me already." She stalked up to him and crossed her arms over her chest.

Broder didn't look up at her for a long moment. Finally he took a bookmark from the table beside him, slid it into the book, closed it carefully, and laid it aside.

Jessa's jaw locked.

At last he looked up at her. "I haven't called them for your own good."

"For my own good?" she sputtered. "How is keeping valuable information from me, information I have been waiting for my entire life, a good thing for me?"

"What do you know about the seidhr?"

"Damn little."

He nodded. "So you don't know why you've been separated from them your entire life. You don't know if they hid you away to grow up completely isolated from their society."

She let out a pent-up breath and stalked over to the massive fireplace and back. "What are you saying . . . that the seidhr hid me on purpose?"

"Someone certainly hid you on purpose, Jessa. We don't

know who or why. Perhaps, for whatever reason, you're in danger from the seidhr. Perhaps it has something to do with your parents, or some quirk of your bloodline. Perhaps they will not like the fact that you are no longer hidden. Perhaps they might mean you harm. In that case, do you think it's a good idea for us to declare your presence here and invite them into my home?"

She paced, chewing her bottom lip. These were good reasons, reasons she hadn't considered, but she wanted so much to delve into the person she was. "Okay, that makes sense."

"Yes."

Coming to a stop in front of him, she spread her hands. "But I have no idea what my abilities are and there's no one here to instruct me."

"I do know a little about what it is to be seidhr."

"A little."

Broder pressed his lips together and stared hard at the fire. "A lot. I know a lot about their magick and how their society is organized."

"Yes, but you're not a witch."

"In the human world both men and women are witches. In seidhr culture, witches are female and men are shamans. It has been that way since before time was recorded. And, no, I'm not seidhr. You would have to take what I know at face value. I may be able to find some written works about them, if you would like to read up."

"I would." Jessa considered him. It wasn't as if she had much of a choice. She had to take what she could get. "I want to know everything."

He inclined his head. "I'll work on that. In the meantime, ask me questions. I may have the answers."

She tipped her head to the side. "The first thing I want to know is why you get that look on your face when you talk about them."

"What look?" He nearly growled the words and the hair stood up on her nape. There was danger here and she didn't know why.

"It's almost like . . . guilt, but it goes deeper than that."
She knew that what she was describing wasn't really from
the look on his face; it came from having an intuitive sense
about him, just as she'd always had intuitive senses about
people. "It's almost like . . . torment, or grief."

"Never mind." This time he really did growl. He pushed
up from his chair. "Don't ask about it again."

She held up her hands in a gesture of surrender. "Okay.
Message received. Can I ask about something else?"

"What?" he barked, making her jump.

"Tell me about the books. You had them in the States and
you have them here. Are you a collector or a reader?"

"Both." He still wouldn't look at her.

She nodded. "Old books are a passion of mine." She
walked over and picked up the book he'd been reading—a
slim, battered volume of Poe's *Tell-Tale Heart*. Dark roman-
ticism. That totally made sense. "Broder, we should talk
about storing these volumes appropriately."

He stalked out of the room.

"Okay, then," she called after him. "We'll talk later."

She watched him go, wondering more powerfully than
ever before what the deal was with the seidhr. She understood his explanation about not uniting her with them yet
and she agreed with it, even though it was painful.

Yet she had a feeling there was more to the story. Broder
didn't want to have anything to do with the seidhr.

Yet apparently that desire didn't extend to her.

She picked up another of the books he'd been thumbing
through. It was open and facedown on the table, which made
her wince. This one was *Adventures of Sinbad* . . . written
in Arabic. Her head came up abruptly and she stared at the
door Broder had just exited through.

There were so many mysteries about this man she wanted
answered.

Book in hand, she followed him out of the library and
into the living room.

Broder stood in the half-darkened living room, staring
into the fire. She stepped into the room, drawn to him even

though she'd promised herself she'd stay away . . . especially when they were alone.

She peered into the flickering flames. "What are you looking at?"

He shifted, locking his gaze on her. "Nothing. I'm thinking."

The tone of his voice warned her not to inquire further. She took another step into the room and lifted the book. "Arabic, Broder?"

He moved toward her, his muscles rolling in that animal-istic way that both repelled and excited her. "I can't fuck. I can't get drunk." He shrugged. "I read. I collect books. I learn languages. I restore old motorcycles and cars because I love them. I do these things so I don't go insane."

And in those short, succinct seven sentences, she learned more about Broder Calderson than she had since she'd met him.

She thought about the cherry red '66 Pontiac GTO they'd driven over from the airport and the classic Harley he'd been on when they first met. She'd caught a glimpse of another obviously older bike in the garage by the keep as well. So, he'd restored those. He hadn't mentioned that before.

"How many languages do you speak?" she asked.

"Fifteen." He said it like it was nothing, and perhaps for a man who'd lived as long he had, it really was nothing.

Suddenly Jessa felt a driving need to sit down. His level of attractiveness had just shot into the stratosphere. He was as strong as a bull and smart, too. He'd just hit all her buttons in a few short sentences. She coughed and cleared her throat. "That's really impressive."

He shrugged a shoulder. "Not really."

She lingered for a moment, out of things to say but happy they were back on friendly terms. She did have to live with the man after all. "I was a lit major in college. Before Margaret died, I was in grad school."

"I know. You want to be a teacher, right? College professor, specifically."

She nodded. "Did you do a background check on me?"

"Of course I did. I need to know everything about you in order to better protect you. I know all of your employment and school history. I'm missing the personal stuff. Share it with me sometime, okay?" He spoke gruffly and wouldn't look at her, leaving her unsure if he was asking to know about her to actually get to know her, or if he was asking for details so he could better protect her.

A part of her desperately hoped it was the former.

"Sure." Hugging herself, she nodded, smiled, and murmured, "Good night," then headed out of the room.

"Jessa."

She stilled. He was close. Way closer than he'd been a moment before. She turned and he was *right there*, close enough to touch. Her heartbeat did the mamba for a second. "Yes?"

He reached out and touched a tendril of her hair. Arousal flared sharply within her. It was amazing how his slightest touch could do that to her. His pupils exploded big and dark. His jaw tightened.

Jessa knew right then she was in trouble.

He wrapped the tendril of hair around his finger as he stepped closer to her. Now she could feel his body heat, catch the faint scent of his cologne and the teasing, subtle aroma of his leather duster.

He snaked his arm around her waist and dragged her up against his chest. "You are mine, Jessa. Stop fighting me. Stop giving me mixed signals." His lips skated over the curve of her jaw and arousal tightened every nerve in her body.

Her eyes fluttered shut and she contemplated giving in. Just this once. His every touch battered at her defenses and she was tired of being strong. He skated his palm over her breast and her nipples peaked against the tight fabric of her sports bra. His mouth found hers and closed over it, giving a groan as if she tasted good.

Her tongue found his and tangled in a hungry back-and-forth as his hand slid over her ass and pressed her against him, forcing his massive erection into her abdomen. The scent of him filled her senses and an image of him driving deep inside her flitted through her mind.

Just once. . . .

He grabbed the hem of her workout pants and yanked down.

Her eyes flew open. She couldn't do this again. She couldn't give in. Memories of Brandon flooded her mind. Denying a man who'd gone this long without sex was a little cruel, maybe, but she couldn't have her heart broken by a meaningless fling again. She couldn't lay all her emotions out on a platter to be destroyed.

"No," she whispered. "Stop. I'm sorry, but . . . stop."

The muscles in Broder's body tightened, but he slid his hand down the curve of her bare behind anyway, skirting between her thighs to rasp over her sex. She sucked in a breath against the wave of need that followed his touch. If he went any further, she would totally lose herself to him— body and maybe soul. She couldn't let that happen. Somewhere deep inside her she sensed that this man had the ability to destroy her in a way Brandon would never have been capable of.

And Brandon had hurt enough.

"Broder, stop."

He nuzzled her throat and made her shiver. Rage and fear surged through her. If he wanted to take what he wanted from her, she had no choice but to surrender.

And that pissed her off.

"I said, *stop!*" She gave him a hard elbow to the appendix.

He grunted and backed away, though she suspected she'd barely wounded him. She turned and bolted from the room, straight out the front door and into the courtyard beyond. Above her night had fallen and the cool air kissed the bare skin of her midriff.

Hugging herself, she walked toward the gates. She wanted to get past them, run a million miles away from here. She knew that would be a stupid move. Beyond those gates were the Blight, just waiting for her to make a misstep so

they could separate her soul from her body. She imagined
them all out there like a pride of lions ready to pounce. She
wasn't sure she could run fast enough.

She stopped right in front of the gates and stared out
into the darkness. Sensing a presence behind her, she stiffened.

"Don't do it," came Broder's deep voice.

"I'm not an idiot. I'm only wishing I could."

He said nothing; he only stood there, a strong, enticing,
protective force at her back. Too bad she wasn't sure which
danger was more threatening—the one in front of her . . .

Or the one behind her.

Roan watched Erik Halvorson climb into his rental car at
the airport. Muscles rolling, the huge man sat behind the
wheel, making the large vehicle look small.

"Och, he's a big one," whispered Molly, who sat behind
him on his motorcycle. "Even bigger than you."

"All the Brotherhood are built like him. That's why we
have to handle this delicately." Molly was a young witch,
but her powers in the arts of *sjónhverfing*, deceiving of the
sight, were strong. The SUV pulled away from the curb and
Roan followed him on his motorcycle, at a distance.

What he was about to do would break the fragile alliance
between the Brotherhood and the seidhr, but Thorgest had
made it clear that he wanted his great-granddaughter at all
costs.

He followed Erik out of the airport and up north, keeping
well behind him and out of his line of sight. He knew where
he was headed, of course. A casting of the runes had told
him of Erik's arrival at Broder Calderson's estate.

And that was just about perfect.

Once they'd made their way into the countryside, Roan
made his move. On a lonely stretch of highway, he edged
closer to Erik's vehicle and signaled for Molly to begin spell
casting. It didn't take long for Erik's SUV to begin to cross
the middle line, the vehicle swaying from side to side as the

huge man became lost in a tangled web of illusion. The members of the Brotherhood were immortal and strong as fuck, but they were not immune to all forms of magick.

The SUV pulled off to the side and Erik stumbled out, leaving the door open and looking dazed. Roan pulled the bike up behind the SUV, but the big guy didn't even see or hear it. It was disarming to realize just how easily someone like Erik Halvorson could be undone with a little mental sleight of hand. It made him proud.

Molly climbed off the bike and went toward him, concentration clear on her face. She was a powerful witch, one of the best they had, but it took a lot of effort to snag someone in an illusion this big.

She crooned at Erik, leading him over to sit on a nearby slope of a hill, smoothing her short black skirt over her black-and-white-striped tights. With her half-black, half-blond hair and her shiny black platform boots, she looked more than a little out of place on the green grass.

Roan walked toward them, then leaned over and plucked a long, sandy-colored hair from Erik's head. Erik hardly moved at all. If the brother had had his senses, Roan was pretty sure his own head would be detached from his shoulders right now.

Roan tucked the hair into the pocket of his jeans. He would need that to work his next bit of shamanistic magick. Shape-shifting.

Nodding at Molly, Roan went for the vehicle. Erik had left it running. How convenient. Before he slid behind the wheel, he glanced at Molly, noticing how she'd cozied up next to Erik. "You'll be all right while I'm gone?" The last thing Molly needed was to have Erik come out of the spell and discover he'd been duped. That would not go well for her.

Molly waved a hand at him. "G'wan, I'll be fine. In fact . . . take your time." She gave a pointed leer at Erik.

Roan started to climb into the SUV, then hesitated. "Don't do anything you shouldn't do, Molly." He paused. "With him."

Molly tried to look shocked, but it fell a little short. "Are you suggesting I might take advantage of the situation?"

"Yes." He gave her a stern look. "Don't."

She sighed and tossed her hair. "As much as this incredible slab of manhood entices me, I don't need to resort to tricks to attract a man."

He believed her. She was beautiful, even with the odd dress she so often chose. Roan nodded. "All the same, be good."

She gave him an angelic smile that he didn't quite believe. "Always."

Roan eased into the car and drove north, toward Broder's estate.

Time for part two of this act. Time to try to get Thorgest's great-granddaughter away from Broder without causing a war between the clans.

ELEVEN

Broder opened the door to find Erik on the other side. He nodded. "Brother."

"I hate planes," Erik grumbled.

Most of the Brotherhood did. He moved aside and allowed Erik to pass into the foyer, then led Erik into the living room, trying to hide his resentment of the fact that Erik had come. He was perfectly capable of protecting Jessa on his own and hated the implication he might need help. Yet Erik had called him the day before and told him he'd be arriving to provide backup and support. The fact that the seidhr were involved complicated everything and made the situation delicate. Broder could handle delicate.

He winced, thinking of a couple times he hadn't done so well with sensitive political issues. Okay, maybe delicacy wasn't one of his strong points.

Erik turned in the middle of the room. "Where's the woman?"

"Jessa is training with Halla. Do you want something to eat or drink?"

Giving his head a sharp shake, he paced to the bookshelves. Broder wondered what was wrong. Erik never failed to ask for whiskey. The fact they couldn't get drunk never seemed to stop them from trying. "Did you contact the seidhr yet?"

"No." Broder frowned. "We talked about that back in

D.C. Remember? I'm not going to contact them until I find out what's up with her. With the Blight targeting her so hard, the last thing we need is the seidhr after her, too."

"Right." Erik glanced at him and nodded. "A good plan." Except he said it like he wasn't totally sure it was.

"Broder, I need—" Jessa breezed into the room wearing a pair of tight-fitting workout pants and a halter top. "Oh, hi, Erik. What are you doing here?"

Erik turned at the sound of her voice and went completely still. He gazed at Jessa as if he'd never seen her before . . . and as if he liked what he saw. He looked at her as if she were something good to eat.

Every protective and possessive fiber in Broder's body went on alert. Loki hadn't constrained Erik's ability to be with women the way he'd constrained Broder's. Erik could have any woman he wanted.

He wasn't getting Jessa.

Broder swallowed the animal-like growl rising from the back of his throat. Erik might be head of the Brotherhood, but that wouldn't stop him from ramming Erik through a wall if he made any move in her direction.

"I'm here to back up Broder," Erik answered. "When the Blight want someone they go to incredible ends to get them. He might need help."

Jessa gave Broder a long look that made him go warm. "I don't think Broder needs backup."

"I'm also here to take you to the seidhr."

"What?" Broder boomed out. "The hell you're taking Jessa to them."

Erik tore his hungry gaze away from Jessa and focused it on him, narrowing his eyes at Broder with a violent intensity. "They want her back. It's time."

"I won't do anything that endangers Jessamine. I won't let you endanger her, either."

"I am the leader of the Brotherhood. I make the decisions. I'm not asking for your permission."

Broder snapped his jaw shut, but it wasn't because he was backing down; it was because he was surprised. In all the centuries he'd known Erik, he'd never once known the man to use his position as leverage. Erik had never needed to—his very presence was leverage. He appeared and men fell in line.

Erik addressed Jessa, who was looking between Broder and Erik and chewing her lower lip thoughtfully. "Don't you want to know your people? Train your magick?"

She took a moment to answer. "Of course I do." Her gaze traveled over Broder. "But, frankly, I trust him and . . . well, I don't trust you."

Broder blinked. She trusted him? Even after all those times he'd tried to get her into his bed?

"Sorry." She winced, glancing at Erik. "But if Broder thinks we should wait until we know more, then I want to wait."

A muscle worked in Erik's jaw. "All right. I see I have to win your faith."

Jessa lingered in the doorway, watching Erik carefully. She didn't respond. That meant yes.

"I need to get my bag out of the rental car," said Erik. "Will you come with me, Jessa? I want to talk to you." He gave Broder a pointed look. "Alone." He strode out of the room toward the front door.

Jessa met Broder's eyes for a long moment before going after Erik.

Broder watched her leave, a tingle at the base of his spine. There was something off about Erik today, but he couldn't put his finger on what it was.

Jessa followed Erik out of the house and to his rented SUV. Ever since she'd first walked into the living room and seen the man, he'd been setting the hair on the nape of her neck on end. Something about him made her uneasy. It was strange. She hadn't had this reaction to him back in D.C. He'd intimidated her with his strength and size, with his mere presence, but he hadn't creeped her out.

Erik looked the same as he had back in the States, though

he wore a pair of jeans and a sweater now, instead of jeans and a T-shirt, and appeared more relaxed than he had at the house in D.C. He acted the same—commanding, overbearing, and forbidding. Just like Broder. Just like all the men of the Brotherhood, she was beginning to suspect.

So why was the man setting off her spidey sense?

There was definitely something odd going on, but maybe it was just her emotional state. Maybe she was just disturbed by the fact that she'd needed to go into hiding from deadly supernatural forces. That was enough to put anyone on edge, right?

"I don't want to make you do anything you don't want to do," said Erik, falling into step beside her. "But I don't understand your unwillingness to join your people."

She stopped walking. Erik halted by the side of the fountain and turned toward her. "I think Broder makes a good point, Erik. We have no idea why I was separated from them in the first place. They could mean me harm."

"Mean you harm?" Erik gave a little laugh as though what she'd said was preposterous. "That's what you think?"

She frowned at him, screwing her face up in an expression of disbelief. "Back in D.C. you *agreed* with Broder." There was definitely something up. Erik didn't strike her as flighty or forgetful. "What's wrong with you?"

Erik began walking to the SUV again. "Long trip."

"I guess. It gave you amnesia."

"Look, I don't think the seidhr mean you harm."

"How do you *know*? We don't know anything about why I was separated from them. Maybe there was a reason."

They reached the SUV and Erik opened the back door. He glanced back at the house . . . a little furtively, in Jessa's opinion. What the hell was that? Erik, *furtive*?

All her alarm bells went off.

"You're not—" She bit off her sentence and yelped as "Erik" grabbed her and tried to push her into the backseat.

She kicked, fought, and scratched, but he had her up against the car and was about three times her size. She managed to work one hand free and popped it up fast and hard, fingers bent back, and took him in the nose with the heel of her palm. Bone snapped and cartilage gave way. Blood gushed. He yelped and swore, and she was able to free herself.

Jessa bolted, but he grabbed her by the upper arm.

Then Broder was there, yanking Erik away from her. She stumbled and fell to her hands and knees. Turning over, she crab-walked out of the way, watching the two men, her stomach in a knot. She expected a clash of the titans, a battle of behemoths, but Broder swung Erik around and punched him in the face once. *That was it.* That one punch sent Erik flying backward to slide along the gravel-strewn courtyard and then collide with the concrete wall of the fountain and go still.

Jessa watched as the illusion of Erik faded to the form of a tousled, dark-haired man with a lean, muscular build, wearing a pair of black jeans and a blue shirt.

She pointed at the prone figure, thick blood leaking from his nose where she'd hit him. She hoped she'd broken his nose. "Who is that?"

Broder stood staring at the man as if in shock. "Shaman," he whispered roughly. "He's a shaman using magick to try and kidnap you. He must have waylaid Erik from the airport, used one of Erik's hairs or something to shape-shift into his form."

"Wait." The words soaked through the befuddlement that had overtaken her brain. "That man is seidhr?"

"Yes."

"And he tried to kidnap me?"

"Yes. They know you're here and they want you."

The words went unspoken—*for some reason.* That was the big question. *Why* did they want her?

Inexplicably, tears rose to prick her eyes. She'd been hoping that her situation wasn't the worst-case scenario, that, somehow, impossibly, her people wanted her back—that she was important to them.

Apparently she *was* important to them, but maybe not in the way she'd been hoping.

She swallowed hard and hugged herself, pushing away the ridiculous sense that she'd been betrayed. "Where do you think Erik is?"

Broder passed a hand over his face. "A shaman would need some type of genetic material to pull off an illusion like this. Like I said, they waylaid him. They're probably holding him somewhere."

She tried to imagine anyone being able to hold Erik against his will and failed. "How would they do that?"

He shrugged. "I'm guessing it's with the help of a witch. She would have the ability to cloud his mind, confuse him for a time, with a skill they call *sjónhverfing*. I can't believe they'd try this with a brother. It breaks the Brotherhood/seidhr alliance and is incredibly reckless." He studied her. "They *really* want you."

She swallowed hard. "Great. Everybody wants me."

He stalked over to her, knelt, and held her face cupped between his strong hands. "Did he hurt you?"

She thought about that for a moment longer than she needed to, still sort of distracted and shaken up. "No. I hurt him first."

His jaw locked as his eyes searched hers. He nodded. "Good."

"There's nothing good about this." She shivered and gazed past him to the bleeding man. She felt betrayed, which was stupid . . . yet there it was.

"There is," answered Broder roughly. He forced her to look at him, take her attention off the treacherous shaman. "And once that shaman wakes up, I'll show you just how much good there can be." His voice held a dark threat. "And I don't mean good for him."

"What do you mean?"

"We'll find out things you've wanted to know for a long time."

She blinked, realization dawning. Oh, right, he would *make* him tell them everything. The man may have tried to kidnap her, but she couldn't wish a pissed-off Broder on anyone. He would hurt that shaman for merely upsetting her.

"What happened?" asked Halla, running out into the courtyard. She stopped short when she caught sight of the shaman.

"Shaman broke in and tried to take Jessa." Broder still hadn't moved his hands from cupping her face or his gaze from hers. She stared into his eyes for a long, deep moment—it was as though she could see forever in there. Pain. So much of it. And fear. He'd been really worried about her.

Suddenly uncomfortable, she pulled away from him and stood.

The sound of a car engine starting up met their ears. A dark figure sat behind the wheel of the SUV. She looked to the prone shaman and saw the image of him—illusion, she guessed—was fading. He'd tricked them. *Again.*

"He's getting away!" yelled Halla, running after the SUV, which had gunned its engine for the closed and locked front gates, tires spitting up gravel.

All of them ran for the SUV—as if they could halt a moving vehicle with their bare hands . . . well, maybe Broder could. The SUV hit the gates with a horrible crash and an ear-splitting groan of twisting metal, forcing them open.

And then the SUV was gone, along with all of Jessa's answers.

She stopped running at the mouth of the twisted gates, watching the dust rise in the wake of the fleeing automobile.

A motorcycle roared out of a nearby garage and went flying past her a moment later.

Halla came up to stand beside her. "We should pray."

"What?"

Halla jerked her chin in the direction of the SUV and the cycle in pursuit. "We should pray for that shaman if Broder catches up to him."

TWELVE

Broder raced after the SUV along the narrow, curving roads near his keep. He couldn't let the shaman get away. This was his one chance to figure out what they wanted with Jessa. The problem was that a motorcycle didn't have much of a shot against an SUV when you compared mass, and he had a feeling they'd soon be dueling for road space.

Luckily he had a really fast bike.

He sidled up alongside the SUV, keeping his eye on the twisting road in front of them. The shaman veered to the left and Broder moved with the vehicle to avoid being bumped off the road, driving in the ditch for a moment. He had a plan for getting the SUV to stop, but it wasn't time yet to make his move.

He knew these roads like the back of his hand and he would bet anything the shaman didn't.

Regaining speed, he sidled up again, only to be almost run off the road once more. He moved to the other side and the SUV swerved right. Back and forth he baited the shaman, doing his best to distract him from the road and push him into driving faster.

There was a particularly hellacious curve coming up. Broder just hoped the shaman survived it.

The shaman headed into the curve way too fast and Broder hung back, letting the road do his work for him. The SUV swerved from side to side as the driver tried to regain control, but it was a lost cause. The vehicle headed into the ditch and hit an embankment, nearly rolling over, but came to a rest on all four tires. Smoke curled from under the hood.

Broder came to a skidding halt by the side of the road and leapt from the back of the bike. The shaman sat stunned behind the wheel.

He yanked the door open, breaking the locks, and hauled the man out. "What the hell do you want with Jessa?" Broder bellowed into the man's face.

Blood trickled from a cut in the shaman's forehead where he'd bashed himself against the steering wheel. His head lolled and his eyes were unfocused.

Broder shook him. "You can die after you answer my question." The man groaned.

"Kill me. I don't care," the man slurred. "Once Thorgest finds out I failed, I'm a dead man anyway."

So the order to kidnap Jessa had come from Thorgest Egilson, the head of the seidhr enclave. Broder snarled into his face. "What do you want with her?"

"She's a powerful witch. She's kin."

"So why try to kidnap her?"

The shaman made an angry hissing sound. "Because she's with *you*, Calderson."

"Do you mean her harm?" It seemed a stupid question. He'd tried to stuff her into the back of a vehicle.

Something emotional moved through the man's eyes and Broder wondered what it could mean. Then the shaman yelled into his face with a surprising amount of anger, "I'm not answering any more of your questions, *brother*."

"Answer my questions and I'll show you mercy."

He smiled. Blood stained his teeth. "My sister died trying to put her entrails back into her stomach. Don't talk to me about compassion or mercy. You know nothing about that, Broder Calderson."

Broder pushed the shaman away violently and turned from him, taking a moment to rein in his rage before he did something that would prevent him from getting the answers he needed. A second later he turned back.

The man was gone.

"Shaman!" he bellowed in the direction of the wrecked vehicle.

No answer. No sign of him. He'd vanished.

Jessa was curled up on the couch near the fire with her legs tucked under her when Broder returned later. He tossed the keys to the motorcycle onto the coffee table with a ringing clatter.

She looked from the keys to his face. "You didn't catch him, right?"

"I caught him, at least for a little while. He used magick to escape."

"Did you find out anything useful?" She sat up a little straighter.

His gaze caught hers and she had a moment to see bare torment in them before he looked away. "Nothing much that pertains to you." His voice sounded hard and cold. "He got away before I could get anything useful out of him."

She took a moment to answer. "Okay."

"I did find out the order came from the highest person in the seidhr power structure. That's definitely pertinent information."

Something in her stomach twisted. She paused, twisting the edge of the blanket over her lap in her hands. "In the excitement over everything else, I totally forgot about this until this afternoon, but right before the demon attacked me in the parking garage I had a strange encounter with a man near the elevators. He told me to be careful—that 'they' knew who I was and that I was being watched."

She had Broder's complete attention now. The raw flash she'd seen in his eyes a moment before was now replaced with the more protective look she'd grown accustomed to seeing when he looked at her.

"He wasn't human, I don't think," she added.

"Was he a shaman?"

She shook her head. "I don't think so. Is it possible he could have been . . . Blight?"

"What would make you think that?"

"He scared me and I got angry. When I showed my temper, his eyes went black . . . totally black, just like the demon who attacked me. But this demon seemed to be warning me, protecting me. Are there good ones? I didn't see any fangs, but the eyes . . . He said his name was Dmitri."

Broder went very still and his eyes narrowed. "Dmitri. I haven't heard that name in a very long time."

"So you know him?"

"Yes."

She waited. And waited. Finally she sighed. "Do you think you could enlighten me a little?"

"Not until I know for sure it was him."

She stood and faced off with him. "I'm sick of being treated like a child. *Tell me* what you know, Broder. Haven't I proven I can handle it?"

He stared down at her with that forbidding, don't-fuck-with-me-or-I-*will*-fuck-with-you way he had. It didn't make her flinch and it didn't scare her. She had him wrapped around her finger and she was just starting to realize that.

She had *him* wrapped around her little finger. Big, strong, immortal warrior. She owned his ass . . . and a fine ass it was, too.

Feeling pretty damn self-satisfied and confident, Jessa raised an eyebrow. "Well?"

"Many years ago"—he paused and thought about it—"*centuries* ago, there was a high-level demon who went rogue. His name was Dmitri."

"Went rogue?"

"He decided he didn't want to play his role in bringing about Ragnarök."

"Oh. I didn't know they had free will."

"The agents in the upper levels of the Blight hierarchy have great intelligence and free will. Dmitri was one such agent." He rubbed a hand over his mouth. "He disappeared. We all thought the Blight had killed him."

"So he's a good guy?"

"No agent of the Blight is a good guy." He paused. "But he could be considered an ally. One we can't really trust."

She gave him a look of indignant ire, although why she felt the need to defend a demon was beyond her. "He warned me I was in danger."

"Then did nothing as you walked right into it."

Her thoughts strayed to the underhanded shaman. "Guess I can't trust anyone these days."

"Wrong. You can trust me."

She relaxed her stance and looked up into his face. He was studying her with that characteristic intensity. "Can I? You want to fuck me."

"I do want to fuck you, *skatten min*. I want your bare skin moving against mine. I want to smell the trace of perfume at the nape of your neck. I want my hands on you, making you moan." He paused, his gaze never leaving hers. "I want to be inside you."

Whoa.

A tremble went through her body as she reacted to his words and the intention in his eyes. She took a step back from him and he caught her, dragging her up against his chest. "Tell me you don't want those things, too, Jessa."

She opened her mouth to say she didn't and her lower lip quivered. It wasn't because she was about to cry—it was because she was having trouble saying no.

He slid his hand around to cup the nape of her neck and dropped his mouth to hers. Right before his lips touched hers, she thought she heard him whisper, "I don't deserve you," but then his mouth touched her and she dissolved into lust and she forgot all about it.

For a man who hadn't been with a woman for a thousand years, Broder had some moves. His kisses made her body ignite and her brain lose at least half its capacity for rational thought. His mouth slid slowly over hers, as though savoring the flavor of her.

She wanted his tongue to penetrate her lips and stroke up against her tongue, but he denied her, teasing her instead. He nipped at her lower lip, dragging it through his teeth slowly until she feared spontaneous combustion.

If she didn't get away from him now, she'd end up on the

couch and the promise she'd made to herself would be broken.

Making a sound of torture, she broke the kiss, though she couldn't quite pull away from his embrace. "Don't you understand? I can't do this, Broder. I'm not this way. I don't have sex with men that I don't have emotional ties with."

Pain clouded his eyes, chasing away the lust. "You think I have no emotion for you?"

"I think you want to fuck me."

He stared down at her for a long moment. "I want more than that. I want you in every way. When I look at you, I see—" He broke off, swearing in some foreign language under his breath.

"What do you see?" she pressed.

"When I call you *skatten min*, it is not just an endearment. You are a treasure, beautiful and precious. If I could lock you away in this keep forever to protect you and keep you close, I would do it." He looked as if he were about to say something else, but instead he released her, turned away, and stalked from the room.

Jessa stood motionless for a moment, her body still singing from the memory of his touch and his nearness, then she rushed after him. She skidded into the foyer to see him disappearing upstairs and took the steps two at a time to get to the top. The corridor was empty when she reached it and his bedroom door was closed.

Standing in front of it, she wilted. Damn it, what had he been about to say?

Broder stood on the other side of his bedroom door, knowing that Jessa was in the corridor. He could feel her presence through to the center of his bones.

When he saw her, he saw his future. That was what he'd wanted to say to her, but he hadn't been able to form the words. It was the truth, but it was an impossible one.

He had forever to live, yet he had no future.

Correction. He had a long future filled with killing, with

death, with punishment. He had a future in which he would go on wishing for his own death, wishing that someone would kill him.

Loki had said Jessa was his reward, but really she was just more punishment. By showing Broder what he couldn't have, Loki had only twisted the knife. Loki had known Broder would fall in love with her and Loki would experience deep pleasure when he took her away.

With every breath Jessa took, she reminded him of everything he wanted, but could never have. With every move she made he regretted his past and longed to be free to share a future filled with life and love with her.

"What's it like, being a Valkyrie?"

Jessa and Halla had taken blankets up onto one of the battlements and were lying in an afternoon of rare sunshine. It was warm, but just barely. Jessa was pretending she was on a beach somewhere.

They'd spent a grueling morning at training and it had left Jessa wondering about what Halla's life must be like. They really never talked about anything personal, just the business at hand and that was usually training.

Halla shrugged and played with the straw stuck into her glass of soda. "The life of a Valkyrie is not much different from that of a witch, except our power lies in physical strength instead of magick. Like the seidhr, we live communally, study together, train together. In our case it's a little like an . . . what is it called . . . an all-female boarding school."

"Sounds like fun."

"It can be, but it's also very hard work. We train hard since we're mortal, unlike the Brotherhood. We can be killed if we're injured badly enough."

"So you battle the Blight like the Brotherhood does, but have a higher casualty rate. Seems unfair."

Halla looked into her drink and poked a melting ice cube. "I'd rather have the risk of death than to be living in eternal torment like the Brotherhood. We have free will; we have our own lives. We love as we will, take vacations, go to the movies if we so choose. The Brotherhood can do none of this. They truly are the damned."

"Broder and Erik sure don't have a sense of humor, that's for certain."

"You wouldn't, either, in their situation. To live at the whim of a god like Loki is not an easy thing."

"Have you met Loki?"

Halla rolled onto her back and sighed. "No, and I'm glad. He's a self-centered bastard. You see him sometimes, in magazines and in the background of celebrity TV shows."

Jessa rose up on her elbows. "Really? Is he an actor or something?"

"No, but he runs in those circles. He's very wealthy and handsome, and he has a certain charm. What is the word . . . charisma? I guess Hollywood is the closest he can get to Asgard. He was banished from that place, you know, and he loved it there."

Jessa nodded. She'd been reading up on her Nordic myth. "Yes, for killing Baldur, the god of truth and light. Loki sounds like a real douche bag."

"Baldur died because Loki wanted to show off his cleverness. Loki is all ego and immaturity. Thor loved Baldur, as did all the gods, so he banished Loki to Earth and set upon him the task of the Brotherhood."

"Which Loki thinks is beneath him."

"A god demoted to that of jail keeper. Yes, he believes it below him."

"So he punishes the inmates."

Halla nodded. "Every opportunity he has."

Jessa was silent for a while, thinking of Loki and the Brotherhood. She turned over onto her stomach and adjusted her sunglasses. Halla had closed her eyes. "Do you know what Broder did to deserve a punishment like the Brotherhood?"

Halla rolled to her stomach, too, and took off her sunglasses. "The original crimes of each of the brothers are well-guarded secrets. I don't know what Broder did, but it involved blood, death. All of the original crimes are heinous things. These men may have found . . . what's the word . . . relegation?"

"I think you might mean redemption."

"Ah, yes, *redemption* sometime throughout the years, but none of them were good men back then. They were all murderers."

Jessa tried to imagine Broder as a man like the ones Halla was describing and shivered. He was protective and caring now, but it wasn't such a big leap to make.

Jessa stepped out into the morning air and inhaled the fresh scent, closing her eyes as it cleansed her lungs. It was a nicer-than-average morning, a bit warmer and clearer of mist. The view, even from where she stood near the front door of the tower, as she'd taken to calling it, was spectacular.

Even better, that morning she'd woken to a box of Jujy-fruits on her bedside table. Smiling, she sipped her coffee. Broder might be as tough as steel on the outside, but the man possessed a compassionate heart.

She hadn't slept well the night before—no big surprise with everything that was going on in her life at the moment. When she'd wondered where Broder had gone, Halla had grunted at her over her coffee and told her to check outside.

The sound of a tool on metal drew her attention to the front gates. *Ah.* There he was. The view had just improved tenfold. Broder was fixing the gate the shaman had busted through. He wore only jeans and a pair of black work boots. Her gaze skated appreciatively over the bunch and flex of the muscles in his arms, back, and chest as he moved.

Goddess help her, but the man was a sin to gaze upon.

Two cups of steaming coffee in her hands, she walked down the sloping driveway to him. He glanced at her with a look on his face that would lead her to believe—if worn by any other man—that he was pissed off. On Broder, she accepted it as his natural expression. If the man ever smiled, she would faint. If he ever laughed, she would probably have a fatal heart attack.

He pointed at the edge of the gate he'd rehung. "Don't step past the boundary."

She halted and looked down at the faint line in the gravel. "Why? What will happen if I do?"

"The protections afforded you here will not shield you." He hefted the other gate like it was made of tissue paper and slid it into the hinges on the stone archway.

Once the second gate was hung, she offered him the cup of coffee. "Want this?"

He nodded and slid the cup from her fingers. She tried to ignore the tingle that went through her when he grazed her fingers with his. He took a long drink as he examined the gate. He wasn't in much of a talkative mood this morning, not that he ever was.

Setting the cup down, he moved to the electrical box. "The shaman did some damage to the gate, but not to the magick that protects this place. You're still safe here."

"I never doubted I was."

"You should."

She shivered, remembering the man trying to shove her into the back of the SUV. "Can the Blight break into this place?"

"No." He paused. "But they have other tricks they can use."

Her blood went cold. "What do you mean?"

Tinkering with the electrical box, he shrugged one broad shoulder. "They are supernatural creatures. The lower-level grunts are just that, grunts, but some of the upper-level demons, they have skills."

"Skills?"

"Powers. Abilities. Not unlike the seidhr. Their abilities vary and can be unpredictable."

"Fabu. And why am I only learning about this now?"

Another shrug, like it was no big deal. "No reason to

worry you. We can't control all the variables. We need to stay vigilant."

She snorted, studying him. The way he'd said that was so flippant. It heated her blood, but this time not with lust. "You say that as if you don't care if they take me."

He moved faster than she'd ever seen another person move. Suddenly she found herself pressed up against the stone wall behind her. The coffee she held sloshed over the side and onto the gravel. "Whoa."

"I care. I *care*, Jessa, more than I've cared in a thousand years. The Blight will need to come through me to get to you. Understand?"

Her heart beat out a staccato rhythm. "I believe you." There was no way she couldn't with the look in his eyes, so intense and earnest. Her voice trembled a little. She swallowed hard. "And that's why I feel safe here despite what happened with the shaman."

He lingered for a moment, his gaze on her mouth, and she thought he might kiss her. Half of her wanted that kiss more than anything in the world, but the other half dreaded it, since every time he kissed her, a little more of her will to resist him shredded away to nothing. Then he would break her heart.

Finally he backed away from her and went back to tinkering with the electrical box.

Her hands shaking, she peered into her now half-empty cup. "I need more coffee."

Broder said nothing.

She stared at the electrical box. "I could help with that, you know."

He stepped back without looking at her. "Go ahead."

Setting her coffee cup down on the gravel, she stepped up to the box and held her hands out. The magick inside her immediately responded to the electrical impulses inside the box and Jessa again made the connection between the electrical impulses in a person's brain. She parsed through the tangled currents and put them in order, repairing the places where the connections were damaged.

When she was done, the green light on the front of the box popped on and she took a step back. "There you go."

Broder nodded at her and went back to work on the gate, turning his back.

Well, then. She collected her coffee cup and made her way back into the house. Apparently that was enough chatting for now.

She turned toward him before she went into the house. "I really want to make you laugh sometime, Broder."

He paused in his work, but said nothing for a long moment. Then he turned his head partway toward her. "I haven't laughed in a very long time. At least, not out of happiness."

"I'm just saying, it's a goal."

He went back to work and she continued into the keep.

Halla was lingering in the foyer when she entered the tower. She had a little grin on her face.

"What?" snapped Jessa as she crossed the floor to the kitchen.

Halla leaned against the railing and shrugged a shoulder. "Nothing."

Jessa shook her head and entered the kitchen, setting the cup down on the counter. Halla followed her in. "That man makes me crazy."

"Not as crazy-making as you do him."

She sorted out the bad grammar. "You think I make him crazy?"

"Like a top. He's just good at not showing it."

Crazy like a top—that was how she felt. Spinning and spinning . . . She leaned on the counter and closed her eyes. "He doesn't show anything, ever, except maybe rage, or aggression. Maybe annoyance once in a while. Lust," she added under her breath. "It's like he's . . . only half cooked."

"It's not all that surprising, is it? Many of the Brotherhood are this way. They're tortured, Jessa, beyond anything you or I could imagine."

Jessa studied Halla. She'd ducked her head and was studying the countertop fiercely. Clearly something weighed heavily on her mind.

"You sound like you speak from experience," said Jessa softly.

"I do," she answered with her head still lowered, "but I don't want to talk about it."

"I get that and totally respect it." She took Halla's hand and the Valkyrie looked up at her in surprise. "But please consider me a friend and know that I'm here anytime you might decide you want to talk about it."

Halla smiled and Jessa noticed a sheen of tears in her eyes. "Thank you."

Jessa slapped the counter. "I want to train today. I need to punch something—*hard*."

"I can help with that," Halla said, all perkiness and grins. "Let's go."

THIRTEEN

After they'd spent a satisfying day of training, Jessa took a long, hot bath. Her body was becoming harder, getting toned, and she could tell her waist was cinching up. Apparently running for her life had managed to do what nothing else in her life had—convince her she needed to be in shape.

She stood, letting the warm water sluice down her body, and grabbed a nearby towel, wrapping it around her torso and then twisting her hair to the top of her head. Humming to herself, she grabbed a bottle of lotion and left the bathroom.

A shadow moved by the window and she gasped in surprise, but instantly went on alert, every muscle ready to defend herself—even if she had to do it in the nude.

The figure walked into the light. It was Broder and she relaxed.

She breezed past him with the lotion bottle in her hand. "The door is made of wood, you know. When you rap your knuckles against it, it makes this really cool knocking sound."

He moved to the side and indicated a pile on the table by the window. "I brought you some information on the seidhr. I just stopped by to drop it off."

Jessa forgot that she was wrapped in only a towel. Leaving the lotion lying on the bed, she went to stand over the sheaf of papers. It was thick. Lots of information in there. She touched it with her forefinger.

"I figured you'd want it," Broder added. "Erik brought it with him."

Erik had found himself sitting all alone on the side of the road not far from the airport after the shaman had tried to abduct her. He'd hitched his way out to the keep right after. How he'd found people willing to pick him up was a mystery to her.

"How'd he have these with him? Didn't he lose all his baggage when the shaman stole his car?"

"He had an external drive tucked into his pocket. I printed the files that were on it."

She nodded absently, deep in thought, still running her fingers over the papers. This was as close as she'd ever been to answers.

Broder moved past her, toward the door.

At the last moment, she caught him by the upper arm. His skin was hot and his upper arm was hard with muscle. The feel of him jolted her out of her distraction and centered her totally on him. "Thank you."

He shrugged. "I hope you find what you're looking for in there."

"It's as close as I'll get to a real witch or shaman." She paused. "Well, at least to one that doesn't want to kidnap me."

He grunted in agreement.

They stood in silence for a long moment, the semidarkness of the room wrapping around them and the fire crackling in the hearth.

She didn't know why she did it; she only knew it was a bad idea. Still, she couldn't stop herself. Rounding the side of his massive body, she came to a stop in front of him. Lifting one hand to cup his jaw, she ran her palm slowly around to the back of his head and then went up onto her tiptoes.

Her breath touched his lips for a moment. She savored those few heartbeats before she leaned in, the warmth of his body near hers and the scent of him filling her senses. Then her mouth touched his, soft at first, then harder.

Broder broke the kiss, staring down at her. She was about to back away when he cupped her cheek with his opposite hand. A part of her wanted to pull from his grip, but another part welcomed the heat of his skin on hers. She fought the urge, as she always did, to give in when Broder touched her. He was damned relentless, this man. Most men would've given up on her by now.

Rubbing his thumb down her cheek, he leaned in so near his breath stirred the fine hairs around her face. His mouth came close to hers and he nipped at her bottom lip, making her shiver. Moving in nearer, he kissed her, pulling her lower lip lazily through his teeth before slanting his mouth over hers and sliding his tongue into her mouth.

Her heart stuttered in her chest and her breath came quick and hard. Like everything about Broder, his kisses were a combination of fierceness and surprising tenderness. Lifting her hands, she touched his upper arms, feeling the tenseness and bulge of the muscles there as he moved. She slid her hands up his broad shoulders to his neck and felt the silky brush of his hair against her fingers.

Gently gripping her hair, he pulled her head to the side, displaying the vulnerable column of her throat, then dropped his mouth to the gentle curve, pressing his lips to her skin. He groaned against her neck and she stifled a small sound of need. With one hand at the small of her back, he dragged her up against his chest.

Broder trembled against her, and then slanted his mouth across hers once more, his tongue pushing aggressively between her lips. She shivered as his tongue stroked up against hers, her body blooming for him. The towel between them became suddenly like so much air. She might as well have been naked.

His hand cupped the nape of her neck as his tongue delved deeper in her mouth. Her knees went weak, but Broder caught her around the waist and held her up. His lips skated over hers, his mouth making love to hers.

Abruptly he broke the kiss and set her away from him. Her body burned as if on fire and Broder looked in the same shape. Without looking at her, he brushed past her and left the room.

After the door had closed behind him, she stood motionless, trying to sort out what had just happened. It had been insane for her to kiss him, maybe even a little cruel, but there had been no way she could have stopped herself.

She stared at the closed door, her body yearning to go after him, but her heart telling her to resist.

Pressing her lips together, she turned to the sheaf of papers. She needed to distract herself from him. Those papers held such promise, but she was so afraid they'd disappoint her.

After she'd slipped into a warm sweater and a pair of soft jersey pants to sleep in, she took the pile of papers and curled up in a chair near the fire with a reading light turned on above her head.

Paging through them she quickly saw that these were mostly notes made by the Brotherhood on the seidhr, specifically about the enclave in the northernmost reaches of Scotland, how it functioned and who was in charge. She held up a grainy picture, printed off a computer file without colored ink, of the man in charge of the enclave. He was old, old even for a shaman, and he'd been in charge for a very, very long time. His name was Thorgest Egilson.

She squinted at the photo, at the merciless set of the man's mouth and the cold glint in his eyes. Jessa was thinking that immortality—or what amounted to it—was not a good thing at all. This guy looked like someone not to be messed with. She wondered if this had been the man who'd ordered her kidnapping. Broder had said it had come from the top.

The printed files told her the nature of seidhr magick. Male and female magick was different, hence the difference in their titles—witch for a female and shaman for a male.

Seidhr magick for a female was of a type that affected the mind by inducing illusion, forgetfulness, fear, sometimes even insanity, on the recipient of the magick. It was referred to as *sjónhverfing*, deception of the mental senses.

That made sense, considering her own ability to Jedi mind trick people into doing what she wanted them to do.

Seidhr women apparently also had special ability in the realm of intuition and precognition. *Huh*. She'd never had anything like that. Too bad. Could have been useful. Maybe she would have seen that demon in the parking garage coming. Of course, she'd had a feeling about the shaman, but it had been too little, too late.

Another little trick Jessa had never experienced was the ability to spin spells into cloth and the laying-on of hands to heal. Maybe that and the intuitive ability were things that needed to be cultivated, trained in a witch.

Witches seemed to be more powerful than shamans and their magick more versatile. For example, spellwork was used for finer magickal work and spells were typically worked by the females. The seidhr women, she noted, seemed to carry more sway in the organization. It made her wonder why the head honcho was a male.

She read on that shamans primarily used runes for their magick. They had the ability to shape-shift into animals or, if they had enough genetic material from the target, to take the shape of a specific human. Yes, she had firsthand experience with that. Shape-shifting was a specialized talent that not all shamans possessed, although most all of the men could at least project their awareness into an animal, or even into another human being, sort of like remote viewing.

Ugh, Jessa thought, *creepy*. The potential for spying was huge. Hopefully the wards protecting Broder's keep would block such activity.

In history, she read on, seidhr males would don animal skins and pound on drums while they used ecstatic dance to work magick. That had to be why they were called shamans.

Late into the night she read about the community of shamans and witches who lived on a large piece of protected land to the north. They were very secretive and tended not to trust any of the other supernatural races, though the Brotherhood and the Valkyrie were technically their allies. They kept close track of all their shamans and witches. The community was small, suffering from a fertility problem that the Valkyrie also seemed to endure. Jessa didn't fault them for their protectiveness; the Blight really wanted them dead.

All of them.

How the hell had she ended up on a different continent? Was she some kind of stain on their bloodline? Was there something about her that was harmful to them or dangerous? What made these people push her away, want to keep her hidden?

She wanted answers so badly.

A longing for her biological mother welled up inside her, making her chest ache. She squeezed her eyes shut against the sudden swell of grief for the woman she'd never known. She shifted on the chair and the papers dropped from her lap.

Slithering down to the floor, she began to gather them, but one particular sheet caught her attention. She held it up, seeing something that was structured like a poem. A closer look revealed that it was a spell for finding a lost object. She studied the ingredients. Mostly it called for various flowers and herbal tinctures. No eye of newt or rodent testicles. But even though they were run-of-the-mill ingredients, Jessa still had no way to gather what she'd need for this spell, at least not easily.

That was a good thing since the witch running through her veins fairly itched to work this magick, mundane though it might be, and she knew she wasn't ready for spell casting. Not by a long shot. Maybe she never would be. Maybe it was too late. Maybe she was too old. The thought depressed her.

Gathering up the papers, she shuffled them together and set them away, then went to stand at the window, pushing aside the heavy drapes to look out at the crumbling ruins of the towers, battlements, and ramparts.

Seeing a smudge of black where it shouldn't be, Jessa did a double take and looked closer. It was gone. She shook her head. Great, now she was seeing things.

She let the drapes fall back into place.

• • •

Broder stared hard at the wall in the kitchen, trying not to punch it. It had taken every ounce of his willpower to walk out of the room when Jessa had kissed him. She had no idea how alluring she was . . . and how crazy she drove him. She was playing with fire and she had no idea just how hot it could burn.

Seeing her in only a towel, her long hair in damp skeins against her skin, had done enough damage. Watching her cross the floor, seeing all that soft, pale skin, her tiny toes painted a light pink . . . All of it had been enough to give a lesser man a heart attack.

But that kiss.

The soft slide of her lips against his, the gentle, sweet flutter of her tongue, the scent and feel of the supple skin of her throat—it had made him harder than steel. All he'd wanted was to rip that towel off her, throw her onto the bed, part her thighs, and bury himself deep inside her. He wanted to lose himself in her, to drown in her skin and kisses and never come up for air.

Erik walked into the room, took one look at Broder, and gave him a wide berth. He headed to the refrigerator, opened it, and pulled out ingredients to make a sandwich. For some reason Broder had headed into this room after leaving Jessa, but all he was doing was standing at the center island, gripping the edge nearly hard enough to rip it free.

"Sandwich?" Erik asked.

Broder grunted at him.

"I see." Erik pulled a plate from the cupboard and started piling bread with ham and cheese. "If you should manage to make more than monosyllabic grunting sounds later and want to tell me why you're trying to destroy the counter, you've always got my ear."

Broder couldn't tell him that he wanted Jessa. He wanted not only her body, but her heart. He couldn't tell Erik how frustrated he was that Jessa could never be his. Most of all he could never tell Erik that Jessa's being a witch was a haunting problem.

So instead of saying any of that, he grunted again and left the room.

Jessa turned over in her bed and groaned. Squinting against the light coming in through the window, she pulled the blanket over herself and tried to go back to sleep. It had been hard to fall asleep after reading through the information about the seidhr.

The light intensified, almost as though a prism were being winked across her closed eyelids, and she opened her eyes, feeling groggy and exhausted. She grunted in frustration. What was that stupid light keeping her awake? She sluggishly pushed the heavy blankets off her, her hair a tangled mess around her head, and shivered in the cool air of the room.

Her muscles slow to warm up, she crawled out of the soft, warm bed and staggered over to close the drapes. Hadn't she closed them before she'd gone to bed? The moonlight was bright tonight. Reaching up to yank the heavy material across the window, she caught sight of a figure swathed in black standing out on the battlements. She blinked hard, trying to process the image through her sleep-clouded mind. Someone was standing out there.

Maybe she hadn't been imagining things earlier that night.

She let the velvet drop from her hand and stared at the black form, the fine hair on the nape of her neck rising. The figure shuffled along the length of the battlements, dressed in a long black cloak.

She shook her head, wondering why she was so fuzzy headed. Her limbs were heavy, almost like she was moving in a sea of molasses. She turned and looked back at her bed. For a moment she thought she saw herself still lying there. Clearly her mind was just as sluggish as her body.

What was going on? She blinked, seeing that the chair

in the corner and the night table beside the bed were both upside down and hanging from the ceiling. The fire was flickering in shades of blue and pink as well.

Ah. That explained a lot. She was dreaming.

This was not the first time she'd become lucid in the middle of a dream. In fact, she'd been doing it since childhood, so she recognized the signs. It was part of the witchiness that was her, she now realized. In fact, she'd even seen mention of witches having a natural inclination toward lucid dreaming in the information Broder had given her.

Now less alarmed by the apparition, she gazed out the window. The figure stopped in the middle of the walkway, reached up, and pushed back the hood of the cloak. Then the person looked up.

It was a woman with white blond hair, done in two old-fashioned plaits, one on either side of her head. Her face was oval and familiar looking, her mouth full and expressive. Her skin was smooth alabaster and she looked to be around Jessa's current age, maybe just a little older. Jessa recognized her from the pictures she'd seen in her aunt's attic. Long hair, brown eyes. Jessa had stared into that face for hours on end. She would know it anywhere.

This was her mother.

Even though Jessa knew this wasn't real, a jolt of emotion still rocked her. She had to remind herself that the figure on the walkway was not connected to her mother at all; instead it was a symbol from her own subconscious. That didn't stop her from racing out of the room, down the steps, and out into the moonlit turnabout, though.

She'd sought to have conversations with figments of her subconscious while she dreamed lucidly before. Sometimes they offered great insight into problems she was facing—and she had no shortage of problems right now. It was a little like do-it-yourself psychoanalysis.

"Mom?" she asked, stepping onto the gravel. The dream was incredibly real; she could hear the crunch under her bare feet and feel the rocks and grit. It even hurt a little.

Nothing. No reply.

She scanned the immediate area and caught sight of a dark, hooded figure on the opposite side of the fountain.

Jessa stepped closer. "Mom?"

In a blink, irrationally, as dreams were, the figure disappeared and reappeared much closer. Another blink and the dream figure stood right in front of her. She sucked in a breath and fought a moment of fear as she stared into the shadowed hood. This was just a dream, she reminded herself, not real. It was important to calm herself, since a rush of adrenaline might wake her sleeping body.

"Mom?" she whispered at the black-hooded figure. It was like staring into the face of a grim reaper.

Silence.

Jessa fidgeted, aware that this dream might be fast becoming a nightmare. Anything could be secreted inside that hood. Even though this was only a dream, it didn't stop her heart from pounding. Consciousness flickered as a result. She could feel her body back in her bed, shifting and whimpering, caught in a bad dream.

How she wanted this to be her mother. She just wanted to talk to her, even if she wasn't real.

Suddenly the hood flipped back to reveal her mother's face. "Beware!" she yelled, the veins on her face and neck nearly bursting and turning icy blue. Her brown eyes bulged with terror. "Beware the Valkyrie!" She reached out toward her, as if to catch hold of her—as if Jessa were about to fall.

Surprise jolted her. She took a step backward . . . slipped, and truly did fall. She wasn't jolted back into consciousness in her bed; that would have been a normal awakening from a lucid dream.

This was not normal.

She plummeted like Alice down the rabbit hole. Darker. Deeper. Shadows enveloped her and she grabbed for something, anything, to slow her descent, but there was only more blackness.

In the blackness there were lighted flashes of a struggle, brief awakenings in her bed as she fought someone weakly who attacked her as she slept.

FOURTEEN

She hit bottom.

"Gurgh." Jessa forced herself to roll to the side and open her eyes. Two people were talking somewhere near her, but she couldn't quite make out what they were saying. Her thought process seemed oddly sluggish, even more than it had in the lucid dream.

Flopping onto her stomach, she dug her fingers into the earth, trying to gain traction on . . . well, she wasn't sure what to do. All she knew was that she was supposed to be in her bed asleep right now, dreaming of her mother in a grim reaper cloak and not out here on the green hills of the Scottish Highlands feeling like she'd been . . . drugged.

Oh, God, had she been drugged?

She groaned, hazy memories filtering through her brain. Frowning, she caught a flash of a dark shape leaning over her bed, the glint of a needle, the upward swoop of her arm to knock it away, a struggle. She'd scratched the tender skin of someone's arms. She'd grabbed hair and pulled. . . .

Jessa flopped onto her back and held up her hands to the moonlight. The long strands she'd yanked out were still curled around her fingers. She squinted, trying to focus, but it was like she'd had one too many beers. In the dim light it was impossible to tell for certain, but she'd bet anything those hairs were dark red.

She let her arm drop to the ground. *Oh, Halla . . . just when I'd started to like you.*

The voices stopped and Jessa knew her window for escape was closing rapidly. Forcing herself to her knees, she tried to move forward, but collapsed after moving only a few feet. Behind her she could hear the footsteps of the thing she knew was hunting her. The only question was whether it was a shaman or an agent of the Blight.

Huge hands lifted her. She swiped him, reminding herself of a puppy being picked up by the scruff of its neck.

"Now, now," clucked the man. "None of that, you silly thing."

"Put . . . me . . . down," she slurred.

"Oh, you'll be put out of your misery soon enough. No worries, lass. I'd drain you now, but I don't want that nasty drug in my body."

Drain? *Ah.* Question answered. This was an agent of the Blight. *Demon.*

Awesome.

"Well," the man continued cheerfully, "shall we be off?" He carried her toward his car like she was a long dress draped over his arms, like she weighed nothing. She was too drugged to fight him and she wondered, even if she hadn't been drugged, what kind of chance would she have?

He'd parked a white cargo van not far down the drive from the gates of Broder's property. For an irrational moment, thanks to the drugs in her veins, she wondered why all criminals and murderers seemed to favor white cargo vans.

He opened the back door, tossed her in like she was a rolled-up carpet. She yelped in pain as she collided with the hard, ridged surface of the van's floor. The agent closed and locked the door, then climbed into the front to start the engine.

The cargo van rumbled to life and began to make its way down the road. Jessa groaned, aching from the impact of being tossed, and rolled onto her back. She wished she could move properly. She wished she could *think* properly. Whatever drugs Halla had given her had really impaired her powers of cognition.

They'd also calmed her down more than she had any right to be.

Distantly, Jessa knew she should be scared right now, terrified, really. The man driving the cargo van wasn't a man at all; he was a demon. Not only was he a demon created from ice in the depths of Hel, he wanted to kill her. That objective, according to Broder, would be driving him now and nothing beyond brute force, or one of Broder's nifty Loki knives, would stop him from achieving it.

She had neither brute force nor a nifty Loki knife.

All these things considered, she shouldn't be counting the black scuff marks on the ceiling of the van right now, she should be either (a) crapping her pants or (b) planning her escape. Ideally, she was pretty sure it was the latter she should doing.

But those scuff marks were so darn interesting. That one over there looked like a giraffe.

The van took a sharp turn to the right. Jessa slid across the floor of the van and slammed into the opposite wall. The jolt cleared her head a little. This damn fog, if only it would lift. She was certain she'd be able to do something awesome if it did.

She forced herself not to be distracted by the scuff marks, or by the enticing lethargic exhaustion that tugged on her. She needed to swim up through this haze of apathy. Looking down at her hands, she saw that he hadn't even bothered to bind them. Her feet were also free. Apparently this guy was really confident the drugs would do their job. Anger pushed away a little more of the cloud around her head.

She was sick of people trying to kill or kidnap her.

Her mind drifted to Broder. He would be pissed when he woke up and discovered she'd disappeared. She wished she could see him in the moment he realized she was gone. He was magnificent when he was pissed and protective.

Broder was just plain magnificent.

She'd never met a man like him in her life and she was pretty sure that if she lived a thousand years, she would never meet his equal. She never should have pushed him away. That had been amazingly stupid. She'd known her life was in danger, so she should have been sowing her wild oats. She should never have teased him, never led him on—not even for a moment. She should have jumped right into bed with him when she'd had the chance, should have just accepted she'd get her heart broken and done it anyway.

No regrets and all that stuff. Not having sex with Broder was a pretty big regret. Now here she was, drugged and held captive by a demon. Her oat-sowing days were drastically numbered.

She couldn't die before she slept with Broder. She just couldn't.

The van took another hard turn and she slid across the floor to slam into the opposite wall. Her head rang with the impact. The hit, combined with her newfound realization that she could have sex with the hottest man in the universe if she survived this, finally lifted the fog.

She pushed carefully to her knees, watching the demon behind the wheel very carefully. It was clear the agent thought she was incapacitated and that was slightly insulting. Carefully, she crawled to the spot behind his seat and looked around for a weapon to use. Just within her reach was a bungee cord that was probably used to secure furniture. Today it would be used to strangle a demon . . . if such a thing was possible.

Oh, she hoped it was possible.

At the very least, maybe she could force the van off the road and somehow escape.

Reaching out, she snatched the bungee cord and stood, looping the cord around the demon's neck and pulling back. The demon yelped and gagged. The van careened from side to side, but she bore down on the demon, using the cord around his throat to anchor herself.

The demon made choking and wheezing sounds, starting to flail. The van jerked to the side violently and drove into a ditch. Jessa lost her footing and her hold on the cord. She collided with the back of the driver's seat and knocked the breath out of herself, then flew backward and landed on her butt, as the van came to an abrupt halt.

She scrambled up, panicking, as she always did when she lost her breath, to see the demon coming at her. He sported a big red welt around his throat from where she'd done her best to choke him and he looked exceptionally pissed off.

Retreating, she soon found herself backed against the rear doors. Her eyes on the demon, her fingers found the handle and jiggled it. It was locked. She turned to give it her full attention, jiggling it harder in desperation. The demon's hands came down on her shoulders and he forced her to face him.

He loomed over her, much taller than she was, eyes blacker than she would imagine a black hole, his fingers digging into her shoulders painfully. His eyes were so deep and so dark, she feared she'd be sucked in and lost forever. He opened his mouth, his fangs glistening sharp white bone and as pointed as daggers. The demon stared at her for one long heartbeat, then he raised his arm and brought it down toward her face.

It cracked against her cheekbone, pain exploded, and everything disappeared.

"Where is Jessa?" Broder roared it through the keep. He'd looked for her everywhere on the grounds and she was nowhere to be found. Either she'd wandered away during the night—which he seriously doubted—or she'd been taken.

Either way, she was gone and that was unacceptable.

Silence reigned.

"Where is Jessa?" he roared again, feeling the veins in his neck pop out. His words echoed through the foyer where he stood and past it, reaching into every corner of the keep.

Halla appeared in the archway leading to the living room and Erik walked from his room to the head of the stairs. Erik stared down at him, his jaw locked and black resignation in his eyes. He knew it, too—Jessa had been taken by the Blight.

"What are you yelling about?" asked Halla. "You're giving me a headache."

He tried to unclench his fists and failed. "Jessa has gone missing."

Halla went very still and the blood drained from her face. Broder was on her in a flash. "Tell me."

"No, it's nothing. I mean, it has to be nothing." Halla looked confused and put a hand to her head. When she did, her sleeve slipped down her arm, revealing long, barely healed furrows.

Broder grabbed her arm and yanked her sleeve the rest of the way up. "What the hell is this?"

"I don't know. I had a nightmare and I woke up with these scratches. . . ." She trailed off, her face going even paler. She shook her head. "No. It cannot be possible."

"Tell me," Broder commanded again. Halla winced and he released her arm, realizing he'd been gripping it way too hard. "Don't leave anything out."

"In the dream, I met an agent of the Blight at the front gate. He gave me a syringe. I went up to Jessa's room and shot her in the arm with it. She fought me, scratched my arms and pulled my hair, but the drug worked fast. Then I carried her to the field next to the keep, where the agent picked her up. She woke up right before the agent collected her and fought a little." Halla looked down at her arm. "I thought it was a dream and I made the scratches myself, in my sleep. No. It's impossible."

"Halla," said Erik, who had come down the stairs to stand beside them, "you're Valkyrie. Since when is the word *impossible* in your vocabulary?"

Halla looked miserable. "I can't believe this. She's probably dead right now and it's my fault."

"No!" The word roared out of Broder, making Halla flinch. Jessa couldn't be dead. And then suddenly Broder knew something he hadn't known in a thousand years.

He knew fear.

He turned away from both of them, rubbing a hand over his mouth and working to get a handle on the tumult of cold emotion within him. His stomach was knotted. "She's not dead. Not yet. We still have time to find her."

"Broder," Erik broke in, "you know as well as anyone that the Blight want her dead. They would have no reason to keep her alive. Use logic. If they'd wanted her alive, they would never have tried so hard to kill her—in the parking garage, the taxicab, the airport. That means, if she was taken last night—"

Broder made an impatient movement with his hand and Erik fell silent. He didn't want to hear anything about logic; he only wanted to hear things that would help him find Jessa—alive. "What did the demon's vehicle look like?"

"Ah . . . it was . . . a white van, like the kind they use for moving furniture."

Broder tore out of the keep.

"Back off." She held out her hand as though it would stop a mad, black-eyed demon from attacking her, all the while glancing around, looking for a weapon. She was in a kitchen; there had to be a knife or something.

"Oh, I'm definitely not backing off." The demon rubbed his long, white hands together with glee. Apparently she was prey and he was enjoying it. He *wanted* her to run.

She'd woken in a small house with a hell of a headache, but still untied. Now she understood why. The demon thought she had no chance to prevail in a battle against him—he was right—and wanted to make her death into a sporting event.

She didn't know where the family was that owned this house. Maybe she didn't want to know. Likely they were more casualties in the war to stop Ragnarök.

There! A butcher's block with knives.

She leapt across the room, only narrowly avoiding the grasp of the demon, and yanked a huge knife from it. No hesitation. She rotated on the ball of her foot and launched it at the demon. It flew end over end and stuck him in the chest, pointy end first.

The demon grunted and looked down at his chest as though completely surprised she'd managed to land the shot.

This had been one of the things Halla had trained her to do. A red spot appeared around the hilt of the embedded knife and quickly grew larger. She watched it, triumphant—but wary. That wound would drop a human man, but this was a demon.

As the demon stared down at the knife, she inched her way out of the kitchen, toward the front door. The demon reached down, grabbed the handle of the knife, and pulled it from his chest as though it didn't even hurt. His blood gushed down his stomach and soaked the front of his jeans. He didn't even grimace.

She bolted for the door, but he was on her in an instant. He grabbed her by the upper arm and yanked her to face him. She came around swinging, her fist hitting his jaw and splitting his lip. His head snapped to the side and she wrenched her arm free of him, staggering and running for the front door. Her fingers had just touched the doorknob when he reached her, tackling her facedown on the floor. She fought hard to twist to her back, so she'd have a chance to fight him.

Punching and kicking like a crazy person, she managed to bring her elbow up and pop him in the chin, following that with a solid thump to the kidney . . . assuming demons had kidneys. Then she hit him in the stab wound. That did it. He rolled off her, bellowing in pain. She scrambled to her feet, but he was blocking her path.

She bolted for one of the bedrooms, hoping like hell there was a lock on the door, but he tackled her again. She landed facedown on the wood floor of the hallway, hitting her forehead. She was covered in his blood. Her fingers left trails of it as she scrabbled on the hardwood in an effort to get away from him. At some point she'd received a cut to her temple and blood gushed from it now, obscuring her vision and turning the world red. She'd never known blood could sting so badly.

Fingernails scratching the floor, she tried to pull herself away from him, but he punched her twice—once on each side—and agony exploded through her, making her cry out.

All she could do was curl up in a fetal position and try not to sob. She could barely draw a breath.

The demon grabbed her by the back of the head and yanked up, bowing her spine, then flipped her to her back. It was clear the demon had had enough of her—playtime was over. She was glad she'd injured the bastard. At least she'd gone down fighting.

Jessa closed her eyes as the thing lowered her to the floor, his fangs pushing through his gums to make horrible daggerlike points. She wished for a reprieve, a last-minute pardon. In a flashing fantasy, she imagined Broder had discovered where the demon had taken her and was ready to burst through the door at any moment, slay her tormentor, and make everything all right again.

But he never came.

Jessa's body was far too bruised and battered to defeat the incredibly strong demon, but she fought him anyway. It was no use. He only bore down on her, keeping her still. Her legs kicked and she made small enraged animal sounds that she barely recognized as coming from herself as he used her hair to pull her head back and expose her throat.

She was pissed. Not scared, definitely not resigned—she was *mad as hell*. She didn't want to die this way.

She didn't want to die.

The demon hovered over her and smiled. Blood from where she'd popped him in the mouth dribbled over his lip and down his fang, making him look even more grotesque than he already did. He loved this. He'd treated her like sport and he'd won. *Of course* he'd won. She wasn't fit prey for a demon. She was a rabbit to a wolf.

Her breath rasped out of her from where he lay across her chest, compressing her lungs. Blood trickled into her eye, making it burn. His eyes burned, too—they looked like tiny black coal fires—as she stared into the endless pits of the demon who was about to murder her.

Killed by an agent of the Blight.

She'd never wondered much about how she'd die. If she had, she was pretty sure death by demon would not have been on her list. She was pretty sure that if she'd had a choice, in her sleep, as an old, satisfied woman, would have been what she'd have chosen.

The demon lowered his mouth to her throat and her breath came faster. Now fear began to mix with the rage. What would death feel like? She focused on a painting of a flock of sheep in a meadow that hung on the wall of the hallway, a tranquil scene that seemed so at odds with what was now happening.

And she felt just like one of those sheep, ready to have its throat cut and become a meal.

The demon's jaw closed around the column of her throat; the fangs pierced her skin, slight at first, then slid in deeper. Pain exploded through her and she bucked beneath his heavy body, a silent scream issuing from her mouth.

The fangs slid even deeper and Jessa knew pain like she'd never known it before. Passing out would be a blessing, but she remained conscious and aware. Unfortunately, since the blood flowed just a moment later. The demon took deep pulls on her neck, sucking the blood and fluid from her veins and into his mouth.

He made a sound as though she tasted delicious. Maybe she did.

It seemed like the feeding went on forever, pain pulsing through her body all the time, but flaring acutely every time the demon drew on her veins. She wished for unconsciousness, something to end the agony.

Little by little the pain ebbed. Soon it was replaced with a floaty, almost dreamy sensation. The room rocked back and forth, as if she were on a boat, or being rocked in her mother's arms—whoever she had been.

Soon her body began to go cold, then even colder.

Soon after that she lost feeling in her arms and legs.

Soon darkness started like a pinpoint in the center of her vision and blackness ate away from that point, destroying, little by little, everything in her line of sight, even the painting.

Soon after that she felt nothing and all the sunshine fled the world.

FIFTEEN

Broder sped down the road leading away from the keep, not knowing if he'd chosen the right direction, just following his gut. He hated that he cared so much about this woman, hated it because to care was to experience fear. He *feared* for her and it was like an icy fist in his stomach. It made him feel helpless and he wasn't used to that.

He hated it.

Up ahead on the road he caught a flash of black. Squinting with the sun in his face, he tried to make it out. It looked like a man.

Broder slowed the bike a small degree and saw it was a figure dressed all in black standing in the middle of the narrow road, blocking his way. Even though he hadn't seen him in over a century, Broder knew who it was right away.

Dmitri.

The motorcycle had barely stopped before Broder leapt off it and barreled toward the demon. Dmitri stood stock-still, unflinching and wholly without fear as Broder grabbed him by the lapels of his black leather coat. "Where is she?" he snarled into his face.

Dmitri lifted a solid black brow and glanced down. "You're damaging my coat."

"I've got a nice pointy knife at the small of my back that can damage a whole lot more than that. *Where is she?*" He knew Dmitri wouldn't be here if he didn't know. Dmitri wanted to help Jessa for reasons Broder didn't have the luxury to examine at the moment.

"Fifteen Bellerock Road."

Broder spun on his heel and left. He didn't ask how Dmitri knew her location or why he'd told him. There was no time.

Jessa could already be dead.

"I canna feel her anymore."

Roan watched Thorgest pace the polished wood floor of the central meeting room. The day had grown dark and cold rain spattered the long windows that ran down one wall. He held out a staying hand. "That doesn't mean—"

"That she's dead?" Thorgest rounded on him. "What else would it mean? I have been able to feel her presence in this country since she landed, even during the nighttime hours when she should have been sleeping. Then, all of a sudden, it disappears. What other conclusion should I draw?"

Roan drew a breath and tried to keep his patience. "Maybe she became frightened and left the country. Have you considered that?"

Thorgest halted and narrowed his eyes at him. "An' whose fault would that be, if it happened? It's as if ye wanted to alert her to our plans with yer bumbling." He turned away, shaking his head. "Never saw the like in all my days."

Roan held his superior's gaze steadily, offering no apology. Maybe somewhere deep within he had wanted her to get away, to alert her to their plans. Abigail would not have wanted her daughter here, under Thorgest's influence. Maybe Roan was carrying out Abigail's will on some subconscious level. His decision to kidnap Jessa had surprised him every bit as much as it had surprised her.

"Bah. It's unlikely she left." Thorgest began pacing again. "The Brotherhood dinna run at the first whiff of trouble. I dinna think Broder whisked her away just because ye mucked it up."

Roan stiffened a little at the reprimand. Thorgest was the

leader of this coven. His power fueled all members' power. If Thorgest was displeased, everyone was displeased.

One day, if Jessa was still alive and if they could get her to the coven, she would be the leader. That was how the authority was passed—from head shaman to head witch, by bloodline, preferably. It was what kept them strong.

"Ye bumbled it up, Roan," continued Thorgest. "Ye know Erik Halvorson. Why dinna ye simply talk to the man? Erik is not Broder Calderson. We have an alliance with him. Tell me why ye chose the path ye chose."

Roan shrugged and lied smoothly. "I sensed she was on to me and I panicked." He had sensed Jessa had begun to realize something was not right, but he hadn't panicked. The urge to push her into the vehicle had simply been impulse. The shortest way to end a big problem.

Thorgest leaned on the table and let out a long, slow breath. "My granddaughter used to name all her dolls Jessamine." He glowered, rheumy eyes fixed on Roan. "If the lass isn't dead, I can't wait to meet her."

"She looks a lot like Abigail."

Thorgest grunted. "Just as long as she doesn't look like Michael." He clenched his fist.

She didn't look like her father at all, in fact. Looking at Jessa, Roan could almost imagine she was his own daughter. If Abigail had chosen him over Michael, maybe she would have been.

But Abigail had been stubborn. She'd had a flicker of love for him in her heart, but he had been her grandfather's choice and, because of that, he'd never stood a chance with her. Abigail had resented her grandfather too much to ever go along with anything he wanted.

"I need to take this into mine own hands. I see that now. It's too important to trust to the likes of ye. Ye better be hoping she dinna die." Thorgest looked down at his wrinkled, callused paw and made a fist. "It's clear I'm the one to do this, so leave off, Roan."

Roan was happy to leave off. He wanted no part of this now that he'd seen Jessa in person. She was too close to

Abigail in both appearance and personality. The whole thing was opening wounds he'd thought long healed. Thorgest had more motivation than he did, anyway.

Thorgest had been head of the coven for far too long. He was old, even for a seidhr, tired, and his power was waning. He needed Jessa to take up the reins. He had sentimental reasons, too, but Thorgest cared more about the coven than anything else. If Jessa came here and decided she didn't want to stay—there'd be hell to pay. No one defied Thorgest Egilson.

And Thorgest wasn't letting another of his kin go. This place would be like the Hotel California to Jessa—she'd be able to enter; but leaving would be entirely a different matter.

Broder burst into the little house on the hill, kicking down the door and sending splinters of wood flying. Immediately his gaze caught a smudge of black disappearing through a doorway. The runes in his coat gave off a pulse and he caught a scent of ice in the air. *Demon.* Broder bolted toward the creature, drawing the knife tucked at the small of his back as he went. Just as he cleared the threshold from the living room to the kitchen, the demon was attempting to exit by the back door.

He threw his blade and it hit the demon right between the shoulder blades. The thing burst into icy fragments, shattering onto the floor with a ringing tinkle. The fragments were larger than usual—that meant the demon was older and more powerful than most, higher up in the hierarchy. He would have to be old and powerful to command magick strong enough to enthrall a Valkyrie.

Not seeing Jessa in the kitchen, he whirled to search the rest of the house. "Jessa!"

No answer. The cold ball in his stomach tightened.

Then he spotted her prone on the floor near the couch. Her skin was the color of alabaster, the unrelenting white broken only by the sick brown of drying blood. It coated her face, matted her hair, streaked her arms and hands. Her lips were blue. A wound gaped in her throat. Her head rested at an odd angle that made his heart pound, as though her neck had been broken. She had a black eye and a nasty gash marked her forehead. She'd fought the bastard, of course. Fought hard.

Broder knelt beside her and felt for a pulse, a riot of unfamiliar emotion tangling through his head and heart— emotion that he didn't know how to deal with. It had been so long since he'd had any. Now there was fear and this other odd sensation wending its way through his chest—grief, he suspected. Her pulse was way too fast, a result of the heart trying to pump a much-reduced amount of blood.

He was just happy she had a pulse.

She'd lost a lot of blood, way too much for a human—or a witch—to survive. He needed to get help or she would die, but traditional human medical care was out of the question. He verified that her neck was not broken. He could move her.

He whipped his cell phone from his back pocket and called Erik. "Get here now," he snarled into the phone after he'd given him the address. After he'd slipped the cell back into his pocket, he gently lifted Jessa into his arms and carried her out the door.

The house the demon had chosen was isolated from the other homes in the neighborhood and that was probably by design. The choice worked to Broder's advantage now as he sank onto the top step to cradle Jessa in his arms.

He brushed her blood-sticky hair away from her forehead, his gaze running over her pale, closed eyelids, and wished like hell he could trade all his strength for just five minutes of truly stellar healing ability. His skills at treating frostbite wouldn't help her much now, but he set to work anyway, clearing up all the places on her body where he could see the demon had laid hands on her. There were way too many.

She couldn't die. *She couldn't.*

Broder had tried to kill himself numerous times over the centuries, but nothing had freed him from Loki's curse. If

Jessa died he would cease to care—about anything. He would stop trying to end his immortality. If she died, he would allow himself to exist under his curse until the end of time. The small amount of emotion he possessed would be extinguished forever.

Without her, everything left inside him that remembered his humanity would perish.

"Broder."

He looked up to find Erik standing in front of him. Erik's gaze flicked from her face to Broder's with concern, then he turned on his heel and started for the car.

Broder loaded her into the vehicle and they raced, tires squealing, away from the house and back to the keep. Broder kept his fingers on her too-fast pulse.

Erik met his gaze in the rearview mirror. "The bastard's dead?" His jaw was locked with anger, his blue eyes flaring with icy hate.

Broder gave a curt nod. "She needs blood and she needs it fast or she'll die."

"We've got it covered. Halla is a universal donor. She's setting things up right now. We figured she'd be down a pint or two if she tangled with an agent."

"Halla—," Broder started to snarl.

"—was under the control of the Blight. The ability that demon possessed is very rare. I've only seen it five times since I became Brotherhood." Erik's lifetime was very long; he'd been the first Loki had ever claimed, over twelve hundred years ago.

Erik's gaze lingered on Jessa's pallid face in the rearview mirror. "Apparently the Blight really want her dead. We may have to reassess her value."

Except Broder already knew her value.

He forcibly unlocked his jaw. "Let's just get her back to the keep. If she dies she won't be of value to anyone."

Broder kept medical equipment on hand at all his residences. One of the things he'd been stupefied by was the improvement of health care over the years. Since he never knew what the day would bring—and it had brought more than one damaged human to him over the years—he was ready to treat her.

They'd given her a blood transfusion via Halla and had also given her fluids. Because Halla was Valkyrie, she was able to give more than a human could and her recovery was quicker. Because Jessa was not human, but seidhr, she was able to undergo a more vigorous and quicker procedure and take more risks. That was good, since if Jessa didn't take the risks, she'd die.

Halla had been visibly emotional through the whole ordeal. The Valkyrie were bred to be strong and never show their emotions, but it was clear that Halla was suffering deeply for her role in this. After producing her blood for transfusion, she'd slunk away, apparently unable to see Jessa so close to death.

There was nothing more they could do for Jessa. Now she lay in her bed, pale, but a little less so. Broder clung to that *less so* in the thready evening hours as he sat at her side, watching the shallow rise and fall of her fragile chest.

He knew, of course, that Jessa wasn't fragile. She'd proven that to him already. But any witch or human—hell, even a member of the Brotherhood—was in deep shit when they went up against a demon. And now, watching Jessa lying there, so still, so pallid, he wanted to smash something— some*one*. A demon.

Armies of them.

Watching her lie there made a mixture of fierce protectiveness and immense failure war within him. This woman had made him feel more emotion in mere days than he had for centuries.

All was silent in the dark room. Outside the moon was coming up and had begun filling the chamber with silver light. He would not leave her side all night. He would not leave her side ever again, fates willing.

Of course his existence was not dictated by the fates, but by one cruel and self-centered god.

Broder bent his head over Jessa's body and whispered, "Loki." It came out low and rough and soft, but he knew Loki could hear him. It was never a question of whether or not he was heard—it was always a question of whether or not Loki deigned to answer.

Silence.

After a moment Broder tipped his head back and yelled, *"Loki!"* with all the pain and rage and fear that constricted his chest.

Jessa didn't move a muscle.

"All right, all right, I'm here. No need to yell."

Broder turned to see Loki standing in the middle of the room, dressed in a black Armani suit. He eased a hand through his perfectly cut dark hair, then adjusted his sparkling cuff links. "Spill it, Broder. I'm on a date with a hot fashion model in Rome right now." He waggled his eyebrows suggestively. "And we just got to the good part."

"The witch is dying."

Loki frowned, as if just now noticing the woman in the bed. He walked closer to her. "What did you do to her?"

"It was the Blight." Broder ground out the words. "You must have known they wanted her when you gave her to me."

"She's a witch; of course they want her." Loki stopped a couple steps from her bedside and looked at Jessa with distaste. Broder clenched his fists. The god pointed at her. "You know she's very valuable to the seidhr, right?"

Broder gave Loki a sharp nod and tried not to snarl. "It would have been nice to have been given that information earlier."

Loki made a mock moue. "But that wouldn't have been any fun."

The gods and their games.

He forced himself not to yell, but it was difficult. "Do something to help her."

Loki laughed. "That's your job. I gave her to you not only so you could . . ." Vaguely, he waved his hand at Broder's pelvis. "But also so you would protect her." He studied Jessa for a moment. "You're not doing a great job, Broder. I hope you've at least dipped your wick."

"Help her, Loki!" Broder bellowed at the top of his lungs at him. "If she's important to the seidhr, she's important to the prevention of Ragnarök."

Loki seemed unperturbed by his outburst. Loki never got mad; he only got even—spectacularly, usually. All malicious humor had left him and his voice was iron hard. "She's your responsibility. She lives or she dies because of you."

In a blink, he was gone.

Broder stared at the empty space where Loki had been standing a moment before. Right now he was probably in a hotel room somewhere, reclining on the bed and watching a supermodel slowly disrobe. Loki didn't care about anyone but himself. He was a god, which meant he was a sociopath. Broder had known that before he'd called him. He should have expected no less.

He leaned back in his chair with a sigh and rubbed his tired face. "Don't die, Jessa."

All he could do was wait.

SIXTEEN

"Don't die, Jessa."

The words filtered through the heavy layers of sleep covering her. They were spoken brutally, in a harsh voice, and with utter truth and deep emotion. The man speaking them wanted her to live more than anything in the world. It sounded as if he would perish if she didn't open her eyes and return to the living. She wasn't sure who he was, but it was nice to have someone care.

Although she wasn't sure she should return. It was so quiet here, so peaceful and calm. She floated in a velvety ocean of nothingness. Only small flickers of emotion teased her once in a while. Other than those pesky flickers of unwanted feeling, she only experienced numbness. It was a place free of fear, uncertainty, and anguish. She wasn't sure she could ever leave. Not if it was to return to the world— where fear, uncertainty, and anguish ruled the day.

Not even if it meant finding out who this intriguing man was and why he wanted her back so badly.

"Don't die."

The words came again, softer this time, a hint of vulnerability mixed in with the aggressive command. This man was hurt in some way, hurt very deeply inside. This man was also strong, stronger than anyone she'd ever known. This man was protective of those he cared about, so protective he would risk anything to keep them safe.

This man was . . . Broder.

The name fluttered through her mind, teasing her with a soft curl of temptation. *Broder.* She remembered him. She remembered the look of hunger in his eyes when he gazed at her. She recalled how . . . when she thought she was about to die . . . how much she'd regretted not allowing herself to grow closer to him. Ah, yes, Broder. An interesting man. An enigma she wanted to solve. Perhaps someone worth returning to the world to see again.

The first tickle of consciousness was excruciating and she almost thrust it away to sink back into the welcoming arms of oblivion. But once she'd made up her mind to return to the world, retreat was not an option. She could only go forward.

So she forced herself upward, breaking through the surface of her tranquil black pool and into the bright light of consciousness. She imagined it must be how being born must seem, emerging from somewhere dark, warm, and soft into bright light and jagged edges. Shock. Pain. Why had she left her safe, quiet, dark place?

Wincing at the pain lingering in her body, she forced her eyelids to part. Momentarily the morning light coming in through the window blinded her, but her pupils adjusted and the room came into focus. A man's face blurred and then came sharper. It was a roughly handsome face. A familiar one. Yet there was something unfamiliar in his eyes. Where normally she saw sexual hunger, torment, and high emotional bleakness, she saw . . . hope.

That flicker of hope in his eyes made leaving her safe, dark pool worth it.

"Jessa?" His voice came out a low, agonized whisper.

Unable to speak, she smiled instead.

Then the events that had brought her to her tranquil pool returned in a rush. Her smile faded. Her eyes unfocused as a series of images flashed through her mind's eye. The struggle. Defending herself. The demon's fangs. The puncture. The suck of her blood into his mouth.

How had she survived?

She reached up and touched her throat, feeling a bandage there. Broder took her hand and gently lowered it to the bed, shaking his head.

Jessa opened her mouth, trying to form words, but only small sounds came out. It was frustrating.

"You almost died," said Broder. "Take it easy." He paused, then seemed to read her mind. She wanted to know what had happened. "The agent had an ability we couldn't anticipate, a very rare skill. He somehow reached Halla when she was sleeping. He forced her to drug you and carry you outside the wards of the keep. She didn't betray you willfully."

Jessa relaxed and nodded. That was good news.

"When I got to the house, you were nearly dead." His eyes went dark. "The agent is ice."

Jessa nodded. "The . . . family?" she managed to rasp out.

He looked confused for a moment, then understood what she was asking. "Erik went back to check on them. There was no sign of any bodies at the house. I think they were lucky enough to not be home when the agent hijacked their house. They won't be happy to return and find all that blood and destruction, but we think they're alive."

Jessa smiled and relaxed into the pillows.

His eyes grew fierce. "Don't ever do that to me again, Jessa. I thought I was going to lose you."

She recalled the timbre of his voice as he asked her to live. "Why . . . ," she rasped slowly, "does my fate matter . . . so much to you?"

He stared at her for a long moment, saying nothing. Finally he rose and walked to the window, staring silently out onto the turrets and battlements where she'd seen the dream image of her mother. Jessa stared at Broder's broad back.

Apparently she wasn't going to get an answer to that. It made her wonder even more.

Jessa woke to a darkened room, the hint of morning peeking from behind the heavy drapes, marking day two of her recovery. She lay for a moment, taking stock of her various aches and pains. Her neck throbbed constantly, even with the nifty painkillers that Broder had somehow produced out of thin air. Her various bumps and bruises, the gash on her head, all of them combined to give her near-constant waking pain.

She welcomed it. After all, the alternative was nothingness— death. She'd take a temporary amount of pain over that any day. It was a small price to pay to keep the rest of her life and she would eventually heal. She'd have scars, of course, but they'd be external and flesh deep. She wasn't giving the Blight any more than that, the bastards.

Shifting in her bed, she moved the covers aside and slid her aching body from beneath them. Her feet hit the smooth hardwood floor.

"Get back into bed."

She jolted, surprised by the low baritone emanating from the corner of the room. "Broder?" She squinted into the low light of the bedroom, just making out his shape in the chair near the fireplace.

It was the same chair he'd been sitting in when she'd gone to sleep the previous evening.

She stood and took a step toward him. "Have you been there all night?"

He rose from the chair and walked toward her. His expression was stormy—his expression was *always* stormy. "Yes. Get back into bed."

"I need to go to the bathroom, and before you ask, no, I don't need help." She pushed past him on shaky legs. She'd give anything for a shower, but she couldn't stand for that long yet. She'd ask him for help with that, but it was too embarrassing.

Broder took her by the upper arm and she didn't object. Losing so much blood had seriously weakened her. Having it replaced with superstrong Valkyrie blood hadn't helped much. "After the bathroom, back into bed."

"Man, you're bossy." Nothing made her bristle more than high-handedness.

"I don't endanger my treasures. I keep them safe and protected, like a dragon guarding jewels."

She'd had a cutting remark ready on her tongue, but it immediately dried up.

After she'd used the bathroom, she settled back into bed. Honestly, she was happy to be there and probably would remain so for the next few days. On her bedside table was a new sheaf of papers. She picked them up. "What's this?"

"I've been trying to gather as much information about the seidhr for you that I can. That was sent by the Valkyrie to me this morning."

She raised an eyebrow and grinned. "Ah, so I see you *did* leave my bedside."

He opened the drapes to let the morning sunlight stream into the room. "Only long enough to print that out," he growled. "I'm not letting you out of my sight again."

"That could get awkward."

"I ordered breakfast for you. It should be up soon. Do you want a bath?"

"More than I want to win the lottery."

He gave her a curt nod. "I'll help you."

She nearly swallowed her tongue. "I think Halla should help me."

"Halla's not getting anywhere close to you without my supervision."

"I can probably wait to—"

He snarled into her face. "I'll be able to resist myself, I promise. You're injured. Do you think I'm an animal?"

"No. I think you're a man with needs."

"I *am* a man with needs. I'm also a man with an incredible amount of control and a woman I want to defend."

Jessa knew it was wrong that those words made her shiver.

He disappeared into the bathroom. A moment later she heard the water start in the bathtub.

Without asking her—Broder wasn't a man who asked, after all—he strode back into the room and gently scooped her into his arms, then carried her into the bathroom. With reservations, she allowed Broder to help her get undressed. He'd already seen it all already, of course, and he wasn't entertaining any of her protests. Honestly, she was too fatigued to put up much of a fight anyway.

His hands were strong, callused . . . and businesslike. She appreciated that. He lifted her like she weighed as much as paper and set her into the warm, soapy water. She sighed in total sensual abandon.

Broder stayed near as she bathed, making sure she didn't pass out, slip into the water, and drown, but he gave her privacy. Right now his behavior was far more like that of a gentleman than an immortal warrior. Jessa was enchanted by both aspects of him.

Just the simple act of taking a bath completely exhausted her and she was glad to have Broder there to help her towel off and climb back into bed. By that time breakfast had arrived. She ate two spoonfuls of oatmeal, one more at Broder's insistence, and fell asleep with the tray still on her lap, feeling warmed and more protected than she'd ever felt in her life.

Broder watched Jessa sleep, just as he'd spent the night watching her. His blood burned with the need to kill that demon all over again, only this time much slower.

Instead of enflaming his libido, Jessa's nude body in her bath had enflamed his rage. He wanted revenge for every bruise and cut on her perfect skin, for every drop of blood that had been consumed.

In his pocket, his cell phone buzzed. He pulled it out and saw the number was unlisted. "Yeah?" he barked into the receiver. His mood was never good, but it was worse than usual.

"Calderson." The voice on the other end was low, smooth. He recognized it.

A muscle in Broder's jaw worked before he answered. "Hello, Dmitri. Funny you should call. I was just sitting here thinking of all the different ways I could painfully kill a demon."

"That's not a very good thank-you." Pause. "As I recall, your little lady would be dead right now if it weren't for me."

"I know you only did it because there's something in it for you. The only question is what."

Dmitri grunted. "Of course you'd think that, Calderson. You're a Brother of the Damned and I'm a demon; never the twain shall meet."

"Never the twain." He growled it.

"Nevertheless, we need to talk. Under the bridge on Kass Lane. One hour." The phone went dead.

Broder pocketed his cell phone, pissed off that Dmitri had gotten the last word. He let his gaze settle on Jessa's sleeping form. As much as he hated to admit it, Dmitri was right—Jessa would be dead right now if it weren't for him. He couldn't blow off this meeting. Maybe Dmitri would know something that could save her life again.

He stood, hating to leave her side, and found Erik. He was talking with Halla in the living room. His gaze rested on the Valkyrie for the barest of moments before she turned her head away, heavy guilt still resting in her pale blue eyes.

Of all the failings possible for a person, weakness was the one most abhorred by the Valkyrie. Halla would consider her susceptibility to the Blight as exactly that.

Broder focused his attention on Erik, allowing Halla privacy in her shame. "Dmitri has contacted me."

Erik nodded. "I thought he might."

"I don't want Jessa to be alone."

"I'll protect her while you're gone, Broder. You have my word."

Broder gave him a curt nod. He trusted Erik completely. Over the centuries they'd had their differences, but Broder counted Erik as more than a comrade in arms; he was as close to a friend as Broder would ever have.

The skies were stormy as he exited the keep, got on his motorcycle, and headed out. By the time he reached the bridge, it was raining. Dmitri leaned against the stone wall beneath the small stone bridge, just like the troll he was. He was smoking, the cherry of his cigarette firing bright in the dim light with every inhalation. Demons didn't have to worry about lung cancer.

Broder guided his bike under the bridge and cut the engine, then ran his hand through his hair. He and his leather duster were soaked. This had better be good.

Dmitri barely acknowledged him as he approached; he only took another long drag on his cigarette, then flicked the butt away. The demon smiled lazily. "Glad you could make it."

"What do you want, Dmitri?" Rain pitter-pattered on the bridge above them, forcing him to raise his voice over the sound.

The demon didn't look at him. He gave a loose, one-shouldered shrug, the leather of his coat creaking. "A decent meal, a good fuck, a million dollars. I'd settle for a thank-you, maybe."

"That better not be why you called me out here."

"It isn't, but I want one anyway. Go on, just say it."

"Hel will burst into flames before I thank a demon."

Dmitri smiled. "What a nice thought."

He hated that they agreed on something. Broder gritted his teeth for a moment. "What do you want? It's the last time I'll ask."

"Then what, you'll leave? Even if I know things about the little lady witch that you don't?"

"You're Blight. How can I trust anything you say?"

Dmitri's eyes hardened. "I may be a demon, but I'm not Blight. Not anymore."

Broder jerked his chin at him. "So you say."

Dmitri pulled out a pack of cigarettes and tapped out another, then lit it. "We might hate each other's guts, Broder, but we have the same goal. Neither one of us wants to see Hel win." He blew smoke out into the damp air.

"Yeah, I've always been a little fuzzy on the details about why you don't want that."

The demon glanced at him and grinned. "My reasons are my own and this isn't kindergarten. No reason to share."

"All these centuries you've been working against your side, but how do we know you're not really working for it?"

"You really think I'm a double agent? I'm flattered you think I could be so cunning."

"To avoid detection by your own kind for this long takes cunning. They all want to kill you, don't they?"

Dmitri smiled slowly. "I'm on everyone's kill list."

"Say what you dragged me out here to say and I'll judge if it's valuable information or whether I can even believe it."

Dmitri made a low scoffing sound and took another drag on his cigarette. "Don't know why I help you, Calderson. Okay, here is it. I know why the Blight have such a hard-on for Jessamine Hamilton."

Broder waited.

The demon blew more smoke. Who knew exactly how much he was blowing? "She's seidhr—"

"Figured that out already, thanks."

The demon glanced at him. "Kissed her, huh? Or maybe—"

Broder made a threatening sound.

Dmitri grinned. "Uh-huh. Anyway, not only is she a witch, she's kin to the leader, Thorgest Egilson. She's Thorgest's great-granddaughter. Your girl is probably a very powerful witch and she's some of the only kin the old fart has. He's been leader of that coven for damn close to fifteen hundred years now and he wants to retire. Carolyn, Jessamine's great-aunt, wants no part of the enclave's leadership, so that leaves only your woman. He needs her to take over for him and he'll stop at nothing to get her. The fate of their coven hangs in the balance. The Blight want her dead before she makes it to the coven or before she figures out how to kill them with magick."

"Do you know why she was separated from her people?"

He shook his head. "Nope."

Broder digested this. "How did you come by this information?"

"I'm not one of the little worker bees anymore, but I'm still plugged into the hive. When the woman grieved the death of her aunt, her magick blossomed. The Blight were like dogs scenting a wild rabbit. They knew right where to find her and she was clueless as a babe. She's strong, Calderson. You need to get her training, but beware that old man. Above all, keep her safe."

But the seidhr had tried to kidnap her. That didn't fit with anything Dmitri was saying. Why would they try to take her that way?

The demon snorted. "Don't ever play poker. I can see the thoughts flitting through your head right now. The seidhr don't like you, Broder." Dmitri paused, then his voice rose suggestively. "They have cause, don't they?"

He remembered back to the words the shaman had snarled at him when he'd asked about the kidnapping. *Because she's with* you, *Calderson.*

Broder moved fast, pinning Dmitri to the wall. The demon didn't even drop his cigarette. Irritatingly, he just grinned into his face like he thought the situation was humorous, although his eyes bled black, giving lie to his unconcerned demeanor. "How do you know about that?"

Dmitri just kept grinning.

Broder let him go and turned away, headed back to his bike.

"You're welcome," Dmitri called behind him.

Jessa sat at a small table and mirror in her room and unraveled the bandage from her throat. Behind her, silhouetted in the doorway, was Broder. He was never very far from her these days. He didn't trust the Blight wouldn't try again to take her from the keep.

She wished she had some amazing ability to heal or something, but apparently witches and shamans healed exactly like humans, though they were stronger in general and could take more injury and withstand worse illness. There was magick to be worked for these things, of course, but she had none. It was a fact that was beginning to vex her more and more. The blood of a Valkyrie had helped. According to Broder it had halved her recovery time, but Jessa couldn't tell. It seemed like a month had passed rather than a week.

Halla was racked with guilt, even though Jessa had forgiven her a million times over the last few days. Halla hadn't known what she was doing; she didn't even need forgiveness.

Unwrapping the last of the bandage, she braced herself to see what the damage was. Squinting as she laid the gauze to the side, she slowly opened her eyes all the way to look at her reflection. Her eyes widened and she gasped.

Broder walked toward her.

She reached up and touched the ugly zigzag of stitches on her throat. She looked like Frankenstein. "It's like he chewed on me." As if she'd been a dog's toy.

Nausea rose up inside her as she remembered. She turned her head away from her reflection, unable to look at what would be a scar once the stitches came out. Every time she looked in the mirror, she'd have a reminder of the horror.

Broder laid a hand on her shoulder and her gaze met his in the mirror. "It's a battle scar, proof that you fought a terrible foe and survived. When you look at the scar, don't see it as something ugly, but as a sign of your strength."

"You saved me, Broder. I couldn't escape that thing and I couldn't defeat it. If it weren't for you, I would have died in that house."

Broder held her gaze for a long moment before answering. "I was there. I saw evidence of the battle you waged against that demon. Believe me, Jessa, you *are* a warrior even if he got the better of you in the end."

She smiled at him in the reflection. Broder was a man of few words, but when he spoke he said the right things.

"Halla is leaving the keep and returning to Norway. She

only stayed this long to make sure you didn't need any more of her blood. Erik and I will handle your training from now on."

"What?" She turned in the chair and faced him. "Is she leaving because of what happened? She can't do that. It wasn't her fault."

"She's leaving because she's the weak link. The Blight do not have mind-control powers of any kind over the Brotherhood. Halla knows that by staying here she's putting you at risk."

"But Erik told me he's only seen an agent with this type of ability five times since he became Brotherhood. You killed that agent, so he's not around to do it again."

"I'd kill him all over again if I could."

"What I mean is, the chances of another agent coming here that has the same ability must be infinitesimal."

"Yes, but there is still a chance. Any chance is too much. You are apparently very important to both the Blight and the seidhr. Maybe you're important enough to send another of their extratalented agents."

Special and she didn't even know why. *Stellar.*

"I wish I was less special to them."

"Me, too." He paused. "I have something to tell you."

The tone of his voice had shifted to wary. The hair on the nape of her neck stood on end. "Oh, hell, it sounds bad. What is it?"

"Maybe nothing. I met with Dmitri the other day."

She frowned. "Dmitri from the parking garage? He's here in Scotland?"

"Yes. He's the one who told me your location after you'd been taken by the demon. If it weren't for him, you probably would have died. I wouldn't have known where to find you without him."

She pushed up slowly and turned to face him. "Why didn't you tell me this earlier?"

He shrugged. "You were recovering and I was handling it."

"Seems like a pretty big detail to omit, Broder. A *demon*

helped you save my life." Why would Dmitri care so much about her welfare, travel all the way to Scotland to help her?

"Yeah, I should have told you."

"Yeah, you *should* have." She poked him in his chest with her index finger. He was like a rock.

"Do you want to hear what he told me or not?"

She relaxed a little and crossed her arms over her chest. "Go on."

"Now, remember, this information came from a demon with murky objectives. I have no idea if it's true or not, but it wouldn't be right to keep the information from you. Just keep in mind the source when you measure the weight."

"Oh, *now* you're worried about full disclosure."

He continued as though she hadn't said anything. "Dmitri told me you're kin to the leader of the seidhr. You're his great-granddaughter. He said that Thorgest wants you because you're destined by your blood to take over leadership of the coven. According to Dmitri, Thorgest Egilson has no one else to take his place and he wants to retire to Florida or something like that."

Her mind tripped over his words. Great-granddaughter to that severe-looking man she'd seen a picture of? "Did Dmitri say how I was separated from them?"

"I asked, but he didn't know. He only told me about your great-grandfather. He also pointed out the obvious; if you're of that particular bloodline your magick is likely very strong."

Jessa sat back down again.

"I don't want you to take this very seriously. At least, not yet. Like I said, we need to consider the source."

"He told you my location—"

"And how did he know it in the first place, Jessa? Have you thought about that?"

He had a good point. She chewed her lower lip.

"He could have been in on that from the beginning, set the whole thing up to win our trust. It would explain how he's survived the Blight all these years. If he defected, they'd want him dead and, as you've seen firsthand, they're relentless. It's suspicious he's survived this long, isn't it?"

"Right. I get it."

"I know you're eager to explore your birthright, but let's take this slow."

She nodded. "Yes, of course."

He started to walk to the door. "Come and say good-bye to Halla. She's packing right now. Your farewell will make her feel better."

She nodded and followed him down to the foyer, where Halla was just organizing her bags. Through the open front door, she could see Erik getting the car ready.

"I really wish you'd stay," said Jessa, approaching the Valkyrie.

Halla straightened from adjusting something on her suitcase and smiled, but Jessa clearly saw the guilt in her eyes. Halla's gaze flicked to the jagged stitches on her throat and away. "I think this is better. I would not like to be the cause of your doom."

"You never could be." Jessa gave the other woman a hug. "You've been a good friend to me here. Well, except for that time you attacked me and called me a wimp."

Halla laughed. "You are not a wimp, Jessa. I just said that because I was jealous of your beauty."

"But not of my fighting ability."

"No." Halla's smile widened. "Definitely not of that." She looked at Broder. "Listen to him, okay? He's very good at teaching defense skills. And you, Broder, be careful with her. She's more fragile than you think."

Jessa watched Halla pick up her suitcase and head out the door, thinking that last comment might not have much to do with self-defense training.

Erik and Broder carried the rest of her luggage out and hoisted it into the back of the car. Halla gave a final wave at Jessa before climbing into the car beside Erik and they pulled away.

She and Broder watched as the car disappeared past the

gates and down the road. Suddenly the silence of the house weighed on her. She was alone with Broder. His warm presence filled her senses and she became very aware of him standing beside her.

If he kissed her now, wanted to touch her . . . she would let him. She was done running away. Done having regrets. Her experience with the demon had shown her the merit in seizing the day and not allowing opportunities to pass her by, even if her heart became broken in the process. That was the risk she'd simply have to take.

But between the moment she became acutely aware of his presence and the moment she decided to give in to her carnal feelings for him, he was gone. She stood alone in the foyer and sighed.

SEVENTEEN

Broder entered the kitchen and stopped short. Arrayed on the center island was a multitude of brightly colored boxes and bags. Jessa stood behind the counter, looking pleased with herself.

This immediately put him on edge.

She smiled. "I hope you're not doing anything tonight."

His eyes narrowed as he took in her outfit, a short black skirt and sweater. Her hair was curled and fell loose over her shoulders and she appeared to be wearing makeup. "What's going on?"

She held up a hand as though to stave off an objection. It was true that he *did* feel an objection coming on. Those cheerful multicolored boxes were not something he had much experience with. "I cleared this with Erik and he's your boss, so you can't say no."

He tilted his head to the side and took a step toward her. "Say no to what?"

With a flourish of her arm, she drew his attention to the various boxes and bags on the counter. "I want to discover what your favorite movie theater candy is. I think it says a lot about a person, you know?"

"Says what"—he moved to the edge of the counter and stared down at all the sugar—"exactly?"

"Says something about their personality, their state of mind, their mental well-being . . . you know, their favorite candy." She twisted the sleeve of her sweater between her fingers. "You don't have a favorite candy and that says a lot about you. But of course, you *do* have one; you just don't know what it is yet." She paused and twisted her sleeve a little more. "I'm babbling, aren't I?"

He nodded.

"I'm kind of nervous."

"Where did you get all of this?"

"Like I said, Erik helped me. He had it flown in from the States for me. I didn't ask for any Jujyfruits, since we've established that you don't like those."

Broder picked up a package of Sugar Babies. "Really." After dropping it to the counter, he eyed a box of Cookie Dough with trepidation.

"There's a part two of the surprise, but that's for later."

Oh, good. "More surprises?"

She nodded, her eyes lighting up. "Come on, this will be fun." A huge smile spread across her face.

He couldn't deny Jessa anything when she smiled that way. Hell, he couldn't deny Jessa anything at any time. He surveyed the mountain of candy. Some of them he knew of, like the Dots, Goobers, Junior Mints, Milk Duds, and Raisinets. It wasn't possible to live in the world and not know of those. Others, like the Sour Patch Kids, were a mystery he wanted to leave undiscovered.

Jessa opened a box of Whoppers and tapped a few out into his hand. "Try them."

He stared down into her palm, where three small chocolate balls lay.

"Oh, please." She sighed. "The big, strong immortal is afraid of candy?"

He shot her a look of disgust, then popped a Whopper into his mouth. It crunched under his teeth and he swallowed it with effort. He grimaced. "Next."

Jessa sighed. "I can tell this is going to take awhile, but I'm up for the challenge." She reached for a bag of something called Buncha Crunch.

He tried everything that Jessa pushed at him and enjoyed

almost none of it. "The Good and Plentys aren't bad," he decided.

She raised a brow. "Is it your favorite?"

"I wouldn't say that."

"Too bad, the Good and Plentys would fit." She gave him an inclusive up-and-down perusal. "You're all kinds of good and plenty." The look in her eyes made candy of a different kind come to mind. "Plus, it's something sweet wrapped in a crunchy outer shell that you need force to get through. Suits you well."

His reaction to the Sour Patch Kids made her break into laughter. "Who thought creating these was a good idea?" he asked, eyeing the yellow package with extreme distaste.

"Whoever he was, he's rich now."

In the end, he decided the Milk Duds, Buncha Crunch, and Sno-Caps were the best.

She nodded. "That makes sense. I'm not surprised to find you're a chocolate fan. Dark, deep, and delicious. So, which one would you buy if you went to the movies?"

He gave her a measured look. "None of them. I'd smuggle in my own dessert."

"Okay, I'll bite. What would you smuggle in?"

"I'll show you." He went to the cupboards and brought forth everything he needed— chocolate, eggs, cream, and sugar, among other things. Then he began to whip up a batch of his favorite sweet.

Jessa took a seat at the counter and rested her hand in her palm as he worked. The sight of him whisking egg yolks seemed to momentarily freeze her brain function. "I thought you couldn't cook."

He stopped whisking and looked at her. "I've been around for a thousand years, Jessa."

"I know. That's why I thought it was so weird. All I ever see you make is toast and sandwiches."

"Been busy."

"So you *can* cook."

"Like a professional." He grinned at her. "I'll make you dinner one night to prove it."

Jessa stared at him, completely mute, mouth open just a little as he heated chocolate on the stovetop behind him.

"What's wrong?" he asked as he finished up the final touches on his dessert and then leaned back, watching her.

"You just . . . *grinned.*"

"I did? Is there some kind of problem with that?"

She shook her head. "No! No problem. I was beginning to think you weren't capable of it. I'm just surprised."

"I'm still human, mostly. My facial muscles are capable of forming all the expressions yours can."

She smiled. "You have dimples. I had no idea."

The dessert was finished. He poured it into a cup and slid it across to her. "Normally it's supposed to chill, but it's good like this, too."

She stared down into the cup. "It's chocolate mousse."

"My favorite."

She picked up the spoon he'd given her and dipped into the confection. "You'd smuggle chocolate mousse into the movies."

He shrugged. "Why not?" Might be hard, but he never went to the movies, so it had never been a consideration.

She lifted her brows. "I'd make a comment right now about how life is too short for anything but the best, but for you and me that's a moot point, right?"

"I think being long-lived gives a man a taste for only the finer things." He held her gaze steadily so she would know he wasn't talking about dessert.

She averted her gaze and took a dollop of the mousse onto her tongue. Groaning as it hit her taste buds, she closed her eyes. "That's like sin made real."

That look of sensual ecstasy on her face made him want to give her more.

Using her spoon to point at the cup, she said, "This is the best chocolate mousse I've ever tasted." She took another bite.

"I told you I could cook."

"I believe you." She paused and set her spoon onto the table. "You surprised me and now I have a surprise for you." She stood, a mischievous look on her face. "Come with me."

"Where are we going?"

"You'll see."

He followed her through the house to one of the rooms at the back of the keep that he didn't use very much. A couch sat in the middle of the room, facing a high white wall. The smell of hot buttered popcorn filled the air.

Jessa turned toward him with a smile on her face. "I'm not allowed to leave the grounds. If I were, I would have taken you to a real movie theater. Things being what they are, Erik helped me do the next best thing."

His gaze went to the projector at the back of room. "We're watching a movie, with popcorn," he observed with a little shock.

"Yes. Maybe one day we'll be able to do it in an actual theater."

The thought of going to a movie with Jessa, of actually being out in public, having fun, was heady. He couldn't remember the last time he'd had fun. The thought of going on a date with Jessa, no threat surrounding them, their focus on each other, made his heart pound and his hands sweat.

He cleared his throat. "What's the movie?"

"*Outlander.*" She beamed at him. "Vikings and aliens all mixed together in a big . . . Viking and alien stew!" She beamed. "There's nothing not to love."

Broder was doubtful, but her enthusiasm was adorable.

She pointed at him. "You just grinned again!"

"I did?"

"Yes." She slid her hand into his. "This is the best night ever. Come on, let's get popcorn."

The movie they watched didn't matter; just spending the evening with Jessa was enough. When the end credits ran, she drowsed with her head resting on his upper arm, tired out easily from her lingering injuries, the empty popcorn bucket at their feet.

He turned off the projector and scooped her into his arms.

"Hey," she protested, winding her arms around his neck, "I can walk, you know."

"I know." He carried her through the darkened house to her room and laid her onto the mattress.

She adjusted herself and lay back into the pillows. "I feel like an invalid," she muttered.

He leaned over her, with an arm on either side of her. "It was an excuse to hold you."

Jessa went very still, staring into his eyes from an inch away. There was a ring of gold around her dark brown pupils. "Okay." Her voice came out a little breathless.

"Thank you for tonight."

"It was my pleasure."

He leaned in and pressed his lips to hers. He wanted more, so much more. Clenching his fist, he contented himself with slipping his tongue into her mouth and easing it up against hers. Her body tightened and her breathing quickened. If he pressed her back into the pillows and demanded more, she would probably give it to him.

Instead he eased back. "Rest now," he murmured, his voice rough from his lust.

"Broder, what does a witch taste like?" she murmured sleepily.

He held her gaze for a long moment before answering. "Most witches taste like peppermint and roses, but you taste like the future I want."

Her drowsy eyes opened wider and she started to say something, but he turned and strode from the room before she had a chance.

"Bring your elbow back, pivot, and punch straight out. It's like a dance."

Jessa turned on the ball of one foot, pulling her elbow back and then punching as Broder had instructed. The tip of the wooden training dagger she held thumped him in the chest, but it was like hitting a heavy sandbag; Broder didn't even feel it. *She* was feeling it . . . in every muscle she possessed. The last week had been a flurry of training, every day from morning until night.

Occasionally Erik stepped in to demand a break for her. She was thankful for his intervention since Broder was such a slave driver. It was as if Broder felt like he was fighting for her life through her training. In actuality, he probably was. And she was fighting for her life by learning how to defend herself. It was for this reason she never complained or asked for a break, no matter that she was still recovering from her ordeal with the demon and became tired more easily than usual.

Broder had given her his dagger, which was why she now trained with a wooden one. She'd protested, knowing that Loki would disapprove and she didn't want Broder to get into trouble, but she couldn't dissuade him of the gift no matter how hard she tried. She kept it sheathed and with her at all times, sometimes wearing it at the small of her back just as Broder did.

Since the attack, Broder had been as hands-off with her as he possibly could be. She'd noticed his reluctance to touch her and was trying very hard not to take it personally. Before the demon attack, he'd pushed her hard in this regard, trying his best to tempt her into bed with him, so the change was odd.

Maybe he'd been turned off by her near-death experience. It certainly wasn't because he feared her fragility. After all, he wouldn't be forcing the training issue so hard if that were the case.

Recently they'd begun training with swords as well. Since one effective way for a human—or seidhr or Valkyrie—to kill a demon was to lop off its head, it made sense that this was a common weapon for the non-Brotherhood to use. She was growing proficient with it, though a Loki dagger was the best weapon. The dagger required no special aim; it was just poke and explode. Pretty simple, really. The only downside was how close you had to get to the target. *No one* wanted to be that close to a demon.

Jessa executed a perfect roundhouse kick for Broder, just the way Halla had taught her. He took a step back and looked impressed.

"Okay," he said, beginning to circle her in a crouched position that made her think of a wolf circling its prey. "It's time."

She raised an eyebrow. "Time for what?"

"Time for you to show me what you've got."

"What do you mean?"

He motioned to her with his fingers curling toward him. "I mean, attack me. Let loose. Try to hurt me."

"I don't want to hurt you."

"You won't. You *can't*. So don't worry about it. Don't think about who I am, just try and hurt me." He jerked his chin at the blunt training sword resting against the wall. "Take my head off, Jessa."

She looked from him to the sword, remembered he was a member of the Brotherhood of the Damned and was as close to indestructible as one could get, and went for the training sword on the wall. The moment her hand touched the smooth, cool metal of the handle, Broder was behind her, lunging. She whirled around, bringing the sword up and impacting his torso with a solid thump.

Broder grunted and backed off, favoring his rib cage. She'd hit him hard, but, hell, he'd invited her to do it.

A moment later and he was stalking her again. Her heart rate ratcheted skyward at the look on his face. He was definitely in the zone, provoking her to attack him out of fear. If this was the way he looked to the Blight, she wasn't sure why they didn't just curl up and die right on the spot.

With a nearly animalistic snarl, he lunged for her. She kicked him in the chest, pushing him back with the flat of her boot, grunting and using every ounce of her muscle to do it. It hardly deterred him. He was on her again, gripping her from behind. Real panic filled her. Even though it was Broder mock-attacking her, it still made all her survival instincts flare to life.

From a place of pure impulse, she punched backward with her elbow, hitting his solar plexus. His grip loosened and she pivoted, sword swinging wide in one hand, bringing the heel of her other hand up toward his nose—and pulling back only at the very last second. She followed the move by bringing the sword around and thumping him soundly in the throat.

Broder stepped back and opened his arms. He smiled widely and purely for the first time since she'd met him. This wasn't a grin, not a smirk—it was a full-on, dazzling smile. His dimples popped and she nearly dropped her sword in surprise. "You just killed me. Good job." He was bleeding from the corner of his mouth and one nostril, and she'd ripped his shirt . . . but he was still smiling.

Apparently the only way to make Broder happy was to inflict bodily harm upon him.

She tried to calm her exerted breathing while looking pointedly away from the rip in his T-shirt that revealed a swath of nicely rippled, muscled chest. "Thanks . . . I guess."

He walked away from her, pulling his T-shirt over his head and using it to wipe his face. Oh, that *so* didn't help. Now there was an even wider swath of muscular chest for her to attempt to not look at.

Swallowing hard, she walked over to replace the sword only to find herself hefted in strong arms. She squealed and thrashed, all the memories of her recent attack rushing to the forefront of her mind and igniting a rush of panic. She knew it was Broder who'd grabbed her, but, again, she couldn't help the brutal survival response that ensued. She fought back with everything she had.

Her heel connected with Broder's shin hard enough to break a human man's bone. He released her, but she wasn't done yet. She dropped to the floor and rotated, kicking up high and catching him in the cheek, making his head whip to the side. While his face was turned away, she jumped on him, landing a punch to the kidneys that made him grunt.

He collapsed and she went with him, punching him again and again. It was the demon all over again, except this time she was winning. It felt good.

Broder rolled over and pinned her down, telling her to calm down.

She relaxed, going limp, and a rush of regret filled her

immediately. She'd cut his cheek in her panicked frenzy and probably inflicted many other injuries. "I'm sorry, Broder."

"Don't be sorry. That's exactly what I wanted to see from you. I surprised you on purpose and you reacted well."

They stared at each other in silence for a long moment in which she became acutely aware of his naked upper torso and how close it was to her.

"You and Halla have taught me well." She tried to make her voice come out steady, but it was hard with him so close to her. "Thank you."

"It probably had a little to do with your attack, too. You're leaner and meaner now, not as ready to take anyone's shit."

"Maybe."

Broder stayed on top of her, though their conversation had ended. He seemed pretty happy to be touching her right now. Wow, she was getting some pretty mixed signals. Did he want her or not?

"Er, Broder? Is there some reason you're still on top of me?"

The haze in his eyes seemed to clear and he rolled away from her. She pushed up, watching with interest the flex of his arms as he pushed to his feet.

"Good work today," he said brusquely, then strode from the room.

Frowning, she stood and followed him through the living room and up the staircase. He was moving so fast, she practically had to run. Right before he went into his bedroom, she caught up to him, laying a hand on his bare upper arm to stop him, then snatching it away as though his skin burned her. Touching him was not a good move; she could still remember the way his body had pressed against hers only minutes before.

"Broder, are you all right?"

He stopped near the entrance of his room, but didn't turn to face her. "I'm okay."

"Really? Then why are you literally running away from me?"

He didn't answer for a moment, but she noticed him make

fists at his sides. "I'm trying to honor your wishes, but it's hard for me not to touch you."

She reached out to place her hand on his arm, hesitated and pulled back a little, then went ahead and did it anyway. Warmth radiated into her palm and she could feel the pulse of his heartbeat through the blood in his veins. It seemed to speed up as she rested her hand on him, and the knowledge that she'd affected him in even such a small way thrilled her.

"Don't touch me," he growled.

"Why not?" Her voice came out shaky. The tone of his voice had become low, rough, and very, very serious. Suddenly it was as though she were baiting a feral animal. Not smart.

He moved so fast she nearly screamed. One second he was standing with his back to her, the next he had her pinned against the wall. It all happened before she could draw a surprised breath. "Because it makes me do things like this."

Her breath left her slowly as she steadied her nerves. "Okay. What's wrong with this?"

"Because it's close to *this*." His gaze dropped to her mouth and studied it hard. A moment later his lips touched hers.

She melted against him, making a shamelessly hungry sound, and pressed her mouth more firmly against his. His hand found the back of her neck and he pulled her against his chest with his other arm, half lifting her, half guiding her into his bedroom and slamming the door closed with his foot.

"And then, *this*," he growled against her mouth. "You're in my bedroom. Now what will you do?"

He released her and she stumbled backward, feeling dazed. Her entire body hummed with excitement from his touch and wanted more. She glanced around, seeing tables, chairs, a wardrobe, and a bed.

Okay, mostly she saw the bed.

"I tried to do as you wished, leave you alone," he said, walking toward her. "Even though every time I looked at you, I felt need burn through my body."

Oh, hell, was it getting hot in here?

"Then Halla left and I was forced to train you." He paused, cocking his head to the side and sweeping his gaze over her. He seemed to unclothe her with merely a look. "Do you know how hard that was for me? I haven't been with a woman for well over a thousand years."

Well over? That was interesting. She wondered what situation he'd been in before Loki that had rendered such a virile Viking without woman.

"Then I am handed a woman who seems fashioned for me by the hand of the goddess Freyja herself. Some days I wonder if you weren't made by her, set upon this earth only to tease me. Maybe Freyja is in league with Loki and her goal is my torment."

She swallowed hard, not sure she'd heard him correctly. "What do you mean by that?"

He took another step closer to her and her heart skipped a beat. "You are perfect, shaped full to please my hands, and you are sweet to my mouth. You have fire in you, with a touch of the vulnerable. You are caring and intelligent and have an adorable inability to marshal your mouth at times. It's an endearing trait. You are the type of woman I would have sought to marry when marriage was an option."

His words sank in and made something light and beautiful flutter through her chest, made her mouth go dry. Never had a man said anything like that to her. Then the last part of what he'd said registered.

. . . *When marriage was an option.*

If she gave in to her desires right now and slept with Broder, she had to do it knowing she would never have more with him. He would never be free to marry her. They could never be together, not for forever. Loki controlled his fate and she didn't have to ask to know that she was not in Loki's plans for Broder. All she would ever have with him was this short time, their bodies joined.

If she fell in love with him, heartbreak would be inevitable.

Broder had stopped a breath's space from her and was

watching her carefully. Perhaps her thought process showed on her face.

She looked up at him, studying the dark depths of his eyes and the contours of his face, the shape of his jaw and the curve of his lips. The cost was high, but she couldn't deny this man.

Right now she would pay any price to have him, even if it was only for a short time. *No regrets.* She knew if she passed this opportunity up, one day she'd regret it.

His shoulders relaxed almost imperceptibly as he saw the difference her thought process made on her face. For a moment they shared a silent conversation that they heard only in their heads.

Jessa, if you want me to hold back, it will hurt, but I will.

No. I want you, no matter what.

EIGHTEEN

He closed the slight distance between them the moment that telepathic conversation finished and she let out a sigh of relief. The conflict within her had ended. She'd made her decision, for better or worse.

Broder walked over and drew her into his arms. Her stomach fluttered, but he seemed calm, confident, even though it had been a long time, a *very* long time, since he'd been with a woman. Of course, was Broder Calderson ever not completely self-assured?

He cupped her cheek in his hand and lowered his mouth to hers, sipping softly at her lips for a moment, then slanting over them and sliding his tongue within to rub up against her tongue.

He pushed her hair away from the delicate shell of her ear and found a sensitive spot right beneath her earlobe. He kissed it lingeringly, then let the tip of his tongue taste it.

Her breathing and heart rate increased, her body quickening at his touch.

"Let's take this slow," he murmured into her ear. "I want to taste every inch of you and commit your flavor to memory."

She shivered and nodded, running her hands up the bulge of his arms and twining her fingers into the silky hair at his nape. Slow, thorough sex with Broder? *Yes, please.*

Broder pulled his shirt over his head and let it drop,

exposing the scarred, yet beautiful, muscled expanse of his upper body. Her heart tap-danced for a moment. She had to touch him, just *had* to. Feeling drugged with need for him, she leaned down and laid a line of kisses from his hard abdomen, muscles rippling under her lips as she went, up his chest to the curve of his neck, inhaling the intoxicating scent of his skin. It fired her blood.

He lifted her shirt over her head and slid the loose jersey pants she'd been training in down to her ankles. She toed off her shoes and stood in only her bra and underwear. His gaze swept down her in appreciation and he eased her back toward the bed.

Soon her bra and underwear were gone, too. He lowered her onto the bed and unbuttoned his jeans. "I'm not letting you get away from me this time, Jessa. You're mine. Mine tonight, mine as long as I can keep you." He held her gaze as he eased his jeans down and off.

Her gaze ate up every magnificent inch of him. His cock was long and thick and looked as hard as steel. Her fingers itched to stroke it.

Realization dawned on her. "We have no condom."

He shook his head. "I cannot impregnate you, nor am I able to carry illness."

Thank all the powers of the universe. "Come here," she murmured roughly, her voice low and husky from the lust coursing through her veins.

He came down over her, his hands on either side of her head, and kissed her slowly, methodically. Then he nudged her head to the side and ran his tongue over the scar that marked her throat. She gasped at the exquisite sensitivity of it.

Working his way down, he sucked one nipple into his mouth, then the other, laving each one until she squirmed on the bed, her sex growing hot and achy.

"Do you like that?" he murmured against her taut nipple. "Do you like it when I touch you, Jessa?"

"Yes," she answered shakily.

With confident hands, Broder turned her over onto her

stomach, kissing and licking his way across her skin as he went, sending quivers of need through her body. She was lost in a haze of sexual bliss with his big body poised above her, his strength making her feel safe and cherished, and his lips and tongue tasting her skin.

Broder gathered her hair up and draped it over the mattress on one side, then leaned down and kissed the nape of her neck. The action tightened her body in places that were much farther down. His tongue flicked out and tasted her skin, then the tip of it dragged down along her spine, slowly, to the base.

"This was always my favorite part of a woman," Broder murmured, and she was reminded again at just how long it had been since he'd been this intimate with another person. The amount of control he displayed was incredible—and amazingly sexy.

She writhed a little and moaned as his tongue explored the base of her spine. She'd never known how sensitive that area of her body was, or maybe it was just Broder—maybe he made every area of her body an erogenous zone. She felt breathless, boneless, and more cherished than she ever had in her life, but she needed . . .

"Broder," she whispered. "*More.*"

"Let me take my time, *skatten min*." He dropped another kiss to the base of her spine, then murmured against her skin, "I may not have had a thousand years of sexual conquests, but I have thought about how I would love you over and over since the first day we met."

Oh . . . guh.

"At least let me touch you." She pushed up and turned over, her hands going to his chest, where she traced her fingers over the definition of muscles and the ripple of his stomach. She touched him like she'd never touched a man before, almost innocently. That was because she'd never touched a man like him before. "God, you're incredible," she breathed.

He shuddered in pleasure at her touch and kissed her hard, his tongue thrusting into her mouth. She returned the kiss greedily, pressing her body against his in order to feel every inch of him that she possibly could.

He broke the kiss, his face hovering above hers. "You're the woman I dreamed of having for the last ten centuries, Jessamine."

Jessa's tongue went dry. She never would have expected this level of tenderness from a man who could snap off a demon's head with his bare hands. She never would have thought that hands that could bring death so indisputably could also bring this kind of pleasure. Her lips pressed close to his, she told him as much.

He eased his hand between her thighs, parting them, and stroked his index finger over her clit. Shivers of ecstasy radiated through her. "These hands are dedicated to protecting you and bringing you pleasure. Nothing else." He caressed her clit over and over, every masterful stroke sending her closer to the razor's edge of a climax. She shuddered against him, her teeth raking her lower lip. "I'm going to make you feel good, Jessa."

"More," she pleaded breathlessly. She closed her eyes.

His thumb rotated on her clit, easing the pressure to control when she climaxed. It made her crazy. "Do you like that? Do you want to come?"

"Please," she whispered.

"Open your eyes and look at me. I want to watch your face while you come."

She opened her eyes and locked her gaze with his.

He moved down an inch from her clit and eased a finger deep inside her, then another, thrusting them in and out. The sensation of it bloomed through her body, rose like heat up her spine. It was just a tease, just a taste of how his long, wide cock would feel inside her. The thought of that—the image of his shaft buried deep inside her, made the brittle crystal edge of a climax taunt her, sending waves of ecstasy through her body.

Knowing just how to push her over that edge, he deepened and lengthened his strokes.

Jessa cried out, her head snapping back. Racking spasms

of pleasure shook her, over and over again. He lengthened it with his fingers, stroking over her clit, so the tail end of her climax bloomed into another, making her moan his name and thrash on the mattress.

He guided her hand to her sex, covering her clit with her fingers and pressing down until pleasure flared, then guided her fingers into her sex. She gasped at the hot, velvet sensation of all those gripping muscles.

"Heaven," Broder murmured hoarsely. "That's what I'm going to feel when I sink into you."

"Please," she whispered. "I want you inside of me, Broder."

He eased her hand away and pressed her wrists above her head on the pillow, forcing her spine to arch and push her breasts up in offering to him. Then he eased her thighs apart and looked his fill of her, exposed and ready on the bed for him, her sex waiting and wanting. Her nipples were as hard as tiny diamonds.

Broder grasped his cock and stroked the full, long length of it. Her heart rate did a little dance as he positioned himself over her and slid the smooth crown inside her.

Jessa gasped at the way only the head of his cock stretched her. She thought for a moment she might come again. Pressing her heels into the mattress, she arched, pushing her hips at him, wanting more, wanting to feel completely possessed and impaled by him.

Broder groaned at her impatience, as though his immense control might be slipping, and pressed his hips toward her, sliding in another few inches. Her muscles stretched even more and she whimpered at the pleasure of it.

She twisted against him and he grabbed her hips, holding her in place. "You're killing me, moving like that. More?" he asked through gritted teeth.

"Yes," she barely managed to respond.

He pushed in another couple inches. "You feel so fucking good," he said drunkenly.

"More," she whispered. "I want every inch of you inside me."

He pushed in until the base of his cock was buried within her. She moaned, her hips moving, needing to feel him thrust. He gave her what she wanted, pulling out slowly and thrusting in again so leisurely she felt every vein and bump of his cock as it glided inside her. He held her hips, keeping her from bucking as he shafted her slowly, then even more slowly.

"Broder," she breathed, her fingernails scraping down his back, "now you're killing me. Faster."

He withdrew and then thrust fast and hard, impaling her to the base of him over and over. Their bodies rocked together on the mattress, finding an erotic rhythm as they came together and parted again and again. She was hot and slick, easing the way of his cock in and out of her.

"That's it," she breathed. "Ah, God, you're going to make me come again."

And she did, pleasure pouring through her body in a powerful wave that stole her breath for a moment. She arched her back and cried his name, her muscles pulsing around his fast-pistoning cock.

Broder came down over her, thrusting into her hard and fast, pressing her hips down on the bed with every thrust. He suckled and licked her neck, groaning out her name. His big body tensed and she sensed he was about to come. He thrust to the base and bit her throat possessively as he came, his cock jumping deep in her body.

After it was over, they lay tangled together in a satisfied heap until Broder rolled to the side and pulled her against him in a spooning position. She noticed with a little smile that she fit perfectly into the curve of his body.

"I hope that was good enough," she whispered.

"What do you mean?" His voice rumbled through her back.

"You waited a thousand years for that. I hope—"

"It was incredible," he growled, kissing her temple. "I want more."

So did she.

Nestling her head against him and the pillow, she twined

her hand with his as he laid his arm protectively around her. She sighed, thinking she could easily stay exactly this way for the rest of her life and be perfectly happy.

She was falling in love with Broder.

She'd known it for a while, of course. After all, this was Broder Calderson—how could she not fall in love with him? She also knew that meant she was headed for a hell of a heartbreak down the road.

Her smile faded a little as she imagined the hollow place she would have in her heart when Loki finally decided their time was up. It could be tonight. It could be tomorrow. Maybe, if they were lucky, it would be a couple of weeks from now.

She'd take two weeks with Broder.

Comforted by the thought, she pushed aside her worries about the future and closed her eyes. Tonight she was safe in Broder's arms. Tomorrow would take care of itself.

Jessa woke to warmth beside her and the events of the previous night flooded her memory, making her even warmer. Opening her eyes, she smiled and stretched, enjoying the sensation of the sleeping body beside her. It wasn't just anyone's body, it was Broder's, the man who cherished her and who kept her safe against all threats.

How lucky she was to have a man like him in her life, even if it would only be for a short time.

The man in question groaned and rolled over onto his back. Jessa shifted onto her side and rested on her elbow, staring down at him. His lashes were a shade darker than his hair and shadowed his cheek. His lips were full and expressive, the mark of an emotional person.

Broder *was* emotional; one could see it teeming beneath the surface. His emotion was tightly leashed, controlled, but it was there in his eyes and in his body language, even though it might be absent from his facial expressions and his tone of voice most of the time.

And, wow, it was there when he made love.

She shivered at the memory. Reaching out, she moved a tendril of hair off his forehead. He moved a little, waking slowly. Not able to resist his warmth, she leaned over and pressed her lips to his. Beneath her, she felt him become aware.

He stiffened for a split second, then relaxed. His arms came around her and he flipped her onto her back, dragging her under his body. She was happy to be there; it was a lovely place with a lovely view.

His warm brown eyes held hers. Deep emotion she couldn't quite read roiled in their depths. This meant something to him, something profound and poignant. "Good morning," he murmured.

"Mmm, yes, it is." She smiled up into his face. She couldn't remember having such a light, happy feeling in her chest. "Best morning I've ever had, maybe."

He returned her smile and she nearly died. The man was handsome all the time, but when he grinned or, God help her, *smiled* he totally rocked her socks. "There are your dimples again."

His smile faded and his thoughts clearly went far away for a moment. "Once, a long time ago, my wife loved my dimples."

She blinked. "Wife?"

He nodded and smiled again. "She's long gone now, no worries."

"No, I know that. It's just . . . I didn't know you'd been married."

"Her name was Agata. We'd only been together for a couple of years. She died before I was cursed by Loki, died in childbirth."

"You had children?"

He shook his head. "No, unfortunately, my infant son died with her."

"I'm so sorry."

"It was a long time ago. I wouldn't say I don't still feel grief when I think of it, but time has salved the wounds. It was a life-changing experience for me back then, though.

If my wife and son had lived, I never would have gone raiding. If I had never gone raiding . . ." He trailed off.

"You never would have been cursed by Loki," she guessed.

"I would have made different decisions." He stared down hungrily at her. "The last thousand years have been hell, but right now I'm glad I endured them because they led to you."

Sorrow threatened her happiness because she knew there was an addendum to that sentence. . . . *Too bad I can't keep you.*

He lowered his mouth to hers and kissed her thoroughly, while his hands drifted down to explore her body. Jessa's thought process went sluggish, the memory of his body on hers still very, *very* fresh in her mind. When he eased his hand between her thighs, she moaned and parted her legs for him.

With her hands and her mouth, she told him silently how much she wanted him inside her again.

Slipping over her body, he pushed her thighs apart, positioned himself, and slid deep within her. Their mouths fused, hands roaming, he rocked in and out of her, taking her slowly in the early light of the morning. Before he was done, she came twice beneath him.

When they were finished, they took a shower together that was entirely too long. They stood under the hot spray of the jets, soaping and rinsing each other clean. Jessa was endlessly fascinated with his body, so hard with muscle and with such soft skin all at the same time. She could spend hours just touching him, exploring every last ridge and valley of his magnificent physique, tracing her fingers over his battle scars. Eventually, however, the water went cold and they got out of the shower and dressed.

Broder hesitated at the door, watching her pull on a sweater.

She smiled, resisted the urge to roll her eyes, and waved him off. "Go get some food. I'll be fine alone for ten minutes." She could tell he was starving. It took a lot of calories to fuel a body as big as his.

Broder went for the door, then stopped, came back, and kissed her. "I'll bring up strawberries." It was her favorite thing to eat in the morning.

She gave him a final kiss, watched him leave the room, then finished getting dressed. The phone rang and she stilled just as she was buttoning her jeans. It wasn't so odd that the phone was ringing, really . . . but it was odd that the phone in question was an unplugged antique.

Taking a few steps closer to it, she studied it. This was beyond creepy, like a scene from a horror movie. The ringing stopped. She relaxed and turned away. A moment later, the phone began ringing again.

When Broder returned, the phone was still ringing. She had drawn her hands into the sleeves of her sweater and remained standing, still staring at the possessed phone. "Broder, that is not a working telephone, right?"

"No." Glancing at her, he set the tray down, went to the phone, and picked up the receiver. "Hello?" he growled. After a moment he set it back down in its cradle. "Apparently they only want to talk to you."

"Oh, how lovely. Who do you think it is?"

Broder said nothing for a moment, then finally said, "It's probably not the Blight. To my knowledge, they don't possess magick of a nature to do that."

And, of course, that left only one other option.

"Do you think . . . it could be my great-grandfather calling?"

Broder's jaw locked. "It could be."

She sat down on the bed, staring at the phone. "If it's not the Blight and whoever doing it is using magick, it has to be him, right?"

Broder's face tightened for a moment in anger. "Yes."

She chewed her lower lip. "What does he want from me?"

"I don't know." His voice was a low growl. "But I'm going to find out."

NINETEEN

Broder entered the fitness room at the back of the keep and found Erik lifting weights. The Brotherhood had all been big men before they'd been damned by Loki. Back then if a man, or a woman, for that matter, wasn't strong and healthy, survival was in question.

The survival of the brothers wasn't at issue, but it was in their best interests to stay in shape in order to battle the Blight. Being in shape meant fewer injuries. Just because they were immortal and had incredible healing ability didn't mean that injuries didn't hurt.

He came to stand in front of Erik. The head of the Brotherhood lowered the weights with a softly ringing clang and sat up, grabbing a nearby towel to wipe off his face. "What is it?"

"I think the seidhr are trying to contact Jessa through magickal means. They can't directly enter my lands unless I allow them inside, but they might attempt to draw her out by another method."

Erik nodded and rubbed a hand over his mouth. "I've tried to contact Thorgest to ask about Jessa, but they're stonewalling me. They want her, but they're not saying why, and they're really pissed that she's under our protection." Erik regarded him for a moment, his blue eyes glittering. "They're especially pissed that it's you who is guarding her. Why is that, Broder?"

He didn't answer.

Erik pressed his lips together in a suspicious, dismissive gesture, clearly sensing that Broder had no interest in sharing. "You are aware of the tension between the seidhr and the Brotherhood. They are not cooperative at the best of times."

And these were definitely not the best of times, since he was involved.

"To protect Jessa, we need to assume the worst. We need to assume they're attempting to use magick to somehow lure her away from us." Broder gritted his teeth.

"Lure her away from you, you mean."

"What do you mean by that?"

Erik leaned forward a little, resting a hand on his thigh. "I mean that it's pretty clear you're close to the woman. You don't want her to leave you."

He didn't. Not ever.

"Sooner or later, you need to let her go. She's seidhr, Broder. Those are her people. If she chooses to go to them, we shouldn't stop her."

"We should if they mean her harm."

"If they meant her harm the shaman who came to the keep would have killed her on the spot. He had plenty of opportunity. Instead he tried to take her unharmed."

Broder grunted. "They wanted to do something to her against her will. That's enough for me." In fact, the rage from the mere idea heated his blood.

Erik gave him a long, measuring look. "Okay."

"What's that supposed to mean?"

He gave an easy, one-shouldered shrug. "It means, okay."

Broder ground his teeth, peeling away the layers of Erik's true meaning expressed in his tone of voice and body language. *Tell the truth. You love her, but you'll have to let her go. You know that. So let her go, Broder. Either it's now or it's later.*

He couldn't let her go. He was a strong man, but he wasn't strong enough for that.

• • •

Jessa nuzzled Broder's chest, sliding her leg along his under the covers. Smiling, she drew her arm over his stomach and cuddled against him. There was nothing better in the world than a warm Broder in bed with her. She was now utterly convinced of this fact.

The night before, he had determined that the best way to protect her from any threats was to watch over her all night long . . . in his bed. She couldn't think of even one downside to that plan.

His hands roamed her body possessively, heating her to near-unmanageable levels. His mouth found hers and he rolled her under his body, pressing her onto the mattress. Her arms twined around his neck, fingers tangling in his hair, then she skated her hands down his back and sides, to cup his incredibly gorgeous rear. His mouth covered hers, his tongue sliding in to rub up against her tongue.

She shifted, forcing him to fit between her legs, and guided his cock inside her. Her back arched and she sighed as he filled her, their bodies coming together yet again in perfect rhythm and erotic fusion.

They tangled together when it was over, Jessa drawing lazy circles on his chest. "I wish we could just stay like this forever. Just forget the Blight, the seidhr, Loki, and send Erik home. We could live here, right? Just you and me."

Broder groaned. "That sounds like paradise."

She rolled over and tucked herself against his side. "Let's just pretend for a while."

They cuddled under the blankets, saying nothing for a long time. Until the phone down the hallway in Jessa's room rang.

Beside her, Broder stiffened.

"Maybe I should just answer it."

It had been ringing on and off for the last two days and nights. A constant, unwelcome reminder that they could pretend she wasn't being hunted by enigmatic, perhaps antagonistic forces, but the reality wasn't far away.

"We should take the phone out of your room," Broder growled.

He hadn't done that yet, though he'd threatened to more than once. Jessa thought she understood why. Ultimately, it was her choice whether or not to answer the phone and perhaps talk to the only blood relative she had. Broder was leaving that door open for her, though she could tell it pained him greatly. If Broder had been a more selfish man, he would have smashed the phone against the wall long ago.

The fact that he hadn't for her sake only made her love him more.

"If you took the phone out, they'd probably just make a statue or a pair of socks ring."

"Maybe."

The phone finally stopped ringing, but the bubble they'd immersed themselves in just moments before was now irreparably popped. Jessa rolled over onto her back. "Maybe we should ask Dmitri what he knows about the situation. He seems to be privy to a lot of information. Maybe he knows more than what he said under the bridge."

Broder sat up at the edge of the bed. "Seek out a demon to ask for help? Jessa, are you serious?"

She pushed to a sitting position. "Of course I'm serious. Anything to clear up this cloud of doubt hanging over us."

Broder shook his head, not answering.

"Broder, I'm ready for any kind of explanation at this point. The seidhr won't talk to the Brotherhood, so what are we supposed to do? Either I answer that phone"—she pointed in the direction of her bedroom—"or we start exploring other options."

"Seeking out help from *a demon* is not an option, Jessa." There was a note of derision in his voice and he said *a demon* the way another person might say *a maggot*.

Jessa sat for a moment, absorbing his hatred. It was understandable that he would hate demons. She hated them, too, but Dmitri had warned her in the parking garage and given Broder information that had saved her life.

She pushed off the bed and stood up, taking the sheet with her. "You are a snob, Broder."

Broder went completely still. Then he stood and turned toward her. "A snob? This has nothing to do with that, Jessa. This has to do with your protection."

"Bullshit. You don't want to have anything to do with Dmitri because he's a demon, even if it could help me."

"You're right. I want nothing to do with demons. Do you know why? *Because they're demons.* Nothing good ever came from a demon and nothing good ever will."

Jessa clenched her fists, fuming. "So, apparently, saving my life wasn't a good thing, then?" She whirled and went for the door, the sheet trailing behind her. God, the man was pigheaded.

"Jessa!" Broder called after her.

"Don't talk to me until you've come to your senses!" she threw over her shoulder at him right before she slammed the door.

She stalked down the hallway, passing Erik, who watched her with acute curiosity as she swept past him with as much dignity as she could muster and entered her bedroom.

Slamming her door shut behind her, she leaned against it, letting out a long, slow breath. Maybe she'd been too harsh. After all, Broder was working off a thousand years of battle against demons. He'd been watching them prey on innocents all that time. She couldn't even imagine the number of dead he must have seen as a result of the Blight. Was it really so surprising that he couldn't trust Dmitri?

She was just frustrated by the lack of movement. With the exception of her new romantic entanglements with Broder, her life right now seemed like it had been put on hold. She'd been working so hard to discover who she was, who her parents had been. Now she felt as though all those answers were close enough to touch. Would she hurt herself if she reached out and took them?

That frustration was at the heart of her blowup at Broder and nothing else.

Sighing, she sought a pair of jeans and a sweater. Once

dressed, she walked to the door. She needed to explain that to Broder and tell him that she understood his reluctance to contact Dmitri . . . but also tell him she didn't agree with it. She had no faith she'd be able to budge him on the issue, however.

Just as she touched the doorknob, the phone rang.

She froze, all the hair on the back of her neck standing on end, her hand still on the knob. It rang again. That could be her great-grandfather. It could be the blood kin she'd never had contact with, a connection she craved.

Yet Jessa knew that just because a person might be related to her that didn't mean the person wouldn't harm her. Therein lay the risk.

Presumably nothing could hurt her through a mere telephone connection, but who knew for certain? Two weeks earlier she never would have thought it was possible for an inanimate object to ring like a telephone, either, or for a shaman to take the form of another person.

Removing her hand from the doorknob, she waited, every ring of the telephone searing her soul. Taking a few steps closer to it, she let it ring a few more times. She reached out toward it, touched the receiver. Hesitating a moment longer, she decided to take the chance.

She picked up the phone and held it to her ear, saying nothing.

"Jessamine Hamilton?" It was a woman's voice. It sounded a lot like the voice from her dream, the one about her mother in the cowl, warning her to watch out for the Valkyrie.

How could that be? Was this . . . her mother?

She could barely speak past the lump in her throat. Her heart pounded out a staccato rhythm. "Yes."

"I'm Carolyn, your great-aunt."

"Ah." Great-aunt, not mother. Of course. *Right.* She swallowed hard. "You're calling me on a phone that is eighty years old and not hooked into the wall."

"Yes, I know. It was the only way to contact you. The wards around the keep make it impossible to enter unless we're allowed in. I'm sorry if it alarmed you." Carolyn had the trace of a Scottish accent, but it sounded mixed with other accents, not unlike Broder's. Perhaps she'd traveled and had lived in many places. Were the seidhr allowed to do that? Jessa's lack of knowledge frustrated her.

"Were you . . ." She trailed off, trying to ask a question that still seemed impossible to her mind, but probably would be nothing to a witch. "Have you ever appeared in my dreams?"

"Yes. It's how I attempted to contact you earlier, but it wasn't successful."

"Thanks for the warning."

"Came too late, I fear."

"I thought you were a dream representation of my mother."

Silence on the other end. "Abigail and I always bore a striking resemblance. You look like her, too, but there's definitely some of your father in you."

"You knew my father?"

"Oh, yes, dear. He was a powerful shaman."

"Wait a minute, how do you know what I look like?"

"We've been watching you. Thorgest, your great-grandfather, knew the moment you set foot on Scottish soil. Once Roan made contact with you, discovered your name, we did the research."

Jessa's voice hardened. "Why did you send that shaman for me?"

"Roan felt he had no other option. You must understand that this is a difficult situation. You're with *him*, Jessa."

"Him, who? Do you mean Broder?"

"Yes. You're in danger with him." Her voice had taken on a chilly, strident quality that made gooseflesh rise along Jessa's arms. "You have no idea the man you're passing time with, or what horrors he's capable of."

"That's silly. Broder is protective, caring. He would never hurt me, not in a million years."

"The magick for this call is fast fading. I'm warning you, Jessa, get out of there. Come to us. We'll guide you." The sound of her voice flickered, cutting out and then growing softer. "Leave Broder's keep and come to us. You'll know where to find us because your blood will tell you. Do it now, Jessa."

"But I have questions. Why is it so urgent I leave now?"

The line was dead. Carolyn was gone.

Jessa lowered the receiver into the cradle and stared down at it. As tempted as she was to meet with her great-aunt in person, she still wasn't sure of their intentions. Broder a threat? Yeah, sure, a threat to the bad guys, but, surely, not to her.

Did that reasoning mean that the seidhr were bad guys? They definitely could be. Why wouldn't they give any straight answers to her questions?

She just couldn't be sure of anything right now. Anything, that was, but herself.

Looking at the stack of papers Broder had been bringing her, she chewed her lower lip thoughtfully. Maybe she couldn't connect in a meaningful way with the seidhr yet, but that didn't mean she couldn't explore who she was on her own.

Broder hovered outside Jessa's door. He could feel her presence beyond the heavy wood and it comforted him. Stubborn woman didn't know what was best for her. She was reckless and impulsive.

Meet with Dmitri and ask him for help? That was crazy. Any risk to Jessa was too big a risk. Couldn't she understand that? He would never rest easy with threats arranged against her. Leaving that phone in her room had been a serious hardship.

Allowing her contact with Dmitri was far worse.

He knocked on the door and it opened right away. Jessa pushed a piece of paper at him. "I need everything on that list, please." Then she turned and went to sit at the little table by the fireplace, riffling through the documents he'd given her.

He read the list she'd thrust at him. Tincture of bladder wrack, the hair of a sloth, scrapings from a mossy rock. "Jessa—"

"Please, Broder." She rounded on him. "This is the only way I can connect to my birthright. Just get me the stuff, okay?"

He studied her for a long moment. She wanted to use untried magick? She, an untried witch? "You mean to work a spell from the information I gave you."

She glanced up at him. "I mean to work magick, yes. I have to do it, Broder, can't you understand? It's like having hives all over my body; I gotta scratch."

He nodded, studying the list again. "I can get these things, with Erik's help."

"Just like that?"

"What do you mean?"

"I was counting on a big argument. You're just going to agree to it?"

He nodded. "You can't connect with the seidhr, so this is the second best thing. I get it."

"You're not afraid I'll blow up the keep?"

He blinked. "A little."

She made a scoffing sound and returned to her papers, shaking her head. "You're about as comforting as a kiss from a gummy bear and a hug from a rainbow, do you know that, Broder?"

He hovered in the doorway, at a loss for words. She seemed unhappy. Dealing with women on this level, he was out of his depth in a major way. Especially one from this century.

A thousand years of fighting demons had never prepared him for this.

Jessa added the last of the crushed evergreen and immediately felt the telltale tingle that signaled the rising of her power. It started in the pit of her stomach, like a nervous quiver.

If she concentrated on it, and didn't fear it, it rose into her chest like a stem growing and flower unfurling to the first rays of sunlight. If she doubted herself, if she feared it, it died with a little gasp that made her queasy.

She had mixed up three different potions so far, smearing the paste into three different "talismans," what were essentially objects of focused power. All of them were items she'd found around the keep. One was a small wooden container, another a silver locket, the third an antique ring that Broder said she could use. Each one had a place where she could dropper a small amount of her concoctions.

She wasn't sure why the mixing of these compounds worked the way they did, but she suspected strongly that the natural magick she carried within her combined with the ingredients and that an ordinary human would end up with only smelly glop.

Sitting back on her heels, she studied the objects, sensing the magick inside her that wanted out, that wanted to get at those talismans and fuel them, make beautiful things happen. Her magick was like a cobra coiled in her chest, ready to strike.

The problem? She had no idea how to invoke the magick within her. The spells weren't clear on that point. All they said were, *invoke the spell.* Well, duh. They'd been written for witches who'd actually had training.

She wished very hard for a book titled *Magick for Dummies.*

It had to be some kind of combination of words that she didn't know. She closed her eyes, hoping for some divine inspiration, but none came.

"It's blood."

"What?" She opened her eyes and looked behind her to see Broder standing in the doorway.

"Or tears." He stepped toward her. "I know that much."

"Oh." She looked down at the talismans. "That makes sense, I guess."

He knelt beside her and she immediately stiffened. Every time he came near her, her body went on high alert and she thirsted for him. His presence was distracting.

"I want to be alone right now. Can you leave, please?" she asked gently, while still staring at the talismans. She didn't want to hurt his feelings—if Broder's feelings could actually be hurt.

"No."

She sighed.

Frowning, he studied each of the talismans in turn. "What do these spells do?"

"Don't worry, they're all innocuous. One blows pink and blue bubbles into the air. I think it's meant as a party favor. Another makes the talisman sing like a bird, also a party favor. The last paints stars on your ceiling for the night."

He nodded. "You picked spells that won't cause harm."

"Well, yeah." She cast him an irritated glance. "What charms did you think I'd pick for my first time out, brain surgery by magick? Have a little faith in me."

"Okay, so pick one."

She frowned.

"What's wrong?"

"I can't remember which one is which."

Broder grunted. "So just pick one. They're all fluffy, so no worries. We'll be surprised."

She winced. "Yeah, we might *really* be surprised."

He looked at her. "You mixed them the right way, didn't you?"

"I was very careful, but I'm flying blind here. Remember, I have no formal training."

"Then invoke one."

"Easy for you to say; you're immortal."

"Just do it, Jessa."

Hesitating with her hand over the three objects, she chose the silver locket and held it up. "I really don't feel like crying, so I guess tears are out of the question."

Broder handed her a small knife.

She used it to prick the top of her index finger, then squeezed out a drop of blood. It welled, then dripped onto the open top of the charm. Immediately the magick within her chest pulsed, flared, and then exploded, sending a ripple of near-sexual pleasure coursing through her.

She gasped and Broder looked at her sidelong.

Clearing her throat—and her mind of a whole host of carnal imagery—she looked down at the talisman. It was glowing a soft blue. "Do you see that?"

Broder stared at it. "See what?"

"The locket is glowing blue."

"Not for me."

Then the blue intensified and was gone. Immediately, the room darkened and a night sky spread across the ceiling. "Oh . . . wow," she breathed.

She rested back on her hands, face raised to the ceiling where a vast constellation spread from the farthest reaches of the room and back to the center. It was like being outside on a cloudless night, away from the city. "It's beautiful."

Broder gazed into the sky spread across the ceiling in silence.

"I always planned to put up little glow-in-the-dark stars in my children's bedrooms. You know the kind?"

"No."

She shook her head. "Of course you don't. Anyway, there are these plastic stars you can buy that simulate stars at night. I had no idea I could do *this*."

They stared at the ceiling for a while in silence.

Finally Broder spoke. "So, you want to have kids someday?"

"Yes. I can, right? I mean, my parents were seidhr, but they had me, so I guess it's possible."

"It's possible, although the fertility rates for the seidhr aren't high."

"I guess the Brotherhood . . ."

"Cannot sire children or contract STDs. Not as long as we carry a sliver."

"Ah. That's right." She swallowed hard, her cheeks growing warm. "You mentioned that before. I guess that's a perk."

"If you're one of the brothers who can have sex, sure. Hasn't done me much good until now."

"Right." She could hear the note of bitterness in his voice. She was the first in a thousand years, but it was nice they didn't need condoms when they made love.

Made love. How stupid. It hadn't been *that* at all. How could it be love when they had no hope of a future? She loved him, but what they were having was just sex. She needed to remember that—it would ease her hurt in the end.

"Broder, what's the last thing you remember from your life . . . before?"

He didn't answer for a moment, then his reply rang out chillingly in the peaceful air with its star-filled sky. "*Blood.* Lots of blood."

Without another word, he got up and left the room, leaving Jessa with goose bumps all over her arms and legs.

TWENTY

"I think it's wrong what they're doing." Molly's voice sounded thready and tired. "If they were doing this to me, I'd be furious. Once she finds out the truth, she will be, too."

Roan watched as Molly hugged herself while she gazed out the second-story stained-glass window. He knew what she saw: The blue tint made the front lawn look dreary.

Roan sighed and rubbed a hand over his face. "Don't let Thorgest or Carolyn hear you say that."

Sam tipped his chair back away from the table and rested his black boots on the top. Roan grimaced at him, but Sam ignored it. "I want to get the fuck out of this place, go back home. Everyone here is crazy."

Sam was a three-hundred-year-old shaman and "home" was actually here in Scotland, but he'd spent the last hundred years in the seidhr enclave located in Baltimore, Maryland. He'd rejected this place a long time ago because of the way Thorgest ruled it. Roan was tempted to leave at times, too. It was his loyalty that kept him here. Sam didn't have that trouble.

Roan walked over to stand beside Molly. She wore a glittery black tutu today, paired with a ruffled blouse with tiny pearl buttons and thigh-high platform boots. "I know his methods can seem cruel sometimes," Roan answered, feeling a bit like the older brother and voice of reason, "but everything he does is for the good of the enclave."

Sam grunted. "I'll take Baltimore over this place any day of the week. I pity both of you."

Roan glanced at him. "You know the Baltimore enclave will lose its protection if Thorgest dies without a successor. You depend on him. We all do. That's why he needs our support, even if his methods are a little Machiavellian."

"A little?" Molly snorted softly beside him. "Please."

"Yeah, can hardly wait until they draw this poor unsuspecting woman into the enclave and chain her to the juggernaut. That will be a proud day for us." Sam grinned.

Roan closed his eyes and marshaled his patience. He didn't like it any more than anyone else. "Maybe she'll *want* to take on the responsibility. Maybe she's more like Thorgest than Abigail. After all, she's never known her biological family; maybe she's yearning for inclusion."

Sam snorted. "Up until the day she meets her dear old great-grandpa, maybe."

"They will convince her to come. You know they'll make her, somehow, someway." Molly turned and looked. "This witch without a drop of training could be our next leader. Doesn't that bother either of you?"

"She's got Egilson blood. She doesn't need any training. Once she's here all that power will rise to the surface and shine like a star. You'll see. She doesn't know it, but all the power is inside her; she just has to trust it. All she needs is a little guidance."

Molly said nothing. She only crossed her arms over her chest and set her jaw. Then she pushed away from the window and started pacing. "I think Carolyn should just suck it up and take the reins."

Carolyn didn't want to stay trapped in Scotland. She was strong enough to travel the world, live away from the seidhr. She was going to do all she could to manipulate Jessa into coming here for her own selfish reasons, because if Jessa didn't take up the reins, she'd be forced to do it. Her freedom would come to an end.

"Keep dreaming." Sam took a handful of small silver balls from his pocket and rolled them around in his hand.

Every last one of them was a charm, separate from the powerful layered talisman he wore on a black cord around his neck. Sam had chosen a pewter wolf for his personal sigil. It was a fitting symbol for him, as long as the wolf was a lone one.

"You've never liked Carolyn," Molly shot at him. "What lies between you two that creates so much friction?"

"Carolyn is a selfish bitch," Sam drawled, coming to his feet. "And my reasons for not trusting her are my own."

Of course, Sam didn't trust anyone. It was the result of his rather unstable upbringing. He and Jessa had a few things in common, although the difference lay in love. Jessa might not have been raised by her biological parents, but she'd had love in abundance. Sam hadn't.

Once they'd obtained her name, they'd done the research. Abigail had made good provision for her daughter in the event of her death. By all accounts, Margaret Hamilton had raised Jessamine well.

"I'm out of here." Sam, now standing, stretched out his impressive height and threw one of the silver balls he held onto the floor. The rune charm exploded into silvery sparks. Light twisted, along with the viewers' minds and Sam shifted into wolf form. It was serious shaman juju and Sam did it well, even if one did need to forgive the showmanship.

The huge gray wolf shook his black mane and glared at both of them in turn, then he turned and leapt out the open window, gone.

"Show-off," groused Molly, her arms crossed over her chest and the toe of one platform boot tapping. They watched him bound into the nearby stand of trees, looking deadly and beautiful all at once.

Roan narrowed his eyes at the swaying branches left in Sam's wake. "He's sold more magick, hasn't he?" Sam had a history of acting as a sort of magickal mercenary. It was against the rules, but Thorgest looked the other way.

She shrugged a shoulder. "How should I know?"

He looked at her. "Come on, I know you're sleeping with him."

Molly gave him a look so cold, he swore his balls frosted a little. "What did you say?"

Bollocks, maybe he was wrong. "Molly—"

She rounded on him, one hand on her hip. "Just because every other witch in the enclave has slept with that whore doesn't mean I have."

"It's just that—"

"Oh, I know what it is. You look at me, look at my clothes, and—"

"Molly . . ."

"And you think I'm a wild child, sleeping around." She flung her arm wide.

"Molly, I'm sorry." He held up a hand. "Really. I was an idiot to presume."

"Yes, you were. And, yes, *of course* Sam has sold more magick. Everyone knows he's a mercenary, for sale to the highest bidder." She rolled her eyes. "You don't have to be sleeping with him to know *that.*" The last part was spoken in a tone that clearly revealed her opinion of Roan's level of intelligence.

She was probably right.

With a final huff of annoyed breath, Molly flounced out the room, tutu bouncing.

"This is for you."

Jessa looked down into her lap and found an expensive-looking burgundy jeweler's box. She touched the top and looked up at Broder. "What is this?"

He pushed a hand through his hair. "Just a little something for your magick."

"Something for my magick?"

"A sigil, if you choose it. It might also be your talisman. Every witch and shaman has a focus object, something they layer their spells on. As long as they have this object on them, touching their skin, specifically, they have access to all the spells the talisman holds. They generally choose an animal or insect as a sigil. Then they find a talisman, a physical thing, like jewelry, that holds the sigil's image or shape."

Jessa opened the box and found a gorgeous sapphire, emerald, ruby, and gold dragonfly pendant on a chain. She gasped. "This is gorgeous."

"A witch's or shaman's sigil is her or his personal symbol of power. You should not feel obligated to take the dragonfly as your sigil just because I gave it to you. It's just temporary, until you can choose your own."

She touched one of the delicate-looking filigreed wings that were tipped with yellow citrine and emerald. It appeared fragile, but she could tell it was actually very strong. "Why a dragonfly?"

"The first thing I thought of when I thought of you was a Jujyfruit." He grinned at her. "But I also think of the dragonfly. It's a symbol of transformation and self-realization."

Jessa rose from the couch and walked over to him. She went up on her tiptoes and gave him a slow kiss on his cheek. "Thank you, Broder. It's probably the best, most thoughtful gift anyone has ever given me."

His body tensed and hers responded, but she forced herself to ease away from him. She slipped the pendant into his hand. "Will you please put it on me?"

The pendant looked extra fragile in his large, rough hand. She doubted his big fingers would even be able to work the clasp, but he managed to open the tiny lobster claw. She turned, pulling her hair up and allowing him to drape the cool chain against the warm flesh of her neck. His fingers brushed her nape and sent shivers down her spine.

She turned, looking down at the dragonfly that lay just above her breasts. "I choose the dragonfly as my sigil. As soon as I know how to layer spells on this talisman, I'll start working on it."

She remained there, standing just in front of him. She simply didn't want to move away. The heat of his body and the scent of him, all of it comforted her. A swell of emotion swamped her for a moment.

How she wanted to keep this man.

Reaching out slowly, she laid her palm against his chest, right over the place where his cold, soul-stealing demon sliver lay. "I know this relationship is doomed. I know that Loki will pull you from me. I want to hold myself away from you, to protect both of us from the future." She raised her gaze to his. "But I'm having trouble with that."

Broder cupped her nape and pulled her face flush against his, holding his mouth a breath's space from hers. "I want you to stay with me."

"I want that, too." Her breath warmed his lips. "I would. Always, if I could."

His gaze dropped to her lips. She could tell that he was fighting the urge to bite her, to mark her. She wanted him to do it. "You make me insane with need for you."

Her lips curled into a mischievous smile. "Likewise, I'm sure." Her hips pressed into his pelvis and she knew he would have her there, *right now*, up against the couch.

His mouth hovered over hers. "There's no going back from this. You touch me, I want you. There's a point when I have trouble stopping and I'm at it. Are you sure?"

She bit her lower lip. "I want you. I want you forever, Broder, but barring that . . . I want you right now."

His hands moved to the small of her back and pulled her shirt over her head. He dropped it to the floor, leaving her clad from the waist up in only her bra, and cupped the back of her head, fisting his fingers in her hair hard, just shy of bringing her pain, and brought his mouth down on hers. His tongue slipped into her mouth and her body tingled, electrified from his touch and what she knew was about to happen.

She pushed his shirt up, revealing his hard, muscled stomach and the amazing sculpted plane of his chest. His skin was warm to her touch, hard steel covered by soft satin. Once his shirt was removed, her fingers went to the button and zipper of his jeans at the same time his fingers went to hers. They fumbled together, both eager to feel bare skin against bare skin. They unclothed each other.

Soon her smooth body slid against his. It nearly made

her purr. Then she jolted, remembering something. "Erik isn't going to walk in on us, is he?"

Broder's full lips curved in a smile. He pushed her back, so she tumbled onto the couch. "He's gone for the morning."

"Good thing." She relaxed back into the pillows.

He stood, his gaze traveling from the crown of her head to the tips of her toes and not missing an inch of bare skin in between. All she wore was the dragonfly pendant. "Have I mentioned lately that you're gorgeous?"

She smiled, her cheeks heating. "A few times."

"Then let me show you." He came down over her body. "With my hands and my tongue and my—"

She gasped as his fingers moved between her legs. "Yes, please show me," she breathed. "I want to be shown."

His lips brushed against hers with gentleness surprising from a man like him. She fought through the fog in her mind, trying to grasp some thread of sanity. It kept slipping away like the memory of a dream in the morning. It didn't help that he was stroking her nipple, making her squirm. Molten pleasure warmed her once more. He touched her as if her body were completely owned by him.

She wished it could be true for forever, instead of on a temporary basis.

Jessa snaked her hand between their bodies, grasped his cock at the base, then pumped him against her palm. He groaned low in his throat. She loved the sounds he made, and loved the feel of him so weighty and hard in her hand. Loved even more that it was *her* touch that made him that way.

Unable to resist the delectable spread of his muscled chest and stomach, she leaned in and scattered kisses along his heated flesh. She licked and sucked her way over the luscious expanse and made her way downward, over his rippled, hard abdomen, finally reaching his cock. It was a beautiful organ. She wanted to lick it, suck it. She laved the smooth head, wanting to feel it against her tongue.

Broder's body went stiff and he let out a low, sexy groan,

letting his head fall back against the headrest of the couch. She licked again, this time tracing her tongue up the full length of it. She wanted to make him come this way, but first she wanted to make him crazy.

"Fuck, Jessa," Broder groaned. "You're teasing me."

She smiled around the head of his cock. He sounded so tortured. Okay, fine. He didn't want her to tease? She sucked him into the warm recesses of her mouth, drew him out, and pushed him back in again very slowly. She couldn't get the whole of him in her mouth, but she did her best, letting her tongue explore him from the base to the crown.

Broder exhaled hard and fisted his hands in her hair, letting loose a string of words in some language she thought must be Norwegian.

Her own body reacted to the act of giving him pleasure, her nipples going hard and a slow, sweet ache beginning between her thighs. She found a measure of control in this act that she enjoyed. He was at her mercy in this moment.

She held all the power now.

Shifting her knees, she set herself to pleasing him, fondling the base of him as she drew his cock deep into her mouth and sucked it in again, over and over. His cock glistened with her saliva. He seemed especially sensitive in the area just under the head of his cock, so she tongued it and rubbed her lips over it, making him groan her name.

"Bad girl. You're going to make me come," he growled.

She grinned up at him. "That's the general idea."

He growled and pulled her up, forcing her onto his lap to straddle him. Clearly he had other ideas. His cock met her sex, but did not slide in. Instead he crushed her to his chest, his fingers tangling in her hair, and kissed her deeply.

Broder let his hand slide down, over her mound, where he stroked her clit with his broad thumb until she gasped into his open mouth. Rotating his thumb against her, he caressed her until she throbbed, until she was up against a looming climax and pleasure poured through her body in waves.

"I want to watch you come," he purred.

She moved her hips, forcing a bit more pressure against his thumb. "I'm close." She closed her eyes, amazing pleasure coursing through her body.

"Not yet, my treasure. I want *you* to watch yourself come as well."

She opened her eyes. "What?"

He guided her to stand up, turned her around, and drew her back down onto his lap, parting her thighs as wide as they would go and hooking her inner knees on the outside of his legs so she couldn't close them. Then he pointed straight ahead of them.

Then she understood. The full-length antique mirror stood directly across from them, reflecting their every move. The mirror's reflection showed her looking bed tousled and well loved. Her nipples were reddened and hard, and her sex appeared pink, excited, and swollen. The image of herself so aroused was strangely erotic.

Broder placed his mouth near her ear and spoke, raising all the tiny hairs along her body. "The reflection of you kneeling between my legs with your mouth on me drove me insane. Now it's your turn."

He cupped her breasts, rolling her nipples between his stroking fingers, making ecstasy shoot straight to her groin. Her hips thrust forward of their own accord, wanting him to fill her. She felt so empty.

"I'm going to make you come, Jessa," he murmured. "I don't want to see your gaze move from that mirror. Understand?"

She nodded, her lips parted slightly and color staining her cheeks. This man was the only one in the world who could make her feel this way—so desperate for his touch. She'd get down on her knees and beg right now if it meant he'd touch her more.

He moved his big hands over her abdomen to her inner thighs. "A little more."

She gave him what he wanted—would give him anything.

He pulled her labia apart, then dipped his finger down,

gathered moisture, and slicked it over her swollen, throbbing clit. "So pretty. So perfect," he murmured, stroking the pad of his finger over it, soft and slow.

She moaned. Jessa's hips jerked involuntarily as she watched him caress her so intimately in the mirror's reflection. His hand looked huge and strong against the slenderness of her thighs. Almost panting, she watched his finger move up and down.

"This will feel even better," he rasped. His voice held the first hint that his incredible level of control might be slipping. She wanted to see him lose it. He pushed two fingers deep inside her sex. "It's hot in there, and so soft." She watched, moaning as his thick digits disappeared into the depths of her and then reappeared over and over as he thrust.

"Do you like that, *skatten min*?" His voice was a deeper rasp now and she could feel the press of his massive erection at her back. This had to be killing him as much as it was killing her.

"Yes," she said breathlessly. "But I want your cock, Broder. I want you to fill me."

He groaned. "*Soon.* Is this going to make you come?"

She made a small, helpless sound at the back of her throat. *"Yes."*

"Come on, baby," he purred. "Give in."

A powerful climax crashed into her, stealing her breath. For a moment she couldn't even moan. She watched her body in the mirror. Her face had flushed and her body shook with gentle, pleasurable spasms, the muscles of her sex pulsing.

Before the waves of her climax had completely ebbed away, he shifted her to the couch, grabbed her hips, and positioned the head of his cock at her entrance. Jessa's breath hissed out as she watched his big body moving over her, then looked down to see his cock push deep inside her. She grabbed his arms and arched her back, panting as he filled her deeper and deeper.

Broder tipped his head back and groaned as he pressed into her farther, stretching her muscles so exquisitely. He pushed in until he was seated to the base of his cock within her. "I'm going to make love to you until you can't see straight, *skatten min*." He pulled back out of her slowly, making her feel every inch of his cock.

She bit her lower lip and moaned. "Yes, please." Her voice came out a breathy, lust-filled whisper. "Take me deep. Take me hard, Broder."

"As you wish."

He grabbed her hips and began to thrust into her just the way she'd asked for. She held on tight to his arms, her fingernails digging in, the relentless, hard slam of him vibrating through her body. With every thrust, the head of his cock sent skitters of pleasure up her spine.

As a climax built to a pitch, she watched the muscles in Broder's shoulders, chest, and arms work. She watched his hips thrust back and forth and the easy glide of his cock in and out of her body.

Then she looked up into his face and her heart dropped out of her chest. Their gazes caught and held. Such emotion roiled in his eyes; it took her breath away. It was as if Broder had added a bit of his own soul to hers as they made love. The knowledge of how much pleasure they gave and received was intoxicating.

Another climax overtook her body, forcing her to break their shared gaze. Arching her back, her head falling against the headrest, she shuddered, moaned, and shook, allowing the orgasm to completely dominate her body. Spasms of pleasure coursed through her, causing her muscles to pulse around Broder's still-thrusting cock.

Broder rasped out a few words in some language she didn't recognize, then closed his eyes and groaned. Jessa felt his cock jump deep inside her.

When it was over and they were both boneless with satisfied sexual lassitude, Broder slid down to the carpet on the floor, taking her with him. Together they snuggled on the soft rug.

Sighing, Jessa smiled and rested her head on his chest. To think that this wouldn't last forever—that they wouldn't always have each other, or that they wouldn't be able to suddenly give in to each other's desires—was unthinkable to her in this moment.

And, for as long as she could, she'd keep it that way.

Jessa hummed to herself as she opened her bedroom door. Broder was talking to Erik in the kitchen, one of the rare times he'd allowed her out of his sight. She entered the twilight-darkened room and sought the sheaf of papers on the table near the fireplace. Tonight she wanted to learn how to layer her new dragonfly talisman, even if it was only with two little parlor trick spells. They were called sun and moon charms, both harmless.

Somewhere behind her in the gloom, a man cleared his throat.

She stilled, all the hair on the back of her neck rising. Then she slowly turned. A man stood at the end of her bed. He wore an expensive-looking gray suit with a tastefully muted tie and a pair of black sunglasses. His dark hair was slicked back from his angular, pretty-boy face and his shoes were shiny and black and had probably cost a bundle. He looked like he had a huge ego.

She knew exactly who this was.

"Hello, Jessamine. So, I see you have my Broder thoroughly bewitched. I didn't think that was possible."

She narrowed her eyes and lifted her chin, her entire body tensing. She understood she was in the presence of a god, but she just couldn't muster any respect. "Any woman would be bewitching to Broder after a thousand years of abstinence."

He took a careful step toward her, putting her on edge. "No, sweet Jessa. One would think so, but one would be wrong. Broder is a much different animal. It could never have been just *any* woman for Broder. It had to be you."

"Are you here to take him away from me?"

"I'm here to encourage you to leave him first."

Her jaw locked. "No."

"I *will* take him from you. He's one of my best." He smiled to show sharp white teeth and spread his perfectly manicured hands. "Do you really think I'm generous enough to let one of my men go, even for such a noble cause as true love?" Loki's voice grew cold and hard. "This is not a fairy tale."

"Gee, and I thought you were such a nice guy."

"I am many things, but *nice guy* isn't one of them." He walked to the side, his polished leather shoes sounding on the polished wood floor. "As I was saying, it's time for you to go. Your people need you and they want you. Broder is afraid to let you go, but there is no need. Your people mean you no harm."

She raised her eyebrows. "I'm supposed to trust you?"

He spread his hands and grinned. "I am a god."

"Exactly." She paused. "I couldn't go to the seidhr even if I wanted to." She gave him a stern look. "My great-aunt told me to leave the keep and start walking, that their magick would guide me to them, but how would I avoid all the bloodthirsty Blight on my way to them?"

"Simple." Loki's perfect lips curled into a perfect smile. "I will protect you if you leave."

"There you go with that trust thing again."

His smile grew larger. "I want you out of Broder's life. *I will protect you* from the Blight should you decide to make your way to the seidhr enclave."

"No need. I'm not going. I'll stay with Broder until the day you take him from me."

"Just go, Jessamine. It will be easier on Broder if you leave before I pull him away from you. If you love him the way I know you do, you'll do the right thing."

"Maybe I think the right thing is to stay with him."

The god smiled. "You know I'll just rip him away anyway, Jessa, and you know, deep down, that every minute you spend with Broder corresponds directly to the weight of your heartache when he's gone. Remember Brandon? It will be *so* much worse than that."

And, just like that, Loki was gone.

TWENTY-ONE

The phone rang in the middle of the night; the phone that wasn't supposed to ring, the one that wasn't even plugged into the wall. Jessa rolled onto her back, the *ring ring* of the phone driving spikes through her head. It was amazing that Broder hadn't woken up. He was right beside her.

She sat up. Or maybe it wasn't amazing at all.

Pushing the blankets away, she left the comforting warmth of Broder's side and answered the phone. "Hello?"

"Hello, Jessa." It was Carolyn again.

"What kind of mojo did you lay on Broder so he wouldn't wake up?" Her voice sounded antagonistic.

"He doesn't need to be a part of this."

"Did you hurt him?"

"All we did was tune the sound of the phone to your ears only. Jessa, it's time you left that house, left Broder, and started the next phase of your life. We want you to come to us."

She chewed her lower lip and glanced at Broder in the bed. The thought of leaving him made her chest heavy and her blood flow sluggish. She couldn't leave him. She was physically unable.

"It's the best thing, for you and for him." Carolyn paused, then she said softly, "You *know* it's for the best."

"Have you and Loki been talking?"

Carolyn said nothing for a long moment. Then finally, "Of course not." Her voice was earnest, a bit offended. "Loki has been good to us . . . with a few exceptions. All the same, Loki is not to be trusted. I don't take advice from him."

"So I shouldn't, either."

"No, you shouldn't. Loki follows his own selfish agenda. Whatever he may have told you to do, you can know it fits his plans."

"He told me to go to you."

She paused. "Well, I hope you do come to us, but not because of Loki. He cares for no one but himself. The gods, they're like humans with vast amounts of power. Loki is what you might call a psychopath."

"Yay for psychopaths with vast amounts of power."

Carolyn laughed. "There are more in this world than you might imagine."

"That explains so much."

"Come home, Jessa. Come now. Just step outside those gates. We'll guide you the rest of the way."

"What about the Blight? They're hunting me." She touched the scar on her neck. "If I leave the keep, they might attack. Loki said he would protect me, but I don't believe him." Just as she didn't believe Carolyn.

"You will be safe. They won't hurt you."

Jessa snorted at her confidence, the memory of her recent ordeal extremely fresh in her mind. "How do *you* know? Do you have some special relationship with the B—" Jessa shivered and blinked, a strange sense of calm stealing over her body. Her skin tingled and the doubt she'd had slid away from her mind.

Why shouldn't she believe Carolyn?

"*Trust us*, Jessamine. We're your family."

"Of course. I'm sorry, Carolyn. If you say I'll be safe, I will be."

"Good. Now come to us, Jessa."

She studied Broder. He lay on his back in the bed, the sheets in a tangle around his waist and his gorgeous chest bared. His hair was strewn dark and tangled on the pillow and one strong arm was thrown up over his head. "I don't know if I can leave him."

"*You must.* Loki will take him from you soon. It will be easier to leave him now, without the tearful farewell. Better for Broder. You want what's best for him, right? Because you love him."

Another little shiver went through Jessa. Carolyn was right. Yet . . .

"I'll think about it." She set the telephone back into the receiver.

She sat on the edge of the bed and shivered, watching the rise and fall of Broder's chest. She believed Carolyn was correct. It was time to go. Time to start the next phase of her life. Time to discover who she truly was.

She touched Broder's chest and he didn't stir. "I love you. I'll always love you, Broder." Loki was right that every moment she spent with him now directly corresponded to the weight of her heartache after they were parted. She imagined the moment it would happen and grief clouded the back of her throat. "I love you, but it's time to let you go," she whispered.

There was no denying that she'd need to eventually.

Jessa rose, found a piece of paper and a pen, and wrote a letter.

A half hour later, a heavy sensation in the center of her chest, she stepped beyond the gates of Broder's keep, the extremely sharp sword she'd taken in a sheath and strapped crosswise at her back for easy access. She'd left Loki's knife for Broder.

She had the assurance of a god and a witch that she would be protected from demons on this journey, but she was used to taking care of herself.

Immediately, a sense of where she needed to go filled her. It was as though an internal compass had started in the center of her chest, leading her in the right direction. Closing her eyes for a moment, she took a deep breath of the chill night air and stared down the dark, narrow road. Her mind strayed to Broder. *How could she leave him this way?* It wasn't right. Both Carolyn and Loki had said this was the best thing for Broder, but how could not saying good-bye be the best thing?

She took a step backward, away from the road.

Right after that moment of doubt slid through her mind, she had another odd shiver, this time stronger. Yes, *of course* this was the right thing to do. Better to cut ties with Broder like this, without an emotional good-bye, and before Loki could yank him away. She didn't want their end to be on Loki's terms.

Touching the comforting weight of the dragonfly pendant that nestled in the hollow of her throat, she stepped onto the next path she'd take in her life.

"I can feel her." Thorgest turned from the large window of the library, where the huge full moon hung pregnant in the early morning sky. "She's on her way here now." He turned and stared pointedly at Roan. "You see? *That's* how it's done. I knew I should have had Carolyn do the job from the beginning."

Roan shifted in the leather chair near the blazing fireplace. Across from him, Carolyn favored him with a smug smile. Roan curled his lip at her and glanced at Thorgest. "I think it's risky. If she finds out she's been manipulated, she'll leave us."

Thorgest narrowed his ice blue eyes at him. "Then I'm guessing the lass best never find out, ye ken?"

Carolyn's eyes hardened. "We did the best thing for the girl. You know that, Roan. She needed to get out of that keep, away from that man. We can give her what she never had, a family." She smiled poisonously. "Thorgest and I are her blood; we want what's best for her."

Yes, except Jessa had had a family—she'd had the woman Jessa thought of as her aunt Margaret, the woman that Abigail and Michael had wanted to raise her in the event of their deaths. Abigail had never wanted Jessa to have *this* family and Roan understood why.

"You want what's best for *you*," Roan retorted, his voice bitter. "Don't deny it, Carolyn."

Carolyn's lip curled into a snarl. She leaned forward and opened her mouth, but Thorgest barked at her, "*Haud yer whist*, the both of ye!" Thorgest turned back to the window. "She'll be here before dawn. Best be ready."

The road stretched into the night, a gravel affair she would have expected to see in rural Alabama, not in the Scottish Highlands. Refuse scattered the road on either side in weed-choked heaps.

Her feet hurt from walking. Hitching rides had brought her close to this place, but she'd had to walk the last five miles of desolate road. Hitching wasn't really her norm. In fact, this was the first time she'd ever done it in her entire life. It had just seemed like the *right thing to do*, as sure as the esoteric sense of direction she had now told her the enclave was somewhere down this road. Magick drove her, she was sure of it. It was a heavy guiding sensation in her chest, leading her to where she needed to be.

She was close to her destination.

But this last bit of the way was enough to make her want to turn back. She shivered a little and held fast. She'd come this far, it was just a bit farther.

She hovered at the mouth of the road, the wind whispering through the branches of nearby trees. Above her the moon was a huge, swollen ball, but clouds covered it sporadically, dimming its light.

If this had been a horror movie she was watching, she would have screamed at the heroine, *Run, run away!* But her great-aunt had led her here and down that path lay the answers to the questions that burned in her mind, and she would risk her life for those answers. She was willing to face the menace of this road and whatever lay at its end to clear up the murkiness of her life's path.

Pulling the sword sheathed across her back as if for reassurance, she took her first step toward the end, both hands tight on the handle. Her shoes crunched in the gravel as she made her way forward, chill air causing the hair at her nape to rise. Somewhere in the distance a dog barked, then another.

Midway down the trash-strewn narrow road, the handle of the sword pulsed against the skin of her palm. She jerked in surprise, nearly dropping it. Peering at the handle in the dim light she noticed it was marked with runes a lot like the ones she'd seen on the inside of Broder's duster.

Her blood turned to slushy ice.

Gripping the warmly pulsing handle, she turned in a tight circle, watching for any sign of movement. Her heart beating out a too-fast rhythm and perspiration slicking her grasp, her gaze flicked from a ripped black trash bag flapping in the breeze to a soaked box that appeared filled with rotted fruit to a decaying, rusted refrigerator turned on its side.

Nothing.

Silence.

The handle of the sword throbbed dully.

Her breath came faster, her body quivering. All her senses told her there was something out there, watching her, stalking her. Then, from the corner of her eye, she saw something dark shoot toward her.

She whirled to face it, sword held high. All the panic left her and into that space rushed every bit of the training she'd received. Her scar throbbed along the length of her neck, reminding her of the stakes.

The demon charged her, white fangs gleaming, and she swung the sword, knowing that if she didn't separate his head from his neck, she'd be his liquid breakfast.

"Jessa?"

Broder murmured her name, turning over to find the bed empty. The pillow was indented and the sheets and blankets were tangled as though she'd just thrown them aside.

Disappointment made him lower his head to the pillow and groan. He'd been looking forward to pulling her against him, giving her a kiss, and seeing where it led. Now that he'd had a taste of her, he couldn't get enough.

She'd probably hit the exercise room already. It was her usual schedule, working out first thing in the morning, though, if so, she'd woken up earlier than usual today. It wasn't even light outside yet.

He forced himself to sit up, needing to go find her. He had things he needed to tell her. Big, heavy things that lay on his heart like hundred-pound weights yet they had all the substance of a fog at dawn. Loki would be the sun that burned away that fog. All the emotion Broder had for Jessa—nothing he said, no matter how much it mattered to him, would make a difference in the end. He was doomed to spend the rest of his life without her.

It didn't matter. He still needed to tell her how he felt.

He found a pair of jeans. Once he'd pulled them on, he turned to walk from the room, but a flash of blue caught his attention before he reached the doorway. On the bedside table an envelope lay propped against the lamp, his name scrawled on the front. A note.

Rage immediately filled him. There was only one reason Jessa would leave a note.

He strode over, ripped the envelope open, and scanned it. She'd gone to the seidhr enclave.

Swearing in four different languages, he tossed the paper to the floor and raced from the room. She could be in danger. He had to get to her before she took a step into that coven.

"Broder, don't you fucking dare."

Broder halted at the sound of Loki's voice behind him. Slowly, he turned to find the god dressed in some polished, expensive suit, with what looked to be a two-hundred-dollar plum-colored tie. "Loki. What an unexpected surprise."

"Spare me the sarcasm. Just where did you think you were headed, Broder?"

His jaw locked.

Loki paced toward him. "You look pissed off. Too pissed to answer." He waved his hand. "Don't bother. I know where you were going and you can stop right there, brother. You know you're forbidden from setting foot in the seidhr enclave."

All the Brotherhood were forbidden, but he, especially, was barred with violent force. Getting the seidhr simply to rune his coat had been a battle.

"What will you do to me if I go anyway?" Broder snorted. "Kill me? Please, do that, Loki. The time is long past that I should be dust in the wind."

Loki favored him with a particularly malicious smile. "Oh, come now, you know I'm far more creative than that. Death is way too easy a punishment for directly disobeying me."

"I love her."

Loki's smile faded, but the cold look in his eyes was even worse. "You gave up your right to love long ago, Broder. Your right to emotion like that was washed away in a deluge of blood spilled by your own hand. Your soul is mine to keep. You can't give it to anyone else." He smiled, brightly this time, as if they were talking about something pleasant. "Anyway, if you really love her, you'll let her go. She's where she needs to be now. She's with her people. Leave her be. All is as it should be."

Broder looked away from Loki, not wanting to accept the truth of those words. *Leave her be.* If he truly loved her, he should do exactly that.

"Ah, I see on your face that I've broken through your thick head. Excellent." Loki's voice sent a chill through the room. "Don't disobey me, Broder. I will freeze the Earth for a thousand years before I let you set foot in the seidhr compound without massive punishment."

And in a blink, he was gone.

Broder stood in the center of the room, staring down at the crumpled letter on the floor.

If you love her . . . leave her be. She's where she needs to be now.

TWENTY-TWO

Jessa leapt out of the way, narrowly missing the swipe of an enormous hand. This was probably a low-level demon and he looked it—an unintelligent grunt. Pivoting on the ball of her foot, she brought her boot around and clipped the thing in the side of the head.

The demon staggered to the side, shaking his ringing head, as she spun away. A split second later he lunged for her again, catching her by her shirt. The material ripped as she lurched to the side and nearly tripped, her sword swinging wildly. Her heart thudded. This was not the time to lose control.

Listing to the side to catch her balance, she madly swiped with the sword, cutting only air. The demon sensed he had her, growled something in a foreign language, and leapt. Staggering backward, she swung again. This time the tip of the blade sliced through fabric, bit into the demon's upper chest. It had been purely luck.

The thing roared, blood coursing down his chest, but this was no Loki blade she wielded; he didn't explode into ice fragments. The wound only seemed to enrage him. He stalked toward her again.

Jessa retreated backward, sword hanging loose in one hand. She had to kill this thing. It was her life or his. She stumbled over a piece of refuse, nearly falling on her ass. The demon smiled, sensing he had her. Whimpering deep in her throat, she slouched her shoulders. *Oh, God, she was going to die.*

The agent's smile widened.

Good. Stupid, gullible thing.

Jessa leapt forward, right into the demon, bringing her fist around into the tender flesh of his nose. The demon howled, his head snapping to the side. Her hand burst with pain, but that was no matter now. With a two-handed grip on the sword handle, she pivoted, bringing the blade around to bite into the nape of his neck with as much force as she could muster. The blade was incredibly sharp and it slid into the demon's flesh like butter.

And stuck a little over halfway through.

She released the handle of the sword and stepped away from the demon, her chest squeezing painfully and little sounds that weren't at all feigned issuing from her throat. She'd taken her shot . . . and failed.

The demon stared at her, wide-eyed, as though surprised to have a sword stuck in his neck. Blood coursed from all three of the wounds she'd inflicted. At least there was that.

At least she'd fought like a banshee for her life.

He took a step toward her, his lip curling, eyes bled black, a snarl ripping from his throat. She closed her eyes and let go. This was it. She was done. The demon's breath teased her face.

Ice exploded all over her and the sound of her sword clattering to the ground met her ears.

She opened her eyes to find ice caught in her hair, splattering her face and clothes. Letting out a small sound of surprise, she stepped backward and slipped in it.

The demon was gone.

Bending down, she snagged up her sword, still too shaky to celebrate her victory. Apparently partway through worked, too. Hallelujah.

Just as she straightened, melting ice slowly sliding down the blade of her sword, she heard a series of low snarls and growls coming from all around her. Her head jerked up. Dogs? Right, she should be so lucky.

Several demons stepped onto the road from their hiding places in the brush.

Jessa stood stock-still for a moment, then bolted down the road as fast as her legs would work. The demons pounded behind her and she ran faster, her chest bursting, her veins pumping. Her only chance was to get to the enclave.

In the lightening early dawn sky she glimpsed the glint of heavy front gates. That had to be it. The seidhr enclave.

Behind her a demon grabbed for her back, his fingertips just brushing her shoulder. *Oh, God,* she chanted in her head. *Please, no.* She pushed herself even harder, using every ounce of her will to widen the gap.

Jessa squinted, seeing a figure in the distance standing in front of the gates. She missed a step and stumbled. That magickal guiding sensation in her chest grew stronger at the sight of this person, whoever he was, and it did seem to be a *he*, by consideration of the build.

This was the person who'd been calling to her. It hadn't been Carolyn at all.

Oh, hell, she hoped he wasn't demon. Had she been tricked? Was this another trap set by the Blight? If it was, she was dead.

She had no choice but to continue, even if she might be running straight into the arms of a high-level agent of the Blight. Veering off the path meant losing momentum, tumbling through trash. Her grip on her sword tightened. All she could do now was run and fight. Fight to the bitter end.

As she drew closer to the figure, she was able to see his face. He was an old man with white hair and a long beard braided into two plaits. His eyes weren't old looking, though. Even from a distance she noted their sharp, bright blueness. This man was an ancient shaman.

This man was Thorgest Egilson, her great-grandfather.

Thorgest raised both his hands, palms facing out. Some force pulsed through the air, seeming to make reality itself bow outward for a moment.

Behind her she heard the now-familiar sound of demons

exploding into ice. In the same moment she reached him, stumbling forward into his arms. She staggered against him, but he held her up with surprisingly steely arms for such an old man. Her sword clattered to the ground at his feet.

Chest heaving, she pushed up away from him, looking over her shoulder. All the demons had exploded at once, leaving the road awash in ice crystals that gleamed and caught the early morning light.

Jessa could say nothing, but it was the most beautiful thing she'd ever seen. Clutching her chest, she concentrated on breathing and staving off a heart attack.

"Welcome, my kin," said the man in a rich baritone. "Welcome, my great-granddaughter." His accent was thickly Scottish.

The first moment she could make a sound, she wheezed, "Thorgest." Her hand hurt like hell from punching the demon. She cradled it, knowing she'd have an awful bruise.

"Yes, my name is Thorgest Egilson."

"Demons," she rasped. "You said I would be safe." She straightened, finally regaining her breath a little.

Thorgest looked unconcerned. He gazed down the road where she'd almost lost her life. She guessed that if you could use magick to explode demons there wasn't much to fear. "One of Loki's tricks, I expect."

She closed her eyes, marshaling a sudden rush of rage. *She hated Loki.*

He motioned to her. "I apologize about the road ye walked, but there's a reason it looks that way. It discourages people from traveling down it, through not only its appearance but also wards. I feared its magick might dissuade ye, but I'm happy to see ye were strong enough to resist."

"It was the demons I was mostly concerned with," she gritted out, gathering her sword from the ground.

She stood, staring down the road in question. Why had she ever left Broder? Her heart ached. It was the dumbest thing she'd ever done. This had been a mistake. She needed to go back to him, demons or no. . . .

She shivered and shook her head. What had she just been

thinking? She couldn't take that kind of a risk. It was far better to stay here, where it was safe.

Jessa turned toward Thorgest. "Did you say wards?" Her ability to think had gone sluggish and slow. She shook her head to try to clear it, but it was hard.

Her great-grandfather motioned to her again. "Come into the compound, Jessa. I ken ye have questions and you need cleaning up."

"I have so many questions."

"And I will answer all of them for ye."

She still didn't move toward him, but she wasn't really sure what was holding her back.

Her great-grandfather shifted his weight and sighed a little. "It's that man, perhaps? Broder Calderson?"

Immediately, she bristled. "You say his name like it's a disease. He's a good man who has been protecting me."

Her great-grandfather snorted. "Protecting ye. Ah, child, I've so much to tell ye."

She didn't move, didn't respond. She didn't like that cold, hard note in his voice. It sent up a warning flag. She especially didn't like it in relation to a man she'd come to care very deeply for.

Her great-grandfather gave a little sigh again. "I see ye've fallen for him. I suppose it's to be expected. The men of the Brotherhood are strong, mysterious, and—"

"That's true, but that's not why I care for him. I'm not that shallow. Broder is far more than a pretty face. He's intelligent, protective, interesting as all hell. He cares more for others than he does for himself and he's the first person in my life, other than Margaret and maybe my best friend, who ever really took the time to know me." Her temper flared, making her take a step back.

Maybe coming here *had* been a mistake.

"All right." Her great-grandfather held out a hand. "I understand. Ye can go back to him whenever ye wish."

Jessa's mouth snapped shut. "Of course I can."

"Please, let's not talk of this man any more right now. I

want to get to know the great-granddaughter I thought long dead."

"You thought I was . . . dead?"

He nodded. "Come with me. Let's talk. I'll answer all yer questions, if ye'll answer mine. I'll finally ken my long-lost kinswoman and, finally, ye will know who ye truly are."

If there had been any question of her not following him down the rest of the road and through the gates she could see in the distance, those words had eradicated it. She fell into step with her great-grandfather and continued the rest of the way into the seidhr enclave.

She barely even felt the snick of the powerful magick that closed behind her as they continued down the road toward a huge set of gates and a tall gray stone wall.

Dawn lightened the horizon in earnest when the gates swung open, revealing anything but the "compound" she'd been imagining in her head. A narrow, curving, tree-lined road stretched from the gates to an enormous gray stone mansion. To both sides of the road lay manicured lawns and in the distance she caught a glimpse of outbuildings. From somewhere on the property, a cow mooed in protest.

"Is that . . . livestock I hear?"

"We grow all our own food here," Thorgest said as they made their way toward the massive house. "Produce our own dairy, eat only organic meat raised right here on the property."

Jessa flinched. That meant they killed their own food, too. "I'm a vegetarian. Margaret raised me that way."

"Ah." Thorgest smiled. "To each her own."

They reached the house. Shouldering her backpack, filled with the few possessions she'd decided to take with her, she climbed the wide stone stairs. The stairs reminded her of something you'd find in front of a huge library in New York City or Los Angeles. Through the front door they entered a posh foyer.

Jessa turned in a circle, whistling low. The floor beneath her feet was made of polished marble, a curving staircase led to the second floor, and an enormous glimmering and twinkling chandelier hung above their heads. It was strange to see a mansion like this way out here in the northernmost reaches of Scotland, even stranger to see it following the trash-strewn road she'd traveled in on.

"Can I ask a rude question?" Her voice echoed through the immense chamber.

"Ye may ask anything ye wish."

"How does the seidhr come by all its money?"

Thorgest laughed, the sound echoing throughout the chamber. "That's a good question, me lass. In the beginning our money came from our magick. Our members have worked for kings and heads of state all throughout the centuries and still do, occasionally. Ever heard of Merlin?"

Jessa's eyes widened. "He was a fictional character."

"Ah, *no*, he wasn't." Thorgest nodded and smiled, his two long beard braids bobbing. "He was a real person and he was one of us. Ye can be proud of yer heritage. But there aren't many of us and we're hunted. So we live communally, for our protection. Our wealth has come from our members, though careful investments over the years have helped us prosper. Come." He motioned at her to follow and crossed the wide marble floor of the foyer to one of the doors leading off from it.

They entered a large room that seemed to be both a library and a meeting room. Books lined tall bookshelves on all the walls and a long, polished wood conference table dominated the center of the room, framed by a huge window. A fire burned in an enormous hearth on the far end of the chamber. Three people stood near it.

As she and Thorgest approached, she spotted Carolyn right away since she looked so much like her biological mother it made her heart try to rise up into her throat. The first man was tall and buff, with sandy brown hair and a strong, handsome face set with intelligent, light blue eyes. She didn't know him.

But the second man she recognized.

• • •

"You."

Roan watched as Jessa's eyes narrowed as soon as she caught sight of him.

"You incredible bastard," she bellowed. "How dare you try and *kidnap* me!" She stalked toward him as she yelled, looking ready to punch him in the face, but instead she jabbed her index finger into his chest. He would have taken the punch, welcomed it. He deserved it.

Gods, but she looked like her mother—all that long, dark blond hair and the fire in her big brown eyes. She was beautiful and she took his breath away, but not with romantic attraction. Compared to him, she was an infant in this world . . . and he'd been in love with her mother. But for a twist of fate, she could be his daughter. All the same, he thought she was magnificent.

This woman was far too good for the likes of a man like Broder Calderson.

He held out a hand to stop her tirade. "Look, I'm not going to apologize for what I did. You had no idea the danger you were living with. You needed out of that keep and away from Broder immediately. It was a desperate move and I failed, but my intentions were good—to protect you from evil."

"Evil?" She whirled to face Thorgest. "What is he talking about?"

Thorgest looked way too satisfied for Roan's taste. Roan realized he may have just given the old man exactly the opening he'd wanted. At the moment he found he was not happy to give Thorgest *anything* he wanted.

Their leader stepped forward. "He's talking about Broder, lass. He's talking about what we need to tell you about him."

"I'm sick of hearing all these vague things about Broder meant to make me afraid of him. He's a good man. He's saved my life time and again. He's protected me and shown me caring. He's supported me more than anyone. *Tell me* why you think he's a dangerous man *right now*. No more ambiguity." She set her hand on her hip and stuck her chin out. That was when Roan saw it. She loved Broder Calderson.

Och, poor lass.

"We're not going to talk about Broder right now. He can wait," Thorgest replied with that same satisfied smile on his face. He knew he had Jessa right where he wanted her. "We're going to talk about your mother."

It was as if all the air left the girl for a moment. When she inhaled, her breath was shaky. Broder, at least for the moment, had been completely forgotten. She took her hand off her hip, her entire demeanor changing. "I want to know everything."

"And I want to tell you everything, lass." Thorgest led her over to the couch and sat.

Jessa hesitated a moment, looking pale and nervous.

"First, let me introduce ye to everyone in the room. Ye've met Roan, my second in command when he isn't arsing things up." Thorgest motioned to Carolyn. "And ye know Carolyn Egilson, yer great-aunt." Carolyn offered Jessa a winning smile that Roan knew all too well was fake.

"That's Sam over there," Thorgest said, motioning to the shaman standing near the fireplace. "He's a powerful shaman and a distant cousin of yours. He spends most his time at the enclave in Baltimore."

Jessa paled. "Baltimore, *Maryland*? I grew up in Cleveland Park, in D.C. There were seidhr right up the road from me and I didn't know it?"

Sam's face had a grim set to it. He probably hated what was going on just as much as Roan did. "We had no idea you were alive, Jessamine. Your mother and father did a good job of hiding you from us."

"Yes, why did they do that, by the way?" She looked at each of them in turn, suspicion tingeing her expression.

"Patience, Jessamine. Your questions will be answered all in good time." Carolyn smiled widely at her.

"Sam, Carolyn, and Roan are here because they're to be

yer teachers." Thorgest smiled. "With yer bloodline, ye're bound to be a powerful witch, but if you dinna get the proper training, all you'll be able to do is tricks fit for entertaining at a child's birthday party. Now, we talk of yer mother."

Roan went for the door. He didn't want to talk about Abigail.

"Wait," called Thorgest. "Stay. Ye have a part in this story, too."

He paused in the doorframe and turned around. "My part to play in this story is just as shameful as the way I tried to take Jessamine from Broder."

Jessa bristled visibly. "I thought you didn't regret it."

"I don't regret the motivation behind the attempt; I regret scaring you."

She made a scoffing sound and crossed her arms over her chest. "Don't worry. Your attempt was so inept it barely frightened me."

Thorgest guffawed. "Lass, ye are very much like your mother. Let me tell ye how."

And with those words Thorgest ensured that Jessa's attention was completely centered on him once again.

"My granddaughter, yer mother . . . her name was Abigail. . . ."

Roan sat in a nearby chair and listened uncomfortably to the story he knew by heart. How Abigail had disobeyed her grandfather by choosing her heart over the man who'd been chosen for her—*him*. In every word that unfurled from Thorgest's tongue, his heart ached again.

Thorgest told her about how much Roan had loved her and how he'd tried to manipulate her into staying here and giving up her relationship with Michael. Roan gritted his teeth, noticing that Thorgest managed to leave out his own cruel manipulations.

"So my mother ran away from here, ran away from you." She narrowed her eyes at Thorgest and then turned to look at Roan. "And you."

Roan shifted in his seat and caught her gaze, holding it intensely. He spoke with all the emotion and conviction he had in his heart when he thought of Jessamine's mother. "I loved Abigail. I wanted her with every breath I took. I would have died for her." He paused. "But she didn't love me back. So, yes, she ran away from me." He paused. "She ran from Thorgest, too."

Thorgest gave him a sharp look, but wisely kept his old yap shut.

"She loved Michael, my father."

Roan nodded. "Truly and deeply." He hated how the pain shone so clearly and brightly in his voice. He wanted to shut it all away, hide it from her. Suddenly he felt naked, not only in front of Jessa, but in front of Thorgest as well . . . and that was unacceptable.

Jessa didn't say a word. She only stared at him as though seeing him for the first time. She blinked and started to say something, but he didn't let her, making a sharp gesture with his arm.

He stood. "I'll be taking my leave now." Then he strode toward the door. He couldn't think of anything more painful than sitting around and listening to a rehash of this particular bit of his history.

Her hand fisted tightly in her lap, Jessa watched Roan leave. His dark gray eyes had held more than a hint of grief when he'd talked of her mother. He'd really loved her, probably still loved her even though she was long dead. Jessa didn't like the empathy she had for him. After all, she took it personally when people tried to stuff her into the backs of SUVs without her consent. Yet there was something complex about Roan.

Something dark. Something in him that hurt, though he tried to mask it. Damage and a deep emotional turmoil.

He reminded her of Broder.

"Don't mind him," said her great-grandfather. "He never got over Abigail. Not even after all these years. Never even took another woman, far as I know."

Blinking as she emerged from her deep train of thought,

she turned her attention back to her great-grandfather. She still couldn't believe she had one, yet when she looked into his face, she saw definite genetic similarities—the almond shape of his eyes, the full curve of his mouth, the pointy chin. "I want to know how they died and how I ended up with my aunt Margaret."

The light went out in Thorgest's eyes. "All we know is that they had a car accident. We thought ye'd died along with them, because we thought Abigail was pregnant with ye at the time. Turns out ye must have been born a little premature."

"But was it really a car accident? Could it have been the Blight?"

Fire flared for a moment in his expression, his jaw going tight. "We have our suspicions it could have been Blight, but there's no way to know for sure. One thing is for certain, we never knew about ye. Abigail made sure of that."

"She didn't want me here."

Of course, she hadn't known that when this odyssey had started. Now that she was here, knowing her mother had fled this man so long ago, she realized that her mother had probably never wanted her to come here and that revelation made her uneasy.

Why hadn't her mom wanted this for her? Her heritage, her people? Was it because of Thorgest? Was she not seeing something, whatever it was her mother had run from?

It was clear her great-grandfather believed in his way or the highway, but how far did his domineering hand stretch?

"As for the woman who raised ye, I'm sorry, lass, but we dinna know anything of that one. Seems yer mother and father were so hell-bent on keeping ye from yer people that they chose her to raise ye without giving ye any knowledge of yer birthright. It was a cruel thing to do."

She bristled, her mouth opening to defend her mother and father, starting to say they'd clearly been trying to protect her from the Blight, nothing more. But as Thorgest stared at her, little by little, her anger faded and she shivered.

Cruel.

He was right, it *had* been cruel. And their action had caused the exact opposite effect, since her lack of knowledge about her heritage had led her here—right where they hadn't wanted her to go.

She relaxed her shoulders, letting her self-righteousness leave her in a slow and steady trickle. Now when she looked at Thorgest she didn't see an overbearing man, determined to control her mother's romantic choices. Now she saw a caring great-grandfather who'd been robbed of a life spent with his family. A poor, tired, broken-down old man who needed her help.

Jessa wasn't sure where this sudden change in her emotions had come from, but they were there nonetheless and suddenly she felt too tired to examine them too closely.

Suddenly nothing mattered but her urge to aid this man in any way she could. She would sacrifice anything to please him, even her final moments with the man she loved.

Knowing exactly what her great-grandfather wanted of her, she settled her hands in her lap and looked up at Thorgest. "I want to stay here to train. I want to become a true witch."

Thorgest's face broke into a wide smile. "Good. That's very good, lass."

"She's done what?" Erik roared the words.

Broder stood in the living room holding Jessa's note clenched in one hand. He'd managed to pull on a pair of boots and a shirt, managed to make it downstairs. Erik was sprawled on the couch, drinking coffee.

"Her letter made it clear that nothing would stop her from joining her people. Loki says she's where she should be, mission accomplished. We need to leave her be." The words physically hurt to say.

The ice-cold fissure that had sat in the center of his chest had begun to melt and heal the moment she'd entered his life. Now that she was gone, it was reclaiming him, inch by agonizing inch. It was like a black hole in the middle of him, slowly consuming all the humanity he'd found again.

"We need to leave her be," Broder repeated in a low, pain-filled voice. "We should leave her be, but I can't." He paused, expecting another outburst from Erik, but it never came. "I'm going after her."

"Loki will burn you alive."

It wasn't a euphemism; Erik meant it literally. Loki could transport them to any number of realms, other than Asgard, for purposes of punishment.

"Wouldn't be the first time. I need to go after her, doesn't matter the cost. Let Loki burn me for a century in the fire pits, it will be worth it." He threw the letter onto the coffee table, then turned and stalked into the foyer, heading for his bike.

"Broder."

He halted in the frame of the front door. Erik had followed him into the foyer. Broder didn't turn to face him, forcing Erik to speak to his back.

"You have no future with Jessa. She knows that and *so do you*. It's why she left. She made it clear in her note. She'll want to stay with her people and, for once, I agree with Loki. She's where she needs to be no matter how much you may not like it. You're sacrificing yourself for nothing."

Broder didn't answer. Erik knew Broder was well aware of this fact. That didn't stop the drive he had to make Jessa his, no matter what. And that was something that Erik couldn't understand.

Broder turned to face him.

Erik saw his response in his expression and dropped his head in defeat. "The enclave is hidden by magick. You'll never find it, not without help, and I can't give you any."

"I'll find it."

Erik let out a low, slow breath. "I'm headed back to D.C. Good luck, brother."

And Broder was gone.

TWENTY-THREE

They gave Jessa a large bedroom on the second floor, decorated in grays and pinks. After Jessa had cleaned up and changed her clothes, an interesting witch named Molly showed her around the house. At least, part of the house. Jessa was pretty sure she would need a decade to explore the whole thing. It had been built over the course of centuries and she could see the sections that were older.

Molly, who was exuberant and friendly and said everything that popped into her head as soon as it popped there, showed Jessa where the dining room was and where she should report for her training, which was to begin the next day.

By twilight, Molly and Jessa were the best of friends. Jessa was grateful to have her and was sorry to see her leave. Once the darkness of twilight closed in around her and mixed with the silence of her bedroom, her misgivings began to push up from the recesses of her mind.

She missed Broder.

Yet every time she thought about going back to him, she immediately shivered and realized it was a bad idea. This was for the best. It really was. She was where she needed to be and Broder was *not* where he should be, but there was no help for that.

Still, she didn't sleep at all. Not even after a hot shower and slipping into a pair of the softest pj's that had ever touched her skin. Not after a cup of delicious noncaffeinated tea that Thorgest had sent up for her. Not even after climbing into the sumptuous, soft four-poster bed and covering herself with the coziest down comforter.

Nothing could make her drift off to dreamland. There was something wrong, bad wrong, something more than just the fact that Broder was not at her side. She couldn't figure out what it was. It pulsed softly just outside her field of awareness and every time she made a grab for it, it slipped through her fingers like water.

It was probably just angst from leaving Broder. Thinking about that brought pain, so she pushed it away and made herself busy thinking of other things. Like not getting lost in this enormous building.

She made her way down the narrow set of stairs at the end of the corridor where her room was located and into the main kitchen. It was very early. Since she hadn't been able to sleep, she had decided just to get up and get on with her day. Maybe she was just excited about being here, excited about finally tapping the talent she had inside her. Maybe that was the source of her unease. After all, even good stress was stress. That was what Aunt Margaret always used to say.

Moving through the empty kitchen, she followed the scent of freshly brewed coffee, found a mug, and poured herself a big serving. Leaning back against the counter, she took a sip of the lovely hot, sugared drink and groaned with pleasure. Sweet, sweet caffeine. There was nothing better than that in the morning . . . unless it was waking up next to the man you loved.

But she'd promised herself not to think about him.

"Good morning, Jessa."

She jerked, startled, and glanced over to find Carolyn sitting at one of the tables. "I didn't see you there. Good morning, Carolyn."

"Sleep well?" Carolyn had a cup of coffee sitting in front of her, too.

Jessa walked over and sat down next to her. "Not really."

"Well, lots of changes. After today you'll be so exhausted you'll sleep like a baby."

"What's today?"

Carolyn smiled. "First day of training." She spotted her pendant, leaned forward, and picked up the dragonfly. "Your sigil is a dragonfly?"

Jessa nodded and slipped the charm from the other woman's fingers, rolling it between her thumb and forefinger. She didn't want Carolyn touching it for some reason she couldn't quite determine.

"Did you get that from your aunt Margaret?"

"No, Broder gave it to me."

Carolyn's smile faded and her expression took on a sour look. "Oh."

Jessa tilted her head to the side. "Why do you all hate him so much?"

Carolyn looked down at the table. "It's not my place to say."

A flare of anger burst through her veins, making her narrow her eyes and lending an edge to her voice. "Then whose would it be?"

"Ask Thorgest. He'll tell you all about it."

Jessa exhaled slowly and looked away from her, a little shiver running through her. "I'm sure you all must have a good reason."

"Oh"—Carolyn leveled her gaze at her—"we do." She eyed the pendant. "Once you find out, you'll throw that into the trash. Why don't you do it right now, save yourself a little heartbreak?"

Another shiver, stronger this time. Jessa clenched the dragonfly in her hand as though trying to hold on to something precious that was rapidly slipping away. She gripped it so hard the points of the wings dug painfully into her skin. "I'm reserving judgment until I hear the story."

Carolyn shrugged. "Fine." She stood. "You'll need something to practice on anyway. Ready to go?"

Jessa took a final sip of her coffee and stood. "I can't wait to get started."

Her great-aunt took her to a room filled with tables, cabinets, stoves, and all sorts of bowls, mixers, test tubes, and cooking implements. It looked like an evil scientist's lab. She told Jessa there were five such rooms in the enclave, but she'd reserved this one for their personal use.

They spent the morning cooking up spells and imbuing Jessa's talisman with them, layer after layer of spells. The process was similar to the one she'd used on her own at Broder's keep, using the papers he'd brought her as instruction. But this time, either because she was with her people in the enclave or because she had a little practice under her belt, it all came easier to her.

This magick was in her blood. It bubbled up from the depths of her. It was as if she'd found a piece of herself that had been missing, that piece that had made her out of step with most of the people she'd ever known, the piece that had made her feel like an outcast from her own life.

Now she understood why she'd always been the outsider. Now that she'd found her people, her magick, all that was over. The broken shards were mended. She was whole, seamless, complete.

In that room with her great-aunt Carolyn, she felt better than she had, perhaps, *ever*, with the exception of the time she'd spent in Broder's arms. Yet every time she thought of him, an odd sensation came over her and her emotions turned away. It was a coping strategy, maybe. Heaven knew, she needed one to deal with his loss. An insulation had formed between her and thoughts of him and she was happy to have it.

Anyway, it was of no matter. What was really important right now was the magick, the enclave, the *seidhr*. She loved it here so much that she was certain she would devote the rest of her life to this place, *her people*. Her mind was focused on that, her new goal.

Even though the charms she and Carolyn layered the talisman with were silly, harmless ones, charms to throw iridescent rainbows across the room, light a candle from ten feet away, or make the limbs of a tree seem to dance, a sense of power filled Jessa. Soon a light filled her eyes and her cheeks glowed a bright healthy pink.

Every time she caught sight of herself in the large mirror hanging on one wall, she barely recognized herself. Never had the woman she saw in the reflection been this satisfied or excited by a possibility for her future. She'd come late to her magick, but she had the rest of her very long life to breathe life into it.

By early afternoon, she was a woman obsessed, absorbing every tidbit and pointer that Carolyn offered her. She was smudged with eleven different kinds of flower dust, coated in mashed and grated minerals, and smeared with various other arcane ingredients she never would have predicted would ever lie in her hands . . . or be used to concoct a spell.

She kept putting off Carolyn when she suggested breaks. She wanted to learn everything in a day, it seemed.

Little by little, Broder completely slipped away.

Roan watched at Thorgest's side through the two-way mirror. Jessa seemed to have no idea she was being watched. She was consumed—obsessed—with the work at hand. From what he'd observed, she had a natural inclination for the magick, not unexpected considering her lineage. Yet she still needed a considerable amount of tutelage if she expected to make anything of herself as a witch.

"She'll make a fine leader," Thorgest said, leaning up against the counter in front of the mirror. "The woman has talent seeping from her very pores, just like every other Egilson to come before her."

Roan nodded. Rubbing his chin, he stared at her, marveling at how much she looked like Abigail.

"Next she'll have a session with Sam," Thorgest said almost to himself. "She and Sam would make a good match. A strong shaman mated to a strong witch. Their babies would be powerful, and assets to our line."

Roan stiffened. "No more matchmaking. You've already

interfered in her life enough. You can't treat your people as if they're brood mares and studs." His thoughts drifted to Abigail and his perverse desire years ago that Thorgest's machinations would work in his case. All they had done was drive Thorgest's granddaughter away from the enclave, and perhaps eventually led to her death.

"It'll be for her own good, Roan," Thorgest mumbled to himself as he watched Jessa through the mirror. "All of this is, and ye know it. Anyway, there's much she can learn from Sam."

Roan said nothing.

Thorgest turned toward him, perhaps sensing the derision and disapproval to which Roan wasn't giving voice. "Do ye have a problem with my plans?"

Roan shifted on his feet and stared past Thorgest, out at Jessa. "I think she craves to find her place, her family. I think she needs to know where she belongs and that people care about her." He paused. "I think if she ever knew how she was being used and the reason why she's here, she would run screaming from this place."

Thorgest snorted. "Years later, I find myself relieved Abigail ran away from ye, Roan. What a sorry, weak shaman ye turned out to be." Then he strode from the room, slamming the door behind him.

Broder eased his motorcycle down another narrow road in the northernmost portion of the Scottish Highlands. Rain fell in a steady beat from the heavy, iron-colored clouds. It didn't matter; he couldn't get any more soaked than he already was.

It had been two days of this. Two days of rain. Two days of searching for the magickally hidden seidhr enclave.

He pulled the bike over to the side of the road at the top of a high hill and stared out across the landscape. Rain ran down his face in rivulets, obscuring his vision.

Erik had clearly thought this endeavor hopeless, but Broder couldn't make himself stop hunting for her. There had to be a way to locate her. After all, Loki hadn't thought it was hopeless. If he had, he would have laughed off the possibility that Broder was going after Jessa. Instead he'd threatened him.

That meant he could find her. He wasn't going to stop until he did.

Wiping a hand across his face, he looked behind him at the sound of a car engine. A small, beat-up white Renault was approaching. It pulled up behind him and the driver rolled down the window.

"Lost then, are ye?" The old man squinted at him. "Yer about a thousand clicks from the nearest town."

"Not lost. Looking for somewhere." Some*one* was more accurate, but that would sound too odd.

"Whereabouts?"

Broder slicked the rain from his hair with one hand, trying to figure out how to answer that question. "I got it under control. Thanks."

"Aye." The old man's gaze flicked up and down his rain-drenched leathers. "Looks like ye do." Broder recognized sarcasm when he heard it.

He started to roll his window up, but Broder decided at the last minute to ask the old guy for help. He lived here. Maybe he could offer a clue. "Know of any garbage dumps near here? Any places with strewn trash? It would be a place not many people would want to go; it would give off a creepy kind of feel. Maybe some people might say it's haunted." He knew he sounded like an idiot to human ears, but he didn't care.

Other than the magickally induced propensity for people to avoid the area where the enclave was located, it was masked as a garbage-strewn place, meant to keep wandering humans away. There were far more strenuous wards in place for Blight, but those didn't affect the Brotherhood.

The old man thought for a long moment, then he nodded. "Aye." He pointed off to the west. "Take this road to the A109, then follow the signs to Galhanscrieg. Drive about fifteen clicks to the north, away from the town. Ye'll come to a place like ye're describing."

"Thank you."

"Want a ride? It'll get ye out of the rain."

"No, I'd rather take my bike."

The man tipped his imaginary hat at him, grinned toothlessly, and started down the road again.

Broder watched the car ramble away. He hoped like hell this was the break he needed.

The rain pattered softly on the huge windows in the room, windows so big they covered almost the whole of two walls. Jessa felt like a turtle in a terrarium. One of the windows was open, for reasons she couldn't determine, letting in a fresh rain-scented breeze.

This was one of the many sitting/meeting rooms in the enclave and where Sam had said he wanted to meet her. Small clusters of couches, tables, and chairs scattered the large room, but it was empty save for both of them.

Sam was awesomely good-looking. His sandy-colored hair fell across his forehead and made his blue eyes seem even bluer. Those eyes were heavy lidded most of the time, and his voice was something like warmed whiskey, making him seem like he had sex on his mind. Really *good* sex. He was like candy, but, although she noted the man's sexiness, she had no interest in him.

No man could hold a candle to Broder and it would be a long time before she would try to find one who could even come close, and Thorgest pushing her at Sam wasn't going to work. She could see right through her great-grandfather and she didn't like it.

Staring out the window for a moment, her thoughts drifted, dangerously, back to the keep. What was she doing here? Why hadn't she soaked up every second she could with Broder? It didn't make sense that she hadn't stayed in the keep until the very end, done everything she could in order to keep him with her. Why had she made the decision to leave again? Why had—

"Jessa?"

She shivered and turned toward Sam. "Sorry."

"You were a million miles away."

"Right. Okay, I'm focused now."

"Good."

He turned his back and walked to the nearby window, unlatched it, and threw it wide. Rain-scented fresh air burst into the room. "Shamanism is a little different in execution from witchcraft." He spoke with his back turned toward her. "But the magick is much the same. There is one major difference, however." He held his hand to the side and she saw a small silver ball glinting there.

He threw the ball to the floor with force. Magick popped and Jessa gasped. Her mind torqued a little—that was the only way to describe the sensation—and Sam transformed. In his place beat the dark wings of a raven. The bird fluttered for a moment in the air, then took off through the open window. His clothes lay in a heap on the floor where he'd stood only a moment earlier.

Jessa leapt from her chair and lunged for the opening, watching him soar off. For a moment, the sky was clear of everything except heavy gray clouds. Then the raven returned, aiming for the window.

She stepped back, allowing the bird through. It landed not far from her and Sam shifted back to human form in a brilliant flash that made her mind bend to the side a little once more. "Holy—"

"Shit," he finished for her with a slow, lazy grin.

Her gaze flicked down. He was naked, his skin glistening wet from the rain. She raised her eyes to his face, her cheeks reddening. "Do you always lose your clothes when you shift?"

He took a step toward her, his lopsided grin hitching up a little at one corner. "No. It's a choice." His eyes glinted mischievously.

Aha.

Sam reached out and touched two fingers to the center of her chest. "Witches have more power than shamans, but shamans can shift. Although select few witches can shift, too. All of them, by the way, have come from *your* bloodline."

Her eyes opened wide. "Seriously?"

Sam grinned, a dimple popping out on one cheek. "Seriously. Want to see if you're one of them?"

And fly into the heavens as a bird? Just as Jessa was about to open her mouth with an enthusiastic *yes*, Thorgest burst into the room. "Sam, we've a security breach."

Sam took a step back. "Blight?"

Thorgest snarled inarticulately. "Worse."

Commotion in the hallway. Raised voices. Scuffling feet. A fistfight. Bodies slamming against the walls of the corridor. Then Broder strode through the doorway, looking as grim and pissed as she'd ever seen him.

TWENTY·FOUR

"Broder!" she yelled. A surge of joy and relief pushed her feet toward him. She ran, meaning to leap right into his arms and ask for his forgiveness. All of a sudden her head was clear of everything but him. She never should have left him. She hadn't been thinking straight.

Sam reached out to snag her and hold her back as she passed, but just missed her. Thorgest intercepted her instead, wrapping his arms around her midsection and swinging her away with wiry strength.

Rage rushed through her veins. She wrenched herself from Thorgest's arms, shooting him a look to kill, and ran the rest of the way to Broder, but the look on his face stopped her dead in her tracks a few paces from him.

His expression held a riot of emotion like she'd never seen on him before. He wore black from head to toe and his wet hair had been slicked back over his skull, throwing the sculpted bones of his face into sharp relief. His gaze took her in like a starving animal confronted with a meal, hot and hungry, but they grew cool when he looked over her head and focused on her great-grandfather.

Behind her she heard a low, menacing growl that made the hair on the back of her neck stand on end, and she looked behind her to find a huge gray wolf standing where Sam had been a moment ago. Sam's teeth were pulled back away from his lips, his sleek wolf head lowered so the whites of his eyes showed and his ears were laid back.

"I tried to stop him," said Roan from the doorway. He was out of breath, his lip bloody, and his shirt was ripped. "Bastard found the enclave and cut right through our wards."

"Maybe that's a good thing. Leave him alone . . . for now," said Thorgest. His voice held a note of satisfaction that Jessa didn't understand. "Broder Calderson, so nice to see ye again after all these years, but I can't say I'm happy you're here, considering yer history with us."

Jessa turned and stared hard at her great-grandfather, who had an irritating smirk on his face. Suddenly she was certain she'd been caught in the middle of a tug-of-war and she didn't know the rules.

Thorgest's gaze flicked to her, then back to Broder. "Now that ye're here, ye can tell Jessa what ye did to her people."

Jessa clenched her hands at her sides against her confusion and the rising animosity in the room. Broder stared at Thorgest as though he wanted to leap across the room and kill him with his bare hands.

"What is going on?" she asked. "Please, someone talk to me."

"Broder?" Her great-grandfather raised his eyebrows. "She's asking for an explanation. Dinna ye want to give her one? If ye love her, ye will."

Broder's gaze dropped to hers and locked. Pain flashed through his eyes so brilliantly that for a moment it gave her chest pains.

"Tell me," she whispered.

But still, he didn't. The emotions that swirled inside her became a storm, making her light-headed. She'd known that Broder had committed some terrible crime in his past. And she'd known the seidhr had no great love for him . . . but she'd never put the two together. Now she realized she should have.

As Broder, mute, his eyes full of guilt, held her gaze, the swirling emotions solidified . . . into anger.

"Broder ne'er told ye the crime that brought him to Loki's untender mercy, did he, Jessa?"

Her gaze still locked with Broder's, she shook her head. She raised her chin. "I think I deserve to know."

"Broder?" Thorgest goaded.

He moved his gaze to holds hers. There was coldness in his eyes that she'd never seen before—never had wanted to see. Coldness and violence. Were they memories? "Do you want to know, Jessa?"

She nodded, her eyes filling with tears. Actually, she wasn't sure if she did. Perhaps ignorance would preserve her memory of the man she loved when Loki had removed him from her life.

Sam gave another low growl.

"I slaughtered them." Broder's voice came out hoarse with barely restrained rage. The muscles in his throat stood out and his body seemed to shake from his effort to hold himself back from attacking Roan, Sam, and Thorgest all at once. "I killed every one of them I could get my hands on. Almost a whole enclave, men and women alike." Brutal, chilling intensity made every word he spoke a dagger point through her chest.

Jessa took a step backward. For the first time since she'd met him, she was afraid of him.

Broder took a step toward her, not allowing her to retreat. "I cleaved their heads from their necks, their arms from their shoulders. I cut them all down. I bathed in their blood and I reveled in it. With sword and ax, I killed them all. Nearly wiped them out of existence in one blood-drenched afternoon."

"Who?" Jessa's voice came out on a weak puff of breath. It was as if all the warm emotion she'd ever had for Broder was ebbing away. It left her cold; it left an empty place where her heart had been. She knew who he was speaking of, of course she did, but she needed to hear the words from his lips. "Who did you kill?"

"You know." His voice was rough and empty sounding at the same time. "The seidhr. Witches and shamans alike."

Silence filled the room like a living thing, sucking out all the air. Jessa stood, staring at Broder, at a loss for words.

Thorgest didn't have any trouble finding something to say. "He killed yer great-great-grandfather, Jessa—my father. He killed my mother. He nearly wiped out our entire genetic line." His gaze swung to Broder. "It must be strange to understand how close ye came to ensuring that Jessa was ne'er born. How many other witches and shamans ne'er saw the light of day because of ye?"

Jessa was still stunned speechless. What had been revealed was like a punch to the gut. She would *rather* have had a fist to the stomach in place of this. It was as if she didn't know Broder at all.

He was a stranger to her.

She'd known his original crime was bad, but she hadn't known it had been anything close to this. The remorseless slaughter of an entire enclave of her people—her blood kin? "Why did you come here?" she finally managed to ask through a constricted throat. Her voice came out sounding as cold as the center of her chest.

Broder jerked as if she'd slapped him. "I came . . . for you."

"Seems a bad idea now, doesn't it?" spat Thorgest.

TWENTY-FIVE

Broder hardly heard Thorgest's words. He knew the old shaman was doing his best to twist the knife in the wound, but it was impossible to make things worse. He saw the truth in Jessa's eyes—she was lost to him in every way.

Now she saw the monster he was. Now she knew his darkest secret.

Of all the women he could have fallen in love with it had to be a witch. . . .

There was more to the story, but it didn't make a difference if she knew it or not. Right now he might as well have been standing in front of her with a bloody sword in one hand and an ax in the other, the carnage he'd wrought in that ancient seidhr enclave all around him. It was as if he truly was back on that day, his side a bleeding, meaty mess and his life leaking out onto the floor.

It hadn't mattered then and it didn't matter now. Without Jessa's love nothing mattered.

"I have no idea who you are," Jessa whispered, ignoring her great-grandfather completely. Broder saw frosty hurt in her eyes, laced with the emotion he never wanted to see on her face when she looked at him—*fear, revulsion*.

The icy black hole in the center of his chest that had been threatening to engulf him since she'd left suddenly swallowed him whole.

"I'll leave," he said, his voice low and rough sounding—

broken. He didn't move, though. Instead he lingered, hoping for one last impossible reprieve, for Jessa to realize he wasn't that man anymore, for her to realize she loved him no matter what. A thousand years had passed. He'd paid for his crimes. If he could take it all back, he would. Couldn't she see how much he'd risked by coming here?

Couldn't she feel how much he loved her?

Optimistic to the bitter end. He never would have guessed he possessed that trait. It had taken Jessa to bring it out of him.

Framed in the doorway, he turned to her and ignored Thorgest's body language that said he wanted to whup his ass. *He could try.* Broder wouldn't mind doing a little whupping of his own and was pretty sure he could take even the master shaman in a fight. He wouldn't give in to the temptation, for Jessa's sake. A final gift to her.

Pushing past Roan, he made his way to the front door.

He wanted to look over his shoulder for one last glimpse of the only woman he'd loved in a thousand years, but he couldn't do it . . . not when she was looking at him that way.

"This can't be happening." Jessa put a hand to her forehead and took a step back. Thorgest and Roan were there in a heartbeat, helping her to ease into a chair.

Sam padded out of the room on huge wolf feet, following Broder, assuring he left the premises, she was certain.

She shivered, unsure about how she felt about Broder leaving.

Everything was a jumble in her mind; her emotions were like tangled balls of yarn and she couldn't separate the skeins. Something about this was off. Something was wrong. She wanted to go after Broder, and yet, what he'd done had been so terrible . . . and oddly *personal* even though it had happened so long before her birth. What he'd done had been unforgivable, even if it had been a thousand years ago and he'd endured a living hell since then to pay for it.

"There, there, lass, let it go," Thorgest said, kneeling

beside her. "He's not worth another thought. Loki is making sure he suffers for what he did."

"I'm caught in a nightmare," she murmured.

"Ye've yer studies here," Thorgest continued. "Ye have us, yer family. Maybe one day ye'll find another man, a better man. Dinna worry yer pretty head over Broder Calderson."

Another man. She grimaced. She didn't want another man.

"A man like Sam, perhaps."

Her grimace deepened.

"Then one day, when ye're ready, ye'll take the reins of this place."

She blinked and looked at her great-grandfather. "What?"

"Thorgest hasn't told you yet." Roan wiped at his lip where Broder had punched him. There was a note of emotion in his voice, something she couldn't identify. "We weren't going to do that until later."

Thorgest seemed to realize he'd said something he shouldn't have, which raised every one of Jessa's red flags. Apparently Roan's comment had warned him he'd trod into dangerous territory. "Tell me what?" Her tone brooked no denial of a straight answer.

"In the seidhr, leadership passes through the bloodline, lass," said Thorgest. "Through our family. Ye're like a princess about to become a queen."

She frowned. "And if I don't want to be queen?"

"It's what you were born to be." Thorgest's voice held a hint of steel that made her bristle. Who was he to dictate the shape of her future? He'd already made it clear he wanted her with Sam. Now this?

She shivered. *Wait a minute.* Of course she wanted to be queen! Who wouldn't want to be a queen? Sam was a different matter, but she could cope with that later. She settled back against the chair. "We'll need to talk a lot more about this."

Yes, *queen.*

Thorgest smiled. "'Course we will, lass."

Roan glared at Thorgest. "You need to make sure Broder has left the enclave." He paused. "As the current leader it's *your* responsibility," he added.

Thorgest hesitated a moment, the lines around his mouth deepening. Clearly he didn't like the note of demand in Roan's voice. But he stood all the same. "Duty calls. I'll be back soon, me lass."

Once Thorgest was gone, Roan knelt before her, his hands on her upper arms, his eyes serious. "You asked the wrong question."

"What?" She looked into his intense face, feeling a little drugged. It had to be the stress. She blinked, trying to clear the cloud hanging around her head.

"You asked Broder the wrong question. You asked him why he came here when you should have asked him *why he did it.*"

"You're confusing me." She shivered and twitched at the same time. What was wrong with her?

"You know why he came here, Jessa, even though Loki will flay the skin from his bones for stepping foot inside the enclave. He did it for you. He did it because he loves you and he can't let you go, no matter the cost."

She bit her lower lip. "I know that, but what he did—"

"Was inconceivable to any normal human brain. He was a berserker of old, Jessa, slaughtering all he saw."

"Exactly. I feel like I don't even know who he is."

"You need to ask yourself why he did it. I'm not saying it excuses it; I'm saying there are things you don't know."

"Like what?"

"Go after him. Ask him."

She thought about that for a moment. Then she shivered. "No. I should stay here."

Roan made a frustrated sound and shook her. "You are a new witch, Jessa, but you're not weak. Find the thread and cut it. *Find your strength.*"

She frowned at him, trying to figure out what he meant.

Thorgest reentered the room, a wide smile on his face. "He's gone, past the wards. Good riddance to 'im, too."

Despair welled up in Jessa's chest. *He was gone.* Likely she would never see him again. But, maybe, if she got up right now and ran . . .

But no.

She looked up at Roan, to find him staring down at her with disappointment on his face. Find the thread and cut it, he'd said. Find the thread of *what*? She parsed the thoughts and emotions crowding her and found a faint one, dying in the back, that she had a feeling should be more prominent. She focused on it.

"I need to see him." Jessa stood.

Thorgest looked at her like she'd grown a second head. "He's gone, lass. Best ye let him go. He's a bad man. Got no place here."

Jessa started to agree with him, then stopped herself. *Find it and cut it.* "I need closure. I need to know why he did it, Thorgest." She walked toward the door, mostly just to see if she could. It was a little like walking through molasses . . . a little like walking through the wards around the enclave.

Did that mean there were wards of some kind between her and Broder? Was there magick affecting her now, keeping her from exercising her free will?

"Ye leave this building, take one step toward that man, ye can never come back, lass." Thorgest's voice boomed behind her, accented with magick to make it seem bigger, deeper, more commanding.

Jessa stopped in her tracks and turned slowly. "Are you threatening me?" She shivered and her anger eased. Realization bloomed.

Oh, hell. There *was* magick affecting her. The thread of it wrapped her will like a piano wire, choking off certain thoughts and emotions . . . the ones Thorgest deemed dangerous.

"It's for yer own good, lass. The man's no good for ye."

She took a step toward her great-grandfather, trying to summon the flash of rage she'd had a moment earlier. She needed that anger now, needed that intense emotion to burn away the enchantment that had been set on her, to cut the thread that was slowly killing her will.

"Just like the spell you've put me under to keep me compliant and easygoing is for my own good, right, Thorgest?"

Thorgest took a step back, the blood draining from his face.

"I just figured it out."

Her great-grandfather shot a look filled with daggers at Roan.

"He didn't tell me." Well, not directly. "I figured it out on my own. How long has it been on me? Who placed it?" She took another step toward him, her rage trickling through her veins a little harder, a little faster. A shiver started and she stopped it dead in its track with a vicious force of her will.

They would never break her.

"Ye leave here to go after that man and ye leave this all behind. Ye'll never be a real witch, Jessa. All you'll be able to manage are tricks fit for a toddler's amusement."

"Don't tell me what I'll be capable of." Another step toward him.

Now her rage was a running river, pushing away every last vestige of the spellwork that had been woven over her. She summoned her strength of will—which had always been a formidable force—and severed that choking thread. She sensed the tatters of the ruined spellwork fluttering harmlessly to the floor all around her.

Thorgest threw an arm wide in an encompassing gesture. "All this can be yers. We need ye to lead the enclave, lass. This can be yer home. This is yer family."

"I had a family. Her name was Margaret, the woman my mother *chose* to raise me in the event of her death." She paused, realization dawning. "It was Carolyn, wasn't it? She placed the magick the night she called me. I understand now. That's why I left the keep, why I left Broder."

Thorgest said nothing and she knew her guess was right. A light of fear had entered his eyes and she wondered why they were so desperate to keep her here. "We're yer blood, lass. We only did what was best for ye."

Jessa looked Thorgest up and down. "*I* decide what's best for me, Thorgest. Right now I've decided that *leaving* is best. I'm out of here." Nodding once at Roan, she turned on her heel and walked out the door.

TWENTY-SIX

It was still raining.

Jessa burst through the front door of the mansion and into a steady downpour. She launched herself down the steps and ran flat out for the main gates. *Please, please, let me not be too late.*

Broder stood on the trash-strewn path just past the gates, beside his motorcycle, with his back to her.

Her fingers curled around the bars of the gates and pulled. They didn't budge. They were locked. "Broder!"

He turned and looked at her as if just waking from a daze. He blinked and the dullness in his eyes cleared. "You should go back in, Jessa. It's over," he yelled over the pounding of the rain. He turned back to his bike.

She pulled on the gates again, but they wouldn't budge. "Broder, wait, I need to talk to you."

He hesitated, then turned and walked toward the gates on the opposite side. Stopping short, he frowned. "This is as close as the wards will allow. They've changed something. I can't take another step."

"Broder," she yelled across the short distance. The rain was really coming down now. "Why did you do it? Why did you go berserker on that enclave?"

"Does it matter?" His voice sounded emotionless. "I did it." He paused. "

Her heart skipped a beat. "Just tell me."

Broder looked up into the heavy, dark clouds, letting the rain hit his face. "My wife went to the witches, asked for a charm to help her conceive, but whatever they did to her, it killed her. Or, at least, I thought so."

"What do you mean?"

He lowered his gaze to hers. "She got pregnant, died in childbirth. The child died, too." He paused. "Some things are better left to nature; sometimes magick shouldn't interfere. It wasn't rational, but I held the seidhr responsible. Before my wife and child had even been buried, I went to the enclave, demanding answers. I yelled, insulted them. I threatened them. They didn't like that, didn't enjoy having accusations of murder flung at them, no matter how unfounded and grief addled they were."

"Is that when you killed them?"

He gave a harsh, stony laugh. "No. They trapped me, kept me for ten years in a cell. Used me like a guinea pig in a lab for magick. They tortured me, drove me insane." He stopped and pushed a hand through his hair. "Then, one day, I escaped."

"And there was hell to pay."

He nodded. "I delivered hell to the seidhr enclave, then—"

"Loki delivered it to you."

"Yeah." He pressed his lips together for a moment. "But I still did it. I slaughtered everyone I saw that day, showed no mercy. I killed innocents."

"You were insane. They'd made you that way."

"Doesn't matter. I did it."

"It's been a thousand years."

He looked up into the clouds again. "And I'm still not worthy of you."

"Says who?"

He lowered his head slowly and caught her gaze. A spark of hope burned in the dark depths of his eyes. "Loki says."

"Fuck him. I love you anyway." Her voice broke on the words. She reached out a hand toward him. He reached out to her, too, but their fingertips could barely brush.

Her gaze held his, her eyes welling with tears.

"I slaughtered your people." His voice sounded dead.

"There were extenuating circumstances. Anyway, turns out some of them really suck." Jessa rattled the gates again, then went for the lock . . . it was open. "Damn it." She took a step back and stared at the high iron bars. More magick. It wasn't letting her pass.

"It's warded," came Thorgest's smug voice from behind them. "Ye'll ne'er get out an' he'll ne'er get back in."

Broder made an angry, snarling sound.

Jessa rounded on the old man. "You can't keep me prisoner in here!"

Thorgest smiled. "It was done the moment ye came here of yer own free will. Powerful magick can be weaved from acts born of free will. Ye gave me all the clay I needed to work with when ye crossed this threshold. Dinna ye ever wonder why ye needed to hitch rides all the way here?"

"I didn't cross it of my own free will! I had a spell on me. Compulsion. It's been choking off certain thoughts and emotions."

"You dared put magick on her?" Broder shouted, his fists clenched. He strained against the warding, but it was impenetrable to him.

Thorgest's smiled widened. He cast a poisonous look at Broder. "Some part of ye wanted to come here. Some part of ye wanted to leave him and come to us. That's all I needed, a sliver of yer will. Now ye're here and he's there. Story done. Ye'll forget this. Train. Become the leader of this enclave one day." He paused, looking satisfied. "Have *Sam's* babies."

"I'm not staying here, Thorgest. I'm not going to be groomed to be some slave to this place. Now I understand why my mother ran."

"Ye'll get over this, Jessamine, see the logic in it. Eventually, ye'll come around."

"Yeah, to killing you in your sleep," Broder interjected.

Thorgest turned his cold eyes to him. "Aye. Ye'd know more than a little about that then, wouldn't ye?"

"About murdering people in their sleep? *No.*" Broder narrowed his eyes and looked so brutal for a moment that Jessa took a step back. "I kill them when they're awake." No one should ever put Broder on their bad side, Jessa decided.

"Let me out of here, Thorgest." Jessa went back to the gates and yanked on them.

"I told ye: If ye leave here, ye'll never be welcome past those wards again."

"Great!" she hurled over her shoulder at him, while still trying to open them. "That's just fine with me!"

"Ye'll never become a true witch."

"Oh, whatever! If to be a witch is to be like you or Carolyn, then good riddance."

"Ye'll be prey to the Blight."

"I'll have Broder to protect me."

"You're forgetting Loki."

Jessa went still. Her gaze went to Broder's on the other side of the iron bars, rain dripping down her face, soaking her clothes and hair. Of course she was forgetting Loki. Broder would never be hers. She turned her attention back to the gate. "I still want out of here. I'll let the Blight kill me before I stay."

"So go." It came from Roan.

She turned and found Roan standing a little behind Thorgest, who had turned to give the shaman the iciest of glares.

"Can I?" she asked him.

Roan shrugged a shoulder loosely. "You broke the magick laid on you by Carolyn; why not break this magick, too?" He paused. "You possess the power to kill Blight, as well. Work on it, maybe you can get it to bloom."

Thorgest said nothing to Roan, but his intentions were clear in his eyes and on his face. Roan was risking a lot in helping her.

So the man had a conscience after all.

She turned back to the gates and studied them. How could she break the warding with absolutely no training? Reaching out, she touched one of the smooth bars, then focused her gaze past it to Broder.

The gates were only a physical—psychological—barrier. They had no lock and would swing free without magick to bind them shut. She wanted to get past them, to the man she loved, and every moment they didn't open was a moment she lost with him. The clock was ticking and her asshole of a great-grandfather was wasting her time. Sorrow welled.

"No," she whispered to herself. "No despair." Sorrow or despair hadn't helped her break Carolyn's magick—*anger had*.

She closed her eyes and tapped into the source of power she'd used when she'd layered the talisman around her neck with Carolyn's help. *Carolyn*, how much she wished she could see her one last time before she got out of here. That woman was in serious need of a piece of her mind . . . of a good right hook to the jaw.

And she *was* getting out of here.

Reaching up, she closed her fist around the dragonfly pendant. It didn't have the magick she needed, but it was the closest she could get to Broder right now—a link, a symbol.

Focusing on her magick—and her rage—she pulled all of it she could up from the depths of her and threw it at the gates. It was messy and clumsy. She fisted her power like a toddler with a fat crayon, making slashes and nonsensical swirls on a blank page. She opened her eyes when it hit and watched in awe as the bars bowed outward in the rain, as though made of rubber, then sprang back into place.

Huh.

She did it again, then again . . . and something binding the gates broke.

"No," snarled Thorgest, "I forbid this." He grabbed for her, but Roan was there, yanking her great-grandfather away from her. They tussled as Jessa lunged for the gates.

Jessa had just grabbed on to the iron bars when magick exploded above her head. Roan wrestled Thorgest to the ground as she pulled on the gates, muttering to herself, *"Please, please, please."*

The gates swung open and Jessa ran to Broder without a

glance backward. He mounted his bike and she jumped on behind him. As he started the motorcycle, she glanced behind her and saw Thorgest shoot a massive amount of magick at Roan, so much that it made her hair stand on end even at a distance. He reminded her of some wizard from a fairy tale—Merlin, perhaps. Fire and smoke exploded.

When it cleared, Roan was gone and only scorch marks showed where he'd been standing in the rain.

A swell of grief swamped Jessa for a moment. Then Thorgest turned his attention to her and Broder. Her throat caught painfully with fear, the memory of all those exploding demons fresh in her mind. She knew she'd been lucky with the gates, but no way could she go toe-to-toe with Thorgest in a magickal battle. "Broder, go faster!"

Broder's bike shot forward, causing her to nearly tumble off the back. She gripped Broder's coat as they sped down the road, away from the enclave. Behind them, magick blew a crater in the pavement. Then one blew closer, and another even closer. Stone exploded, bits of shrapnel flying, raining down on their heads. A crater opened up just under Broder's back tire, nearly making him lose control of the cycle.

The bike flew down the road until the gates were only a speck behind them and Thorgest was gone forever. They shot out of the mouth of the creepy garbage-strewn road and into the sweet, fresh air of the Scottish Highlands.

Freedom. Safety.

Jessa relaxed against Broder's back, a tear squeezing out of her eye. So, that was that. Done. The rain was finally beginning to stop. How fitting.

Broder pulled over to the side of the road and cut the engine. They were both drenched and she was shivering. At least this time the shivering wasn't from manipulative magick, but a result of good, honest chilly air.

Broder pulled her off the back of the bike and dragged her up against his chest, nestling his nose in her hair. He said nothing, but that was okay. Everything that needed to be said was in the warmth of his body and the way he held her.

He loved her more than anything in this world, would do anything for her, risk anything.

She laid her head against his chest and listened to the thrum of his strong heartbeat. For one thousand years that heart had beat. It was the heart of a warrior, of a man who'd been damned, of a Viking—of the man she loved. In his arms, she wasn't chilly any longer.

He pulled her away from him and stared into her eyes. "You heard everything I did to that enclave."

"Yes." She paused. "When you were doing it, did you know? I mean, were you aware? You were described as a—"

"Berserker. I was in a berserker rage. I didn't know what I was doing but, Jessa, when it was done I didn't regret it."

She nodded and swallowed hard, looking away from him. "Okay." She couldn't get the images out of her head—what the carnage must have looked like. It was hard to imagine Broder as a stone-cold killer, mowing down everyone in his path indiscriminately.

He tipped her chin up, forcing her to look at him. "I regret it now, and not because I've spent a thousand years paying for it, but because I've had a thousand years to think about it. I am sick of death, sick of killing, even the killing of the Blight. If I could take back what I did that day, even after what they did to me—I would."

Her body relaxed a little.

"I thought I'd lost you, Jessa."

"Never."

"Stay with me." It was an order, issued in a low, gruff voice.

"Forever, if they let me."

But they wouldn't. They both knew that.

Something dark moved in his eyes, then he lowered his head and kissed her. His tongue eased into her mouth and brushed up against hers. She shuddered against him, her body responding instantly. Molding her body to his, she told him without words how much she needed him right now. They both knew they had a limited time together and they had no idea when it would end.

He scooped her into his arms and carried her over the rise of a nearby hill. Setting her on her feet, he swept off his worn leather duster and laid it on the wet grass, then eased her down on top of it. They were both soaked; the coat was saturated; everything was wet. She should have been cold, but not with Broder hovering over her body, covering her, protecting her.

Her fingers fumbled desperately with the button and zipper on his jeans, even as he also attempted to get her jeans off her. Slowly, inch by inch, they managed to drag fabric over damp skin. Somehow they managed to get most of their clothes off—the important pieces, anyway.

TWENTY-SEVEN

The rain. The wet duster. The hard earth beneath them. None of that mattered now. Her entire reality had narrowed to the feel of his body rubbing against the bare skin of her thighs, the pressure of his chest against hers.

Pushing her hands underneath the hem of his sweater, she ran her fingers over his hard body, exploring the way the muscles of his back bunched as he moved, running her hands over his amazing rear, his lean hips, and strong thighs. She almost purred as she moved her fingers over the hard, warm, and leanly muscled expanse of his chest. Sinking into every movement, every moment, every breath they took, she tried to memorize each inch of his body so she could keep the memory with her forever.

Broder gave her one last, mind-numbing kiss, then moved down her body, pushing her damp sweater up to kiss her abdomen, then moving lower still. He eased her thighs apart and laid a long kiss to first one inner thigh, then the other.

Groaning with anticipation, she allowed her head to fall back as she sank her fingers into the silky hair at the nape of his neck. He ran the tip of his tongue slowly over her inner thigh—right at the soft, tender place where it met her sex. A moment later, he slid his tongue directly to the center.

She let out a long, slow breath as his tongue skated over her most intimate of areas. He took his time, delivering a slow, thought-robbing amount of pleasure that left her incapable of anything but the most minimal level of cognition. Pleasure ruled her now, pleasure mixed with love.

Finally she shuddered beneath him and came, his name on her lips. Then he was there, between her thighs, pressing the head of his cock inside. He pushed in little by little, slowly letting her have an inch of him at a time. She was ready for him; he didn't need to take such care. It was as though he savored her, melting into every moment the way she was doing, to hold them close and keep for some lonely night in the future. He also knew their moments would be coming to an end.

Finally he hilted deep within her.

He stayed that way, completely sunk within her body and staring down at her in the late afternoon light. Jessa gazed up at him, thinking she might get lost in the depths of emotion showing in his dark eyes.

Broder moved a tendril of hair away from her face in a gesture of complete love and caring. Tears filled her eyes and several rolled down her cheeks. She hated that she was crying, but she couldn't make it stop. The emotion coursing between them was too great and their impending separation too awful to consider.

Hilted deep inside her body, he lowered his head and kissed her forehead very gently. Gentleness from this man was a gift, unique and special. Tenderness from a man this big and strong, so brutal and protective in a fight, was the most erotic thing Jessa had ever experienced. He took her mouth in a masterful, possessive kiss, drawing a small sound from her throat.

Then he began to move inside her. Slowly at first. So slowly it made her moan, made her see stars, made blissful waves of sexual ecstasy crash through her body. Then his thrusts grew harder, faster.

His gaze locked with hers as their bodies moved together as though they were one being. She had the odd, flashing sensation that the sliver of frozen Blight buried deep in his chest was melting, easing away until there was nothing of it left. Little by little her love was overpowering the magick that bound him. Broder closed his eyes and sighed, as though he felt it, too.

She wished it could be true, but it was just the power of the moment, their combined desire. A fantasy they both shared.

"I love you," she whispered.

He buried his face in the curve of her neck and whispered it back to her, over and over.

Her climax came from the very depths of her. It overwhelmed everything else. The pleasurable waves filled her, took the very breath from her. She couldn't scream, couldn't moan, couldn't do anything but lose herself to it.

Lose herself totally and utterly to him.

When it was over, they lay still linked for a long time, as if a warm bubble had settled over them—a magickal barrier that separated them from the rest of the world. If they moved, it would pop.

Jessa never wanted to move. Not ever again.

But eventually the chilly, damp earth reached through even their strong bubble of love and Jessa began shivering violently. Broder kissed her softly, and then pulled her from the ground, helping her to dress in her still-damp clothes, telling her they needed to get to somewhere warm. They made their way over the rise to the motorcycle.

Loki was standing near Broder's bike, dressed in a suit and looking like a Ken doll, completely out of place in the Scottish countryside. Smiling, he opened his arms wide. "Broder! Jessamine! It's so good to see you."

Broder and Jessa stopped on top of the hill and Broder's hand entwined with hers. They both stood stock-still, watching the god with trepidation and tight muscles.

When they made no reply, Loki walked toward them, his fancy, expensive loafers squishing into the wet grass. He smiled as though happy to see them. "Well, Broder, how did you enjoy your furlough? Was it pleasurable for you?"

Broder's grip on her hand increased.

"Don't torment him, Loki. He knows it's time to go." She had to be brave and let Broder leave. She knew all too well that if Broder fought Loki, things would not go well for him. However, from the feel of Broder's stiff body beside her, his leaving without a fight was unlikely.

Loki's smile tightened a bit. "Really? I suppose he does know that. He also knew that it's forbidden for a Brother of the Damned to step foot on the land of the seidhr. Especially *this* particular brother."

Jessa looked up at Broder. She'd figured as much, but from the note in Loki's voice she realized that his punishment might be more than a simple slap on the wrist.

She leveled her gaze at Loki. "Don't touch him." Her voice sounded hard, but she knew she was like a kitten baring her teeth at a lion.

Loki laughed at her, but his eyes were cold. "None of your business."

"He's suffered enough."

"*I* say when he's suffered enough. The time has come for you to say good-bye. I'll give you a second." He crossed his arms over his chest and tapped his foot. "Okay, time's up."

"I'm not leaving her." Broder's voice came out a low, dangerous growl.

"The hell you're not. You got your treat, Broder, now back to reality."

Broder growled and lunged at Loki with intense ferocity, covering the ground that separated them like a bullet.

Loki raised his hand as though bored. Clearly he'd been waiting for Broder to attack him. Now he was going to employ magick of some kind, Jessa supposed.

But nothing happened. No magick sparked. Broder kept coming.

Loki's eyes widened in shock as Broder barreled toward him, tackling him to the rain-soaked earth with a thump. Jessa yelped and clasped a hand over her mouth. Broder rolled off the man, looking surprised. Clearly Broder hadn't thought he'd actually be able to do it.

Loki gasped on the ground, clutching his chest. "What in the name of Hel—"

Broder lunged at him again, but Loki disappeared,

reappearing again a short distance away and dressed in a fresh, new suit.

Loki straightened his lapels. "Broder, you appear to be missing something." His voice shook almost imperceptibly. He was clearly disturbed.

What did it take to shake up a god?

Broder pushed to his feet and touched his chest. Then he raised his gaze to Jessa's.

Jessa's eyes widened. "Is Broder free?" she asked Loki.

"No," Loki snarled at her. "I didn't fucking free him, so that means he isn't fucking free."

"I freed him," came a low, melodious voice to their right.

TWENTY-EIGHT

They all turned to find the most beautiful woman Jessa had ever seen. She had long, deep electric ruby hair, shimmering in the light like threads drawn from the stars and planets above. Her dewy, flawless, pale skin glistened almost iridescently, and she had enormous blue eyes that seemed able to swallow a person whole. A shimmery pale gold gown swathed her slender body.

This had to be a goddess, Jessa decided.

"What the fuck, Freyja?" Loki blew out a breath as though totally put out. He set a hand to his hip and stuck out his lower lip like a pouting child.

Jessa looked between Loki and . . . Freyja, thinking for a moment she'd lost her mind. This was *Freyja*, as in *the* Freyja—the Norse goddess of love? Jessa took a shaky step backward, just catching herself from collapsing to the ground.

"Broder Calderson's sliver has been removed." Freyja's voice gave Jessa shivers. It was beautiful, but in a marble sort of way—cold and untouchable—yet light and compelling. Alluring, yet dangerous. Oddly, her voice seemed like love itself. "He has suffered enough, feels genuine repentance for his original crime, and has found love. He is not yours any longer, Loki."

Broder met Jessa's gaze across the distance that separated them. Could it be possible?

Loki stomped his foot. "You can't do this, Freyja! The Brotherhood is *my* dominion and you can't interfere."

Freyja smiled and lifted one slim shoulder. "Watch me."

Jessa struggled to remember what she'd read recently about the Norse pantheon. Freyja was pretty high up, higher than Loki, if memory served.

Loki pinched the bridge of his nose. "Freyja, I am trying to end a threat here. A threat to *you*, my beautiful one. To all we hold dear—"

"From now on, any Brother of the Damned who has redeemed himself of his original crime and who finds genuine love will be freed from punishment. This will be the second way they can dissolve the sliver of Blight that pierces them. A loophole of sorts." She paused, her mouth curving into a sweet smile. "*Odin* agrees."

Loki's face turned red and his body seemed to quiver for a moment with rage. "You cannot do this, Freyja!"

"It is done." She turned her attention to Broder. "Broder Calderson, you are free from the Brotherhood of the Damned. Your sliver has been removed. You are completely human again, but your lifeline is now tied to Jessamine's. You will live as she lives, love as she loves, die as she dies. May you know happiness."

Then she was gone.

Jessa and Broder stared at each other in shock, while Loki threw a fit. The god stomped his feet, exclaiming in languages that Jessa couldn't even begin to decipher.

Broder took a step toward her, but Loki snarled and attacked him. They scuffled, fists flying. Loki landed a punch high on Broder's cheekbone, making his head snap to the side.

The god bounced backward like a boxer on the balls of his feet. "With the sliver goes your extra strength and healing ability. How does it feel to be normal again, brother? Kind of jarring, isn't it?"

Broder staggered to the side and gave his head a sharp shake. "I'm not your brother anymore, Loki."

Loki bounced up to him and sneered close into Broder's face. "Give me back my dagger."

Broder stepped toward him, close enough to kiss. "Try and take it from me."

"I'm going to give you an ass kicking that'll—"

Broder brought his head down hard and fast, connecting with Loki's nose. Loki howled, blood spurting from his nostrils. Jessa brought a hand to her mouth, surprised to see that the god could bleed just like a mortal.

"How dare you!" Loki held his nose, blood gushing beneath his fingers. "Now you're really asking for it," he bawled, his voice pinched and nasal sounding. He raised his hands and the air crackled with power. Jessa bet this time whatever magick Loki was cooking would work.

She gripped her pendant and sought one of her spells, wishing like hell she had more than fluffy little charms stored on it. Murmuring under her breath, she peeled off a layer of magick. A bright burst of white light exploded in front of Loki's eyes, making him yelp with surprise.

Broder chose that moment to take advantage of Loki's distraction. He turned and kicked Loki hard in the hip, then he brought his massive fist up and punched him sharply in the side of the head. Broder's movements were smooth and easy, oddly beautiful, like a dance.

Loki staggered backward, looking stunned.

Stepping toward the man, Broder grabbed the back of his neck like he might a kitten, twisted, and pushed him down to the ground in a flurry of flailing arms and legs. "Take a nap, Loki," Broder growled a moment before his massive fist connected with Loki's head.

Loki went limp, as if his bones had turned to water, and lay still.

Jessa stood, her hands still curled around the pendant, magick still faintly tickling her palm. She knew she appeared stunned—eyes wide, lips parted.

"Jessa?" Broder approached her, reaching out with one hand as though he feared she'd bolt at any moment.

Her shock broke and she launched herself into his arms. He caught her around the waist, lifting her, and she twined her legs around his midsection, burying her face in his chest and inhaling the wonderful scent of him.

This time she didn't need to memorize that scent. Anytime she wanted it, all she'd have to do was this—hug him, kiss him.

Broder was hers to love forever.

He held her and kissed her all over her face, then slanted his mouth across hers and took her in a deep, possessive kiss that seemed meant to mark her soul with his. Finally, her feet touched the ground again and she clasped his hand as they walked toward his bike, stepping over Loki's prone body.

"Will he be okay?" she asked, glancing back.

He shrugged. "He's a god."

"Why did he stick around for that beating?"

"Ego. And probably surprise. Whatever the reason, I'm glad he did. That felt good." He flashed a grin.

Blood marked his lip where Loki had landed a punch. "It is true you no longer have your fantastic healing ability and strength."

"It's true, but I have something better. It's a good trade-off."

They mounted his bike and he started it up. The engine roared to life, then settled into a kittenish purr, sounding as satisfied and happy as she felt. "What will we do now?"

Broder shrugged again. "We'll figure it out." Then he pulled away from the gravel at the side of the road and started them on their journey.

A brand-new one.

Jessa rested her chin on Broder's shoulder, smiled, and closed her eyes as they traveled off into the muted oranges and reds of the setting sun, the wind tangling her hair.